# JEFFREY ARCHER

'. . . ranks in the top ten storytellers in the world'
**Los Angeles Times**

'. . . is a storyteller in the class and style of
Alexandre Dumas'
**Washington Post**

'. . . has a great gift for storytelling'
**Susan Howatch**

'. . . is Britain's number one storyteller'
**Pete Murray**

'. . . is the greatest storyteller of our age'
**Manchester Evening News**

'. . . is a storyteller in the style of Galsworthy'
**Yorkshire Post**

'If the Nobel Prize were awarded for storytelling
Jeffrey Archer could go and collect his'
**Newcastle Evening Chronicle**

Jeffrey Archer is a master storyteller, the author of six novels which have all been worldwide bestsellers. NOT A PENNY MORE, NOT A PENNY LESS was his first book which achieved instant success. Next came the tense and terrifying thriller SHALL WE TELL THE PRESIDENT? followed by A QUIVER FULL OF ARROWS, a collection of short stories. After this came the triumphant bestseller KANE AND ABEL and its superb sequel THE PRODIGAL DAUGHTER. His latest novel is FIRST AMONG EQUALS, the story of four men's battle to control our lives. This revised and updated version of SHALL WE TELL THE PRESIDENT? sets the novel in the 1990s and continues the story of Florentyna Kane.

Jeffrey Archer was born in 1940 and educated at Wellington School and Brasenose College, Oxford. He represented Oxford, Somerset and Great Britain in the 100 metres in the early sixties, and became the youngest member of the House of Commons when he won the by-election at Louth in 1969. He wrote his first novel NOT A PENNY MORE, NOT A PENNY LESS, on leaving the House in 1974. In September 1985 he was appointed Deputy Chairman of the Conservative Party. He is married with two children and lives in London and Cambridge.

# SHALL WE TELL THE PRESIDENT?

## JEFFREY ARCHER

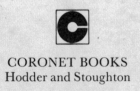

CORONET BOOKS
Hodder and Stoughton

Copyright © 1977 by Jeffrey Archer

Revised edition copyright © 1985 by Jeffrey Archer
First published in Great Britain 1977 by Jonathan Cape Ltd

*First Coronet Edition September 1978*
*Reprinted 1978 twice*
*Reprinted 1979 twice*
*Sixth impression, reset October 1980*
*Reprinted 1981 six times*
*Reprinted 1982 three times*
*Reprinted 1983 five times*
*Reprinted 1984 three times*
*Reprinted 1985 twice*
*Revised Edition March 1986*
*Reprinted 1986 twice*
*This impression June 1986*

**British Library C.I.P.**

Archer, Jeffrey
   Shall we tell the President? – Rev. ed.
   I. Title
   823'.914[S]       TR6051.R285

   ISBN 0-340-39344-0

Printed and bound in Great Britain for
Hodder and Stoughton Paperbacks, a
division of Hodder and Stoughton Ltd.,
Mill Road, Dunton Green, Sevenoaks,
Kent (Editorial Office: 47 Bedford
Square, London, WC1 3DP) by
Cox & Wyman Ltd., Reading.
Photoset by Rowland
Phototypesetting Ltd.,
Bury St Edmunds, Suffolk

To Adrian and Anne

# Author's Note to Revised Edition

When I first wrote *Shall We Tell the President?* I set the story six or seven years in the future. Now that that future date lies in the past, some of the story's credibility becomes impaired.

Since that time too I have written *The Prodigal Daughter* in which the chief character, Florentyna Kane, becomes the first woman President of the United States. It therefore seems logical to me, in recasting *Shall We Tell the President?*, to introduce my fictional president rather than keep the real-life name of Edward M. Kennedy who was the focus of the original novel. This gives it a natural link to *The Prodigal Daughter* and also to *Kane and Abel*.

I have not altered the essential story of *Shall We Tell the President?* but a number of significant changes as well as minor ones, have been made in this revised, re-set edition.

*Jeffrey Archer*

# WASHINGTON D.C.

0     Mile     1

THE PRESIDENT'S ROUTE

7th STREET
6th STREET

N STREET
M STREET

1st STREET

E STREET

Union Station

Peace Monument

Russell Buildings

Dirksen Buildings

Archives    **CAPITOL**

EAST CAPITOL STREET

Library of Congress

INDEPENDENCE AVENUE

D.C. Armory

6th STREET
7th STREET

Rayburn Building

1st STREET

PENNSYLVANIA AVENUE

Woodrow Wilson Medical Center

G STREET

Arena Stage

**MARK'S HOUSE**

RIVER

CHANNEL

ANACOSTIA

# Tuesday afternoon, 20 January

## 12:26 pm

"I, Florentyna Kane, do solemnly swear . . ."

*"I, Florentyna Kane, do solemnly swear . . ."*

". . . that I will faithfully execute the office of the President of the United States . . ."

*". . . that I will faithfully execute the office of the President of the United States . . ."*

". . . and will to the best of my ability, preserve, protect and defend the Constitution of the United States. So help me God."

*". . . and will to the best of my ability, preserve, protect and defend the Constitution of the United States. So help me God."*

Her hand still resting on the Douay Bible, the forty-third President smiled at the First Gentleman. It was the end of one struggle and the beginning of another. Florentyna Kane knew about struggles. Her first struggle had been to be elected to Congress, then the Senate and finally four years later when she had become the first woman Vice President of the United States. After a fierce primary campaign, she had only narrowly managed to defeat Senator Ralph Brooks on the fifth ballot at the Democratic National Convention in June. In November she survived an even fiercer battle with the Republican candidate, a former congressman from New York. Florentyna Kane was elected President by 105,000 votes, a mere one per cent, the smallest margin in American history, smaller even than the 118,000 that John F. Kennedy had gained over Richard Nixon back in 1960.

While the applause died down, the President waited for the twenty-one-gun salute to come to an end. Florentyna Kane cleared her throat and faced fifty thousand attentive citizens on the Capitol Plaza and two hundred million more somewhere out there beyond the television transmitters. There was no need today for the blankets and heavy coats which normally accompanied these occasions. The weather was unusually mild for late January, and the crowded grassy area facing the east front of the Capitol, although soggy, was no longer white from the Christmas snow.

"Vice President Bradley, Mr Chief Justice, President Carter, President Reagan, Reverend clergy, fellow citizens."

The First Gentleman looked on, smiling occasionally to himself as he recognised some of the words and phrases he had contributed to his wife's speech.

Their day had begun at about 6:30 am. Neither had slept very well after the splendid pre-Inaugural concert given in their honour the previous evening. Florentyna Kane had gone over her presidential address for the final time, underlining the salient words in red, making only minor changes.

When she rose that morning, Florentyna wasted no time in selecting a blue dress from her wardrobe. She pinned on the tiny brooch her first husband, Richard, had given her just before he had died.

Every time Florentyna wore that brooch she remembered him; how he had been unable to catch the plane that day because of a strike by maintenance workers but still hired a car to be sure he could be by Florentyna's side when she addressed the Harvard commencement.

Richard never did hear that speech, the one *Newsweek* described as a launching pad for the Presidency – because by the time she had reached the hospital he was dead.

2

She snapped back into the real world of which she was the most powerful leader on earth. But still without enough power to bring Richard back. Florentyna checked herself in the mirror. She felt confident. After all, she had already been President for nearly two years since the unexpected death of President Parkin. Historians would be surprised to discover that she had learned of the President's death while trying to sink a four-foot putt against her oldest friend and future husband, Edward Winchester.

They had both stopped their match when the helicopters had circled overhead. When one of them had landed a Marines Captain had jumped out and run towards her, saluted and said, "Madam President, the President is dead." Now the American people had confirmed that they were willing to continue living with a woman in the White House. For the first time in its history, the United States had elected a woman to the most coveted position in its political life in her own right. She glanced out of the bedroom window at the broad placid expanse of the Potomac River, glinting in the early-morning sunlight.

She left the bedroom and went straight to the private dining-room where her husband Edward was chatting to her children William and Annabel. Florentyna kissed all three of them before they sat down to breakfast.

They laughed about the past and talked about the future but when the clock struck eight the President left them to go to the Oval Office. Her Chief of Staff, Janet Brown, was sitting outside in the corridor waiting for her.

"Good morning, Madam President."

"Good morning, Janet. Everything under control?" She smiled at her.

"I think so, Madam."

"Good. Why don't you run my day as usual? Don't worry about me, I'll just follow your instructions. What do you want me to do first?"

"There are 842 telegrams and 2,412 letters but they

will have to wait, except for the Heads of State. I'll have replies ready for them by twelve o'clock."

"Date them today, they'll like that, and I'll sign every one of them as soon as they are ready."

"Yes, Madam. I also have your schedule. You start the official day with coffee at eleven with the former Presidents Reagan and Carter, then you will be driven to the Inauguration. After the Inauguration, you'll attend a luncheon at the Senate before reviewing the Inaugural Parade in front of the White House."

Janet Brown passed her a sheaf of three-by-five index cards, stapled together, as she had done for fifteen years since she joined her staff when Florentyna had first been elected to Congress. They summarised the President's hour-by-hour schedule; there was rather less on them than usual. Florentyna glanced over the cards, and thanked her Chief of Staff. Edward Winchester appeared at the door. He smiled as he always did, with a mixture of love and admiration, when she turned towards him. She had never once regretted her almost impulsive decision to marry him after the eighteenth hole on that extraordinary day she was told of President Parkin's death, and she felt for certain that Richard would have approved.

"I'll be working on my papers until eleven," she told him. He nodded and left to prepare himself for the day ahead.

A crowd of well-wishers was already gathering outside the White House.

"I wish it would ra'n," confided H. Stuart Knight, the head of the Secret Service, to his aide; it was also one of the most important days of his life. "I know the vast majority of people are harmless, but these occasions give me the jitters."

The crowd numbered about one hundred and fifty; fifty of them belonged to Mr Knight. The advance car that always goes five minutes ahead of a President was already meticulously checking the route to the White

4

House; Secret Service men were watching small gatherings of people along the way, some waving flags; they were there to witness the Inauguration, and would one day tell their grandchildren how they had seen Florentyna Kane being inaugurated as President of the United States.

At 10:59 the butler opened the front door and the crowds began to cheer.

The President and her husband waved to the smiling eyes and only sensed by experience and professional instinct that fifty people were not looking towards them.

Two black limousines came to a noiseless stop at the North Entrance of the White House at 11:00 am. The Marine Honour Guard stood at attention and saluted the two ex-Presidents and their wives as they were greeted by President Kane on the Portico, a privilege normally accorded only to visiting Heads of State. The President herself guided them through to the library for coffee with Edward, William and Annabel.

The older of the ex-Presidents was grumbling that if he were frail it was because he had had to rely on his wife's cooking for the past eight years. "She hasn't dirtied a frying pan in ages, but she's improving every day. To make sure, I've given her a copy of *The New York Times Cook Book*; it's about the only one of their publications that didn't criticise me." Florentyna laughed nervously. She wanted to get on with the official proceedings, but she was conscious that the ex-Presidents were enjoying being back in the White House so she pretended to listen attentively, donning a mask that was second nature to her after nearly twenty years in politics.

"Madam President . . ." Florentyna had to think quickly to prevent anyone noticing her instinctive response to the words. "It's one minute past midday." She looked up at her press secretary, rose from her chair, and led the ex-Presidents and their wives to the steps of the White House. The Marine band struck up "Hail to the Chief" for the last time. At one o'clock they would play it again for the first time.

The two former Presidents were escorted to the first car of the motorcade, a black, bubble-topped, bullet-proof limousine. The Speaker of the House, Jim Wright, and the Senate Majority Leader, Robert Byrd, representing the Congress, were already seated in the second car. Directly behind the limousine there were two cars filled with Secret Service men. Florentyna and Edward occupied the fifth car in line. Vice President Bradley of New Jersey and his wife rode in the next car.

H. Stuart Knight was going through one more routine check. His fifty men had now grown to a hundred. By noon, counting the local police and the FBI contingent, there would be five hundred. Not forgetting the boys from the CIA, Knight thought ruefully. They certainly didn't tell him whether they were going to be there or not, and even he could not always spot them in a crowd. He listened to the cheering of the onlookers reaching a crescendo as the presidential limousine pulled out, on its way to the Capitol.

Edward chatted amiably but Florentyna's thoughts were elsewhere. She waved mechanically at the crowds lining Pennsylvania Avenue, but her mind was once again going over her speech. The renovated Willard Hotel, seven office buildings under construction, the tiered housing units that resembled an Indian cliff-dwelling, the new shops and restaurants and the wide landscaped sidewalks passed by. The J. Edgar Hoover Building, which housed the FBI, still named after its first Director, despite several efforts by certain senators to have the name changed. How this street had been transformed in fifteen years.

They approached the Capitol and Edward interrupted the President's reverie. "May God be with you, darling." She smiled and gripped his hand. The six cars came to a stop.

President Kane entered the Capitol on the ground floor. Edward waited behind for a moment as he thanked the chauffeur. Those who stepped out of the other cars were quickly surrounded by Secret Service agents and, waving to the crowd, they made their way separately to their seats on the platform. Meanwhile the chief usher was taking President Kane quietly through the tunnel into the reception area, Marines saluting at every ten paces. There she was greeted by Vice President Bradley. The two of them stood talking of nothing, neither of them taking in the other's reply.

The two ex-Presidents came through the tunnel smiling. For the first time the older President was looking his age, his hair seemed to have turned grey overnight. Once again, he and Florentyna went through the formality of shaking hands with one another; they were to do it seven times that day. The chief usher guided them through a small reception room on to the platform. For this, as for all Presidential inaugurations, a temporary platform had been erected on the east steps of the Capitol. The crowds rose and cheered for over a minute as the President and the ex-Presidents waved; finally they sat in silence and waited for the ceremony to begin.

"My fellow Americans, as I take office the problems facing the United States across the world are vast and threatening. In South Africa, pitiless civil war rages between black and white; in the Middle East the ravages of last year's battles are being repaired, but both sides are rebuilding their armaments rather than their schools, their hospitals or their farms. On the borders between China and India, and between Russia and Pakistan, there is the potential for war among four of the most populous nations on earth. South America veers between extreme right and extreme left, but neither extreme seems to be able to improve the living conditions of their peoples. Two of the original signatories of the North Atlantic Treaty Organisation, France and Italy, are on the verge of withdrawing from that pact.

"In 1949, President Harry S. Truman announced that the United States stood ready with all its might and resources to defend the forces of freedom wherever they might be endangered. Today, some would say that this act of magnanimity has resulted in failure, that America was, and is, too weak to assume the full burden of world leadership. In the face of repeated international crises, any American citizen might well ask why he should care about events so far from home, and why he should feel any responsibility for the defence of freedom outside the United States.

"I do not have to answer these doubts in my own words. 'No man is an island,' John Donne wrote more than three and a half centuries ago. 'Every man is a piece of the continent.' The United States stretches from the Atlantic to the Pacific and from the Arctic to the Equator. 'I am involved in mankind; and therefore never send to know for whom the bell tolls; it tolls for thee.'"

Edward liked that part of the speech. It expressed so well his own feelings. He had wondered, though, whether the audience would respond with the same enthusiasm as they had greeted Florentyna's flights of rhetoric in the past. The thunderous applause assaulting his ears in wave after wave reassured him. The magic was still working.

"At home, we will create a medical service that will be the envy of the free world. It will allow all citizens an equal opportunity for the finest medical advice and help. No American must be allowed to die because he cannot afford to live."

Many Democrats had voted against Florentyna Kane because of her attitude towards Medicare. As one hoary old G.P. had said to her, "Americans must learn to stand on their own two feet." "How can they if they're already flat on their backs?" retorted Florentyna. "God deliver us from a woman President," replied the doctor, and voted Republican.

"But the main platform of this administration will be in the field of law and order, and to this end I intend to present to Congress a bill that will make the sale of firearms without a licence illegal."

8

The applause from the crowd was not quite so spontaneous.

Florentyna raised her head. "And so I say to you, my fellow citizens, let the end of this century be an era in which the United States leads the world in justice as well as in power, in care as well as enterprise, an era in which the United States declares war – war on disease, war on discrimination, and war on poverty."

The President sat down; in a single motion, the entire audience rose to its feet.

The sixteen-minute speech had been interrupted by applause on ten occasions. But as the nation's Chief Executive turned from the microphone, now assured that the crowd was with her, her eyes were no longer on the cheering mass. She scanned the dignitaries on the platform for the one person she wanted to see. She walked over to her husband, kissed him on the cheek, and then took his arm before they were accompanied from the platform by the briskly efficient usher.

H. Stuart Knight hated things that didn't run on schedule, and today nothing had been on time. Everybody was going to be at least thirty minutes late for the lunch.

Seventy-six guests stood as the President entered the room. These were the men and women who now controlled the Democratic party. The Northern establishment who had decided to back the lady were now present, with the exception of those who had supported Senator Ralph Brooks.

Some of those at the luncheon were already members of her cabinet, and everyone present had played some part in returning her to the White House.

The President had neither the opportunity nor the inclination to eat her lunch; everyone wanted to talk to her at once. The menu had been specially made up of her favourite dishes, starting with lobster bisque and going on to roast beef. Finally, the chef's *pièce de résistance* was produced, an iced chocolate cake, in the form of the White House. Edward watched his wife ignore the neat wedge of the Oval Office placed in front of her. "That's why she never needs to slim," commented Marian Edelman, who was the surprise appointment as Attorney General. Marian had been telling Edward about the importance of children's rights. Edward tried to listen; perhaps another day.

By the time the last wing of the White House had been demolished and the last hand pumped, the President and her party were forty-five minutes late for the Inaugural Parade. When they did arrive at the reviewing stand in front of the White House, the most relieved to see them, among the crowd of two hundred thousand, was the Presidential Guard of Honour, who had been standing at attention for just over an hour. Once the President had taken her seat the parade began. The State contingent in the military unit marched past, and the United States Marine Band played everything from Sousa to "God Bless America". Floats from each state, some, like that of Illinois, commemorating events from Florentyna's Polish background, added colour and a lighter touch to what for her was not only a serious occasion but a solemn one.

She still felt this was the only nation on earth that could entrust its highest office to the daughter of an immigrant.

When the three-hour-long parade was finally over and the last float had disappeared down the avenue, Janet Brown, Florentyna Kane's Chief of Staff, leaned over and asked the President what she would like to do between now and the first Inaugural Ball.

"Sign all those cabinet appointments, the letters to the Heads of State, and clear my desk for tomorrow," was the immediate reply. "That should take care of the first four years."

The President returned directly into the White House. As she walked through the South Portico, the Marine band struck up "Hail to the Chief". The President had taken off her coat even before she reached the Oval Office. She sat herself firmly behind the imposing oak and leather desk. She paused for a moment, looking around the room. Everything was as she wanted it; behind her there was the picture of Richard and William playing touch football. In front of her, a paperweight with the quotation from George Bernard Shaw which Annabel quoted so often: "Some men see things as they are and say, why; I dream things that never were and say, why not." On Florentyna's left was the Presidential flag, on her right the flag of the United States. Dominating the middle of the desk was a replica of the Baron Hotel, Warsaw, made out of papier mâché by William when he was fourteen. Coal was burning in the fireplace. A portrait of Abraham Lincoln stared down at the newly sworn-in President while outside the bay windows, the green lawns swept in an unbroken stretch to the Washington Monument. The President smiled. She was back at home.

Florentyna Kane reached for a pile of official papers and glanced over the names of those who would serve in her cabinet; there were over thirty appointments to be made. The President signed each one with a flourish. The final one was Janet Brown as Chief of Staff. The President ordered that they be sent down to the Congress immediately. Her press secretary picked up the pieces of paper that would dictate the next four years in the history of America and said, "Thank you, Madam President," and then added, "What would you like to tackle next?"

"Always start with the biggest problem is what Lincoln advised, so let's go over the draft legislation for the Gun Control bill."

The President's press secretary shuddered, for she knew only too well that the battle in the House over the next two years was likely to be every bit as vicious and hard-fought as the Civil War Lincoln had faced. So many people still regarded the possession of arms as their inalienable birthright. She only prayed that it all would not end the same way, as a House Divided.

# Thursday evening, 3 March
# (two years later)

## 5:45 pm

Nick Stames wanted to go home. He had been at work since seven that morning and it was already 5:45 pm. He couldn't remember if he had eaten lunch; his wife, Norma, had been grumbling again that he never got home in time for dinner, or, if he did, it was so late that her dinner was no longer worth eating. Come to think of it, when did he last find time to finish a meal? Norma stayed in bed when he left for the office at 6:30 am. Now that the children were away at school, her only real task was to cook dinner for him. He couldn't win; if he had been a failure, she would have complained about that, too, and he was, goddamn it, by anybody's standards, a success; the youngest special agent in charge of a Field Office in the FBI and you don't get a job like that at the age of forty-one by being at home on time for dinner every night. In any case, Nick loved the job. It was his mistress; at least his wife could be thankful for that.

Nick Stames had been head of the Washington Field Office for nine years. The third largest Field Office in America, although it covered the smallest territory – only sixty-one square miles of Washington, D.C. – it had twenty-two squads; twelve criminal, ten security. Hell, he was policing the capital of the world. Of course, he must be expected to be late sometimes. Still, tonight he intended to make a special effort. When he had the time to do so, he adored his wife. He was going to be home on time this evening. He picked up his internal phone and called his Criminal Co-ordinator, Grant Nanna.

"Grant."

"Boss."

"I'm going home."

"I didn't know you had one."

"Not you, too."

Nick Stames put the phone down, and pushed his hand through his long dark hair. He would have made a better movie criminal than FBI agent, since everything about him was dark – dark eyes, dark skin, dark hair, even a dark suit and dark shoes, but the last two were true of any special agent. On his lapel he wore a pin depicting the flags of the United States and of Greece.

Once, a few years ago, he had been offered promotion and a chance to cross the street to the Bureau Head-quarters and join the Director as one of his thirteen assistants. Being an assistant chained to a desk wasn't his style, so he stayed put. The move would have taken him from a slum to a palace; the Washington Field Office is housed on floors four, five, and eight of the Old Post Office Building on Pennsylvania Avenue, and the rooms are a little like railroad coaches. They would have been condemned as slums if they had been sited in the ghetto.

As the sun began to disappear behind the tall buildings, Nick's gloomy office grew darker. He walked over to the light switch. "Don't Be Fuelish," commented a fluores-cent label glued to the switch. Just as the constant move-ment of men and women in dark sober suits in and out of the Old Post Office Building revealed the location of the FBI Washington Field Office, so this government graffito served notice that the czars of the Federal Energy Administration inhabited two floors of the cavernous building on Pennsylvania Avenue.

Nick stared out of his window across the street at the new FBI Headquarters, which had been completed in

1976, a great ugly monster with elevators that were larger than his office. He didn't let it bother him. He'd reached Grade 18 in the service, and only the Director was paid more than he was. In any case, he was not going to sit behind a desk until they retired him with a pair of gold handcuffs. He wanted to be in constant touch with the agent in the street, feel the pulse of the Bureau. He would stay put at the Washington Field Office and die standing up, not sitting down. Once again, he touched the intercom. "Julie, I'm on my way home."

Julie Bayers looked up and glanced at her watch as if it were lunchtime.

"Yes, sir," she said, sounding disbelieving.

As he passed through the office he grinned at her. "Moussaka, rice pilaf, and the wife; don't tell the Mafia." Nick managed to get one foot out of the door before his private phone rang. One more step and he would have made it to the open lift, but Nick never could resist the ring of a phone. Julie rose and began to walk towards his office. As she did so Nick admired, as he always did, the quick flash of leg. "It's all right, Julie. I'll get it." He strode back into his room and picked up the ringing telephone.

"Stames."

"Good evening, sir. Lieutenant Blake, Metropolitan Police."

"Hey, Dave, congratulations on your promotion. I haven't seen you in . . ." he paused, ". . . it must be five years, you were only a sergeant. How are you?"

"Thank you, sir, I'm doing just fine."

"Well, Lieutenant, moved into big-time crime, now have you? Picked up a fourteen-year-old stealing a pack of chewing gum and need my best men to find where the suspect has hidden the goods?"

Blake laughed. "Not quite that bad, Mr Stames. I have a guy in Woodrow Wilson Medical Center who wants to meet the head of the FBI, says he has something vitally important to tell him."

14

"I know the feeling, I'd love to meet him myself. Do you know whether he's one of our usual informers, Dave?"

"No, sir."

"What's his name?"

"Angelo Casefikis." Blake spelled out the name for Stames.

"Any description?" asked Stames.

"No. I only spoke to him on the phone. All he would say is it will be worse for America if the FBI doesn't listen."

"Did he now? Hold on while I check the name. He could be a nut."

Nick Stames pressed a button to connect him with the Duty Officer. "Who's on duty?"

"Paul Fredericks, boss."

"Paul, get out the nut box."

The nut box, as it was affectionately known in the Bureau, was a collection of white index cards containing the names of all the people who liked to call up in the middle of the night and claim that the Martians had landed in their back yards, or that they had discovered a CIA plot to take over the world.

Special Agent Fredericks was back on the line, the nut box in front of him.

"Right, boss. What's his name?"

"Angelo Casefikis," said Stames.

"A crazy Greek," said Fredericks. "You never know with these foreigners."

"Greeks aren't foreigners," snapped Stames. His name, before it was shortened, had been Nick Stamatakis. He never did forgive his father, God rest his soul, for anglicising a magnificent Hellenic surname.

"Sorry, sir. No name like that in the nut box or the informants' file. Did this guy mention any agent's name that he knows?"

"No, he just wanted the head of the FBI."

"Don't we all?"

"No more cracks from you, Paul, or you'll be on complaint duty for more than the statutory week."

Each agent in the Field Office did one week a year on the nut box, answering the phone all night, fending off canny Martians, foiling dastardly CIA coups, and, above all, never embarrassing the Bureau. Every agent dreaded it. Paul Fredericks put the phone down quickly. Two weeks on this job and you could write out one of the little white cards with your own name on it.

"Well, have you formed any view?" said Stames to Blake as he wearily took a cigarette out of his left desk drawer. "How did he sound?"

"Frantic and incoherent. I sent one of my rookies to see him, but he couldn't get anything out of him other than that America ought to listen to what he's got to say. He seemed genuinely frightened. He's got a gunshot wound in his leg and there may be complications. It's infected; apparently he left it for some days before he went to the hospital."

"How did he get himself shot?"

"Don't know yet. We're still trying to locate witnesses, but we haven't come up with anything so far, and Casefikis won't give us the time of day."

"Wants the FBI, does he? Only the best, eh?" said Stames. He regretted the remark the moment he said it; but it was too late. He didn't attempt to cover himself. "Thank you, Lieutenant," he said. "I'll put someone on it immediately and brief you in the morning." Stames put the telephone down. Six o'clock already – why had he turned back? Damn the phone. Grant Nanna would have handled the job just as well and he wouldn't have made that thoughtless remark about wanting the best. There was enough friction between the FBI and the Metropolitan Police without his adding to it. Nick picked up his intercom phone and buzzed the head of the Criminal Section.

"Grant."

"I thought you said you had to be home."

"Come into my office for a moment, will you?"

"Sure, be right there, boss."

Grant Nanna appeared a few seconds later along with his trademark cigar. He had put on his jacket which he only did when he saw Nick in his office.

Nanna's career had a storybook quality. He was born in El Campo, Texas, and received a BA from Baylor. From there, he went on to get a law degree at SMU. As a young agent assigned to the Pittsburgh Field Office, Nanna met his future wife, Betty, an FBI stenographer. They had four sons, all of whom had attended Virginia Polytechnic Institute: two engineers, a doctor, and a dentist. Nanna had been an agent for over thirty years. Twelve more than Nick. In fact, Nick had been a rookie agent under him. Nanna held no grudge, since he was head of the Criminal Section, and greatly respected Nick – as he called him in private.

"What's the problem, boss?"

Stames looked up as Nanna entered the office. He noted that his five-feet-nine, fifty-five-year-old, robust, cigar-chewing Criminal Co-ordinator was certainly not "desirable", as Bureau weight requirements demanded. A man of five-feet-nine was required to keep his weight between a hundred and fifty-four and a hundred and sixty-one pounds. Nanna had always cringed when the quarterly weigh-in of all FBI agents came due. Many times he had been forced to purge his body of excess pounds for that most serious transgression of Bureau rules, especially during the Hoover era, when "desirability" meant lean and mean.

Who cares, thought Stames. Grant's knowledge and experience were worth a dozen slender, young athletic agents who can be found in the Washington Field Office halls every day. As he had done a hundred times before, he told himself he would deal with Nanna's weight problem another day.

Nick repeated the story of the strange Greek in Woodrow Wilson Medical Center as it had been relayed to him by Lieutenant Blake. "I want you to send down two men. Who's on duty tonight?"

"Aspirin, but if you suspect it might be an informer, boss, I certainly can't send him."

"Aspirin" was the nickname of the oldest agent still employed in the WFO. After his early years under Hoover, he played everything by the book, which gave most people a headache. He was due to retire at the end of the year and exasperation was now being replaced by nostalgia.

"No, don't send Aspirin. Send two youngsters."

"How about Calvert and Andrews?"

"Agreed," replied Stames. "If you brief them right away, I can still make it in time for dinner. Call me at home if it turns out to be anything special."

Grant Nanna left the office, and Nick smiled a second flirtatious goodbye to his secretary. She was the only attractive thing in the WFO. Julie looked up and smiled nonchalantly. "I don't mind working for an FBI agent, but there is no way I would ever marry one," she told her little mirror in the top drawer.

Grant Nanna returned to his office and picked up the extension phone to the Criminal Room.

"Send in Calvert and Andrews."

"Yes, sir."

There was a firm knock on the door. Two special agents entered. Barry Calvert was big by anybody's standards, six-feet-six in his stockinged feet and not many people had seen him that way. At thirty-two, he was thought to be one of the most ambitious young men in the Criminal Section. He was wearing a dark green jacket, dark nondescript trousers, and clumpy black leather brogues. His brown hair was cut short and parted neatly on the right. His tear-drop aviator glasses had been his sign of nonconformity. He was always on duty long after the official check-out time of 5:30 and not just because he was fighting his way up the ladder. He loved the job. He didn't love anybody else, so far as his colleagues knew, or at least not on more than a temporary basis. Calvert was a Midwesterner by birth and he had entered the FBI after leaving college with a BA in sociology from Indiana University and then took the fifteen-week course at Quantico, the FBI Academy. From every angle, he was the archetypal FBI man.

By contrast, Mark Andrews had been one of the more unusual FBI entrants. After majoring in history at Yale he finished his education at Yale Law School, and then decided he wanted some adventure for a few years before he joined a law firm. He felt it would be useful to learn about criminals and the police from the inside. He didn't give this as his reason for applying to the Bureau – no one is supposed to regard the Bureau as an academic experiment. In fact, Hoover had regarded it so much as a career that he did not allow agents who left the service ever to return. At six feet Mark Andrews looked small next to Calvert. He had a fresh, open face with clear blue eyes and a mop of curly fair hair long enough to skim his shirt collar. At twenty-eight he was one of the youngest agents in the department. His clothes were always smartly fashionable and sometimes not quite regulation. Nick Stames had once caught him in a red sports jacket and brown trousers and relieved him from duty so that he could return home and dress properly. Never embarrass the Bureau. Mark's charm got him out of a lot of trouble in the Criminal Section, but he had a steadiness of purpose which more than made up for the Ivy League education and manner. He was self-confident, but never pushy or concerned about his own advancement. He didn't let anyone in the Bureau know about his career plan.

Grant Nanna went over the story of the frightened man waiting for them in Woodrow Wilson.

"Black?" queried Calvert.

"No, Greek."

Calvert's surprise showed in his face. Eighty per cent of the inhabitants of Washington were black, and ninety-eight per cent of those arrested on criminal charges were black. One of the reasons the infamous break-in at the Watergate had been suspicious from the beginning to those who knew Washington at all well was the fact that no blacks were involved, though no agents had admitted it.

"Okay, Barry, think you can handle it?"

"Sure, you want a report on your desk by tomorrow morning?"

"No, the boss wants you to contact him direct if it turns out to be anything special, otherwise just file a report overnight." Nanna's telephone rang. "Mr Stames on the radio line from his car for you, sir," said Polly, the night switchboard operator.

"He never lets up, does he?" Grant confided to the two junior agents, covering the mouthpiece of the phone with his palm.

"Hi, boss."

"Grant, did I say that the Greek had a bullet wound in his leg, and it was infected?"

"Yes, boss."

"Right, do me a favour will you? Call Father Gregory at my church, Saint Constantine and Saint Helen, and ask him to go over to the hospital and see him."

"Anything you say."

"And get yourself home, Grant. Aspirin can handle the office tonight."

"I was just going, boss."

The line went dead.

"Okay, you two – on your way." The two special agents headed down the dirty grey corridor and into the service elevator. It looked, as always, as if it required a crank to start it. Finally outside on Pennsylvania Avenue, they picked up a Bureau car.

Mark guided the dark blue Ford sedan down Pennsylvania Avenue past the National Archives and the Mellon Gallery. He circled around the lush Capitol grounds and picked up Independence Avenue going towards the south-east section of Washington. As the two agents waited for a light to change at 1st Street, near the Library of Congress, Barry scowled at the rush-hour traffic and looked at his watch.

"Why didn't they put Aspirin on this damn assignment?"

"Who'd send Aspirin to a hospital?" replied Mark.

Mark smiled. The two men had established an immediate rapport when they first met at the FBI Academy at Quantico. On the first day of the training course, every trainee received a telegram confirming his appointment. Each new agent was then asked to check the telegram of the person on his right and his left for authenticity. The manoeuvre was intended to emphasise the need for extreme caution. Mark had glanced at Barry's telegram and handed it back with a grin. "I guess you're legit," he said, "if FBI regulations allow King Kong in the ranks."

"Listen," Calvert had replied, reading Mark's telegram intently. "You may just need King Kong one day, Mr Andrews."

The light turned green, but a car ahead of Mark and Barry in the inside lane wanted to make a left turn on 1st Street. For the moment, the two impatient FBI men were trapped in a line of traffic.

"What do you imagine this guy could tell us?"

"I hope he has something on the downtown bank job," replied Barry. "I'm still the case agent, and I still don't have any leads after three weeks. Stames is beginning to get uptight about it."

"No, can't be that, not with a bullet in his leg. He's more likely to be another candidate for the nut box. Wife probably shot him for not being home on time for his stuffed vine leaves."

"You know, the boss would only send a priest to a fellow Greek. You and I could wallow in hell as far as he's concerned."

They both laughed. They knew if either of them were to

land in trouble, Nick Stames would move the Washington Monument stone by stone if he thought it would help. As the car continued down Independence Avenue into the heart of south-east Washington, the traffic gradually diminished. A few minutes later, they passed 19th Street and the D.C. Armory and reached Woodrow Wilson Medical Center. They found the visitors' parking lot and Calvert double-checked the lock on every door. Nothing is more embarrassing for an agent than to have his car stolen and then for the Metropolitan Police to call and ask if he could come and collect it. It was the quickest way to a month on the nut box.

The entrance to the hospital was old and dingy, and the corridors grey and bleak. The girl on night duty at the reception desk told them that Casefikis was on the fourth floor, in Room 4308. Both agents were surprised by the lack of security. They didn't have to show their credentials, and they were allowed to wander around the building as if they were a couple of interns. No one gave them a second look. Perhaps, as agents, they had become too security conscious.

The elevator took them gradually, grudgingly, to the fourth floor. A man on crutches and a woman in a wheelchair shared the elevator, chatting to one another as though they had a lot of time to spare, oblivious to the slowness of the elevator. When they arrived at the fourth floor, Calvert walked over to a nurse and asked for the doctor on duty.

"I think Dr Dexter has gone off duty, but I'll check," the staff nurse said and bustled away. She didn't get a visit from the FBI every day and the shorter one with the clear blue eyes was so good-looking. The nurse and the doctor returned together down the corridor. Dr Dexter came as a surprise to both Calvert and Andrews. They introduced themselves. It must have been the legs, Mark decided. The last time he had seen legs like that was when the Yale Cinema Club had shown a re-run of Anne Bancroft in *The Graduate*. It was the first time he had ever really looked at a woman's legs, and he hadn't stopped looking since.

"Elizabeth Dexter, MD" was stamped in black on a piece of red plastic that adorned her starched white coat. Underneath it, Mark could see a red silk shirt and a stylish skirt of black crepe that fell below her knees. Dr Dexter was of medium height and slender to the point of fragility. She wore no make-up, so far as Mark could tell; certainly her clear skin and dark eyes were in no need of any help. This trip was turning out to be worthwhile, after all. Barry, on the other hand, showed no interest whatever in the pretty doctor and asked to see the file on Casefikis. Mark thought quickly for an opening gambit.

"Are you related to Senator Dexter?" he asked, slightly emphasising the word Senator.

"Yes, he's my father," she said flatly, obviously used to the question and rather bored by it – and by those who imagined it was important.

"I heard him lecture in my final year at Yale Law," said Mark, forging ahead, realising he was now showing off, but he realised that Calvert would finish that damn report in a matter of moments.

"Oh, were you at Yale, too?" she asked. "When did you graduate?"

"Three years ago, Law School," replied Mark.

"We might even have met. I left Yale Med last year."

"If I had met you before, Dr Dexter, I would not have forgotten."

"When you two Ivy Leaguers have finished swapping life histories," Barry Calvert interrupted, "this Mid-westerner would like to get on with his job."

Yes, thought Mark, Barry will end up as Director one day.

"What can you tell us about this man, Dr Dexter?" asked Calvert.

"Very little, I'm afraid," the doctor replied, taking back the file on Casefikis. "He came in of his own volition and reported a gun wound. The wound was septic and looked as if it had been exposed for about a week; I wish he had come in earlier. I removed the bullet this morning. As you know, Mr Calvert, it is our duty to inform the police immediately when a patient comes in with a gunshot wound, and so we phoned your boys at the Metropolitan Police."

"Not our boys," corrected Mark.

"I'm sorry," replied Dr Dexter rather formally. "To a doctor, a policeman is a policeman."

"And to a policeman, an MD is an MD, but you also have specialties – orthopaedics, gynaecology, neurology – don't you? You don't mean to tell me I look like one of those flatfoots from the Met Police?"

Dr Dexter was not to be beguiled into a flattering response. She opened the manilla folder. "All we know is that he is Greek by origin and his name is Angelo Casefikis. He has never been registered in this hospital before. He gave his age as thirty-eight . . . Not a lot to go on, I'm afraid."

"Fine, it's as much as we usually get. Thank you, Dr Dexter," said Calvert. "Can we see him now?"

"Of course. Please follow me." Elizabeth Dexter turned and led them down the corridor.

The two men followed her, Barry looking for the door marked 4308, Mark looking at her legs. When they arrived, they peered through the small window and saw two men in the room, Angelo Casefikis and a cheerful-looking black, who was staring at a television set which emitted no sound. Calvert turned to Dr Dexter.

"Would it be possible to see him alone, Dr Dexter?"

"Why?" she asked.

"We don't know what he is going to tell us, and he may not wish to be overheard."

"Well, don't worry yourself," said Dr Dexter, and laughed. "My favourite mailman, Benjamin Reynolds, who is in the next bed is as deaf as a post, and until we operate on him next week, he won't be able to hear

Gabriel's horn on the Day of Judgement, let alone a state secret."

Calvert smiled for the first time. "He'd make a hell of a witness."

The doctor ushered Calvert and Andrews into the room, then turned and left them. See you soon, lovely lady, Mark promised himself. Calvert looked at Benjamin Reynolds suspiciously, but the black mailman merely gave him a big happy smile, waved, and continued to watch the soundless *$25,000 Pyramid*; nonetheless, Barry Calvert stood on that side of the bed and blocked his view of Casefikis in case he could lip-read. Barry thought of everything.

"Mr Casefikis?"

"Yes."

Casefikis was a grey, sick-looking individual of medium build, with a prominent nose, bushy eyebrows, and an anxious expression that never left his face. His hair was thick, dark, and unkempt. His hands seemed particularly large on the white bedspread, and the veins stood out prominently. His face was darkened by several days of unshaven beard. One leg was heavily bandaged and rested on the cover of the bed. His eyes darted nervously from one man to the other.

"I am Special Agent Calvert and this is Special Agent Andrews. We are officers with the Federal Bureau of Investigation. We understand you wanted to see us."

Both men withdrew their FBI credentials from their right inside coat pockets, and displayed them to Casefikis while holding the credentials in their left hands. Even such a seemingly insignificant manoeuvre was carefully taught to all new FBI agents so that their "strong hand" would be free to withdraw and fire when necessary.

Casefikis studied their credentials with a puzzled frown, pressing his tongue over his lips, obviously not knowing what to look for. The agent's signature must pass partly over the seal of the Department of Justice to insure authenticity. He looked at Mark's card number,

3302, and his badge number, 1721. He didn't speak, as if wondering where to start, or perhaps whether to change his mind and say nothing at all. He stared at Mark, clearly the more sympathetic, and began his tale.

"I never been in any trouble with police before," he said. "Not with any of police."

Neither agent smiled or spoke.

"But I in big mess now and, by God, I need help."

Calvert stepped in. "Why do you need our help?"

"I am illegal immigrant and so is wife. We both Greek nationals, we came in Baltimore on ship and we been working here two years. We've nothing to go back to."

It came out in spurts and dashes.

"I have information to trade if we not deported."

"We can't make that sort –" began Mark.

Barry touched Mark's arm. "If it's important and you are able to help us solve a crime, we will speak to the Immigration authorities. We can promise no more than that."

Mark mused; with six million illegal immigrants in the United States, another couple was not going to sink the boat.

Casefikis looked desperate. "I needed job, I needed money, you understand?"

Both men understood. They faced the same problem a dozen times a week behind a dozen different faces.

"When I offered this job as waiter in restaurant, my wife very pleased. On second week I was given special job to serve lunch in a hotel room for big man. The only trouble that the man wanted waiter who not speak English. My English very bad so bossman tell me I could go, keep my mouth shut, speak only Greek. For twenty dollars I say yes. We go in back of van to hotel – I think in Georgetown. When we arrive I sent to kitchen, join staff in basement. I dress and start taking food to private dining-room. There five-six men and I heard big man say I no speak English. So they talk on. I don't listen. Very last cup of coffee, when start talking about President

26

Kane, I like Kane, I listen. I heard say, 'We have to blow her away.' Another man say: 'The best day would still be 10 March, the way we planned it.' And then I heard: 'I agree with Senator, let's get rid of the bitch.' Someone was staring at me, so I left room. When I downstairs washing up, one man came in and shouted, 'Hey, you, catch this.' I looked around put arms up. All at once he start come for me. I run for door and down street. He shoot gun at me, I feel bit pain in leg but I able to get away because he older, big and slower than me. I hear him shout but I knew he couldn't catch me. I scared. I get home pretty damn quick, and wife and I move out that night and hide out of town with friend from Greece. Hoped all would be okay, but my leg got bad after few days so Ariana made me come to hospital and call for you because my friend tell they come around to my place look for me because if they find me they kill me." He stopped, breathed deeply, his unshaven face covered in sweat, and looked at the two men imploringly.

"What's your full name?" said Calvert, sounding about as excited as he would if he were issuing a traffic ticket.

"Angelo Mexis Casefikis."

Calvert made him spell it in full.

"Where do you live?"

"Now at Blue Ridge Manor Apartments, 11501 Elkin Street, Wheaton. Home of my friend, good man, please don't give trouble."

"When did this incident take place?"

"Last Thursday," Casefikis said instantly.

Calvert checked the date. "24 February?"

The Greek shrugged. "Last Thursday," he repeated.

"Where is the restaurant you were working in?"

"A few streets from me. It called Golden Duck."

Calvert continued taking notes. "And where was this hotel you were taken to?"

"Don't know, in Georgetown. Maybe could take you there when out of hospital."

"Now, Mr Casefikis, please be careful about this. Was

there anyone else working at this luncheon who might have overheard the conversation in that room?"

"No, sir. I only waiter attend in room."

"Have you told anyone what you overheard? Your wife? The friend whose house you're staying at? Anyone?"

"No, sir. Only you. No tell wife what I hear. No tell no one, too scared."

Calvert continued to interview, asking for descriptions of the other men in the room and making the Greek repeat everything to see if the story remained the same. It did. Mark looked on silently.

"Okay, Mr Casefikis, that's all we can do for this evening. We'll return in the morning and have you sign a written statement."

"But they going to kill me. They going to kill me."

"No need to worry, Mr Casefikis. We'll put a police guard on your room as soon as possible; no one is going to kill you."

Casefikis dropped his eyes, not reassured.

"We'll see you again in the morning," said Calvert, closing his notebook. "You just get some rest. Good night, Mr Casefikis."

Calvert glanced back at a happy Benjamin, still deeply absorbed in *$25,000 Pyramid* with no words, just money. He waved again at them and smiled, showing all three of his teeth, two black and one gold. Calvert and Andrews returned to the corridor.

"I don't believe a word of it," Barry said immediately. "With his English, he could easily have got hold of the wrong end of the stick. It was probably quite innocent. People curse the President all the time. My father does, but that doesn't mean he would kill her."

"Maybe, but what about that gunshot wound? That's for real," said Mark.

"I know. I guess that's the one thing that worries me," Barry said. "It could just be a cover for something completely different. I think I'll speak to the boss to be on the safe side."

Calvert headed for the pay phone by the side of the elevator and took out two quarters. All agents carry a pocketful of quarters; there are no special telephone privileges for members of the Bureau.

"Well, was he hoping to rob Fort Knox?" Elizabeth Dexter's voice startled Mark, although he had half-expected her to return. She was obviously on her way home: the white coat had been replaced by a red jacket.

"Not exactly," replied Mark. "We'll have to come around tomorrow morning to tidy things up; probably get him to sign a written statement and take his finger-prints, then we'll pick up the gold."

"Fine," she said. "Dr Delgado will be on duty tomorrow." She smiled sweetly. "You'll like her, too."

"Is this hospital entirely staffed by beautiful lady doctors?" said Mark. "How does one get to stay the night?"

"Well," she said, "the flu is the fashionable disease this month. Even President Kane has had it."

Calvert looked around sharply at the mention of the President's name. Elizabeth Dexter glanced at her watch.

"I've just completed two hours' unpaid overtime," she said. "If you don't have any more questions, Mr Andrews, I ought to get home now." She smiled and turned to go, her heels tapping sharply against the tiled floor.

"Just one more question, Dr Dexter," said Mark, fol-lowing her around the corner beyond the range of Barry Calvert's disapproving eyes and ears. "What would you say to having dinner with me later tonight?"

"What would I say?" she said teasingly. "Let me see, I think I'd accept gracefully and not too eagerly. It might be interesting to find out what G-men are really like."

"We bite," said Mark. They smiled at each other. "Okay, it's 7:15 now. If you're willing to take a chance on it, I could probably pick you up by 8:30."

Elizabeth jotted her address and phone number on a page of his diary.

29

"So you're a left-hander, are you, Liz?"

The dark eyes flashed momentarily up to meet his. "Only my lovers call me Liz," she said, and was gone.

"It's Calvert, boss. I can't make my mind up about this one. I don't know if he's a jerk or for real so I'd like to run it past you."

"Fine, Barry. Shoot."

"Well, it could be serious, or just a hoax. He may even be nothing more than a small-time thief trying to get off the hook for something bigger. But I can't be sure. And if every word he said turned out to be true, I figured you ought to know immediately." Barry relayed the salient parts of the interview without mentioning the Senator, stressing that there was an added factor he did not want to discuss over the phone.

"What are you trying to do, get me in the divorce courts – I suppose I'll have to come back to the office," said Nick Stames, avoiding his wife's expression of annoyance. "Okay, okay. Thank God I got to eat at least some of the moussaka. I'll see you in thirty minutes, Barry."

"Right, boss."

Calvert depressed the telephone cradle with his hand momentarily and then dialled the Metropolitan Police. Two more quarters, leaving sixteen in his pockets. He often thought the quickest way to check out an FBI agent would be to make him turn his pockets inside out; if he produced twenty quarters, he was a genuine member of the Bureau.

"Lieutenant Blake is on the front desk. I'll put you right through."

"Lieutenant Blake."

"Special Agent Calvert. We've seen your Greek and we'd like you to put a guard on his room. He's scared to hell about something so we don't want to take any chances."

"He's not my Greek, damn it," said Blake. "Can't you use one of your own fancy guys?"

"There's no one we can spare at the moment, Lieutenant."

"I'm not exactly overstaffed myself, for God's sake. What do you think we're running, the Shoreham Hotel? Oh hell, I'll do what I can. But they won't be able to get there for a couple of hours."

"Fine. Thanks for your help, Lieutenant. I'll brief my office." Barry replaced the receiver.

Mark Andrews and Barry Calvert waited for the elevator, which was just as slow and reluctant to take them down as it had been to take them up. Neither of them spoke until they were inside the dark blue Ford.

"Stames is coming back to hear the story," said Calvert. "I can't imagine he'll want to take it any further, but we'd better keep him informed. Then maybe we can call it a day."

Mark glanced at his watch; another hour and forty-five minutes' overtime, technically the maximum allowed an agent on any one day.

"I hope so," said Mark. "I just got myself a date."

"Anyone we know?"

"The beautiful Dr Dexter."

Barry raised his eyebrows. "Don't let the boss know. If he thought you picked up someone while you were on duty, he'd send you for a spell in the salt mines in Butte, Montana."

"I didn't realise that they had salt mines in Butte, Montana."

"Only FBI agents who really screw it up know there are salt mines in Butte."

Mark drove back to downtown Washington while Barry wrote up his report of the interview. It was 7:40 by the time they had returned to the Old Post Office Building, and Mark found the parking lot almost empty. By this time at night most civilised people were at home doing civilised things, like eating moussaka. Stames's car was already there. Goddamn him. They took the elevator to the fifth floor and went into Stames's reception room.

It looked empty without Julie. Calvert knocked quietly on the chief's door and the two agents walked in. Stames looked up. He had already found a hundred and one things to do since he'd been back, almost as if he had forgotten that he had specifically come back to see them.

"Right, Barry. Let's have it from the top, slowly and accurately."

Calvert recounted exactly what had happened from the moment they had arrived at Woodrow Wilson to the moment he had asked the Metropolitan Police to put a guard on the room to protect the Greek. Mark was impressed by Barry's total recall. At no point had he exaggerated or revealed any personal prejudice. Stames lowered his head for a few moments and then suddenly turned to Mark.

"Do you want to add anything?" he asked.

"Not really, sir. It was all a bit melodramatic. Although he didn't come over as a liar, he was certainly frightened. Also there's no trace of him in any of our files. I radioed the Night Super for a name check. Negative on Casefikis."

Nick picked up the phone and asked to be put through to Bureau Headquarters. "Give me the National Computer Information Center, Polly." He was put straight through. A young woman answered the phone.

"Stames, Washington Field Office. Would you please have the following suspect checked out on the computer immediately? – Angelo Casefikis: Caucasian; male; Greek ancestry; height, five feet nine inches; weight, about a hundred and sixty-five pounds; hair, dark brown; eyes, brown; age; thirty-eight; no distinguishing marks or scars known; no identifying numbers known." He was reading from the report Calvert had placed in front of him. He waited silently.

"If his story is true," Mark said, "we should have no listing for him at all."

"If it's true," said Calvert.

Stames continued to wait. The days of waiting to find

out who was in the FBI files and who wasn't had long gone. The girl came back on the line.

"We have nothing on a Casefikis, Angelo. We don't even have a Casefikis. The best the computer can offer is a Casegikis who was born in 1901. Sorry I can't help, Mr Stames."

"Thanks very much." Stames put the phone down. "Okay boys, for the moment let's give Casefikis the benefit of the doubt. Let's assume he is telling the truth and that this is a serious investigation. We have no trace of him in any of our files, so we'd better start believing his story until it's disproved; he just might be on to something, and if he is, then it goes way above me. Tomorrow morning, Barry, I want you back at the hospital with a fingerprint expert; take his prints in case he is giving a false name, put them through the identification computer right away and make sure you get a full written statement, signed. Then check the Met files for any shooting incidents on 24 February he could have been involved in. As soon as we can get him out, I want him in an ambulance showing us where that luncheon took place. Push the hospital into agreeing to that tomorrow morning, if possible. To date, he's not under arrest or wanted for any crime we know about, so don't go too far, not that he strikes me as a man who would know much about his rights.

"Mark," Stames said, turning his head, "I want you to go back to the hospital immediately and make sure the Met are there. If not, stay with Casefikis until they do arrive. In the morning, go round to the Golden Duck and check him out. I'm going to make a provisional appointment for us to see the Director tomorrow morning, at 10:00 am, which will give you enough time to report back to me. And if, when we check the fingerprints through the identification computer, nothing comes up at all, and the hotel and the restaurant exist, we may be in a whole heap of trouble. If that's the case, I'm not taking it one inch further without the Director knowing.

For the moment, I want nothing in writing. Don't hand in your official memorandum until tomorrow morning. Above all, don't mention that a senator could be involved to anybody – and that includes Grant Nanna. It's possible tomorrow, after we have seen the Director, that we will do no more than make a full report and hand the whole thing over to the Secret Service. Don't forget the clear division of responsibility – the Secret Service guards the President, we cover federal crime. If a senator is involved, it's us; if the President's involved, it's them. We'll let the Director decide the finer points – I'm not getting involved in Capitol Hill, that's the Director's baby, and with only seven days to play with, we don't have time to sit and discuss the academic niceties."

Stames picked up the red phone which put him straight through to the Director's office.

"Nick Stames, WFO."

"Good evening," said a low, quiet voice. Mrs McGregor, a dedicated servant of the Director of the Federal Bureau of Investigation, was still on duty. It was said that even Hoover had been slightly frightened of her.

"Mrs McGregor, I'd like to make a provisional appointment for myself and Special Agents Calvert and Andrews to see the Director for fifteen minutes, if that's possible. Anytime between 9:00 am and 11.00 am tomorrow. It's likely that after further investigation tonight and early tomorrow, I won't need to bother him."

Mrs McGregor consulted the Director's desk diary. "The Director is going to a meeting of police chiefs at eleven but he is expected in the office at 8:30 and he has nothing marked in his diary before eleven. I'll pencil you in for 10:30, Mr Stames. Do you want me to tell the Director what the subject of your discussion will be?"

"I'd prefer not to."

Mrs McGregor never pressed or asked a second question. She knew if Stames called, it was important. He saw the Director ten times a year on a social basis, but only three or four times a year on a professional basis, and he was not in the habit of wasting the Director's time.

"Thank you, Mr Stames. 10:30 tomorrow morning, unless you cancel beforehand."

Nick put the phone down and looked at his two men.

"Okay, we're fixed to see the Director at 10:30. Barry, why don't you give me a lift home, then you can take yourself off afterwards, and pick me up again first thing in the morning. That'll give us another chance to go over the details again." Barry nodded. "Mark, you get straight back to the hospital."

Mark had allowed his mind to slip away to visualise Elizabeth Dexter walking down the corridor of Woodrow Wilson towards him, red silk collar over the white medical coat, black skirt swinging. He was doing this with his eyes open and the result was quite pleasant. He smiled.

"Andrews, what the hell is so amusing about a reported threat on the President's life?" Stames demanded.

"Sorry, sir. You just shot my social life down in flames. Would it be okay if I use my own car? I was hoping to go directly from the hospital to dinner."

"Yes, that's fine. We'll use the duty car and see you first thing in the morning. Get your tail in gear, Mark, and hope the Met makes it before breakfast." Mark looked at his watch. "Christ, it's already 8:00 pm."

Mark left the office slightly annoyed. Even if the Met were there when he arrived, he would still be late for Elizabeth Dexter. Still, he could always call her from the hospital.

"Like a plate of warmed-up moussaka, Barry, and a bottle of retsina?"

"It was more than I was expecting, boss."

The two men left the office. Stames mentally checked off the items on his nightly routine.

"Barry, will you double-check that Aspirin is on duty, as you go out, and tell him we won't be back again tonight."

Calvert made a detour to the Criminal Room and

delivered the message to Aspirin. He was doing the crossword from *The Washington Star*. He had finished three clues; it was going to be a long night. Barry caught up with Nick Stames as he stepped into the blue Ford.

"Yes, boss, he's working away."

They looked at each other, a night of headaches. Barry got in the driver's seat, slid it back as far as it would go, and adjusted the seat belt. They moved quietly up Constitution Avenue, then past the White House on to the E Street Expressway, and on towards Memorial Bridge.

"If Casefikis is on to something, we've got one hell of a week ahead of us," said Nick Stames. "Did he seem sure of the date for the assassination attempt?"

"When I questioned him a second time about the details, he repeated 10 March, in Washington."

"Hum-uh, seven days, not very long. Wonder what the Director will make of it," said Stames.

"Hand it over to the Secret Police, if he's got any sense," Barry said.

"Ah, let's forget it for the moment. Let's concentrate on warmed-over moussaka and deal with tomorrow when tomorrow comes."

The car came to a halt at a traffic light, just beyond the White House, where a bearded, long-haired, dirty youth, who had been picketing the home of the President, stood with a large poster advising the world: BEWARE THE END IS NIGH. Stames glanced at it and nodded to Barry.

"That's all we need tonight."

They passed under Virginia Avenue on the Expressway and sped across Memorial Bridge. A black 3.5 Lincoln passed them at about seventy miles an hour.

"Bet the Met pick him up," said Stames.

"Probably late for Dulles Airport," replied Barry.

The traffic was light, the rush-hour well behind them and when they turned on to George Washington Parkway they managed to stay in top gear. The Parkway, which follows the Potomac along the wooded Virginia shore, was dark and winding. Barry's reflexes were as fast as any man's in the service and Stames, although older, saw exactly what happened at the same time. A Buick, large and black, started to overtake them on their left. Calvert glanced towards it and when he looked forward again an instant later, another car, a black Lincoln, had swung in front of them on the wrong side of the highway. He thought he heard a rifle shot. Barry wrenched the wheel towards the centre of the road but it didn't respond. Both cars hit him at once, but he still managed to take one of them with him down the rocky slope. They gathered speed until they hit the surface of the river with a thud. Nick thought as he struggled in vain to open the door that the sinking seemed grotesquely slow, but inevitable.

The black Buick continued down the highway as if nothing had happened; past a car skidding to a halt, carrying a young couple, two terrified witnesses to the accident. They leapt out of their car and ran to the edge of the slope. There was nothing they could do but watch helplessly for the few seconds it took the blue Ford sedan and the Lincoln to sink out of sight.

"Jee-sus, did you see what happened ahead?" said the young man.

"Not really. I just saw the two cars go over the top. What do we do now, Jim?"

"Get the police fast."

Man and wife ran back to their car.

# Thursday evening, 3 March

## 8:15 pm

"Hello, Liz."

There was a moment's pause at the other end of the phone.

"Hello, G-man. Aren't you getting a little ahead of yourself?"

"Only wishful thinking. Listen, Elizabeth, I've had to come back to the hospital and keep an eye on your Mr Casefikis until the police arrive. It's just possible that he could be in some danger, so we're having to put a guard on him which means I'm bound to be late for our date. Do you mind waiting?"

"No, I won't starve. I always have lunch with my father on Thursdays, and he's a big eater."

"That's good. Because I think you need to be fed. You look as though you might be hard to find in the dark. I'm still trying to get the flu, incidentally."

She laughed warmly. "See you later."

Mark put the telephone back on the hook and walked over to the elevator, and pressed the arrow on the Up-button.

He only hoped the Met policeman had arrived and was already on duty. Christ. How long was the elevator going to take to return to the ground floor? Patients must have died just waiting for it. Eventually the doors slid open and a burly Greek Orthodox priest hurried out and past him. He could have sworn it was a Greek Orthodox priest, from the high dark hat and long trailing veil and the Orthodox Cross around his neck, although something about the priest struck Mark as strange, but he couldn't put his finger on it. He stood, puzzling for a moment, staring at his retreating back and only just managing to jump into the elevator before the doors closed. He pressed the fourth-floor button several times. Come on, come on. Get going, you bastard, but it had no ears for Mark, and proceeded upward at the same stately pace as it had earlier in the afternoon. It cared nothing for his date with Elizabeth Dexter. The door opened slowly, and he went through the widening gap sideways and ran down the corridor to Room 4308 but there was no sign of any policeman. In fact, the corridor was deserted. It looked as if he were going to be stuck there for some time. He peered through the little window in the door at the two men, asleep in their beds, the voiceless television set was still on giving out a square of light. Mark left to look for the staff nurse and eventually found her tucked away in the head nurse's office enjoying a cup of coffee. She was pleased to see that it was the better-looking of the two FBI men who had returned.

"Has anyone come from the Metropolitan Police to keep an eye on Room 4308?"

"No, no one's been anywhere near the place tonight. Silent as the grave. Were you expecting someone?"

"Yes, damn it. Guess I'll have to wait. Do you think I could take a chair? I'm going to have to stick around till an officer from the Metropolitan Police comes. I hope I won't be in your way."

"You won't be in my way. You can stay as long as you like. I'll see if I can find you a nice comfortable chair." She put her mug down. "Would you like some coffee?"

"I certainly would." Mark looked at her more carefully. It might be an evening with the nurse rather than the doctor. Mark decided he had better go back and check the room first, reassure Casefikis, if he were still awake, and then call the Met and ask where the hell their man was. He walked slowly to the door a second time; he felt no need to hurry now. He opened the door quietly. It was pitch black except for the light from the TV, and his eyes were not quite focused. He glanced at the two of them in bed. They were quite still. He wouldn't have bothered to look any further if it hadn't been for the dripping.

Drip, drip, drip.

It sounded like tap water but he couldn't remember a tap.

Drip, drip.

He moved quietly to the bedside of Angelo Casefikis, and glanced down.

Drip, drip.

Warm fresh blood was flowing over the bottom sheet, trickling from Casefikis's mouth, his dark eyes bulged from their sockets, his tongue was hanging loose and swollen. His throat had been cut, ear to ear, just below the chin line. The blood was starting to make a pool on the floor. Mark was standing in it. He felt his legs sink, and he was barely able to grip the side of the bed and stop himself falling. He lurched over towards the deaf man. Mark's eyes were now focused, and he retched loudly. The postman's head was hanging loose from the rest of his body; only the colour of his skin showed that they were once connected. Mark managed to scramble out of the door and get to the pay phone, his heartbeat thudding madly in his ears. He could feel his shirt clinging to his body. His hands were covered with blood. He fumbled ineffectually for a couple of quarters. He dialled Homicide and gave the bare outline of what had happened. This time they wouldn't be casual about sending someone. The nurse on duty returned with a cup of coffee.

"Are you okay? You look a bit pale," she said, and then she saw his hands and screamed.

"Don't go into Room 4308 whatever you do. Don't let

anyone into that room unless I say so. Send me a doctor immediately."

The nurse thrust the cup of coffee at him, forcing him to take it, and ran down the corridor. Mark made himself go back into Room 4308, although his presence was irrelevant. There was nothing he could do except wait. He switched on the lights and went over to the bathroom; he tried to remove the worst of the blood and vomit from himself and his clothes. Mark heard the swinging door and rushed back into the room. Another young, white-coated female doctor . . . "Alicia Delgado, MD" said her plastic label.

"Don't touch anything," said Mark.

Dr Delgado stared at him and then the bodies, and groaned.

"Don't touch anything," repeated Mark, "until Homicide arrive; they will be here shortly."

"Who are you?" she asked.

"Special Agent Mark Andrews, FBI." He instinctively took out his wallet and showed his credentials.

"Do we just stand here staring at each other or are you going to allow me to do something about this mess?"

"Nothing until Homicide has completed their investigation and given clearance. Let's get out of here." He passed her and pushed the door with his shoulder, not touching anything.

They were back in the corridor.

Mark instructed Dr Delgado to wait outside the door and to allow no one else inside while he phoned the Metropolitan Police again.

She nodded reluctantly.

He went over to the pay phone, two more quarters; he dialled the Metropolitan Police and asked for Lieutenant Blake.

"Lieutenant Blake went home about an hour ago. Can I help you?"

"When had you been planning to send someone over to guard Room 4308 at Woodrow Wilson Medical Center?"

"Who's speaking?"

"Andrews, FBI, Washington Field Office." Mark repeated the details of the double murder.

"Well, our man should be with you now. He left the office over half an hour ago. I'll inform Homicide immediately."

"I've already done that," snapped Mark.

He put the phone down and collapsed into a nearby chair. The corridor was now full of white coats. Two gurneys were being wheeled up to Room 4308. They were all waiting. What was the right thing to do?

Two more quarters, he dialled Nick Stames's home. The phone seemed to ring for a long time. Why didn't he answer? Eventually a female voice came on.

Mustn't show panic, he thought, holding on to the phone box. "Good evening, Mrs Stames. It's Mark Andrews. Can I speak to your husband?" An even tone, no sign of stress.

"I'm afraid Nick is not home, Mark. He went back to the office about two hours ago. Funny, he said he was going to see you and Barry Calvert."

"Yes, we saw him, but he left the office to go back home about forty minutes ago."

"Well, he hasn't arrived yet. He only managed to finish the first course of his dinner and said he would come straight back. No sign of him. Maybe he returned to the office. Why don't you try him there?"

"Yes, of course. Sorry to have bothered you." Mark hung up, looked over to check that no one had gone into Room 4308. No one had. He put two more quarters in and phoned the office. Polly was on duty.

"Mark Andrews. Put me through to Mr Stames, quickly, please."

"Mr Stames and Special Agent Calvert left about forty-five minutes ago – on their way home, I think, Mr Andrews."

"That can't be right. It can't be right."

"Yes, they did leave, sir. I saw them go."

"Could you double-check?"

"If you say so, Mr Andrews."

Mark waited, it seemed to him, for an interminable time. What should he be doing? He was only one man, where was everyone else? What was he supposed to do? Christ, nothing in his training covered this – the FBI are meant to arrive twenty-four hours after a crime, not during it.

"There's no answer, Mr Andrews."

"Thanks, Polly."

Mark looked desperately at the ceiling for inspiration. He had been briefed not to tell anybody about the earlier events of the evening, not to say a word whatever the circumstances until after Stames's meeting with the Director. He must find Stames; he must find Calvert. He must find somebody he could talk to. Two more quarters. He tried Barry Calvert. The phone rang and rang. No reply from the bachelor apartment. Same two quarters. He called Norma Stames again. "Mrs Stames, Mark Andrews. Sorry to trouble you again. The moment your husband and Mr Calvert arrive, please have them call me at Woodrow Wilson."

"Yes, I'll tell Nick as soon as he comes in. They probably stopped off on the way."

"Yes, of course, I hadn't thought of that. Maybe the best thing will be for me to go back downtown as soon as the relief arrives. So perhaps they could contact me there. Thank you, Mrs Stames." He hung up the receiver.

As he put the phone down Mark saw the Met policeman jauntily walking towards him down the middle of the now crowded corridor, an Ed McBain novel under his arm. Mark thought of bawling him out for his late arrival, but what was the point. No use crying over spilt blood he thought, morbidly, and began to feel sick again. He took the young officer aside, and briefed him on the killings, giving no details of why the two men were important, only of what had happened. He asked him to inform his chief and added that the Homicide Squad were on their way, again adding no details. The policeman called his own duty officer, and reported all he had been told, matter-of-factly. The Washington Metropolitan Police handled over six hundred murders a year.

The medical personnel were all waiting impatiently; it was going to be a long wait. Professional bustle seemed to have replaced the early panic. Mark still wasn't sure where to turn, what to do. Where was Stames? Where was Calvert? Where the hell was anybody?

He went over to the policeman again, who was explaining in detail why no one must enter the room . . . they were not convinced but waited; Mark told him he was leaving for the Field Office. He still gave him no clue why Casefikis had been important. The Metropolitan policeman felt he had things under control. Homicide would be there at any moment. He told Mark they'd want to talk to him later that night. Mark nodded and left him.

When he arrived back at his car, he took the flashing red light out of the side compartment and fixed it to the roof, placing the switch into its special slot. He was going to get back to the office, at top speed, to people he knew, to reality, to men who would make some sense out of his nightmare.

Mark flicked on the car radio. "WFO 180 in service. Please try and locate Mr Stames and Mr Calvert. Urgent. I am returning to Field Office immediately."

"Yes, Mr Andrews."

"WFO 180 out of service."

Twelve minutes later, he arrived at the Washington Field Office and parked his car. He ran to the elevator. The operator took him up. He rushed out.

"Aspirin, Aspirin. Who the hell's on duty tonight?"

"I'm the only one on tonight, boy, I'm here on my own," said Aspirin, looking over his glasses, rather bored. "What's the matter?"

"Where's Stames? Where's Calvert?" Mark demanded.

44

"They went home just over an hour ago."

Oh hell, what should he do now? Aspirin was not a man to confide in, but he was the only person Mark could seek any advice from. And although Stames had carefully instructed him not to speak to anyone about the details until they had seen the Director, this was an emergency. He wouldn't give away any of the details, he would just find out what a Hoover man would have done.

"I have to find Stames and Calvert, wherever they are. Any suggestions?"

"Well, first of all, have you tried the car radio stations?" asked Aspirin.

"I asked Polly to check. I'll try her again."

Mark picked up the nearest phone. "Polly, did you locate Mr Stames or Mr Calvert on the car radio?"

"Still trying, sir."

He seemed to wait endlessly, endlessly; and nothing happened. "What's going on, Polly, what's going on?"

"I'm trying as hard as I can, sir. All I can get is a buzzing sound."

"Try One, Two, Three, or Four. Doesn't matter what you try. Try every station."

"Yes, sir. I can only do one at a time. There are four stations and I can only do one at a time."

Mark realised he was panicking. It was time to sit down and think things through. The end of the world hadn't come – or had it?

"They're not on One, sir. Not on Two. Why would they be on Three or Four at this time of night? They're only on their way home."

"I don't care where they're going. Just find them. Try again."

"Okay, okay." She tried Three. She tried Four. She had to have authorisation to break the code for Five and Six. Mark looked at Aspirin. The duty officer was authorised to break the code.

"This is an emergency – I swear to you it's an emergency."

Aspirin told Polly to try Five and Six. Five and Six are Federal Communications Commission to the FBI. They are known by the initial KGB: it always amused FBI men to have KGB as their network call code. But at that moment it didn't seem particularly funny. There was no reply to be had on KGB 5. Then KGB 6 was raised; likewise nothing. Now what, dear God, now what? Where did he turn next? Aspirin looked at him inquiringly, not really wanting to get involved.

"Always remember, son, C-Y-A. That's the ticket. C-Y-A."

"Covering your ass will not help me to locate Mr Stames," said Mark, forcing himself to speak calmly. "It doesn't matter, Aspirin, you get back to your crossword puzzle."

Mark left him and went into the men's room, cupped his hands under the tap and washed his mouth out; he still smelled of vomit and blood. He cleaned up as best he could. He returned to the Criminal Room, sat down, and counted to ten very slowly. He had to make up his mind what to do, and then to carry it out, come what may. Something had probably happened to Stames and Calvert, he knew something had happened to the black postman and the Greek. Perhaps he should try and get in touch with the Director, although it was an extreme course. A man of Mark's rank, two years out of training, didn't just pick up a phone and call the Director. In any case he could still keep Stames's appointment with the Director at 10:30 the next morning. 10:30 the next morning. That was half a day away. More than twelve hours of not knowing what to do. Nursing a secret that he had been told not to discuss with anyone. Holding information he couldn't impart to anybody else.

The phone rang and he heard Polly's voice. He prayed it would be Stames, but his prayer was not answered.

"Hey, Mr Andrews, are you still there? I've got Homicide on the line. Captain Hogan wants to talk to you."

"Andrews?"

"Yes, Captain."

"What can you tell me?"

Mark reported truthfully that Casefikis was an illegal immigrant who had delayed seeking treatment for his leg, and untruthfully that he alleged he had been shot by a crook who had subjected him to blackmail, threatening exposure of his illegal entry into the States. A full written report would be sent around to his office by tomorrow morning.

The detective sounded disbelieving.

"Are you holding out on me, son? What was the FBI doing there in the first place? There's going to be one hell of a scene if I find out you're withholding information. I wouldn't hesitate to roast your ass over the hottest coals in Washington."

Mark thought of Stames's repeated injunctions about secrecy.

"No, I'm not withholding information," he said in a raised voice; he knew he was trembling and could hardly have sounded less convincing. The Homicide detective grumbled to himself, asked a few more questions, and hung up. Mark put the phone down. The receiver was clammy with sweat, his clothes still stuck to him. He tried Norma Stames again; still the boss hadn't reached home. He called Polly again, and asked her to go through the whole routine with the radio channels again; still nothing except a buzzing sound on Channel One. Finally, Mark abandoned the telephone and told Aspirin he was leaving. Aspirin didn't seem interested.

Mark headed for the elevator and walked quickly to his car. Must get on to home ground. Then call the Director. Once again he was speeding through the streets towards his home.

It wasn't the most luxurious part of town, but the renovated south-west section of Washington was home for many young, single professionals. It was on the waterfront near the Arena Stage, conveniently located next to a

Metro station. Pleasant, lively, not too expensive – the place suited Mark perfectly.

As soon as he reached his apartment, he ran up the stairs, burst through the door and picked up the phone. After several rings, the Bureau answered. "Director's office. Duty officer speaking."

Mark drew a deep breath.

"My name is Special Agent Andrews, Washington Field Office," Mark began slowly. "I want to speak to the Director, priority and immediate."

The Director, it seemed, was dining with the Attorney General at her home. Mark asked for the telephone number. Did he have special authority to contact the Director at this time of night? He had special authority, he had an appointment with him at 10:30 tomorrow morning and, for God's sake, he had special authority.

The man must have sensed Andrews was desperate.

"I'll call you right back, if you'll give me your number."

Andrews knew that this was simply to check that he was an FBI agent and that he was scheduled to see the Director in the morning. The phone rang after one minute and the duty officer was back.

"The Director is still with the Attorney General. Her private number is 761-4386."

Mark dialled the number.

"Mrs Edelman's residence," said a deferential voice.

"This is Special Agent Mark Andrews," he began. "I need to speak to the Director of the Federal Bureau of Investigation."

He said it slowly, he said it clearly, although he was still trembling. The reply came back from a man whose biggest worry that night had been that the potatoes had taken longer than expected.

"Will you hold the line one moment please, sir?"

He waited, he waited, he waited.

A new voice said: "Tyson here."

Mark drew a deep breath and plunged in.

"My name is Special Agent Mark Andrews. I have an

appointment to see you with SAC Stames and Special Agent Calvert at 10:30 tomorrow morning. You don't know the details, sir, because it was made through Mrs McGregor after you had left your office. I have to see you immediately, you may wish to call me back. I'm at home.''

"Yes, Andrews," said Tyson. "I'll call you back. What is your number?"

Mark gave it.

"Young man," Tyson said, "this had better be a priority."

"It is, sir."

Mark waited again. One minute passed, and then another. Had Tyson dismissed him as a fool? What was going on? Three minutes passed. Four minutes passed; he was obviously checking more thoroughly than his duty officer had done.

The phone rang. Mark jumped.

"Hi, Mark, it's Roger. Want to come out for a beer?"

"Not now, Roger, not now." He slammed the phone down.

It rang again immediately.

"Right, Andrews, what do you have to tell me? Make it quick and to the point."

"I want to see you now, sir. I need fifteen minutes of your time and I need you to tell me what the hell to do."

He regretted "hell" the moment he had said it.

"Very well, if it's that urgent. Do you know where the Attorney General lives?"

"No, sir."

"Take this down: 2942 Edgewood Street, Arlington."

Mark put the phone down, wrote the address carefully in block capitals on the inside of a matchbook advertising life insurance, and called Aspirin, who just couldn't get 7-across.

"If anything happens, I'll be on my car radio; you can get me there, I'll leave the line on Channel Two open the whole time. Something's wrong with Channel One."

Aspirin sniffed: the young agents took themselves far too seriously nowadays. It wouldn't have happened under J. Edgar Hoover, shouldn't be allowed to happen now. Still, he only had one more year and then retirement. He returned to the crossword. 7-across, ten letters: gathering of those in favour of buccaneering. Aspirin started to think.

Mark Andrews was thinking too as he rushed into the elevator, into the street, into his car, and moved off at speed to Arlington. He raced up East Basin Drive to Independence Avenue, past the Lincoln Memorial to get on to Memorial Bridge. He drove as fast as possible through the early night, cursing the people calmly strolling across the road on this mild, pleasant evening, casually on their way to nowhere in particular, cursing the people who took no notice of the flashing red light he had affixed to the car roof, cursing all the way. Where was Stames? Where was Barry? What the hell was going on? Would the Director think he was crazy?

He crossed Memorial Bridge and took the G.W. Parkway exit. A tie-up. He couldn't move an inch. Probably an accident. A goddamn accident right now. That was all he needed. He pulled into the centre lane and leaned on his horn. Most people assumed he was connected with the police rescue team: most people let him by. Eventually he made it to the group of police cars and rescue-squad ambulances. A young Metropolitan policeman approached the car. "Are you on this detail?"

"No. FBI. I've got to get to Arlington. Emergency."

He flashed his credentials. The policeman ushered him through. He raced away from the accident. Goddamn accident. Once he was clear of it, the traffic became light. Fifteen minutes later, he arrived at 2942 Edgewood Street, Arlington. One last check with Polly at the Washington Field Office on the car phone. No, neither Stames nor Calvert had called in.

Mark jumped out of the car. Before he had taken a step, a Secret Service man stopped him. Mark showed his credentials and said that he had an appointment with the Director. The Secret Service man courteously asked him to wait by his car. After consultation at the door, Mark was shown into a small room just on the right of the hall which was obviously used as a study. The Director came in. Mark stood up.

"Good evening, Director."

"Good evening, Andrews. You've interrupted a very important dinner. I hope you know what you are doing."

The Director was cold and abrupt, clearly displeased at being summoned to a meeting by an unknown junior agent.

Mark went through the whole story from the first meeting with Stames through to his decision to go over everybody's head. The Director's face remained impassive throughout the long recital. It was still impassive when Mark had finished. Mark's only thought was: I've done the wrong thing. He should have gone on trying to reach Stames and Calvert. They were probably home by now. He waited, a little sweat appearing on his forehead. Perhaps this was his last day in the FBI. The Director's first words took him by surprise.

"You did exactly the right thing, Andrews. I'd have made the same decision in your place. It must have taken guts to bring the whole thing to me." He looked hard at Mark. "You're absolutely certain only Stames, Calvert, you, and I know all the details of what happened this evening? No one from the Secret Service, and no one from the Metropolitan Police Department?"

"That's correct, sir, just the four of us."

"And the three of you already have an appointment with me at 10:30 tomorrow morning?"

"Yes, sir."

"Good. Take this down."

Mark took out a pad from his inside coat pocket.

"You have the Attorney General's number here?"

"Yes, sir."

"And my number at home is 721-4069. Learn them

and then destroy them. Now I'll tell you exactly what you do next. Go back to the Washington Field Office. Check on Stames and Calvert again. Call the morgue, call the hospitals, call the highway police. If nothing turns up, I'll see you in my office at 8:30 tomorrow morning, not 10:30. That's your first job. Second, get me the names of the Homicide officers working on this detail with the Metropolitan Police. Now tell me if I have this right – you told them nothing about the reason you went to see Casefikis?"

"Nothing, sir."

"Good."

The Attorney General put her head around the door.

"Everything under control, Halt?"

"Fine, thanks, Marian. I don't think you've met Special Agent Andrews of the Washington Field Office."

"No. Nice to meet you, Mr Andrews."

"Good evening, ma'am."

"Will you be long, Halt?"

"No, I'll be back as soon as I've finished briefing Andrews."

"Anything special?"

"No, nothing to worry about."

The Director had obviously decided nobody was going to be told the story until he got to the bottom of it himself.

"Where was I?"

"You told me to return to the Washington Field Office, sir, and check on Stames and Calvert."

"Yes."

"And then to call the morgue, the hospitals, and the highway police."

"Right."

"And you told me to check on the Homicide officers, get their names."

"Right. Take down the following: check the names of all hospital employees and visitors, as well as any other persons who can be identified as having been in the vicinity of Room 4308 between the time the two occupants were known to be alive and the time you found them dead. Check the names of the two dead men through NCIC and Bureau indexes for any background information we may have. Get fingerprints of all persons on duty and all visitors and all others who can be identified as having been near Room 4308, as well as fingerprints of the two dead men. We will need all these prints both for elimination purposes and possible suspect identification. If you don't find Stames and Calvert, as I said, see me at 8:30 in my office tomorrow morning. If anything else arises tonight, you call me here or at home. Don't hesitate. If it's after 11:30, I'll be home. If you call me on the phone, use a code name – now let me think – Julius – let's hope it's not prophetic, and give me your number. Make sure you use a pay phone and I'll call you back immediately. Don't bother me before 7:15 in the morning, unless it's really important. Have you understood all that?"

"Yes, sir."

"Right. I think I'll get back to dinner."

Mark stood up, ready to leave. The Director put a hand on his shoulder.

"Don't worry, young man. These things happen from time to time and you made the right decision. You showed a lot of self-possession in a lousy situation. Now get on with the job."

"Yes, sir."

Mark was relieved that someone else knew what he was going through; someone else with far bigger shoulders was there to share it.

On his way back to the FBI office, he picked up the car microphone. "WFO 180 in service. Any word from Mr Stames?"

"Nothing yet, WFO 180, but I'll keep trying."

Aspirin was still there when he arrived, unaware that Mark had just been talking with the Director of the FBI. Aspirin had met all four directors at cocktail parties, though none of them would have remembered his name.

"Emergency over, son?"

"Yes," Mark said, lying. "Have we heard from Stames or Calvert?" He tried not to sound anxious.

"No, must have dropped in somewhere on the way home. Never you worry. The little sheep will find their way back without you to hold their tails."

Mark did worry. He went to his office and picked up the phone. Polly had still heard nothing. Just a buzz that continued on Channel One. He called Norma Stames, still no news. Mrs Stames asked if there might be anything to worry about.

"Nothing at all." Another lie. Was he sounding too unconcerned? "We just can't find out which bar he's ended up in."

She laughed, but she knew Nick never frequented bars.

Mark tried Calvert; still no reply from the bachelor apartment. He knew in his bones something was wrong. He just didn't know what. At least the Director was there, and the Director knew everything now. He glanced at his watch: 11:15. Where had the night gone? And where was it going? 11:15. What was he supposed to have done tonight? Hell. He had persuaded a beautiful girl to have dinner with him. Yet again, he picked up the telephone. At least she would be safely at home, where she ought to be.

"Hello."

"Hello, Elizabeth, it's Mark Andrews. I'm really sorry about not making it tonight. Something happened that got way out of my control."

The tension in his voice was apparent.

"Don't worry," she said lightly. "You warned me you were unreliable."

"I hope you'll let me take a raincheck. Hopefully, in the morning, I can sort things out. I'll probably see you then."

"In the morning?" she said. "If you're thinking of the hospital, I'm off duty tomorrow."

Mark hesitated, thinking quickly of what he could

prudently say. "Well, that may be best. I am afraid it's not good news. Casefikis and the other man in his room were brutally murdered tonight. The Met is following it up, but we have nothing to go on."

"Murdered? Both of them? Why? Who? Casefikis wasn't killed without reason, was he?" The words came out in a torrent. "What's going on, for heaven's sake? No, don't answer that. You wouldn't tell me the truth in any case."

"I wouldn't waste my time lying to you, Elizabeth. Look, I've had it for tonight, and I owe you a big steak for messing up your evening. Can I call you some time soon?"

"I'd like that. Murder isn't food for the appetite, though. I hope you catch the men responsible. We see the results of a great deal of violence at Woodrow Wilson, but it isn't usually inflicted within our walls."

"I know. I'm sorry it involves you. Good night, Elizabeth. Sleep well."

"And you, Mark. If you can."

Mark put the phone down, and immediately the burden of the day's events returned. What now? There was nothing practicable he could do before 8:30, except keep in touch on the radio phone until he was home. There was no point just sitting there looking out of the window, feeling helpless, sick, and alone. He went in to Aspirin, told him he was going home, and that he'd call in every fifteen minutes because he was still anxious to speak to Stames and Calvert. Aspirin didn't even look up.

"Fine," he said, his mind fully occupied by the crossword puzzle. He had completed eleven clues, a sure sign it was a quiet evening.

Mark drove down Pennsylvania Avenue towards his apartment. At the first traffic circle, a tourist who didn't know he had the right of way was holding up traffic. Damn him, thought Mark. Visitors to Washington who hadn't mastered the knack of cutting out at the right turn-off could end up circling round and round many more times than originally planned. Eventually, Mark managed to get around the circle and back on Pennsylvania Avenue. He continued to drive slowly towards his home, at the Tiber Island Apartments, his thoughts heavy and anxious. He turned on the car radio for the midnight news; must take his mind off it somehow. There were no big stories that night and the newscaster sounded rather bored; the President had held a press conference about the Gun Control bill, and the situation in South Africa seemed to be getting worse. Then the local news; there had been an automobile accident on the G.W. Parkway and it involved two cars, both of which were being hauled out of the river by cranes, under floodlights. One of the cars was a black Lincoln, the other a blue Ford sedan, according to eyewitnesses, a married couple from Jacksonville vacationing in the Washington area. No other details as yet.

A blue Ford sedan. Although he had not really been concentrating, it kept repeating itself in his brain – a blue Ford sedan? Oh no, God, please no. He veered right off 9th Street on to Maine Avenue, narrowly missing a fire hydrant, and raced back towards Memorial Bridge, where he had been only two hours before. The roads were clearer now and he was back in a few minutes. At the scene of the accident the Metropolitan Police were still thick on the ground and one lane of the G.W. was closed off by barriers. Mark parked the car on the grassy verge and ran up to the barrier. He showed his FBI credentials and was taken to the officer in charge; he explained that he feared one of the cars involved might have been driven by an agent from the FBI. Any details yet?

"Still haven't got them out," the inspector replied. "We only have two witnesses to the accident, if it was an accident. Apparently there was some very funny driving going on. They should be up in about thirty minutes. All you can do is wait."

Mark went over to the side of the road to watch the vast cranes and tiny frogmen groping around in the river under vast klieg lights. The thirty minutes wasn't thirty minutes; he shivered in the cold, waiting and watching. It was forty minutes, it was fifty minutes, it was over an hour before the black Lincoln came out. Inside the car was one body. Cautious man, he was wearing a seat belt. The police moved in immediately. Mark went back to the officer in charge and asked how long before the second car.

"Not long. That Lincoln wasn't your car, then?"

"No," said Mark.

Ten minutes, twenty minutes, he saw the top of the second car, a dark blue car; he saw the side of the car, one of the windows fractionally opened; he saw the whole of the car. Two men were in it. He saw the licence plate. For a second time that night, Mark felt sick. Almost crying, he ran back to the officer in charge and gave the names of the two men in the car, and then ran on to a pay phone at the side of the road. It was a long way. He dialled the number, checking his watch as he did so; it was nearly one o'clock. After one ring he heard a tired voice say, "Yes."

Mark said, "Julius."

The voice said, "What is your number?"

He gave it. Thirty seconds later, the telephone rang.

"Well, Andrews. It's one o'clock in the morning."

"I know, sir, it's Stames and Calvert, they're dead."

There was a moment's hesitation, the voice was awake now.

"Are you certain?"

"Yes, sir."

Mark gave the details of the car crash, trying to keep the weariness and emotion out of his voice.

"Call your office immediately, Andrews," Tyson said, "without releasing any of the details that you gave me this evening. Only tell them about the car crash – nothing more. Then get any further information about it you can from the police. See me in my office at 7:30, not 8:30;

come through the wide entrance on the far side of the building; there will be a man waiting there for you. He'll be expecting you; don't be late. Go home now and try to get some sleep and keep yourself out of sight until tomorrow. Don't worry, Andrews. Two of us know, and I'll put agents on the routine checks that I gave you to do earlier."

The phone clicked. Mark called Aspirin, what a night for him to have to be on duty, told him about Stames and Calvert, hanging up abruptly before Aspirin could ask any questions. He returned to his car and drove home slowly through the night. There was hardly another car on the streets and the early-morning mist gave everything an unearthly look.

At the entrance to his apartment garage he saw Simon, the young black attendant, who liked Mark and, even more, Mark's Mercedes. Mark had blown a small legacy from his aunt on the car just after graduating from college, but never regretted his extravagance. Simon knew Mark had no assigned spot in the garage and always offered to park his car for him – anything for a chance to drive the magnificent silver Mercedes SLC 580. Mark usually exchanged a few bantering words with Simon; tonight he passed him the keys without even looking at him.

"I'll need it at seven in the morning," he said, already walking away. "Okay, man," came back the reply.

Mark heard Simon restart the car with a soft whoosh before the elevator door closed behind him. He arrived at his apartment; three rooms, all empty. He locked the door, and then bolted it, something he had never done before. He walked around the room slowly, undressed, throwing his sour-smelling shirt into the laundry hamper. He washed for the third time that night and then went to bed, to stare up at the white ceiling. He tried to make some sense out of the night's events; he tried to sleep. Six hours passed, and if he slept it was never for more than a few minutes.

*

Someone else who didn't sleep that night for more than a few minutes was tossing and turning in her bed at the White House.

Abraham Lincoln, John F. Kennedy, Martin Luther King, John Lennon and Robert Kennedy. How many citizens distinguished and unknown needed to sacrifice their lives before the House would pass a bill to outlaw such self-destruction?

"Who else must die?" she remarked. "If I myself there is no hour so fit as . . ."

She turned over and looked at Edward whose expression left no doubt that such morbid thoughts were not on his mind.

# Friday morning, 4 March

## 6:27 am

Eventually Mark could stand it no longer and at 6:30 am he rose, showered, and put on a clean shirt and a fresh suit. From his apartment window, he looked out across the Washington Channel to East Potomac Park and went over in his mind all that had happened yesterday. In a few weeks the cherry trees would bloom. In a few weeks . . .

He closed the apartment door behind him, glad simply to be on the move again. Simon gave him the car keys; he had managed to find a space for the Mercedes in one of the private parking lots.

Mark drove the car slowly up 6th Street, turned left on G and right on 7th. No traffic at this time of morning except trucks. He passed the Hirshhorn Museum as he crossed into Independence Avenue. At the intersection of 7th and Pennsylvania, next to the National Archives, Mark came to a halt at a red light. He felt an eerie sense of nothing being out of the ordinary, as though the previous day had been a bad dream. He would arrive at the office and Nick Stames and Barry Calvert would be there as usual. The vision evaporated as he looked to his left. At one end of the deserted avenue, he could see the White House grounds and patches of the white building through the trees. To his right, at the other end of the avenue, stood the Capitol, gleaming in the early morning sunshine. And between the two, between Caesar and Cassius, thought Mark, stood the FBI Building. Alone in the middle, he mused, the Director and himself, playing with destiny.

Mark drove the car down the ramp at the back of FBI Headquarters and parked. A young man in a dark blue blazer, grey flannels, dark shoes, and a smart blue tie, the regulation uniform of the Bureau, awaited him. An anonymous man, thought Mark, who looked far too neat to have just got up. Mark Andrews showed him his identification. The young man led him towards the elevator without saying a word; it took them to the seventh floor, where Mark was noiselessly escorted to a small room and asked to wait.

He sat in the reception room, next to the Director's office, with the inevitable out-of-date copies of *Time* and *Newsweek*; he might have been at the dentist's. It was the first time in his life that he would rather have been at his dentist's. He pondered the events of the last fourteen hours. He'd gone from being a man with no responsibility enjoying the second of five eventful years in the FBI to one who was staring into the jaws of a tiger. His only previous trip to the Bureau itself had been for his interview; they hadn't told him that this could happen. They had talked of salaries, bonuses, holidays, a worthwhile and fulfilling job, serving the nation, nothing about immigrant Greeks and black postmen with their throats cut, nothing about friends being drowned in the Potomac. He paced around the room trying to compose his thoughts; yesterday should have been his day off, but he had decided he could do with the overtime pay. Perhaps another agent would have got back to the hospital more quickly and forestalled the double murder. Perhaps if he had driven the Ford sedan last night, it would have been he, not Stames and Calvert, in the Potomac. Perhaps ... Mark closed his eyes and felt an involuntary shiver run down his spine. He made an effort to disregard the panicky fear that had kept him awake all night – perhaps it would be his turn next.

His eyes came to rest on a plaque on the wall, which stated that, in over sixty years of the FBI's history, only thirty-four people had been killed while on duty; on only one occasion had two officers died on the same day. Yesterday made that out-of-date. Mark's eyes continued moving around the wall and settled on a large picture of the Supreme Court; government and the law hand-in-hand. On his left were the five directors, Hoover, Gray, Ruckelshaus, Kelley, and now the redoubtable H. A. L. Tyson, known to everyone in the Bureau by the acronym Halt. Apparently, no one except his secretary, Mrs McGregor, knew his first name. It had become a long-standing joke in the Bureau. When you joined the FBI, you paid one dollar to Mrs McGregor, who had served the Director for twenty-seven years, and told her what you thought the Director's first name was. If you got it right, you won the pool. The kitty had now reached $3,516. Mark had guessed Hector. Mrs McGregor had laughed and the pool was one dollar the richer. If you wanted a second guess, that cost you another dollar, but if you got it wrong, you paid a ten-dollar fine. Quite a few people tried the second time and the kitty grew larger as each new victim arrived.

Mark had had what he thought was the bright idea of checking the Criminal Fingerprints File. The FBI fingerprints records fall into three categories – military, civil, and criminal, and all FBI agents have their prints in the criminal file. This insures that they are able to trace any FBI agent who turns criminal, or to eliminate an agent's prints at the scene of a crime; these records are very rarely used. Mark had considered himself very clever as he asked to see Tyson's card. The Director's card was handed to him by an assistant from the Fingerprints Department. It read – "Height: 6′1″; Weight: 180 lbs; Hair; brown; Occupation: Director of FBI; Name: Tyson, H. A. L." No forename given. The assistant, another anonymous man in a blue suit, had smiled sourly at Mark and had said, loud enough for Mark to hear, as he returned the card to its file, "One more sucker who thought he was going to make a quick three thousand bucks."

Because the Bureau had become more political during the last decade the appointment of a professional law enforcement officer was a figure whom Congress found very easy to endorse. Law enforcement was in Tyson's blood. His great-grandfather had been a Wells Fargo man, riding shotgun on the stage between San Francisco and Seattle in the other Washington. His grandfather had been mayor of Boston and its chief of police, a rare combination, and his father before his retirement had been a distinguished Massachusetts attorney. That the great-grandson had followed family tradition, and ended up as Director of the Federal Bureau of Investigation, surprised no one. The anecdotes about him were legion and Mark wondered just how many of them were apocryphal.

There was no doubt that Tyson had scored the winning touchdown in his final Harvard–Yale game because it was there on record, as indeed was the fact that he was the only white man to box on the 1956 American Olympic team in Melbourne. Whether he had actually said to the late President Nixon that he would rather serve the devil than direct the FBI under his presidency, no one could be sure, but it was certainly a story the Kane camp made no effort to suppress.

His wife had died five years earlier of multiple sclerosis. He had nursed her for twenty years with a fierce loyalty.

He feared no man and his reputation for honesty and straight talking had raised him above most government employees in the eyes of the nation. After a period of malaise, following Hoover's death, Halt Tyson had restored the Bureau to the prestige it had enjoyed in the 1930s and 1940s. Tyson was one of the reasons Mark had been happy to commit five years of his life to the FBI.

Mark began to fidget with the middle button of his jacket, as all FBI agents tend to do. It had been drummed into him in the fifteen-week course at Quantico that jacket buttons should always be undone, allowing access to the gun, on the hip holster, never on a shoulder strap. It annoyed Mark that the television series about the FBI always got that wrong. Whenever an FBI man sensed danger, he would fiddle with that middle button to make sure his coat was open. Mark sensed fear, fear of the unknown, fear of H. A. L. Tyson, fear which an accessible Smith and Wesson could not cure.

The anonymous young man with the vigilant look and the dark blue blazer returned.

"The Director will see you now."

Mark rose, felt unsteady, braced himself, rubbed his hands against his trousers to remove the sweat from his palms and followed the anonymous man through the outer office and into the Director's inner sanctum. The Director glanced up, waved him to a chair, and waited for the anonymous man to leave the room and close the door. Even seated, the Director was a bull of a man with a large head placed squarely on massive shoulders. Bushy eyebrows matched his careless, wiry brown hair; it was so curly you might have thought it was a wig if it hadn't been H. A. L. Tyson. His big hands remained splayed on the surface as though the desk might try to get away. The delicate Queen Anne desk was quite subdued by the grip of the Director. His cheeks were red, not the red of alcohol, but the red of good and bad weather. Slightly back from the Director's chair stood another man, muscular, clean-shaven, and silent, a policeman's policeman.

The Director spoke. "Andrews, this is Assistant Director Matthew Rogers. I have briefed him on the events following Casefikis's death: we will be putting several agents on the investigation with you." The Director's grey eyes were piercing – piercing Mark. "I lost two of my best men yesterday, Andrews, and nothing – I repeat, nothing – will stop me from finding out who was respon-

sible, even if it was the President herself, you understand."

"Yes, sir," Mark said very quietly.

"You will have gathered from the press releases we
gave that the public is under the impression that what
happened yesterday evening was just another automobile
accident. No journalist has connected the murders in
Woodrow Wilson Medical Center with the deaths of my
agents. Why should they, with a murder every twenty-six
minutes in America?"

A Metropolitan Police file marked "Chief of Metropolitan Police" was by his side; even they were under
control.

"We, Mr Andrews . . ."

It made Mark feel slightly royal.

". . . we are not going to disillusion them. I have been
going over carefully what you told me last night. I'll
summarise the situation as I see it. Please feel free to
interrupt me whenever you want to."

Under normal circumstances, Mark would have
laughed.

The Director was looking at the file.

"The Greek immigrant wanted to see the head of the
FBI," he continued. "Perhaps I should have granted his
request, had I known about it." He looked up. "Still, the
facts: Casefikis made an oral statement to you at Woodrow Wilson, and the gist of it was that he believed that
there was a plot in motion to assassinate the President
of the United States on 10 March; he overheard this
information while waiting on a private lunch in a Georgetown hotel, at which he thought a US senator was present.
Is that correct so far, Andrews?"

"Yes, sir".

Once more the Director looked down at the file.

"The police took prints of the dead man, and he hasn't
shown up in our files or in the Metropolitan Police files.
So for the moment we must act on the assumption,
after last night's four killings, that everything the Greek

immigrant told us was in good faith. He may not have got the story entirely accurately, but he certainly was on to something big enough to cause four murders in one night. I think we may also assume that whoever the people are behind these diabolical events, they believe they are now in the clear and that they have killed anyone who might have known of their plans. You may consider yourself lucky, young man."

"Yes, sir."

"I suppose it had crossed your mind that they thought it was you in the blue Ford sedan?"

Mark nodded. He had thought of little else for the past ten hours; he hoped Norma Stames would never think of it.

"I want these conspirators to think they are now in the clear and for that reason, I am going to allow the President's schedule for the week to continue as planned, at least for the moment."

Mark ventured a question. "But, sir, won't that put her in grave danger?"

"Andrews, somebody, somewhere, and it may be a United States senator, is planning to assassinate the President; so far, he has been prepared to murder two of my best agents, a Greek who might have recognised him, and a deaf postman whose only connection with the matter was that he may have been able to identify Casefikis's killer. If we rush in now with the heavy artillery, then we will scare them off. We have almost nothing to go on; we would be unlikely to discover their identities. And if we did, we certainly wouldn't be able to nail them. Our only hope of catching them is to let the bastards think they are in the clear – right up to the last moment. That way, we just might get them. It's possible they have already been frightened off, but I think not. They have used such violent means to keep their intentions secret they must have some overriding reason for wanting the President out of the way within seven days. We must find out what the reason is."

"Shall we tell the President?"

"No, no, not yet. God knows, over the past two years she's had enough problems with the Gun Control bill without having to look over her shoulder trying to figure out which senator is Mark Antony and which is Brutus."

"So what do we do for the next six days?"

"You and I will have to find Cassius. And he may not be the one with the lean and hungry look."

"What if we don't find him?" asked Mark.

"God help America."

"And if we do?"

"You may have to kill him."

Mark thought for a moment. He'd never killed anybody in his life; come to think of it, he hadn't knowingly killed anything at all. He didn't like stepping on insects. And the thought that the first person he might kill could be a US senator was, to say the least, daunting.

"Don't look so worried, Andrews. It probably won't come to that. Now let me tell you exactly what I intend to do. I'm going to brief Stuart Knight, the head of the Secret Service, that two of my officers were investigating a man claiming that the President of the United States was going to be assassinated some time within the next month. However, I have no intention of letting him know that a senator may be involved; and I won't tell him that two of our men died because of it; that's not his problem. It may actually have nothing to do with a senator, and I'm not having a whole bunch of people staring at their elected representatives wondering which one of them is a criminal."

The Assistant Director cleared his throat and spoke for the first time. "Some of us think that anyway."

The Director continued unswervingly. "This morning, Andrews, you will write a report on Casefikis's information and the circumstances of his murder, and you will hand it in to Grant Nanna. Do not include the subsequent murders of Stames and Calvert: no one must connect these two events. Report the threat on the President's life but not the possibility that a senator is involved. Is that how you would play it, Matt?"

"Yes, sir," said Rogers. "If we voice our suspicions to people who don't need to know them, we will run the risk of provoking a security operation that will make the assassins run for cover; then we would simply have to pick up our marbles and start over – if we were lucky enough to get a second chance."

"Right," said the Director. "So this is how we'll proceed, Andrews. There are one hundred senators. One of them provides our only link with the conspirators. It's going to be your task to pinpoint that man. The Assistant Director will have a couple of junior men follow up the few other leads that we have. No need for them to know the details, Matt. To start with, check out the Golden Duck Restaurant."

"And every hotel in Georgetown, to see which one put on a private luncheon party on 24 February," said Rogers. "And the hospital. Maybe someone saw suspicious characters hanging around the parking lot or the corridors; the assassins must have seen our Ford there while Calvert and you, Andrews, were interviewing Casefikis. I think that's about all we can do for the moment."

"I agree," said the Director. "Okay, thanks, Matt, I won't take up any more of your time. Please let me have anything you turn up immediately."

"Sure," said the Assistant Director. He nodded at Mark and left the room.

Mark had sat silently, impressed by the clarity with which the Director had grasped the details of the case; his mind must be like a filing cabinet.

The Director pressed a button on his intercom.

"Coffee for two, please, Mrs McGregor."

"Yes, sir."

"Now, Andrews, you come into the Bureau at seven o'clock every morning and report to me. Should any emergency arise, call me, using the code name Julius. I will use the same code name when calling you. When you hear the word 'Julius', break off whatever you are doing. Do you understand?"

"Yes, sir."

"Now, a most important point. If, in any circumstances, I die or disappear, you brief only the Attorney General, and Rogers will take care of the rest. If you die, young man, you can leave the decision to me." He smiled for the first time – it was not Mark's idea of a joke. "I see from the files that you're entitled to two weeks' leave. Well take it, starting at noon today. I don't want you to exist officially for at least a week. Grant Nanna has already been briefed that you have been seconded to me," continued the Director. "You may have to tolerate me night and day for six days, young man, and no one other than my late wife has had that problem before."

"And you me, sir," was Mark's quick and unthinking reply.

He waited for his head to be bitten off; instead the Director smiled again.

Mrs McGregor appeared with the coffee, served them, and left. The Director drank his coffee in one swallow and began to pace around the room as if it were a cage; Mark did not move, though his eyes never left Tyson. His massive frame and great shoulders heaved up and down, his large head with its bushy hair rocking from side to side. He was going through what the boys called the thought process.

"The first thing you're to do, Andrews, is find out which senators were in Washington on 24 February. As it was near the weekend, most of those dummies would have been floating all over the country, making speeches or vacationing with their pampered children."

What endeared the Director to everyone was not that he said it behind their backs but that he said it even more explicitly to their faces. Mark smiled and began to relax.

"When we have that list, we'll try and figure out what they have in common. Separate the Republicans from the Democrats, and then put them under party headings as to interests, public and private. After that, we have to find out which ones have any connection with President Kane, past or present, friendly or unfriendly. Your report will cover all these details and be ready for our meeting tomorrow morning. Understood?"

"Yes, sir."

"Now there's something else I want you to understand, Andrews. As I am sure you know, for the past decade, the FBI has been in a very sensitive political position. Those watchdogs in Congress are just waiting for us to exceed our legitimate authority. If we in any way cast suspicion upon a member of Congress, without indisputable evidence of his guilt, they will hang, draw and quarter the Bureau. And rightly so, in my opinion. Police agencies in a democracy must prove that they can be trusted not to subvert the political process. Purer than Caesar's wife. Understood?"

"Yes, sir."

"From today we have six days, from tomorrow five, and I want to catch this man and his friends red-handed. So neither of us will be on statutory overtime."

"No, sir."

The Director returned to his desk and summoned Mrs McGregor.

"Mrs McGregor, this is Special Agent Andrews, who'll be working closely with me on an extremely sensitive investigation for the next six days. Whenever he wants to see me, let him come right in; if I'm with anybody but Mr Rogers, notify me immediately – no red tape, no waiting."

"Yes, sir."

"And I'd appreciate it if you didn't mention this to anybody else."

"Of course not, Mr Tyson."

The Director turned to Mark. "Now you go back to the WFO and start working. I'll see you in this office at seven o'clock tomorrow morning."

Mark stood up. He didn't finish his coffee; perhaps by

70

the sixth day he would feel free to say so. He shook hands with the Director and headed towards the door. Just as he reached it, the Director added: "Andrews, I hope you'll be very careful. Keep looking over both shoulders at once."

Mark shivered and moved quickly out of the room, down the corridor, keeping his back firmly to the wall when he reached the elevator, and walking along the sides of the passage on the ground floor, where he ran into a group of tourists who were studying pictures of the Ten Most Wanted Criminals in America. Next week, would one of them be a senator?

When he reached the street, he dodged the traffic until he arrived at the Washington Field Office, on the other side of Pennsylvania Avenue. It wouldn't quite be like home this morning. Two men were missing, and they weren't going to be able to replace them with a training manual. The flag on top of the FBI Building and the flag on top of the Old Post Office Building were at half-mast; two of their agents were dead.

Mark went straight into Grant Nanna's office; he had aged ten years overnight. For him, two friends had died, one who worked under him and one who worked above him.

"Sit down, Mark."

"Thank you, sir."

"The Director has already spoken to me this morning. I didn't ask any questions. I understand you're taking a two-week leave as of noon today, and that you are writing me a memorandum on what happened at the hospital. I have to pass it on to higher authorities and that will be the end of it as far as the WFO is concerned, because Homicide will take over. They are also trying to tell me Nick and Barry died in a car accident."

"Yes, sir," said Mark.

"I don't believe a goddamn word of it," said Nanna. "Now you're in the middle of this, somehow, and maybe you can nail the bastards who did it. When you find

71

them, grind their balls into powder and then call me so that I can come help you, because if I lay my hands on those bastards . . ."

Mark looked at Grant Nanna, and then tactfully away again, waiting until his superior had regained control of his face and voice.

"Now, you're not allowed to contact me once you leave this office, but if I can help at any time, just call me. Don't let the Director know, he'd kill us both if he found out. Get going, Mark."

Mark left quickly and went to his office. He sat down and wrote out his report exactly as the Director had instructed, bland and brief. He took it back to Nanna, who flicked through it and tossed it into the out-box. "Neat little whitewash job you've done there, Mark."

Mark didn't speak. He signed out of the Washington Field Office, the one place in which he felt secure. He'd be on his own for six days. Ambitious men always wanted to see a few years ahead, to know the shape of their careers; Mark would have settled for a week.

The Director pressed a button. The anonymous man in the dark blue blazer and light grey trousers entered the room.

"Yes, sir."

"I want a full surveillance on Andrews, night and day; six men on three shifts reporting to me every morning. I want detailed background on him, his education, girl friends, associates, habits, hobbies, religion, organisational affiliations, everything by tomorrow morning, 6:45. Understood?"

"Yes, sir."

Aware that Senate staff members would be suspicious of an FBI agent who asked for information about their employers, Mark began his research at the Library of Congress. As he climbed the long flight of steps, he remembered a scene from *All the President's Men*, in which

Woodward and Bernstein had spent innumerable fruitless hours searching for a few slips of paper in the bowels of the building. They had been trying to find proof that E. Howard Hunt had checked out materials on Edward M. Kennedy. And for an FBI agent on the trail of a killer, just as for the investigative reporters, it would be tedious research, not glamorous assignments, that would make the difference between success and failure.

Mark opened the door marked "Readers Only" and strolled into the Main Reading Room, a huge, circular, domed room decorated in muted tones of gold, beige, rust, and bronze. The ground floor was filled with rows of dark, curved wooden desks, arranged in concentric circles around the reference area in the centre of the room. On the second floor, visible from the reading area through graceful arches, were thousands of books. Mark approached the reference desk and, in the hushed tones appropriate to all libraries, asked the Clerk where he could find current issues of the *Congressional Record*.

"Room 244. Law Library Reading Room."

"How do I get there?"

"Go back past the card catalogue to the other side of the building and take an elevator to the second floor."

Mark managed to find the Law Library, a white, rectangular room with three tiers of bookshelves on the left-hand side. After questioning another clerk, he located the *Congressional Record* on one of the dark brown reference shelves along the right-hand wall. He carried the unbound volume marked 24 February, to a long, deserted table and began the tedious weeding-out process.

After leafing through the digest of Senate business for half an hour, Mark realised that he was in luck. Many senators had apparently left Washington for the weekend, because a check of the roll calls on 24 February revealed that, of the one hundred senators, the number present on the floor never exceeded sixty. And the bills which were voted on were sufficiently important to command the presence of those senators who might have been hiding in the nooks and crannies of the Senate or the city. When he had eliminated those senators who were listed by the Whips of each party as "absent because of illness" or "necessarily absent", and added those who were merely "detained on official business", Mark was left with sixty-two senators who were definitely in Washington on 24 February. He then double-checked the other thirty-eight senators, one by one, a long and tiresome task. All of them had for some reason been out of Washington that day.

He glanced at his watch: 12:15. He couldn't afford to take time off for lunch.

# Friday afternoon, 4 March

## 12:30 pm

Three men had arrived. None of them liked one another; only the common bond of financial reward could have got them into the same room. The first went by the name of Tony; he'd had so many names that nobody could be sure what his real name was, except perhaps his mother, and she hadn't seen him in the twenty years since he had left Sicily to join his father, her husband, in the States. Her husband had left twenty years before that; the cycle repeated itself.

Tony's FBI criminal file described him as five-feet-eight, a hundred and forty-six pounds, medium build, black hair, straight nose, brown eyes, no distinguishing features, arrested and charged once in connection with a bank robbery; first offence, two-year jail sentence. What the rap sheet did not reveal was that Tony was a brilliant driver; he had proved that yesterday and if that fool of a German had kept his head, there would have been four people in the room now instead of three. He had told the boss, "If you're going to employ a German, have him build the damn car, never let him drive it." The boss hadn't listened and the German had been dragged out of the bottom of the Potomac. Next time they'd use Tony's cousin Mario. At least then there would be another human on the team; you couldn't count the ex-cop and the little Jap who never said a word.

Tony glanced at Xan Tho Huc, who only spoke when asked a direct question. He was actually Vietnamese, but he had finally escaped to Japan in 1979. Everyone would have known his name if he had entered the Los Angeles Olympics, because nobody could have stopped him from getting the gold medal for rifle shooting, but Xan had decided, with his chosen career in mind, he had better keep a low profile and withdraw from the Japanese Olympic trials. His coach tried to get him to change his mind, but without success. To Tony, Xan remained a goddamn Jap, though he grudgingly admitted to himself he knew no other man who could fire ten shots into a three-inch square at eight hundred yards. The size of Florentyna Kane's forehead.

The Nip sat staring at him, motionless. Xan's appearance helped him in his work. No one expected that the slight frame, only about five-feet-two and a hundred and ten pounds, was that of a superlative marksman. Most people still associated marksmanship with hulking cowboys and lantern-jawed Caucasians. If you had been told this man was a ruthless killer, you would have assumed he worked with his hands, with a garrote or nunchaki, or even with poison. Among the three, Xan was the only one who carried a personal grudge. As a child he had seen his parents butchered by the Americans in Vietnam. They had spoken warmly of the Yanks and had supported them until the bullets tore into their bodies. They had left him for dead. A target almost too small to hit. From that moment he had vowed in silent torment to avenge his loss. He escaped to Japan and there, for two years after the fall of Saigon, he had lain low, getting a job in a Chinese restaurant, and participating in the US Government Program for Vietnamese refugees. Then he had gone with the offer of practical assistance to some of his old contacts in the Vietnamese intelligence community. With the US presence so scaled down in Asia, and the Communists needing fewer killers, and more lawyers, they had been sorry but they had no work for him. So Xan had begun freelancing in Japan. In 1981, he obtained Japanese citizenship, a passport, and started his new career.

Unlike Tony, Xan did not resent the others he was working with. He simply didn't think about them. He had been hired, willingly, to perform a professional task, a task for which he would be well paid and that would at last avenge, at least in part, the outraged bodies of his parents. The others had limited roles to play in support of his operation. Provided they played them with a minimum of foolish error, he would perform his part flawlessly, and within a few days, he would be back in the Orient. Bangkok or Manila, perhaps, Singapore. Xan hadn't decided yet. When this one was over, he would need – and would be able to afford – a long rest.

The third man in the room, Ralph Matson, was perhaps the most dangerous of the three. Six-feet-two tall and broad, with a big nose and heavy chin, he was the most dangerous because he was highly intelligent. After five years as a special agent with the Federal Bureau of Investigation, he found an easy way out after Hoover's death; loyalty to the Chief and all that garbage. By then, he had learned enough to take advantage of everything the Bureau had taught him about criminology. He had started with a little blackmail, men who had not wanted their FBI records made public, but now he had moved on to bigger things. He trusted no man – the Bureau had also taught him that – certainly not the stupid wop, who under pressure might drive backward rather than forward, or the silent slant-eyed yellow hit man.

Still nobody spoke.

The door swung open. Three heads turned, three heads that were used to danger and did not care for surprises; they relaxed again immediately when they saw the two men enter.

The younger of the two was smoking. He took the seat at the head of the table as befits a chairman; the other man sat down next to Matson, keeping the Chairman on his right. They nodded acknowledgment, no more. The younger man, Peter Nicholson on his voter-registration card, Pyotr Nicolaivich by birth certificate, looked for all the world like the reputable head of a successful cosmetics company. His suit revealed that he went to Chester Barrie. His shoes were Loeb's. His tie Ted Lapidus. His criminal record revealed nothing. That was why he was at the head of the table. He didn't look upon himself as a criminal; he looked upon himself as a man who wished to maintain the status quo.

He was one of a small group of Southern millionaires who had made their money in the small-arms trade. Theirs was a giant business: it was the right of every American citizen under Amendment Two of the Constitution to bear arms, and one in every four American males exercised that right. A regular pistol or revolver could be had for as little as $100 but the fancy shotguns and rifles that were a status symbol to many patriots could fetch as much as $10,000. The Chairman and his ilk sold handguns by the millions and shotguns by the tens of thousands. It had not been hard to persuade Ronald Reagan to leave the arms trade alone, but they knew they were never going to convince Florentyna Kane. The Gun Control bill had already squeaked through the House, and unless some drastic action were taken, there was undoubtedly going to be the same result in the Senate. To preserve the status quo, therefore, the Chairman sat at the head of their table.

He opened the meeting formally, as any regular chairman would, by asking for reports from his men in the field. First Matson.

The big nose bobbed, the heavy jaw moved.

"I was tuned into the FBI's Channel One." During his years as an FBI agent, preparing for a career in crime, Matson had stolen one of the Bureau's special portable walkie-talkies. He had signed it out for some routine purpose and then reported that it was lost. He was reprimanded and had to reimburse the Bureau; it had been a small price to pay for the privilege of listening to FBI communications. "I knew the Greek waiter was hiding somewhere in Washington, and I suspected that because of his leg injury, he would eventually have to go to one of D.C.'s five hospitals. I guessed he wouldn't end up with a private doctor, too expensive. Then I heard that bastard Stames come up on Channel One."

"Cut out the profanity, if you please," said the Chairman.

Stames had given Matson four reprimands during his service with the FBI. Matson did not mourn his death. He started again.

"I heard Stames come up on Channel One, on his way to Woodrow Wilson Medical Center, to ask a Father Gregory to go to the Greek. It was a long shot, of course, but I remembered that Stames was a Greek himself, and it wasn't hard to trace Father Gregory. I just caught him as he was about to leave. I told him the Greek had been discharged from the hospital and that his services would no longer be needed. And thanked him. With Stames dead, no one is likely to follow that one up and, if they do, they won't be any the wiser. I then went to the nearest Greek Orthodox church and stole the vestments, a hat, a veil, and a cross and I drove to Woodrow Wilson. By the time I arrived, Stames and Calvert had already left. I learned from the receptionist on duty that the two men from the FBI had returned to their office. I didn't ask for too much detail as I didn't want to be remembered. I discovered which room Casefikis was in and it was simple to reach there unnoticed. I slipped in. He was sound asleep. I cut his throat."

The Senator winced.

"There was a nigger in the bed next to him, we couldn't take the risk. He might have overheard everything, and he might have given a description of me, so I cut his throat too."

The Senator felt sick. He hadn't wanted these men to

79

die. The Chairman had showed no emotion, the difference between a professional and an amateur.

"Then I called Tony in the car. He drove to the Washington Field Office and saw Stames and Calvert coming out of the building together. I then contacted you, boss, and Tony carried out your orders."

The Chairman passed over a packet. It was one hundred one-hundred-dollar bills. All American employees are paid by seniority and achievement; it was no different in the criminal world.

"Tony."

"When the two men left the Old Post Office Building, we followed them as instructed. They went over Memorial Bridge. The German passed them and managed to get well ahead of them. As soon as I realised they were turning up on to the G.W. Parkway, as we thought they would, I informed Gerbach on the walkie-talkie. He was waiting in a clump of trees on the middle strip, with his lights off, about a mile ahead. He turned on his lights and came down from the top of the hill on the wrong side of the divided highway. He swung in front of the Feds' car just after it crossed Windy Run Bridge. I accelerated and overtook on the left-hand side of the car. I hit them with a glancing sideways blow at about seventy miles an hour, just as that damn-fool German hit them head-on. You know the rest, boss. If he had kept his cool," Tony finished contemptuously, "the German would be here today to make his report in person."

"What did you do with the car?"

"I went to Mario's workshop, changed the engine block and the licence plates, repaired the damage to the fender, sprayed it, and dumped it. The owner probably wouldn't recognise his own car if he saw it."

"Where did you dump it?"

"New York. The Bronx."

"Good. With a murder there every four hours, they don't have a lot of time to check on missing cars."

The Chairman flicked a packet over the table. Three

thousand dollars in used fifties. "Stay sober, Tony, we'll be needing you again." He refrained from saying what assignment number two would be; he simply said, "Xan". He stubbed out his cigarette and lit another one. All eyes turned to the silent Vietnamese. His English was good, though heavily accentuated. He tended, like so many educated Orientals, to omit the definite article, giving his speech a curious staccato effect.

"I was in car with Tony whole evening when we got your orders to eliminate two men in Ford sedan. We followed them over bridge and up freeway and when German swung across path of Ford, I blew both back tyres in under three seconds, just before Tony bounced them. They had no chance of controlling car after that."

"How can you be so sure it was under three seconds?"

"I'd been averaging two-point-eight in practice all day."

Silence. The Chairman passed yet another packet. Another one hundred fifties, twenty-five hundred dollars for each shot.

"Do you have any questions, Senator?"

The Senator did not look up, but shook his head slightly.

The Chairman spoke. "From the press reports and from our further investigation, it looks as if nobody has connected the two incidents, but the FBI just aren't that stupid. We have to hope that we eliminated everybody who heard anything Casefikis might have said, if he had anything to say in the first place. We may just be oversensitive. One thing's for certain, we eliminated everybody connected with that hospital. But we still can't be sure if the Greek knew anything worth repeating."

"May I say something, boss?"

The Chairman looked up. Nobody spoke unless it was relevant, most unusual for an American board meeting. The Chairman let Matson have the floor.

"One thing worries me, boss. Why would Nick Stames be going to Woodrow Wilson?"

They all stared at him, not quite sure what he meant.

"We know from my inquiries and my contacts that Calvert was there, but we don't actually know that Stames was there. All we know is that two agents went and that Stames asked Father Gregory to go. We know Stames was on his way home with Calvert, but my experience tells me that Stames wouldn't go to the hospital himself; he'd send somebody else –"

"Even if he thought it were a serious matter?" interrupted the Chairman.

"He wouldn't know it was a serious matter, boss. He wouldn't have known until the agents had reported back to him."

The Chairman shrugged. "The facts point to Stames going to the hospital with Calvert. He left the Washington Field Office with Calvert driving the same car that left the hospital."

"I know, boss, but I don't like it; I know that we've covered all the angles, but it's possible that three or more men left the Washington Field Office and that there is still at least one agent running around who knows what actually happened."

"It seems unlikely," said the Senator. "As you will discover when you hear my report."

The lips compressed in the heavy jaw.

"You're not happy are you, Matson?"

"No, sir."

"Very well, check it out. If you come up with anything report back to me."

The Chairman never left a stone unturned. He looked at the Senator.

The Senator despised these men. They were so small-minded, so greedy. They only understood money, and Kane was going to take it away from them. How their violence had frightened and sickened him. He should never have allowed that smooth-talking plausible bastard Nicholson to pump so much into his secret campaign funds, although God knows he would never have been elected without the money. Lots of money, and such a small price to pay at the time: steadfast opposition to any gun control proposals. Hell, he was genuinely opposed to gun control anyway. But assassinating the President to stop the bill, by God, it was lunacy, but the Chairman had him by the balls. "Co-operate, or be exposed, my friend," he had said silkily. The Senator had spent half a lifetime sweating to reach the Senate and what's more, he did a damned good job there. If they stopped him now he would be finished. A public scandal. He couldn't face it. "Co-operate, my friend, for your own good. All we need is some inside information, and your presence at the Capitol on 10 March. Be reasonable, my friend, why ruin your whole life for a Polish woman?" The Senator cleared his throat.

"It is highly unlikely that the FBI knows any details about our plans. As Mr Matson knows, if the Bureau had anything to go on, any reason to think that this supposed threat is any different from a thousand others the President has received, the Secret Service would have been informed immediately. And my secretary has ascertained that the President's schedule for this week remains unchanged. All her appointments will be kept. She will go to the Capitol on the morning of 10 March for a special address to the Senate –"

"But that's exactly the point," Matson interrupted with a contemptuous sneer. "All threats against the President, no matter how far-fetched, are routinely reported to the Secret Service. If they haven't reported anything, it must mean that –"

"It may mean that they don't know a thing, Matson," said the Chairman firmly. "I told you to look into it. Now let the Senator answer a more important question: If the FBI knew the details, would they tell the President?"

The Senator hesitated. "No, I don't think so, or only if they were absolutely certain of danger on a particular day; otherwise they'd go ahead as planned. If every threat or suggestion of a threat were taken seriously, the

President would never be able to leave the White House. The Secret Service report to Congress last year showed that there were 1,572 threats against the President's life, but thorough investigations revealed that there were no actual known attempts."

The Chairman nodded. "Either they know everything or they know nothing."

Matson persisted. "I am still a member of the Society of Former 'Special Agents and I attended a meeting yesterday, and no one there knew a damn thing. Someone would have heard something by now. Later, I had a drink with Grant Nanna, who was my old boss at the Washington Field Office, and he seemed almost uninterested, which I found strange. I thought Stames was a friend of his, but I obviously couldn't push it too far, since Stames was no friend of mine. I'm still worried. It doesn't make sense that Stames went to the hospital and no one in the Bureau is saying anything about his death."

"Okay, okay," said the Chairman. "If we don't get her on 10 March, we may as well quit now. We go ahead as if nothing had happened, unless we hear any rumbles – and that's in your hands, Matson. We'll be there on the day, unless you stop us. Now let's plan ahead. First I'll go over Kane's schedule for that day. Kane" – no one in that room except for the Senator ever called her the President – "leaves the White House at 10 am. She passes the FBI Building at three minutes past, she passes the Peace Monument at the north-west corner of the Capitol grounds at five minutes past. She gets out of her car at the east front of the Capitol at six minutes past. Normally, she would go in the private entrance, but the Senator has assured us that she will milk this visit for all it's worth. It takes her forty-five seconds to walk from the car to the top of the Capitol steps. We know that Xan can easily complete the job in forty-five seconds. I will be watching at the corner of Pennsylvania Avenue when Kane passes the FBI Building. Tony will be there with a car, in case of an emergency, and the Senator will be on the Capitol steps to stall her, if we need more time. The most important part of the operation is Xan's, which we have worked out to a split second. So listen and listen carefully. I have arranged for Xan to be on the construction crew working on the renovation of the front of the Capitol. And, believe me, with that union it was no mean feat to place an Oriental. Take over, Xan."

Xan looked up. He had said nothing since his last invitation to speak.

"Construction on west front of Capitol has been going on for nearly six months. No one is more enthusiastic about it than Kane. She wants it finished in time for her second Inaugural." He grinned. All eyes were upon the little man, intent on his every word. "I have been part of work force now for just over four weeks. I am in charge of checking all supplies that come on to site, which means I am in site office. From there, it has not been hard to discover movements of everybody connected with construction. The guards are not from FBI, Secret Service, or from CIA, but from Government Building Security Service. They are usually a lot older than normal agents, often retired from one of services. There are sixteen in all, and they work in fours on four shifts. I know where they drink, smoke, play cards, everything; no one is very interested in site because at moment it overlooks nothing and it's on least-used side of Capitol. A little petty theft from site but not much else to excite guards." Xan had total silence. "Right in middle of site is biggest American Hoist Co. crane in world, number 11-3-10, specially designed for lifting new parts of Capitol into place. Fully extended, it is 322 feet, almost double regulation height allowed in Washington buildings. Nobody expect us on west side, and nobody figure we can see that far. On top is small covered platform for general maintenance of pulleys, used only when it is flat and parallel to ground, but platform becomes like a small box in effect. It is four feet long, two feet three inches in width, and one foot five inches in height. I have slept there for last three nights.

I see everything, no one can see me, not even White House helicopter."

There was a stunned silence.

"How do you get up there?" asked the Senator.

"Like cat, Senator. I climb. An advantage of being very small. I go up just after midnight and come down at five. I overlook all Washington and no one see me."

"Do you have a good view of the Capitol steps from such a small platform?" asked the Chairman.

"Perhaps it will take four seconds," Xan replied. "View allows me to see Whte House as no one has ever seen it. I could have killed Kane twice last week. When she make official visits, it will be easy. I can't miss –"

"What about the other workers on Thursday? They may want to use the crane," the Senator interrupted.

This time the Chairman smiled. "There will be a strike next Thursday, my friend. Something to do with unfair rates for overtime, no work while Kane is visiting the Capitol to emphasise their point. One thing is certain, with no one on the site other than some ageing guards, nobody will be eager to climb to the top of a crane that is all but open to the world. From the ground it doesn't look as if a mouse could hide up there, let alone a human being." The Chairman paused. "Xan flies to Vienna tomorrow and will be back in time to report the results of his trip at our final meeting next Wednesday. By the way, Xan, have you got your can of yellow paint?"

"Yes, stole one from site."

The Chairman looked around the table – silence. "Good, we seem to be well organised. Thank you, Xan."

"I don't like it," mumbled Matson. "Something's wrong. It's all too easy, it's all too clever."

"The FBI has taught you to be overly suspicious, Matson. You'll discover that we're better prepared than they are, because we know what we're going to do and they don't. Fear not, you'll be able to attend Kane's funeral."

Matson's big chin moved up and down. "You're the guy that wants her dead," he said sourly.

"And you're being paid to see it happens," said the Chairman. "Right, we meet again in five days to go over the final plan. You will be told where to report on Wednesday morning. Xan will have returned from Austria long before then."

The Chairman smiled and lit another cigarette. The Senator slipped out. Five minutes later, Matson left. Five minutes later, Tony left. Five minutes later, Xan left. Five minutes later, the Chairman ordered lunch.

# Friday afternoon, 4 March

## 4:00 pm

Mark was too hungry to work efficiently any longer, so he left the Library in search of some food. When the elevator stopped, the opening doors provided a view of the card catalogue: "Harrison-Health" confronted him. Some sub-conscious word association triggered in his mind the welcome vision of the beautiful, witty girl he had met the previous day, walking along the corridor in her black skirt and red shirt, heels tapping on the tiles. A big grin spread across Mark's face. It was amazing the pleasure it gave him just to know he could call her and rearrange the date, unusual for him to find just how much he wanted to.

Mark found the snack bar and munched his way through a hamburger, letting his mind recall all the things she had said, and the way she had looked while she was saying them. He decided to call Woodrow Wilson.

"I'm sorry, Dr Dexter is not on duty today," said a nurse. "Can Dr Delgado help?"

"No thank you," said Mark. "I'm afraid she can't." He took out his diary, and dialled Elizabeth Dexter's home number. He was delighted to find her in.

"Hello, Elizabeth. It's Mark Andrews. Any hope of givng you dinner tonight?"

"Promises, promises. I continue to live in the hope of a real meal."

"Not a laughing matter," said Mark, almost to himself.

"You sound a bit low, Mark. Perhaps you really do have a touch of flu."

"No, I don't think it's flu, just thinking of you makes it hard to breathe. I'd better hang up now, before I turn blue."

It was good to hear her laugh.

"Why don't you come by about eight?"

"Fine. See you around eight, Elizabeth."

"Take care, Mark."

He put the telephone down, suddenly conscious that once again he was smiling from ear to ear. He glanced at his watch: 4:30. Good. Three more hours in the Library, then he could go in pursuit of her. He returned to his reference books and continued to make biographical notes on the sixty-two senators.

His mind drifted for a moment to the President. This wasn't just any President. This was the first woman President. But what could he learn from the last presidential assassination of John F. Kennedy. Were there any senators involved with those deaths? Or was this another lunatic working on his own? All the evidence on this inquiry so far pointed to teamwork. Lee Harvey Oswald, long since dead, and still there was no convincing explanation of his assassination or, for that matter, of Robert Kennedy's.

Some people still claimed the CIA was behind President Kennedy's death because he had threatened to hang them out to dry in 1961, after the Bay of Pigs fiasco. Others said Castro had arranged the murder in revenge; it was known that Oswald had an interview with the Cuban ambassador in Mexico two weeks before the assassination, and the CIA had known about that all along. Thirty years after the event, and still no one could be certain.

A smart guy from L.A., Jay Sandberg, who had roomed with Mark at law school, had maintained that the conspiracy reached the top, even the top of the FBI: they knew the truth but said nothing.

Maybe Tyson and Rogers were two of those who knew the truth and had sent him out on useless errands to keep him occupied: he hadn't been able to tell anyone the details of yesterday's events, not even Grant Nanna.

If there were a conspiracy, whom could he turn to? Only one person might listen and that was the President, and there was no way of getting to her. He'd have to call Jay Sandberg, who had made a study of presidential assassinations. If anyone would have a theory, it would be Sandberg. Mark retraced his steps to the pay phone, checked Sandberg's home number in New York, and dialled the ten digits. A woman's voice answered the telephone.

"Hello," she said coolly. Mark could visualise the cloud of cocaine smoke that went with the voice.

"Hello, I'm trying to reach Jay Sandberg."

"Oh." More cocaine smoke. "He's still at work."

"Can you tell me his number?" asked Mark.

After more smoke, she gave it to him, and the phone clicked.

Sheeesh, Mark said to himself, Upper East Side women.

A very different voice, warm Irish-American, answered the phone next.

"Sullivan and Cromwell."

Mark recognised the prestigious New York law firm. Other people were getting ahead in the world.

"Can I speak to Jay Sandberg?"

"I'll connect you, sir."

"Sandberg."

"Hi, Jay, it's Mark Andrews. Glad I caught you. I'm calling from Washington."

"Hello, Mark, nice to hear from you. How's life for a G-man? Rat-a-tat-tat and all that."

"It can be," said Mark, "sometimes. Jay, I need some advice on where to find the facts on political assassination attempts, particularly the one in Massachusetts in 1979; do you remember it?"

"Sure do. Three people arrested; let me think." Sandberg paused. "All released as harmless. One died in an auto accident in 1980, another was knifed in a brawl in San Francisco, later died in 1981, and the third disappeared mysteriously last year. I tell you it was another conspiracy."

"Who this time?"

"Mafia wanted Edward Kennedy out of the way in '76 so they could avoid an inquiry he was pressing for into the death of those two hoodlums, Sam Giancana and John Rosselli; they don't love President Kane now with the way she is running the Gun Control bill."

"Mafia? Gun Control bill? Where do I start looking for the facts?" asked Mark.

"I can tell you it's not in the Warren Commission Report or any of the later inquiries. Your best bet is *The Yankee and Cowboy Wars* by Carl Oglesby – you'll find it all there."

Mark made a note.

"Thanks for your help, Jay. I'll get back to you if it doesn't cover everything. How are things in New York?"

"Oh, fine, just fine. I'm one of about a million lawyers interpreting the constitution at an exorbitant fee. Let's get together soon, Mark."

"Sure, next time I'm in New York."

Mark went back to the Library thoughtfully. It could be CIA, it could be Mafia, it could be a nut, it could be anyone – even Halt Tyson. He asked the girl for the Carl Oglesby book. A well-thumbed volume beginning to come apart was supplied. Sheed Andrews & McMeel, Inc., 6700 Squibb Road, Mission, Kansas. It was going to make good reading, but for now it was back to the senators' life histories. Mark spent two more hours trying to eliminate senators or find motives for any of them wanting President Kane out of the way: he wasn't getting very far.

"You'll have to leave now, sir," said the young librarian, her arms full of books, looking as if she would like to go home. "I'm afraid we lock up at 7:30."

"Can you give me two more minutes? I'm very nearly through."

"I guess so," she said, staggering away under a load of Senate Reports, 1971–73, which few but herself would ever handle.

Mark glanced over his notes. There were some very prominent names among the sixty-two "suspects", men like Alan Cranston of California, often described as the "liberal whip" of the Senate; Ralph Brooks of Massachusetts, whom Florentyna Kane had defeated at the Democratic Convention. Majority Leader Robert C. Byrd of West Virginia. Henry Dexter of Connecticut. Elizabeth's father, he shuddered at the thought. Sam Nunn, the respected senator for Georgia, Robert Harrison of South Carolina, an urbane, educated man with a reputation for parliamentary skill; Marvin Thornton, who occupied the seat vacated by Edward Kennedy in 1980; Mark O. Hatfield, the liberal and devout Republican from Oregon; Hayden Woodson of Arkansas, one of the new breed of Southern Republicans; William Cain of Nebraska, a staunch conservative who had run as an independent in the 1980 election; and Birch Bayh of Indiana, the man who had pulled Ted Kennedy from a plane wreck in 1967, and probably saved his life. Sixty-two men under suspicion, thought Mark. And six days to go. And the evidence must be iron-clad. There was little more he could do that day.

Every government building was closing. He just hoped the Director had covered as much and could bring the sixty-two names down to a sensible number quickly. Sixty-two names; six days.

He returned to his car in the public parking lot. Six dollars a day for the privilege of being on vacation. He paid the attendant, eased the car out on Pennsylvania Avenue, and headed down 9th Street back towards his apartment in N Street, SW, the worst of the rush-hour behind him. Simon was there, and Mark tossed him the car keys. "I'm going out again as soon as I've changed," Mark called over his shoulder as he went up to his eighth-floor apartment.

He showered and shaved quickly and put on a more casual suit than the one he had worn for the Director. Now for the good part of the day.

When he came back down, the car was turned around so that Mark could, to quote Simon, make a quick get-away. He drove to Georgetown, turned right on 30th, and parked outside Elizabeth Dexter's house. A small red-brick town house, very chic. Either she was doing well for herself or her father had bought it for her. Her father, he couldn't help remembering . . .

She looked even more beautiful on the doorstep than she had in his imagination. That was good. She wore a long red dress with a high collar. It set off her dark hair and deep brown eyes.

"Are you going to come in, or are you just going to stand there looking like a delivery boy?"

"I'm just going to stand here and admire you," he said. "You know, Doctor, I've always been attracted to beautiful, clever women. Do you think that says something about me?"

She laughed and led him into the pretty house.

"Come and sit down. You look as though you could do with a drink." She poured him the beer he asked for. When she sat down, her eyes were serious.

"I don't suppose you want to talk about the horrible thing that happened to my mailman."

"No," said Mark. "I'd prefer not to, for a number of reasons."

Her face showed understanding.

"I hope you'll catch the bastard who killed him." Again, those dark eyes flashed to meet his. She got up to turn over the record on the stereo. "How do you like this kind of music?" she asked lightly.

"I'm not much on Haydn," he said. "I'm a Mahler freak. And Beethoven, Aznavour. And you?"

She blushed slightly.

"When you didn't turn up last night, I called your office to see if you were there."

Mark was surprised and pleased.

"Finally I got through to a girl in your department. You were out at the time, and besides she said you were very busy, so I didn't leave a message."

"That's Polly," said Mark. "She's very protective."

"And pretty?" She smiled with the confidence of one who knows she is good-looking.

"Good from far but far from good," said Mark. "Let's forget Polly. Come on, you ought to be hungry by now, and I'm not going to give you that steak I keep promising you. I've booked a table for nine o'clock at Tio Pepe."

"Lovely," she said. "Since you managed to get your car parked, why don't we walk?"

"Great."

It was a clear, cool evening and Mark enjoyed the fresh air. What he didn't enjoy was the continual urge to look over his shoulder.

"Looking for another woman already?" she teased.

"No," said Mark. "Why should I look any further?" He spoke lightly, but he knew he hadn't fooled her. He changed the subject abruptly. "How do you like your work?"

"My work?" Elizabeth seemed surprised, as though she never thought of it in those terms. "My life, you mean? It's just about my entire life. Or has been so far."

She glanced up at Mark with a sombre expression on her face. "I hate the hospital. It's a big bureaucracy, old and dirty and a lot of the people there, petty administrative types, don't really care about helping people. To them it's just another way of earning a living. Only yesterday I had to threaten to resign in order to convince the Utilisation Committee to let an old man remain in the hospital. He had no home to go back to."

They walked down 30th Street, and Elizabeth continued to tell him about her work. She spoke with spirit, and Mark listened to her with pleasure. She showed a pleasant self-assurance, as she told him about a soulful Yugoslav who would sing incomprehensible Slavic songs of love and of longing as she inspected his ulcerated armpit and who had finally, in a misplaced gesture of passion, seized her left ear and licked it.

Mark laughed and took her arm as he guided her into the restuarant. "You ought to demand combat pay," he said.

"Oh, I wouldn't have complained, other than to tell him that his singing was always out of tune."

The hostess led them upstairs to a table in the centre of the room, near where the floor show would be performed. Mark rejected it in favour of a table in the far corner. He did not ask Elizabeth which seat she would prefer. He sat down with his back to the wall, making a lame excuse about wanting to be away from the noise so he could talk to her. Mark was sure that this girl would not fall too easily for that sort of blarney; she knew something was wrong and she sensed his edginess, but she did not pry.

A young waiter asked them if they would like a cocktail. Elizabeth asked for a Margarita, Mark for a spritzer.

"What's a spritzer?" asked Elizabeth.

"Not very Spanish, half white wine, half soda, lots of ice. Stirred but not shaken. Sort of a poor man's James Bond."

The pleasant atmosphere of the restaurant helped to dispel some of Mark's tension; he relaxed slightly for the first time in twenty-four hours. They chatted about movies, music, and books, and then about Yale. Her face, often animated, was sometimes serene but always lovely in the candlelight. Mark was enchanted by her. For all her intelligence and self-sufficiency, she had a touching fragility and femininity.

As they ate their paella Mark asked Elizabeth why her father had become a senator, about his career, and her childhood in Connecticut. The subject seemed to make her uneasy. Mark couldn't help remembering that her father was still on the list. He tried to shift the conversation to her mother. Elizabeth avoided his eyes and even, he thought, turned pale. For the first time, a tiny ripple of suspicion disturbed his affectionate vision of Elizabeth, and made him worry momentarily. She was the first beautiful thing that had happened for quite a while, and he didn't want to distrust her. Was it possible? Could she be involved? No, of course not. He tried to put it out of his mind.

The Spanish floor show came on and was performed with enthusiasm. Mark and Elizabeth listened and watched, unable to speak to each other above the noise. Mark was happy enough just to sit and be with her; her face was turned away as she looked at the dancers. When the floor show eventually ended, they had both long finished the paella. They ordered dessert and coffee.

"Would you like a cigar?"

Elizabeth smiled. "No, thanks. We don't have to ape men's vile habits as well as their good ones."

"Like that," said Mark. "You're going to be the first woman Surgeon General, I suppose?"

"No, I'm not," she said demurely. "I'll probably be the second or third."

Mark laughed. "I'd better get back to the Bureau, and do great things. Just to keep up with you."

"And it may well be a woman who stops you becoming Director of the FBI," Elizabeth added.

"No, it won't be a woman that stops me becoming Director of the FBI," said Mark, but he didn't explain.

"Your coffee, señorita, señor."

If Mark had ever wanted to sleep with a woman on the first date, this was the occasion, but he knew it wasn't going to happen.

He paid the bill, left a generous tip for the waiter, and congratulated the girl from the floor show, who was sitting in a corner drinking coffee.

When they left the restaurant Mark found the night had a chill edge. Once again he began looking nervously around him, trying not to make it too obvious to Elizabeth. He took her hand as they crossed the street, and didn't let it go when they reached the other side. They walked on, chatting intermittently, both aware of what was happening. He wanted to hold on to her. Lately, he had been seeing a lot of women, but with none of them had he held their hand either before or afterwards. Gradually his mood darkened again. Perhaps fear was making him excessively sentimental.

A car was driving up behind them. Mark stiffened with anticipation. Elizabeth didn't appear to notice. It slowed down. It was going slower as it neared them. It stopped just beside them. Mark undid his middle button and fidgeted, more worried for Elizabeth than for himself. The doors of the car opened suddenly and out jumped four teenagers, two girls, two boys. They darted into a Hamburger Haven. Sweat appeared on Mark's forehead. He shook free of Elizabeth's touch. She stared at him. "Something's very wrong, isn't it?"

"Yes," he said. "Just don't ask me about it."

She sought his hand again, held it firmly, and they walked on. The oppression of the horrible events of the previous day bore down on Mark and he did not speak again. When they arrived at her front door, he was back in the world which was shared only by him and the hulking, shadowy figure of Halt Tyson.

"Well, you have been most charming this evening, when you've actually been here," she said smilingly.

Mark shook himself. "I'm really sorry."

"Would you like to come in for coffee?"

"Yes and no. Can I take another raincheck on that? I don't feel like good company right now."

He still had several things to do before he saw the Director at 7:00 am and it was already midnight. Also he hadn't slept properly for a day and a half.

"Can I call you tomorrow?"

"I'd like that," she said. "Be sure to keep in touch, whatever happens."

Mark would carry those few words around with him like a talisman for the next few days. He could recall her every word and its accompanying gesture. Were they said in fun, were they said seriously, were they said teasingly? Lately, it hadn't been fashionable to fall in love; very few people seemed to be getting married and a lot of people who had were getting divorced. Was he really going to fall madly in love in the middle of all this?

He kissed her on the cheek and turned to leave, his eyes darting up and down the road again. She whispered after him:

"I hope you find the man who killed my mailman and your Greek."

Your Greek, your Greek, Greek Orthodox priest, Father Gregory. God in heaven, why hadn't he thought of it before? He'd forgotten Elizabeth for a moment as he started to run towards his car. He turned to wave; she was staring at him with a puzzled expression, wondering what she had said. Mark leaped into the car and drove as fast as he could to his apartment. He must find Father Gregory's number. Greek Orthodox priest, what did he look like, the one who came out of the elevator, what did he look like; it was all coming back, there had been something unusual with him: what the hell was it? His clothes? No, they were fine, or was it his face? His face was wrong somehow. Of course. Of course. How could he have been so stupid. When he arrived home, he called the Washington Field Office immediately. Polly, on the switchboard, was surprised to hear him.

"Aren't you on leave?"

"Yes, sort of. Do you have Father Gregory's number?"

"Who is Father Gregory?"

"A Greek Orthodox priest whom Mr Stames used to contact occasionally; I think he was his local priest."

"Yes, you're right. Now I remember."

Mark waited.

She checked Stames's Rolodex and gave him the number. Mark wrote it down, and replaced the phone. Of course, of course, of course. How stupid of him. It was so obvious. Well past midnight, but he had to call. He dialled the number. The telephone rang several times before it was answered.

"Father Gregory?"

"Yes."

"Do all Greek Orthodox priests have beards?"

"Yes, as a rule. Who is this asking such a damn silly question in the middle of the night?"

Mark apologised. "My name is Special Agent Mark Andrews. I worked under Nick Stames."

The man at the other end, who had sounded sleepy, immediately woke up. "I understand, young man. What can I do for you?"

"Father Gregory, last night Mr Stames's secretary called you and asked you to go to Woodrow Wilson to check a Greek who had a bullet wound in his leg?"

"Yes, that's right – I remember, Mr Andrews. But somebody else called about thirty minutes later, just as I was leaving, in fact, to tell me I needn't bother because Mr Casefikis had been discharged from the hospital."

"He'd been what?" Mark's voice rose with each word.

"Discharged from the hospital."

"Did the caller say who he was?"

"No, the man gave no other details. I assumed he was from your office."

"Father Gregory, can I see you tomorrow morning at eight o'clock?"

"Yes, of course, my son."

"And can you be sure you don't talk to anybody else about this phone call, whoever they say they are?"

"If that is your wish, my son."

"Thank you, Father."

Mark dropped the telephone and tried to concentrate. He was taller than I was, so he was over six feet. He was dark, or was that just his priest's robes? No, he had dark hair, he had a big nose, I remember he had a big nose, eyes, no I can't remember his eyes, he had a big nose, a heavy chin, a heavy chin. Mark wrote everything down he could remember. A big heavy man, taller than me, big nose, heavy chin, big nose, heavy . . . he collapsed. His head fell on the desk and he slept.

# Saturday morning, 5 March

## 6:32 am

Mark had awoken, but he wasn't awake. His head was swimming with incoherent thoughts. The first vision to flash across his mind was Elizabeth; he smiled. The second was Nick Stames; he frowned. The third was the Director. Mark woke with a start and sat up, trying to focus his eyes on his watch. All he could see was the second hand moving: 6:35. Hell. He shot up from the chair, his stiff neck and back hurting him; he was still dressed. He threw off his clothes and rushed into the bathroom and showered, without taking time to adjust the water temperature. Goddamn freezing. At least it woke him up and made him forget Elizabeth. He jumped out of the shower and grabbed a towel: 6:40. After throwing the lather on his face, he shaved too quickly, mowing down the stubble on his chain. Damn it, three nicks; the aftershave lotion stung viciously: 6:43. He dressed: clean shirt, same cuff links, clean socks, same shoes, clean suit, same tie. A quick look in the mirror: two nicks still bleeding slightly, the hell with it. He bundled the papers on his desk into his briefcase and ran for the elevator. First piece of luck, it was on the top floor. Downstairs: 6:46.

"Hi, Simon."

The young black garage attendant didn't move. He was dozing in his little cubbyhole at the garage entrance.

"Morning Mark. Hell, man, is it eight o'clock already?"

"No, thirteen minutes to seven."

"What are you up to? Moonlighting?" asked Simon, rubbing his eyes and handing over the car keys. Mark smiled, but didn't have time to answer. Simon dozed off again.

Car starts first time. Reliable Mercedes. Moves on to the road: 6:48. Must stay below speed limit. Never embarrass the Bureau. At 6th Street, held up by lights: 6:50. Cut across G Street, up 7th, more lights. Cross Independence Avenue: 6:53. Corner of 7th and Pennsylvania. Can see FBI Building: 6:55. Down ramp, park, show FBI pass to garage guard, run for elevator: 6:57; elevator to seventh floor: 6:58. Along the corridor, turn right, Room 7074, straight in, past Mrs McGregor as instructed. She barely glances up; knock on door of Director's office; no reply; go in as instructed. No Director: 6:59; sink into easy chair. Director going to be late; smile of satisfaction. Thirty seconds to seven: glance around room, casually, as if been waiting for hours. Eyes land on grandfather clock. Strikes: one, two, three, four, five, six, seven.

The door opened, and the Director marched in. "Good morning, Andrews." He did not look at Mark, but at the clock on the wall. "It's always a little fast." Silence. The Old Post Office Tower clock struck seven.

The Director settled into his chair, and once again the large hands took possession of the desk.

"We'll start with my news first, Andrews. We have just received some identification on the Lincoln that went into the Potomac with Stames and Calvert."

The Director opened a new manilla file marked "Eyes only" and glanced at its contents. What was in the file that Mark didn't know about and ought to know about?

"Nothing solid to go on. Hans-Dieter Gerbach, German. Bonn has reported that he was a minor figure in the Munich rackets until five years ago, then they lost track of him. There is some evidence to suggest he was in Rhodesia and even hitched up with the CIA for a while. The White-Lightning Brigade. The CIA is not being helpful on him. I can't see much information coming from them before Thursday. Sometimes I wonder whose side they're on. In 1980, Gerbach turned up in New York, but there's nothing there except rumours and street talk, no record to go on. It would have helped if he'd lived."

Mark thought of the slit throats in Woodrow Wilson Medical Center and wondered.

"The interesting fact to emerge from the car crash is that both back tyres of Stames's and Calvert's car have small holes in them. They could have been the result of the fall down the bank, but our laboratory boys think they are bullet holes. If they are, whoever did the shooting makes Wyatt Earp look like a boy scout."

The Director spoke into his intercom. "Have Assistant Director Rogers join us please, Mrs McGregor."

"Yes, sir."

"Mr Rogers's men have found the catering outfit Casefikis was working for, for what that's worth."

The Assistant Director knocked and entered. The Director indicated a chair. Rogers smiled at Mark and sat down.

"Let's have the details, Matt."

"Well, sir, the owner of the Golden Duck wasn't exactly co-operative. Seemed to think I was after him for contravening employers' regulations. I threatened to shut him down if he didn't talk. Finally he admitted to employing a man matching Casefikis's description on 24 February. He sent Casefikis to serve at a small luncheon party in one of the rooms at the Georgetown Inn on Wisconsin Avenue. The man who made the arrangement was a Lorenzo Rossi. He insisted on a waiter who couldn't speak English. Paid in cash. We've run Rossi through all the computers – nothing. Obviously a false name. Same story at the Georgetown Inn. The proprietor said the room had been hired for the day of 24 February by a Mr Rossi, food to be supplied, but no service, cash paid in advance. Rossi was about five-feet-eight, dark complexion, no distinguishing features, dark hair, sunglasses. The proprietor thought he "seemed Italian". No one at the hotel knows or cares who the hell went to lunch in that room that day. I'm afraid it doesn't get us very far."

"I agree. I suppose we could pull every Italian answering that description off the street," said the Director. "If we had five years, not five days. Did you turn up anything new at the hospital, Matt?"

"It's a hell of a mess, sir. The place is full of people coming and going, all day and most of the night. The staff all work shifts. They don't even know their own colleagues, let alone outsiders. You could wander around there all day with a torchlight in your hand and no one would stop you unless they wanted a light."

"That figures," said Tyson. "Right, Andrews, what have you been up to for the past twenty-four hours?"

Mark opened his regulation blue plastic portfolio. He reported that there were sixty-two senators left, the other thirty-eight accounted for, most of them having been a long way from Washington on 24 February. He passed the list of names over to the Director, who glanced through them.

"Some pretty big fish still left in the muddy pond, Andrews. Go on."

Mark proceeded to outline his encounter with the Greek Orthodox priest. He expected a sharp reprimand for failing to remember the matter of the beard immediately. He was not disappointed. Chastened, he continued: "I am seeing Father Gregory at eight o'clock this morning, and I thought I would go on to see Casefikis's widow afterwards. I don't think either will have much to offer, but I imagine you want those leads followed up, sir. After that I intended to return to the Library of Congress to try and figure out why any of those sixty-two senators might wish to see an end of President Kane."

"Well, to start with, put them in categories," said the Director. "First political party, then committees, then outside interests, then their personal knowledge of the President. Don't forget, Andrews, we do know that our man had lunch in Georgetown on 24 February and that should bring the numbers down."

"But sir, presumably they all had lunch on 24 February."

"Exactly, Andrews, but not all in private. Many of them would have been seen in a public place or lunched officially, with constituents or federal employees or lobbyists. You have to find out who did what, without letting the senator we're after get suspicious."

"How do you suggest I go about doing that, sir?"

"Simple," replied the Director. "You call each of the senators' secretaries and ask if the boss would be free to attend a luncheon on –" he paused "– 'The Problems of Urban Environment'. Yes, I like that. Give them a date, say 5 May, then ask if they attended either the one given on," the Director glanced at his calendar, "17 January or 24 February, as some senators who had accepted didn't attend, and one or two turned up without invitations. Then say a written invitation will follow. All the secretaries will put it out of their minds unless you write, and if any of them does remember on 5 May, it will be too late for us to care. One thing is certain: no senator will be letting his secretary know that he is planning to kill the President."

The Assistant Director grimaced slightly. "If he gets caught, sir, all hell will break loose. We'll be back in the dirty-tricks department."

"No, Matt, if I tell the President one of her precious brethren is going to knife her in the back, she won't see anything particularly pleasant in that trick."

"We haven't got any real proof, sir," said Mark.

"Then you had better find it, Andrews, or we'll all be looking for a new job, trust my judgement."

Trust my judgement, Mark thought.

"All we have is one strong lead," the Director continued. "That a senator may be involved, but we have only five days left. If we fail next Thursday, there will be enough time during the next twenty years to study the inquiry and you, Andrews, will be able to make a fortune writing a book about it."

Mark looked apprehensive.

"Andrews, don't get too worried. I have briefed the head of the Secret Service. I told him no more and no less than was in your report, as we agreed yesterday, so that gives us a clear run right through to 10 March. I'm working on a contingency plan, in case we don't know who Cassius is before then; but I won't bore you with it now. I have also talked to the boys from Homicide; they have come up with very little that can help us. It may interest you to know that they have seen Casefikis's wife already. Their brains seem to work a little faster than yours, Andrews."

"Perhaps they don't have as much on their minds," said the Assistant Director.

"Maybe not. Okay, go see her if you think it might help. You may pick up something they missed. Cheer up, you've covered a lot of ground. Perhaps this morning's investigation will give us some new leads to work on. I think that covers everything for now. Right, Andrews, don't let me waste any more of your time."

"No, sir."

Mark rose.

"I'm sorry, I forgot to offer you coffee, Andrews."

I didn't manage to drink it the last time, Mark wanted to say. He left as the Director ordered coffee for himself and the Assistant Director. He decided that he too could do with some breakfast and a chance to collect his thoughts. He went in search of the Bureau cafeteria.

The Director drank his coffee and asked Mrs McGregor to send in his personal assistant. The anonymous man appeared almost instantly, a grey folder under his arm.

He didn't have to ask the Director what it was that he wanted. He placed the folder on the table in front of him, and left without speaking.

"Thank you," said the Director to the closing door.

He turned the cover of the folder and browsed through it for twenty minutes, a chuckle here, and a grunt there, the odd comment to Matthew Rogers. There were facts in it about Mark Andrews of which Mark himself would have been unaware. The Director finished his second cup of coffee, closed the file, and locked it in the personal drawer of the Queen Anne desk. Queen Anne had never held as many secrets as that desk.

Mark finished a much better breakfast than he could have hoped for at the Washington Field Office. There, you had to go across the street to the Lunch Connection, because the snack bar downstairs was so abominable, much in keeping with the rest of the building. Not that he wouldn't have liked to return to it now instead of the underground garage to pick up his car. He didn't notice the man across the street who watched him leave, but he did wonder whether the blue Ford sedan that stayed in his rear-view mirror so long was there by chance. If it wasn't, who was watching whom, who was trying to protect whom?

He arrived at Father Gregory's church just before 8:00 am and they walked together to the priest's house. The priest's half-rim glasses squatted on the end of a stubby nose. His large, red cheeks and even larger basketball belly led the uncharitable to conclude that Father Gregory had found much to solace him on earth while he waited for the eternal kingdom of heaven. Mark told him that he had already breakfasted, but it didn't stop the Father from frying two eggs and bacon, plus toast, marmalade, and a cup of coffee. Father Gregory could add very little to what he had told Mark on the telephone the previous night, and he sighed deeply when he was reminded of the two deaths at the hospital.

"Yes, I read the details in the *Post*." When they talked about Nick Stames, a light came into his grey eyes; it was clear that priest and policeman had shared a few secrets, this was no jolly old Jesus freak.

"Is there any connection between Nick's death and the accident in the hospital?" Father Gregory asked suddenly.

The question took Mark by surprise. There was a shrewd brain behind the half-rim glasses. Lying to a priest, Greek Orthodox or otherwise, seemed somehow worse than the usual lies which were intended to protect the Bureau from the general public.

"Absolutely none," said Mark. "Just one of those horrible auto accidents."

"Just one of those weird coincidences?" said Father Gregory quizzically, peering at Mark over the top of his glasses. "Is that right?" he sounded almost as unconvinced as Grant Nanna. He continued: "There's one more thing I would like to mention. Although it's hard to remember exactly what the man said when he called me and told me not to bother to go to the hospital, I'm fairly certain he was a well-educated man. I feel sure by the way he carried it off that he was a professional man, and I am not sure what I mean by that; it's just the strange feeling that he had made that sort of call before; there was something professional about him."

Father Gregory repeated the phrase to himself – "Something professional about him" – and so did Mark, while he was in the car on the way to the house in which Mrs Casefikis was staying. It was the home of the friend who had harboured her wounded husband.

Mark drove down Connecticut Avenue, past the Washington Hilton and the National Zoo, into Maryland. Patches of bright, yellow forsythia had begun to appear along the road. Connecticut Avenue turned into University Boulevard, and Mark found himself in Wheaton, a suburban satellite of stores, restaurants, gas stations, and a few apartment buildings. Stopped by a red light near

Wheaton Plaza, Mark checked his notes. 11501 Elkin Street. He was looking for the Blue Ridge Manor Apartments. Fancy name for a group of squat, three-storey faded-brick buildings lining Blue Ridge and Elkin streets. As he approached 11501, Mark looked for a parking space. No luck. He hovered for a moment, then decided to park in front of a fire hydrant. He draped the radio microphone carefully over his rear-view mirror, so that any observant meter maid or policeman would know that this was an official car on official business.

Ariana Casefikis burst into tears at the mere sight of Mark's badge. She looked frail; only twenty-nine, her clothes unkempt, her hair all over the place, her eyes grey and still full of tears. The lines on her face showed where the tears had been running, running for two days. She and Mark were about the same age. She didn't have a country, and now she didn't have a husband. What was going to happen to her? If Mark had felt alone, he was certainly better off than this poor woman.

Mrs Casefikis's English turned out to be rather better than her husband's. She had already seen two policemen. She told them that she knew nothing. First the nice man from the Metropolitan Police who had broken the news to her and been so understanding, then the Homicide lieutenant who had come a little later and been much firmer, wanting to know things she hadn't the faintest clue about, and now a visit from the FBI. Her husband had never been in trouble before and she didn't know who shot him or why anybody would want to. He was a gentle, kind man. Mark believed her.

He also assured her that she had no immediate cause for worry and that he would deal personally with the Immigration Office and the Welfare people about getting her some income. It seemed to cheer her up and make her a little more responsive.

"Now please try to think carefully, Mrs Casefikis. Have you any idea where your husband was working on 23 or

24 February, the Wednesday and Thursday of last week, and did he tell you anything about his work?"

She had no idea. Angelo never told her what he was up to and half the jobs were casual and only for the day, because he couldn't risk staying on without a work permit, being an illegal immigrant. Mark was getting nowhere, but it wasn't her fault.

"Will I be able to stay in America?"

"I'll do everything I can to help, Mrs Casefikis. That I promise you. I'll talk to a Greek Orthodox priest I know about finding some money to tide you over till I've seen the Welfare people."

Mark opened the door, despondent about the lack of any hard information either from Father Grègory or from Ariana Casefikis.

"The priest already give me money."

Mark stopped in his tracks, turned slowly, and faced her. He tried to show no particular interest.

"Which priest was that?" he asked casually.

"He said he help. Man who came to visit yesterday. Nice man, very nice, very kind. He give me fifty dollars."

Mark turned cold. The man had been ahead of him again. Father Gregory was right, there was something professional about him.

"Can you describe him, Mrs Casefikis?"

"What do you mean?"

"What did he look like?"

"Oh, he was a big man, very dark, I think," she began.

Mark tried to remain offhand. It must have been the man who had passed him in the elevator, the man who had earlier kept Father Gregory from going to the hospital and who, if Mrs Casefikis had known anything at all about the plot, would no doubt have dispatched her to join her husband.

"Did he have a beard, Mrs Casefikis?"

"Of course he did," she hesitated, "but I can't remember him having one."

Mark asked her to stay in the house, not to leave under

any circumstances. He made an excuse that he was going to check on the Welfare situation and talk to the Immigration officials. He was learning how to lie. The clean-shaven Greek Orthodox priest was teaching him.

He jumped into the car and drove a few hundred yards to the nearest pay phone on Georgia Avenue. He dialled the Director's private line. The Director picked up the phone.

"Julius."

"What is your number?" asked the Director.

Thirty seconds later the phone rang. Mark went over the story carefully.

"I'll send an Identikit man down to you immediately. You go back there and hold her hand. And, Andrews, try to think on your feet. I'd like that fifty dollars. Was it one bill, or several? There may just be a fingerprint on them." The telephone clicked. Mark frowned. If the phony Greek Orthodox priest weren't always two steps ahead of him, the Director was.

Mark returned to Mrs Casefikis and told her that her case would be dealt with at the highest level; he must remember to speak to the Director about it at the next meeting, he made a note about it on his pad. Back to the casual voice again.

"Are you sure it was fifty dollars, Mrs Casefikis?"

"Oh, yes, I don't see a fifty-dollar bill every day, and I was most thankful at the time."

"Can you remember what you did with it?"

"Yes, I went and bought food from the supermarket just before they closed."

"Which supermarket, Mrs Casefikis?"

"Wheaton Supermarket. Up the street."

"When was that?"

"Yesterday evening about six o'clock."

Mark realised that there wasn't a moment to lose. If it weren't already too late.

"Mrs Casefikis, a man will be coming, a colleague of

mine, a friend, from the FBI, to ask you to describe the kind Father who gave you the money. It will help us greatly if you can remember as much about him as possible. You have nothing to worry about because we're doing everything we can to help you."

Mark hesitated, took out his wallet and gave her fifty dollars. She smiled for the first time.

"Now, Mrs Casefikis, I want you to do just one last thing for me. If the Greek priest ever comes to visit again, don't tell him about our conversation, just call me at this number."

Mark handed her a card. Ariana Casefikis nodded, but her lacklustre grey eyes followed Mark to his car. She didn't understand, or know which man to trust: hadn't they both given her fifty dollars?

Mark pulled into a parking space in front of the Wheaton Supermarket. A huge sign in the window announced that cases of cold beer were sold inside. Above the window was a blue and white cardboard representation of the dome of the Capitol. Five days, thought Mark. He went into the store. It was a small family enterprise, privately owned, not part of a chain. Beer lined one wall, wine the other, and in between were four rows of canned and frozen foods. A meat counter stretched the length of the rear wall. The butcher seemed to be minding the store alone. Mark hurried towards him, starting to ask the question before he reached the counter.

"Could I please see the manager?"

The butcher eyed him suspiciously. "What for?"

Mark showed his credentials.

The butcher shrugged and yelled over his shoulder, "Hey, Flavio. FBI. Wants to see you."

Several seconds later, the manager, a large red-faced Italian, appeared in the doorway to the left of the meat counter. "Yeah? What can I do for you, Mr, uh . . ."

"Andrews, FBI." Mark showed his credentials once again.

"Yeah, okay. What do you want, Mr Andrews? I'm

Flavio Guida. This is my place. I run a good, honest place."

"Yes, of course, Mr Guida. I'm simply hoping you can help me. I'm investigating a case of stolen money, and we have reason to believe that a stolen fifty-dollar bill was spent in this supermarket yesterday and we wonder now if there is any way of tracing it."

"Well, my money is collected every night," said the manager. "It's put into the safe and deposited in the bank first thing in the morning. It would have gone to the bank about an hour ago, and I think –"

"But it's Saturday," Mark said.

"No problem. My bank is open till noon on Saturday. It's just a few doors down."

Mark thought on his feet.

"Would you please accompany me to the bank immediately, Mr Guida?"

Guida looked at his watch and then at Mark Andrews.

"Okay. Give me just half a minute."

He shouted to an invisible woman in the back of the store to keep an eye on the cash register. Together he and Mark walked to the corner of Georgia and Hickers. Guida was obviously getting quite excited by the whole episode.

At the bank Mark went immediately to the chief cashier. The money had been handed over thirty minutes before to one of his tellers, a Mrs Townsend. She still had it in piles ready for sorting. It was next on her list. She hadn't had time to do so yet, she said rather apologetically. No need to feel sorry, thought Mark. The supermarket's take for the day had been just over five thousand dollars. There were twenty-eight fifty-dollar bills. Christ Almighty, the Director was going to tear him apart, or to be more exact, the fingerprint experts were. Mark counted the fifty-dollar notes using gloves supplied by Mrs Townsend and put them on one side – he agreed there were twenty-eight. He signed for them, gave the receipt to the chief cashier, and assured him they would be returned in the very near future. The bank manager came over and took charge of the receipt and the situation.

"Don't FBI men usually work in pairs?"

Mark blushed. "Yes, sir, but this is a special assignment."

"I would like to check," said the manager. "You are asking me to release one thousand four hundred dollars on your word."

"Of course, sir, please do check."

Mark had to think quickly. He couldn't ask the manager of a local bank to ring the Director of the FBI. It would be like charging your gasoline to the account of Henry Ford.

"Why don't you ring the FBI's Washington Field Office, sir, ask for the head of the Criminal Section. Mr Grant Nanna."

"I'll do just that."

Mark gave him the number, but he ignored it and looked it up for himself in the Washington directory. He got right through to Nanna. Thank God he was there.

"I have a young man from your Field Office with me. His name is Mark Andrews. He says he has the authority to take away twenty-eight fifty-dollar bills. Something to do with stolen money."

Nanna also had to think quickly. Deny the allegation, defy the alligator – Nick Stames's old motto.

Mark, meanwhile, offered up a little prayer.

"That's correct, sir," said Nanna. "He has been instructed by me to pick up those notes. I hope you will release them immediately. They will be returned as soon as possible."

"Thank you, Mr Nanna. I'm sorry to have bothered you. I just felt I ought just to check; you never can be sure nowadays."

"No bother, sir, a wise precaution. We wish everybody were as careful." The first truth he'd uttered, thought Grant Nanna.

The bank manager replaced the receiver, put the pile

of fifty-dollar bills in a brown envelope, accepted the receipt, and shook hands with Mark apologetically.

"You understand I had to check?"

"Of course," said Mark. "I would have done the same myself."

He thanked Mr Guida and the manager and asked them both not to mention the matter to anybody. They nodded with the air of those who know their duty.

Mark returned to the FBI Building immediately and went straight to the Director's office. Mrs McGregor nodded at him. A quiet knock on the door, and he went in.

"Sorry to interrupt you, sir."

"Not at all, Andrews. Have a seat. We were just finishing."

Matthew Rogers rose and looked carefully at Andrews and smiled.

"I'll try and have the answers for you by lunch, Director," he said, and left.

"Well, young man, do you have our Senator in the car downstairs?"

"No, sir, but I do have these."

Mark opened the brown envelope and put twenty-eight fifty-dollar bills on the table.

"Been robbing a bank, have you? A federal charge, Andrews."

"Almost, sir. One of these notes, as you know, was given to Mrs Casefikis by the man posing as the Greek Orthodox priest."

"Well, that will be a nice little conundrum for our fingerprint boys; fifty-six sides with hundreds, perhaps thousands of prints on them. It's a long shot and it will take a considerable time, but it's worth a try." He was careful not to touch the notes. "I'll have Sommerton deal with it immediately. We'll also need Mrs Casefikis's prints. I'll also put one of our agents on her house in case the big man returns." The Director was writing and talking at the same time. "It's just like the old days when I ran a field office. I do believe I'd enjoy it if it weren't so serious."

"Can I mention just one other thing while I'm here, sir?"

"Yes, say whatever you want to, Andrews." Tyson didn't look up, just continued writing.

"Mrs Casefikis is worried about her status in this country. She has no money, no job, and now no husband. She may well have given us a vital lead and she has certainly been as co-operative as possible. I think we might help."

The Director pressed a button.

"Ask Sommerton from Fingerprints to come up immediately, and send Elliott in."

Ah, thought Mark, the anonymous man has a name.

"I'll do what I can. I'll see you Monday at seven, Andrews. I'll be home all weekend if you need me. Don't stop working."

"Yes, sir."

Mark left. He stopped at the Riggs Bank and changed fifteen dollars into quarters. The teller looked at him curiously.

"Have your own pinball machine, do you?"

Mark smiled.

He spent the rest of the morning and most of the afternoon with a diminishing pile of quarters, calling the weekend-duty secretaries of the sixty-two senators who had been in Washington on 24 February. All of them were most gratified that their senator should be invited to an Environmental Conference; the Director was no fool. At the end of sixty-two phone calls, his ears were numb. Mark studied the results . . . thirty senators had eaten in the office or with constituents, fifteen had not told their secretaries where they were having lunch or had mentioned some vague "appointment", and seventeen had attended luncheons hosted by groups as varied as the National Press Club, Common Cause, and the NAACP. One secretary even thought her boss had been at that particular Environmental Luncheon on 24 February. Mark hadn't been able to think of a reply to that.

With the Director's help he was now down to fifteen senators.

He returned to the Library of Congress, and once again made for the quiet reference room. The librarian did not seem the least bit suspicious of all his questions about particular senators and committees and procedure in the Senate; she was used to graduate students who were just as demanding and far less courteous.

Mark went back to the shelf that held the *Congressional Record*. It was easy to find 24 February: it was the only thumbed number in the pile of unbound latest issues. He checked through the fifteen remaining names. On that day, there had been one committee in session, the Foreign Relations Committee; three senators on his list of fifteen were members of that committee, and all three had spoken in committee that morning, according to the *Record*. The Senate itself had debated two issues that day: the allocation of funds in the Energy Department for solar-energy research, and the Gun Control bill. Some of the remaining twelve had spoken on one or both issues on the floor of the Senate: there was no way of eliminating any of the fifteen, damn it. He listed the fifteen names on fifteen sheets of paper, and read through the *Congressional Record* for every day from 24 February to 3 March. By each name he noted the senator's presence or absence from the Senate on each working day. Painstakingly, he built up each senator's schedule; there were many gaps. It was evident that senators do not spend all their time in the Senate.

The young librarian was at his elbow. Mark glanced at the clock: 7:30. Throwing-out time. Time to forget the senators and to see Elizabeth. He called her at home.

"Hello, lovely lady. I think it must be time to eat again.

I haven't had anything since breakfast. Will you take pity on my debilitated state, Doctor, and eat with me?"

"And do what with you, Mark? I've just washed my hair. I think I must have soap in my ears."

"Eat with me, I said. That will do for the moment. I just might think of something else later."

"I just might say no later," she said sweetly. "How's the breathing?"

"Coming on nicely, thank you, but if I go on thinking what I am thinking right now, I may break out in pimples."

"What do you want me to do, pour cold water in the phone?"

"No, just eat with me. I'll pick you up in half an hour, hair wet or dry."

They found a small restaurant called Mr Smith's in Georgetown. Mark was more familiar with it in the summer, when one could sit at a table in the garden at the back. It was crowded with people in their twenties. The perfect place to sit for hours and talk.

"God," said Elizabeth. "This is just like being back at college; I thought we had grown out of that."

"I'm glad you appreciate it," Mark smiled.

"It's all so predictable. Folksy wooden floors, butcher-block tables, plants. Bach flute sonatas. Next time we'll try McDonald's."

Mark couldn't think of a reply, and was saved only by the appearance of a menu.

"Can you imagine, four years at Yale, and I still don't know what *ratatouille* is," said Elizabeth.

"I know what it is, but I wasn't sure how to pronounce it."

They both ordered chicken, baked potato, and salad.

"Look, Mark, there, that ghastly Senator Thornton with a girl young enough to be his daughter."

"Perhaps she is his daughter."

"No civilised man would bring his daughter here." She smiled at him.

"He's a friend of your father's, isn't he?"

"Yes, how do you know that?" asked Elizabeth.

"Common knowledge." Mark already regretted his question.

"Well, I'd describe him as more of a business associate. He makes his money manufacturing guns. Not the most attractive occupation."

"But your father owns part of a gun company."

"Daddy? Yes, I don't approve of that either, but he blames it on my grandfather who founded the firm. I used to argue with him about it when I was at school. Told him to sell his stock and invest it in something socially useful, saw myself as a sort Major Barbara."

"How is your dinner?" a hovering waiter asked.

"Um, just great, thanks," said Elizabeth looking up. "You know, Mark, I once called my father a war criminal."

"But he was against the war, I thought."

"You seem to know an awful lot about my father," said Elizabeth looking at him suspiciously.

Not enough, thought Mark, and how much could you really tell me? If Elizabeth picked up any sign of his anxiety, she didn't register it but simply continued.

"He voted to approve the MX missile, and I didn't sit at the same table with him for almost a month. I don't think he even noticed."

"How about your mother?" asked Mark.

"She died when I was fourteen, which may be why I'm so close to my father," Elizabeth said. She looked down at her hands in her lap, evidently wanting to drop the subject. Her dark hair shone as it fell across her forehead.

"You have very beautiful hair," Mark said softly. "I wanted to touch it when I first saw you. I still do."

She smiled. "I like curly hair better." She leaned her chin on her cupped hands and looked at him mischievously. "You'll look fantastic when you're forty and fashionably grey at the temples. Provided you don't lose it all first, of course. Did you know that men who lose their hair at the crown are sexy, those who lose it at the temples, think, and those who lose it all over, think they are sexy?"

"If I go bald at the crown, will you accept that as a declaration of intent?"

"I'm willing to wait but not that long."

On the way back to her house he stopped, put his arm around her and kissed her, hesitantly at first, unsure of how she would respond.

"You know, my knees are feeling weak, Elizabeth," he murmured into her soft, warm hair. "What are you going to do with your latest victim?"

She walked on without speaking for a little way.

"Get you some knee pads," she said.

They walked on hand in hand, silently, happily, slowly. Three not very romantic men were following them.

In the pretty living-room, on the cream-coloured sofa, he kissed her again.

The three unromantic men waited in the shadows outside.

She sat alone in the Oval Office going over the clauses in the bill one by one, searching for any line that still might trip her up when the bill was voted on tomorrow.

She looked up suddenly startled to see her husband standing in front of her, a mug of steaming cocoa in his hand.

"An early night won't harm your chances of influencing that lot," he said pointing towards the Capitol.

She smiled, "Darling Edward, where would I be without your common sense?"

# Sunday morning, 6 March

## 9:00 am

Mark spent Sunday morning putting the finishing touches to his report for the Director. He began by tidying his desk; he could never think clearly unless everything was in place. Mark gathered all his notes together and put them in a logical sequence. He completed the task by two o'clock, without noticing that he had missed lunch. Slowly he wrote down the names of the fifteen senators who were left, six under the heading Foreign Relations Committee, nine under Gun Control bill – Judiciary Committee. He stared at the lists, hoping for inspiration but none came. One of these men was a killer and there were only four days left to find out which one. He put the papers into his briefcase, which he locked in his desk.

He went into the kitchen and made himself a sandwich. He looked at his watch. What could he do that would be useful for the rest of the day? Elizabeth was on duty at the hospital. He picked up the phone and dialled the number. She could only spare a minute, due in the operating theatre at three o'clock.

"Okay, Doctor, this won't take long and it shouldn't hurt. I can't call you every day just to tell you that you are lovely and intelligent and that you drive me crazy, so listen carefully."

"I'm listening, Mark."

"Okay. You are beautiful and bright and I'm crazy about you . . . What, no reply?"

"Oh, I thought there might be more. I'll say something nice in return when I'm three inches away from you, not three miles."

"Better make it soon, or I am going to crack up. Off you go, and cut out someone else's heart."

She laughed. "It's an ingrown toenail actually . . ."

She hung up. Mark roamed about the room, his mind jumping from fifteen senators, to Elizabeth, back to one Senator. Wasn't it going just a little too well with Elizabeth? Was one Senator looking for him, rather than the other way around? He cursed and poured himself a Michelob. His mind switched to Barry Calvert; on Sunday afternoons they usually played squash. Then to Nick Stames, Stames who had unknowingly taken his place. If Stames were alive now, what would he do? . . . A remark that Stames had made at the office party last Christmas came flashing across Mark's mind: "If I'm not available, the second best crime man in this goddamn country is George Stampouzis of *The New York Times*" – another Greek, naturally. "He must know more about the Mafia and the CIA than almost anyone on either side of the law."

Mark dialled Information in New York, and asked for the number, not quite sure where it was leading him. The operator gave it to him.

"Thank you."

"You're very welcome."

He dialled it.

"Crime desk, George Stampouzis, please." They put him through.

"Stampouzis," said a voice. They don't waste words on *The New York Times*.

"Good afternoon. My name is Mark Andrews. I'm calling from Washington. I was a friend of Nick Stames; in fact, he was my boss."

The voice changed. "Yes, I heard about the terrible accident, if it was an accident. What can I do for you?"

"I need some inside information. Can I fly up and see you immediately?"

"Does it concern Nick?"

"Yes."

"Then yes. Meet me at eight o'clock, north-east corner of Twenty-first and Park Avenue South?"

"I'll be there," said Mark looking at his watch.

"And I'll be waiting for you."

The Eastern Airlines shuttle flight arrived a few minutes after seven. Mark made his way through the crowd milling around the baggage pickup and headed for the taxi stand. A potbellied, middle-aged, unshaven New Yorker with an unlit cigar stub bobbing up and down in his mouth drove him towards Manhattan. He never stopped talking the whole way, a monologue that required few replies. Mark could have used the time to compose his thoughts.

"This country's full of shit," said the bobbing cigar.

"Yes," said Mark.

"And this city is nothing more than a garbage hole."

"Yes," said Mark.

"And that daughter of a bitch Kane's to blame. They ought to string her up."

Mark froze. It was probably said a thousand times a day; someone in Washington was saying it and meaning it.

The cab driver pulled up to the curb.

"Eighteen dollars even," said the bobbing cigar.

Mark put a ten and two fives into the little plastic drawer in the protective screen that divided driver from passenger, and climbed out. A heavy-set man in his mid-fifties and wearing a tweed overcoat, headed towards him. Mark shivered. He had forgotten how cold New York could be in March.

"Andrews?"

"Yes. Good guess."

"When you spend your life studying criminals, you

begin to think like them." He was taking in Mark's suit. "G-men are certainly dressing better than they did in my day."

Mark looked embarrassed. Stampouzis must know that an FBI agent was paid almost double the salary of a New York cop.

"You like Italian food?" He didn't wait for Mark's reply. "I'll take you to one of Nick's old favourites." He was already on the move. They walked the long block in silence, Mark's step hesitating as he passed each restaurant entrance. Suddenly, Stampouzis disappeared into a doorway. Mark followed him through a run-down bar full of men who were leaning on the counter and drinking heavily. Men who had no wives to go home to, or if they did, didn't want to.

Once through the bar, they entered a pleasant, brick-walled dining area. A tall, thin Italian guided them to a corner table: obviously Stampouzis was a favoured customer. Stampouzis didn't bother with the menu.

"I recommend the shrimp marinara. After that, you're on your own."

Mark took his advice and added a *piccata al limone* and half a carafe of Chianti. Stampouzis drank Colt 45. They talked of trivia while they ate. Mark knew the residual Mediterranean creed after two years with Nick Stames – never let business interfere with the enjoyment of good food. In any case, Stampouzis was still sizing him up, and Mark needed his confidence. When Stampouzis had finished an enormous portion of zabaglione and settled down to a double espresso with Sambuca on the side, he looked up at Mark and spoke in a different tone.

"You worked for a great man, a rare lawman. If one tenth of the FBI were as conscientious and intelligent as Nick Stames, you would have something to be pleased about in that brick coliseum of yours."

Mark looked at him, about to speak.

"No, don't add anything about Nick; that's why you're here, and don't ask me to change my opinion of the

Bureau. I've been a crime reporter for over thirty years and the only change I've seen in the FBI and the Mafia is that they are both bigger and stronger." He poured the Sambuca into his coffee, and took a noisy gulp. "Okay. How can I help?"

"Everything off the record," said Mark.

"Agreed," said Stampouzis. "For both our sakes."

"I need two pieces of information. First, are there any senators with close connections in organised crime and second, what is the attitude of the mob to the Gun Control bill?"

"You don't want much, do you?" said the Greek sarcastically. "Where shall I begin? The first is easier to answer directly, because the truth is that half the senators have loose connections with organised crime, by which I mean the Mafia, however out-of-date that is. Some don't even realise it but if you include accepting campaign contributions from businessmen and large corporations directly or indirectly associated with crime, then every President is a criminal. But when the Mafia needs a senator they do it through a third party, and even that's rare."

"Why?" queried Mark.

"The Mafia needs clout at the state level, in courts, with deals, local by-laws, all that. They're just not interested in foreign treaties and the approval of Supreme Court justices. In a more general way, there are some senators who owe their success to links with the Mafia, the ones who have started as civil court judges or state assembly-men and received direct financial backing from the Mafia. It's possible they didn't even realise it; some people don't check too carefully when they are trying to get elected. Added to this are cases like Arizona and Nevada, where the Mafia runs a legit business, but God help any outsiders who try to join in. Finally, in the case of the Democratic party, there's organised labour, especially the Teamsters Union. There you are, Mark, thirty years' experience in ten minutes."

"Great background. Now can I ask you some specifics.

If I name fifteen senators, will you indicate if they could fall into any of the categories you have mentioned?" Mark asked.

"Maybe. Try me. I'll go as far as I feel I can. Just don't push me."

"Bradley."

"Never," said Stampouzis.

"Thornton."

He didn't move a muscle.

"Bayh."

"Not that I have ever heard."

"Harrison."

"No idea. I don't know much about South Carolina politics."

"Nunn."

'Sam Sunday-School? Scout's Honour Nunn? You've got to be kidding."

"Brooks."

"Hates the President but I don't think he'd go that far."

Mark went down the list. Stevenson, Biden, Moynihan, Woodson, Clark, Mathias. Stampouzis shook his head silently.

"Dexter."

He hesitated. Mark tried not to tense.

"Trouble, yes," Stampouzis began. "But Mafia, no."

He must have heard Mark sigh. Mark was anxious to know what the trouble was; he waited but Stampouzis didn't add anything.

"Byrd."

"Majority leader. Not his style."

"Pearson."

"You're joking."

"Thank you," said Mark. He paused. "Now to the Mafia's attitude towards the Gun Control bill."

"I'm not certain at the moment," began Stampouzis. "The Mafia is no longer monolithic. It's too big for that and there has been a lot of internal disagreement lately.

The old-timers are dead set against it because of the obvious difficulty of getting guns legally in the future, but they are more frightened by the riders to the bill, like mandatory sentences for carrying an unregistered gun. The Feds will love that; for them it's the best thing since tax evasion. They will be able to stop any known criminal, search him, and if he is carrying an unregistered gun, which he is almost certain to be, wham, he's in the court-house. On the other hand, some of the young Turks are looking forward to it, a modern-day Prohibition for them. They will supply unregistered guns to unorganised hoodlums and any mad radical who wants one, another source of income for the mob. They also believe the police won't be able to enforce the law and the cleaning-up period will take a decade. Does that get near to answering the question?"

"Yes, very near," said Mark.

"Now, my turn to ask you a question, Mark."

"Same rules?"

"Same rules. Are these questions directly connected with Nick's death?"

"Yes," said Mark.

"I won't ask any more then, because I know what to ask and you're going to have to lie. Let's just make a deal. If this breaks into something big, you'll see I get an exclusive over those bastards from the *Post*."

"Agreed," said Mark.

Stampouzis smiled and signed the check; the last comment had made Mark Andrews a legitimate expense.

Mark looked at his watch; with luck he would make the last shuttle from La Guardia. Stampouzis rose and walked to the door; the bar was still full of men drinking heavily, the same men with the same wives. Once on the street, Mark hailed a cab. This time, a young black pulled up beside him.

"I'm halfway there," said Stampouzis, puzzling Mark. "If I pick up anything that I think might help, I'll call you."

Mark thanked him and climbed into the cab.

"La Guardia, please."

Mark rolled down the window, Stampouzis stared in briefly.

"It's not for you, it's for Nick." He was gone.

The journey back to the airport was silent.

When Mark eventually reached his own apartment, he tried to put the pieces together in his mind ready for the Director the following morning. He glanced at his watch. Christ, it was already the following morning.

# Monday morning, 7 March

## 7:00 am

The Director listened to the results of Mark's research in attentive silence and then added his own unexpected piece of information.

"Andrews, we may be able to narrow your list of fifteen senators even further. Last Thursday morning a couple of agents picked up an unauthorised transmission on one of our KGB channels. Either temporary interference from some commercial station caused us to tune in a different frequency momentarily or else some guy is in possession of an illegal transmitter for our frequency. The only thing our boys heard was: 'Come in, Tony. I just dropped the Senator back for his committee meeting and I'm . . .' The voice stopped transmitting abruptly and we couldn't find it again. Perhaps the conspirators had been listening in on our conversations, and this time one of them without thinking started to transmit on our frequency as well; it's easy enough to do. The agents who heard it filed a report concerning the illegal use of our frequency without realising its particular significance."

Mark was leaning forward in his chair.

"Yes, Andrews," said the Director. "I know what's going through your mind: 10:30 am. The message was sent at 10:30 am."

"10:30 am, 3 March," said Mark urgently. "Let me just check . . . which committees were already in progress

. . ." He opened his file. "Dirksen Building . . . that hour
. . . I have the details at hand somewhere, I know,"
he continued as he flicked through his papers. "Three
possibilities, sir. The Foreign Relations and Government
Operations committees were in session that morning. On
the floor of the Senate they were debating the Gun Control
bill: that seems to be taking up a lot of their time right
now."

"Now we may be getting somewhere," said the Director. "Can you tell from your records how many of your
fifteen were in the Capitol on 3 March and what they
were up to?"

Mark leafed through the fifteen sheets of paper and
slowly divided them into two piles. "Well, it isn't conclusive, sir, but I have no record of these eight" – he placed
his hand on one of the piles – "being in the Senate
that morning. The remaining seven were definitely there.
None on the Government Operations Committee. Two
on Foreign Relations – Pearson and Nunn, sir. The
other five are Brooks, Byrd, Dexter, Harrison and
Thornton. They were all on the floor. And they were
all on the Judiciary Committee, Gun Control bill, as
well."

The Director grimaced. "Well, as you say, Andrews,
it's hardly conclusive. But it's all we have, so you concentrate on those seven. With only four days, it's a chance
we will have to take. Don't get too excited just because
we had one lucky break, and double-check that those
eight could not have been in Dirksen that morning. Now,
I am not going to risk putting seven senators under
surveillance. Those folks on the Hill are suspicious
enough of the FBI as it is. We'll have to use different
tactics. Politically, we can't take a chance on a full-scale
investigation. I'm afraid we'll have to find our man by
using the only clues we're certain of – where he was on
Thursday, 24 February at lunchtime, and this 10:30
Judiciary Committee meeting last week. So don't bother
with the motive – we needn't waste time second-guessing

that, Andrews. Just keep looking for ways of narrowing the list, and spend the rest of the day at the Foreign Relations Committee and the floor of the Senate. Talk to the staff directors. There is nothing they don't know – public or private – about the senators."

"Yes, sir."

"And one more thing. I'm having dinner with the President tonight so I may be able to glean some information from her which could help us reduce the number of suspects."

"Will you tell the President, sir?"

The Director of the FBI paused. "No, I don't think so. I still believe we have the problem under control. I see no reason for worrying her at this stage, certainly not before I'm convinced we're likely to fail."

Finally the Director passed over an Identikit picture of the Greek priest. "Mrs Casefikis's version," he said. "What do you think of it?"

"It's not a bad likeness at all," said Mark. "Maybe a little fleshier around the jaws than that. Those men really know their job."

"What worries me," said the Director, "is that I've seen that damn face before. So many criminals have come across my path that to remember one of them is almost impossible. Maybe it will come to me."

"I do hope it comes before Thursday, sir," said Mark, without thinking.

"So do I," Tyson replied grimly.

"And to think I was only twenty-four hours behind him. It hurts."

"Think yourself lucky, young man. If you had been ahead of him, I think Ariana Casefikis would now be dead and so might you. I've still got a man on Mrs Casefikis's home just in case he returns, but I think he is far too professional a bastard to risk that."

Mark agreed. "Professional bastard," he repeated.

The red light on the internal telephone winked.

"Yes, Mrs McGregor?"

"You'll be late for your appointment with Senator Hart."

"Thank you, Mrs McGregor." He put the phone down. "I'll see you at the same time tomorrow, Mark." It was the first time he called him Mark. "Leave no stone unturned; only four days left."

Mark took the elevator down and left the building by his usual route. He didn't notice he was being followed from the other side of the street. He went to the Senate Office Building and made appointments to see the staff directors of the Foreign Relations and Judiciary committees. The earliest either could manage was the following morning. Mark returned to the Library of Congress to research more thoroughly the personal histories of the seven senators left on his list. They were a rather varied bunch, from all over the country, with little in common; one of them had nothing in common with the other six, but which one? Nunn – it didn't add up. Thornton – Stampouzis obviously didn't care for him but what did that prove. Byrd – surely not the majority leader? Harrison – Stampouzis said he was against the Gun Control bill, but so was almost half the Senate. Dexter – what was the trouble Stampouzis wouldn't tell him about? Perhaps Elizabeth would enlighten him tonight. Ralph Brooks, a strangely intense, driven man and certainly lacking any affection for Kane, that was for sure. Pearson – if he turned out to be the villain, no one would believe it: thirty-three years in the Senate, and always playing honest Casca in public and private.

Mark sighed – the long weary sigh of a man who has come to an impasse. He glanced at his watch: 10:45; he must leave immediately if he were to be on time. He returned the various periodicals, *Congressional Records*, and Ralph Nader reports to the librarian, and hurried across the street to the parking lot to pick up his car. He drove quickly down Constitution Avenue and over Memorial Bridge – how many times had he done that this week? Mark glanced in his rear-view mirror and thought he recognised the car behind him, or was it just the memory of last Thursday?

Mark parked his car at the side of the road. Two Secret Service men stopped him. He produced his credentials and walked slowly down the path just in time to join a hundred and fifty other mourners standing around two graves, freshly dug to receive two men who a week ago were more alive than most of the people attending their burial. The Vice President, former Senator Bill Bradley, was representing the President. He stood next to Norma Stames, a frail figure in black, being supported by her two sons. Hank, the eldest, stood next to a giant of a man, who must have been Barry Calvert's father. Next was the Director, who glanced around and saw Mark, but didn't acknowledge him. The game was being played out even at the graveside.

Father Gregory's vestments fluttered slightly in the cold breeze. The hem was muddy, for it had rained all night. A young chaplain in white surplice and black cassock stood silently at his side.

"I am the image of Thine inexpressible glory, even though I bear the wounds of sin," Father Gregory intoned.

His weeping wife bent forward and kissed Nick Stames's pale cheek and the coffin was closed. As Father Gregory prayed, Stames's and Calvert's coffins were lowered slowly, slowly into their graves. Mark watched sadly: it might have been him going down, down; it should have been him.

"With the saints give rest, O Christ, to the souls of Thy servants, where there is neither sickness nor sorrow, nor sighing, but Life everlasting."

The final blessing was given, the Orthodox made the sign of the cross and the mourners began to disperse.

After the service Father Gregory was speaking warmly of his friend Nick Stames and expressed the hope that he and his colleague Barry Calvert had not died without purpose; he seemed to be looking at Mark as he said it.

Mark saw Nanna, Aspirin, Julie, and the anonymous man, but realised he mustn't speak to them. He slipped quietly away. Let the others mourn the dead: his job was to find their living murderers.

Mark drove back to the Senate, more determined than ever to find out which senator should have been present at the poignant double funeral. Had he stayed a little longer, he would have seen Matson talking casually to Grant Nanna, saying what a good man Stames was and what a loss he would be to law enforcement.

Mark spent the afternoon at the Foreign Relations Committee listening to Pearson and Nunn. If it were either of them, they were cool customers, going about their job without any outward signs of anxiety. Mark wanted to cross their names off the list but he needed one more fact confirmed before he could. When Pearson finally sat down, Mark felt limp. He also needed to relax tonight if he were going to survive the next three days. He left the committee room and called Elizabeth to confirm their dinner date. He then called the Director's office and gave Mrs McGregor the telephone numbers at which he could be reached: the restaurant, his home, Elizabeth's home. Mrs McGregor took the numbers down without comment.

Two cars tailed him on his way back: a blue Ford sedan and a black Buick. When he arrived home, he tossed the car keys to Simon, dismissed the oppressive but familiar sensation of being continually watched, and started thinking of more pleasant things, an evening with Elizabeth.

# 6:30 pm

Mark walked down the street thinking about the evening ahead of him. Already I adore that girl. That's the one thing I am certain of at the moment. If only I could get rid of the nagging doubt about her father – even about her.

He went into Blackistone's and ordered a dozen roses, eleven red, one white. The girl handed him a card and an envelope. Quickly, he wrote Elizabeth's name and address on the envelope, and he pondered the blank card, fragments of sentences and poems flashing through his mind. Finally, he smiled. He wrote, carefully:

Happly I think on thee, and then my state,
Like to the lark at break of day arising
From sullen earth, sings hymns at heaven's gate.
    P.S. Modern version. Is it at long last love?


"Have them sent at once, please."
"Yes, sir."
Good. Back home. What to wear? A dark suit? Too formal. The light blue suit? Too much like a gay, should never have bought it in the first place. The double-breasted suit – latest thing. Shirt. White, casual, no tie. Blue, formal, tie. White wins. Too virginal? Blue wins. Shoes: black slip-on or laces? Slip-on wins. Socks: simple choice, dark blue. Summing up: denim suit, blue shirt, dark blue tie, dark blue socks, black slip-on shoes. Leave clothes neatly on bed. Shower and wash hair – I like curly hair better. Damn, soap in eyes. Grope for towel, soap out, drop towel, out of shower. Towel around waist. Shave; twice in one day. Shave very carefully. No blood. Aftershave. Dry hair madly with towel. Curls all over the place. Back to bedroom. Dress carefully. Get tie exactly – that won't do, tie again. Better, this time. Pull up zipper – could stand to lose inch around waist. Check in mirror. Seen worse. To hell with modesty, have seen a whole lot worse. Check money, credit cards. No gun. All set. Bolt door. Press button for elevator.

"Can I have my keys, please, Simon?"

"Well, goddamn." Simon's eyes opened very wide. "Found yourself a new fox!"

"You better not wait up, because if I fail, Simon, I'll probably jump on top of you."

"Thanks for the warning, Mark. Tough it out, man."

Beautiful evening, climb into car, check watch: 7:34.


The Director checked his dinner jacket again.

I miss Ruth. Housekeeper does a great job, but not the same thing at all. Pour a scotch, check clothes. Tuxedo just pressed – a little out of fashion. Dress shirt back from the cleaners. Black tie to be tied. Black shoes, black socks, white handkerchief – all in order. Turn on shower. Ah, how to get something useful out of the President? Damn, where's the soap? Have to get out of shower and soak bathmat and towel. Only one towel. Grab soap, revolting smell. Nowadays, they must only make it for gays. Wish I could still get army surplus. Out of the shower. Overweight; I need to lose about fifteen pounds. Body too white. Hide it quickly and forget. Shave. Good old trusty cutthroat. Never shave twice a day except when dining with the President. Good. No damage. Get dressed. Fly buttons; hate zippers. Now to tie black tie. Damn it. Ruth could always do it the first time, perfectly. Try again. At last. Check wallet. Don't really need money, credit cards, or anything else. Unless the President's going through hard times. Tell housekeeper I'll be back about eleven. Put on overcoat. Special agent there with car, as always.

"Good evening, Sam, beautiful evening."

The only chauffeur in the employ of the FBI opened the back door of the Ford sedan.

Climb into car, check watch: 7:45.


Drive slowly – lots of time – don't want to be there early – never seems to be any traffic when you have all the time in the world – hope roses have arrived – take longer route to Georgetown, past Lincoln Memorial and up Rock Creek and Potomac Parkway – it's prettier – at least con yourself that's why you're doing it. Don't run yellow lights, even though man behind you is obviously late and gesticulating. Obey the law – con yourself again – you'd shoot through the lights if you were running late for her. Never embarrass the Bureau. Careful of trolley lines in Georgetown, so easy to skid on them. Turn right at end of street and find parking space. Circle slowly looking for perfect spot – no such thing. Double-park and hope no traffic cop's around. Stroll nonchalantly towards house – bet she's still in the tub. Check watch: 8:04. Perfect. Ring doorbell.

"We're running a bit late, Sam." Perhaps unwise to say that because he'll break the speed limit and might embarrass the Bureau. Why is there so much traffic when you're in a hurry? Damn Mercedes in front of us at the circle, stopping even before the lights turned red. Why have a car that can do 120 mph if you don't even want to do thirty? Good, the Mercedes has turned off towards Georgetown. Probably one of the beautiful people. Down Pennsylvania Avenue. At last the White House in sight. Turn on to West Executive Avenue. Waved on by guard at gate. Pull up to West Portico. Met by Secret Service man in dinner jacket. His tie looks better than mine. Bet it's a clip-on. No, come to think of it, it's regulation to have to tie them in the White House. Damn it, the man must be married. Didn't do it himself. Follow him through foyer to West Wing Reception Room past Remington sculpture. Met by another Secret Service man also in dinner jacket. Also better tie. I give up. Escorted to elevator. Check watch: 8:06. Not bad. Enter West Sitting Hall.

"Good evening, Madam President."

"Hello, lovely lady."
She looks beautiful in that blue dress. Fantastic creature. How could I have any suspicions about her?
"Hello, Mark."

"That's a terrific dress you're wearing."

"Thank you. Would you like to come in for a minute?"

"No, I think we'd better go, I'm double-parked."

"Fine, I'll just grab my coat."

Open car door for her. Why didn't I just take her by the hand into the bedroom and make mad passionate love to her? I would have happily settled for a sandwich. That way we could do what we both want to do and save a lot of time and trouble.

"Did you have a good day?"

"Very busy. How about you, Mark?"

Oh, managed to think about you for a few hours while I got some work done, but it wasn't easy.

"Busy as all hell. I wasn't sure I was going to be able to make it."

Start car, right on M Street to Wisconsin. No parking spaces. Past Roy Rogers' Family Restaurant. Let's just get some chicken legs and head back home.

"Aah, success."

Hell, where did that Volkswagen come from?

"What lousy luck. You'll find another one."

"Yes, but four hundred yards away from the restaurant."

"The walk will do us good."

Did the roses come? I'll put that florist's girl in jail in the morning if she forgot to send them.

"Oh, Mark, how thoughtless of me not to mention it before; thank you for those glorious roses. Are you the white one? And the Shakespeare?"

"Think nothing of it, lovely lady."

Liar. So you liked the Shakespeare, but what was your answer to the Cole Porter? Enter supersmooth French restaurant. Rive Gauche. Gauche is right. A Fed in a place like this? Bet it'll cost an arm and a leg. Full of snotty waiters with their hands out. What the hell, it's only money.

"Did you know that this place is responsible for making Washington the French-restaurant capital of America?"

Trying to impress her with a little inside dope.

"No, why?"

"Well, the owner keeps bringing his chefs over from France. One by one they quit and go off to start their own restaurants."

"You G-men really do carry around a store of useless information."

Look for the maître d'.

"Table in the name of Andrews."

"Good evening, Mr Andrews. How nice to see you."

Damn man's never seen me before and probably will never see me again. Which table is he going to give me? Not too bad. She might even believe I've been here before. Slip him a five-dollar bill.

"Thank you, sir. Enjoy your dinner."

They settled back in the deep red leather chairs. The restaurant was crowded.

"Good evening. Would you care for an aperitif, sir?"

"What will you have, Elizabeth?"

"Campari and soda, please."

"One Campari and soda and I'll have a spritzer."

Glance at menu. Chef Michel Laudier. The restaurant motto: *Fluctuat nec mergitur.* Oh, I'll *mergitur*, all right, cover charges, service charges. Ouch. And she has no way of knowing. This is one of those sexy places where the man is given a menu with the prices.

"I'll have a first course, but only if you'll join me."

"Of course, I'm going to have one, lovely lady."

"Good, I'll have the avocado . . ."

Without prawns?

". . . with prawns, and then . . ."

. . . Caesar salad?

". . . the filet mignon Henri IV – rare, please."

$20.50. To hell with it, she's worth every penny. I think I'll have the same.

"Have you decided, sir?"

"Yes, we'll both have the avocado with prawns and the fillet mignon Henri IV, rare."

"Would you care to look at the wine list?"

No, thank you, I'll have a beer.

"Would you like some wine, Elizabeth?"

"That would be lovely, Mark."

"A bottle of Hospice de Beaune, *soixante-dix-huit*, please."

I bet he can tell the only damn French I learned at school was the numbers.

"Very good, sir."

The first course arrived and so did the sommelier with the wine.

If you think you're going to sell us two bottles, you damn frog, think again.

"Shall I serve the wine, sir?"

"Not yet, thank you. Open it and then serve it with the main course."

"Certainly, sir."

"Your avocado, Mademoiselle."

Prawns go before the fall.


"Good evening, Halt. How's life at the Bureau?"

"We're surviving, Madam."

What banal remarks the mighty make to each other.

The Director glanced around the pleasant blue and gold room. H. Stuart Knight, the head of the Secret Service, stood alone at the far end. On the sofa, by the window overlooking the West Wing and the Executive Office Building, sat the Attorney General, Marian Edelman, talking to Senator Birch Bayh, the man who had succeeded Ted Kennedy as chairman of the Judiciary Committee. The hackneyed phrase "boyish good looks", which had been applied to Bayh constantly during his campaigning in the 1976 Democratic presidential primaries, was still an accurate description. The thin, gaunt senator from Texas, Marvin Thornton, hovered over his colleague and Marian Edelman.

My God, let me have men about me that are fat . . .

"You see I've invited Thornton."

"Yes, Madam."

"We must try and talk him round on the Gun Control bill."

The West Sitting Hall was a comfortable room on the family floor of the White House, adjacent to the First Gentleman's dressing-room. It was an honour to be entertained in this part of the White House. And to eat in the small dining-room, rather than the President's dining-room downstairs, was a special privilege, since the former was usually reserved for strictly family dining. The fact that the President's husband was absent only confirmed how private this occasion had to be.

"What will you drink, Halt?"

"Scotch on the rocks."

"Scotch on the rocks for the Director and an orange juice for me. I'm watching my weight."

Doesn't she know orange juice is the last thing to drink if you're dieting?

"How are the votes stacking up, Madam?"

"Well, the numbers are forty-eight for and forty-seven against at the moment, but it's got to go through on the tenth or I'll have to forget the whole thing until the next session. That's my biggest worry at the moment, what with my European tour and the New Hampshire primary less than a year off. I would have to drop the bill until I was re-elected and I can't afford it to be the main election issue. I want it out of the way and seen to be working before then."

"Then let's hope it passes on the tenth, because it would certainly make my job easier, Madam President."

"Marian's too. Another drink, Halt?"

"No, thank you, Madam."

"Shall we go in to dinner?"

The President led her five guests into the dining-room. The wallpaper in the room depicted scenes from the American Revolution. It was furnished in the Federal style of the early nineteenth century.

*I never get bored with the beauty of the White House.*

The Director gazed at the plaster-composition mantel designed by Robert Welford of Philadelphia in 1815. It bore the famous report of Commodore Oliver Hazard Perry after the Battle of Lake Erie during the War of 1812: "We have met the enemy, and they are ours."

"Five thousand people passed through this building today," H. Stuart Knight was saying. "Nobody really grasps the security problems. This building may be the home of the President, but it still belongs to the people and that makes one continuous democratic head-ache."

*If he knew everything . . .*

The President sat at the head of the table, the Attorney General at the other end, Bayh and Thornton on one side, the Director and Knight on the other. The first course was avocado with prawns.

*I always get sick when I eat prawns.*

"It's good to see my law officers together," said the President. "I want to take this opportunity to discuss the Gun Control bill, which I remain determined will pass on 10 March. That's why I invited Birch and Marvin here tonight, because their support will influence the fate of this bill."

*10 March again. Perhaps Cassius has to keep to a deadline. Seem to remember Thornton being firmly against this bill, and he's on Andrews' list of seven.*

"The rural states are going to be a problem, Madam President," Marian Edelman was saying. "They won't be willing to hand over their guns all that readily."

"A long amnesty period, say about six months, might be the answer," the Director offered. "So the law remains unaffected for a statutory period. It's what always happens after a war. And the public relations boys can keep announcing that hundreds of weapons have been handed in to local police stations."

"Good thinking, Halt," said the President.

"It's going to be a hell of an operation," said the

Attorney General, "with seven million members of the National Rifle Association and probably fifty million fire-arms in America."

No one disagreed with that conclusion.

The second course arrived.

Dover sole. Obviously the President is serious about her diet.


"Coffee or brandy, sir?"

"Don't let's bother," said Elizabeth, touching Mark's hand gently. "Let's have it at home."

"Nice idea."

He smiled into her eyes and tried to guess what was going on in her mind . . .

"No, thank you. Just the check."

The waiter scurried away obediently.

They always scurry away obediently when you ask for the check. She hasn't let go of my hand.

"A delicious meal, Mark. Thank you very much."

"Yes, we must come here again sometime."

The check arrived. Mark glanced at it in rueful bemuse-ment.

$87.20, plus tax. If you can understand how a res-taurant gets to its final figure you deserve to be Secretary of the Treasury. Hand over the American Express Card. The little piece of blue paper comes back to sign. Make it up to $100.00 and forget it until the envelope marked American Express arrives in the mail.

"Good night, Mr Andrews." Much bowing and scraping. "I hope we will see you and Mademoiselle again soon."

"Yes, indeed."

You'll need a very good memory to recognise me next time I come. Open car door for Elizabeth. Will I do this when we're married? Christ, I'm thinking about marriage.

"I think I must have eaten too much. I'm rather sleepy."

Now what does that mean? You could take that about twenty different ways.

"Oh, really, I feel ready for anything."

A bit clumsy, maybe. Look for parking space again. Good. There's one right in front of the house and no Volkswagen to stop me grabbing it. Open car door for Elizabeth. She fumbles with front door keys. Into kitchen. Kettle on.

"What a nice kitchen."

Silly remark.

"I'm glad you like it."

Equally silly.

Into living-room.

Good, there are the roses.

"Hello, Samantha. Come and meet Mark."

Christ Almighty, she has a roommate.

Samantha rubbed up against Mark's leg and purred.

Relief. Samantha is Siamese, not American.

"Where shall I sit?"

"Anywhere."

She's no help at all.

"Black or with cream, darling?"

"Darling." The odds must be better than 50–50.

"Black, please, with one sugar."

"Amuse yourself till the water boils. I'll only be a few minutes."


"More coffee, Halt?"

"No thank you, Madam, I have to be getting home, if you'll excuse me."

"I'll walk you to the door. There are one or two things I'd like to discuss with you."

"Yes, of course, Madam President."

The Marines at the West Entrance came to attention. A man in a dinner jacket hovered in the shadows behind the pillars.

"I'll need your backing a hundred per cent for this Gun Control bill, Halt. The committee is bound to be

144

pushing for your views. And although the numbers are just with us on the floor of the House, I don't want any last-minute hiccups; I'm running out of time."

"I'll be with you, Madam. I've wanted it ever since the death of John F. Kennedy."

"Have you any particular worries about it, Halt?"

"No, Madam. You deal with the politics and sign the bill, and I'll see that the law is enforced."

"Any advice, perhaps?"

"No, I don't think so . . ."

Beware the ides of March.

". . . although it's always puzzled me, Madam President, why in the end you left the bill this late. If something goes wrong on 10 March and if you were to lose next year's election, we would all be back at square one."

"I know, Halt, but I had to decide between my Medicare bill, which was a controversial enough way to start an administration, and pushing a Gun Control bill through at the same time; I might have ended up losing both. To tell you the truth, it had been my intention to start the bill in committee a year earlier, but no one could have anticipated Nigeria attacking South Africa without warning, and America finally having to decide where she stood on that continent."

"You sure stuck your neck out on that one, Madam President, and I confess at the time I thought you were wrong."

"I know, Halt. I had a few sleepless nights myself. But, getting back to the Gun Control bill: don't ever forget that Dexter and Thornton have run the most successful two-man filibuster in the history of the Senate. By 10 March, this damn bill will have been going the rounds for nearly two years despite the tacit support of Senator Byrd as Majority Leader. But I'm not too worried. I still believe we'll pull it off. I can't foresee anything that can stop it now, can you, Halt?"

The Director hesitated. "No, Madam."

The first lie I have ever told the Chief. Would an

investigating commission believe my reasons if the President is assassinated in three days' time?

"Good night, Halt, and thank you."

"Good night, Madam President, and thank you for an excellent dinner."

The Director stepped out, and into his car. The special agent in the driver's seat looked around at him.

"An important message has just come in for you, sir. Could you return to the Bureau immediately?"

Not again.

"All right, but it might be simpler to keep a bed in the place, except someone would accuse me of trying to live rent-free on taxpayers' money."

The driver laughed; the Director had obviously had a good dinner, which was more than he had.


Elizabeth brought the coffee in and sat down by him.

Only the brave deserve the fair. Lift arm casually, place at the back of the couch, touch her hair lightly.

Elizabeth rose. "Oh, I nearly forgot. Would you like a brandy?"

No, I don't want a brandy. I want you to come back.

"No, thank you."

She settled back into Mark's shoulder.

Can't kiss her while she's got the coffee cup in her hand. Ah, she's put the cup down. Hell, she's up again.

"Let's have some music."

No thank you.

"Great idea."

"How about 'In Memory of Sinatra'?"

"Great."

. . . "This time we almost made the pieces fit . . . didn't we . . . gal?"

It's got to be absolutely the wrong song. Ah, she's back. Try the kiss again. Damn, still more coffee. The cup's down at last. Gentle. Yes, very nice. Christ, she's beautiful. Long kiss – are her eyes open? – no, closed. She's enjoying it – good – longer and even better.

"Would you like some more coffee, Mark?"

No no no no no no no.

"No, thank you."

Another long kiss. Start moving hand across back –
I've been this far before with her – can't possibly be any
objection – move hand to leg – pause – what fabulous
legs and she's got two of them. Take hand off leg and
concentrate on kissing.

"Mark, there's something I have to tell you."

Oh, Christ! It's the wrong time of the month. That's
all I need now.

"Uh-mh?"

"I adore you."

"I adore you too, darling."

He unzipped her skirt, and began to caress her gently.
She began to move her hand up his leg.

Heaven is about to happen.

Ring, ring, ring, ring.

Jee-sus!

"It's for you, Mark."

"Andrews?"

"Sir."

"Julius."

Shit.

"I'm coming."

# Tuesday morning, 8 March

## 1:00 am

The man standing at the corner of the churchyard was
trying to keep warm in the chill of the early March
morning by slapping himself on the back. He had once
seen Gene Hackman do it in a movie and it had worked.
It wasn't working. Perhaps he needed the big Warner
Brothers arc light Hackman had had to help him. He
considered the matter, while he continued slapping.

There were actually two men on surveillance, Special
Agent Kevin O'Malley and Assistant Field Supervisor
Pierce Thompson, both selected by Tyson for their ability
and discretion. Neither had shown any sign of surprise
when the Director had instructed them to tail a fellow
FBI man and report back to Elliott. It had been a long
wait for Mark to emerge from Elizabeth's house, and
O'Malley didn't blame him. Pierce left the churchyard
and joined his colleague.

"Hey, Kevin, have you noticed that someone else is
tailing Andrews for us?"

"Yeah. Matson. Why?"

"I thought he was retired."

"He is. I just assumed old Halt was making sure."

"I guess you're right but I wonder why Tyson didn't
tell us."

"Because the whole operation's pretty irregular. No
one seems to be telling anyone anything. You could
always ask Elliott."

"You ask Elliott. You might as well ask the Lincoln Memorial."

"Or you could ask the Director."

"No, thank you."

A few minutes passed by.

"Think we should talk to Matson?"

"You remember the special orders. No contact with anyone. He probably has the same orders, and he would report us without thinking about it. He's that sort of bastard."

O'Malley was the first to see Mark leaving the house and could have sworn he was carrying one shoe. He was right and Mark was running, so he began to follow him. Must avoid getting burned, thought O'Malley. Mark stopped at the pay phone; his pursuer disappeared into some new shadows, to continue his vain attempts to keep warm. He was thankful for the brisk walk, which had helped a little.

Mark had only two quarters; the others were all lying uselessly on the floor by the side of Elizabeth's couch. Where had the Director phoned from? Could it have been the Bureau? That didn't make sense, what would he be doing there at this time of night? Wasn't he supposed to be with the President? Mark looked at his watch. Hell, 1:15. He must be at home; if he isn't I'll be out of quarters. Mark put on his other shoe. Easy slip-on. He cursed, and tossed one of the quarters; George Washington, I call the Bureau. *E pluribus unum*, then I call him at home. The coin landed – George Washington. Mark dialled the Director's private number at the Bureau.

"Yes."

God bless George Washington.

"Julius?"

"Come in immediately."

That didn't sound very friendly. Perhaps he had just returned from the President with some important new information, or maybe something at the dinner had given him indigestion.

Mark walked quickly to his car, checking his shirt buttons and tie as he went. His socks felt uncomfortable, as if one of the heels were in the arch of his foot. He passed the man in the shadows, who watched as Mark returned to his car and hesitated. Should he return to Elizabeth and say, say what? He looked up at the light in the window, took a deep breath, cursed again, and fell into the bucket seat of the Mercedes. There hadn't even been time for a cold shower.

It took only a few minutes to reach the Bureau. There was very little traffic, and with the streets so quiet, the computerised lights meant no stopping.

Mark parked the car in the basement garage of the FBI and immediately there was the anonymous man, the anonymous man who obviously was waiting for him. Didn't he ever go to bed? A harbinger of bad tidings, probably, but he didn't let him know, because as usual he didn't speak. Perhaps he's a eunuch, Mark thought. Lucky man. They shared the elevator to the seventh floor. The anonymous man led him noiselessly to the Director's office; wonder what he does for a hobby, thought Mark. Probably a prompter at the National Theater for the Deaf.

"Mr Andrews, sir."

The Director offered no greeting. He was still in evening clothes and looked as black as thunder.

"Sit down, Andrews."

Back to Andrews, thought Mark.

"If I could take you out into the parking lot, stick you up against the wall, and shoot you, I would."

Mark tried to look innocent; it had usually worked with Nick Stames. It didn't seem to cut any ice with the Director.

"You stupid, unthinking, irresponsible, reckless idiot."

Mark decided he was more frightened of the Director than he was of those who might be trying to kill him.

"You've compromised me, the Bureau, and the President," continued the Director. Mark could hear his heart pounding. If he could have counted it, it would have been a hundred and twenty. Tyson was still in full cry. "If I could suspend you or just dismiss you, if only I could do something as simple as that. How many senators are there left, Andrews?"

"Seven, sir."

"Name them."

"Brooks, Harrison, Thornton, Byrd, Nunn, Dex . . . Dexter, and . . . " Mark went white.

*"Summa cum laude* at Yale, and you have the naïvete of a boy scout. When we first saw you with Dr Elizabeth Dexter, we, in our stupidity, knowing she was the doctor on duty on the evening of 3 March at Woodrow Wilson, assumed in our stupidity" – he repeated it even more pointedly – "that you were on to a lead, but now we discover that not only is she the daughter of one of the seven senators whom we suspect of wanting to murder the President but, as if that's not enough, we find out you're having an affair with her."

Mark wanted to protest but couldn't get his lips to move.

"Can you deny you've slept with her, Andrews?"

"Yes, sir, I can," Mark said very quietly.

The Director was momentarily dumbfounded. "Young man, we wired the place; we know exactly what went on."

Mark leaped out of his chair, stunned dismay yielding to fierce anger. "I couldn't have denied it," he cried, "if you hadn't interrupted me. Have you forgotten what it feels like to love someone, if you ever knew? Fuck your Bureau, and I don't use that word that often, and fuck you. I've been working sixteen hours a day and I'm not getting any sleep at night. Someone may be trying to murder me and I find that you, the only man I've trusted, have ordered your anonymous pimps to play Peeping Tom at my expense. I hope you all roast in hell. I'd rather join the Mafia because I'm sure they let their people have it off occasionally."

151

Mark was angrier than he had ever been in his life. He collapsed back into the chair, and waited for the consequences. His only strength was that he no longer cared. The Director was equally silent. He walked to the window and stared out. Then he turned slowly; the heavy shoulders, the large head were turning towards him. This is it, thought Mark.

The Director stopped about a yard away from him, looking him square in the eyes, the way he had done from the first moment they had met.

"Forgive me," said the Director. "I've been thoughtless but I'm becoming paranoid about the whole problem. I've just left the President, healthy, fit, full of plans for the future of this country, only to be told that her one hope of carrying out those dreams is sleeping with the daughter of one of the seven men who might at this very moment be planning to assassinate her. I didn't think much further than that."

A big man, thought Mark.

The Director's eyes hadn't left him .

"Let's pray it's not Dexter. Because if it is, Mark, you may well be in considerable danger." He paused again. "By the way, those anonymous pimps have been guarding you night and day, also on a sixteen-hour day, without a break. Some of them even have wives and children. Now we both know the truth. Let's get back to work, Mark, and let's try and stay sane for three more days. Just remember to tell me everything."

Mark had won. No, Mark had lost.

"There are seven senators left." The words were slow and tired, the man was still on edge. Mark had never seen him like this and doubted that many members of the Bureau had.

"My discussions with the President have confirmed my suspicion that the link between 10 March and the Senator is the Gun Control bill. The chairman of the Judiciary Committee, who handled the planning stages of the bill, was there – Senator Bayh. He's still on the list. You had better see what he and our other suspects on that committee had to say about the bill – but keep your eye on Pearson and Nunn at Foreign Relations as well." He paused. "Only three days to go. I intend to stick to my original plan and let things run just as they are for the moment. I'm still in a position to cancel the President's schedule for the tenth at the very last minute. Do you wish to add anything, Mark?"

"No, sir."

"What are your plans?"

"I am seeing the staff directors of both the Foreign Relations and Judiciary committees tomorrow, sir. I may have a clearer idea then on how to approach the problem and what to be looking for."

"Good. Follow them both up meticulously, just in case I've missed something."

"Yes, sir."

"We've had our fingerprint men working overtime on those twenty-eight bills; at the moment, they are only looking for the prints of Mrs Casefikis. That way at least we will know which one might have our man's on it. They have found over a thousand prints, so far, but none fit Mrs Casefikis's. I'll brief you the moment I hear anything. Now let's call it a day, we're both bushed. Don't bother to come in at seven tomorrow" – the Director looked at his watch – "I mean today. Make it 7:00 am on Wednesday and make it on time because then we'll have only one full day left."

Mark knew he was being invited to leave but there was something he wanted to say. The Director looked up and sensed it immediately.

"Save it, Mark. Go home and get some rest. I'm a tired old man, but I would like those bastards, each and every one of them, behind bars on Thursday night. For your sake, I hope to God Dexter isn't involved. But don't close your eyes to anything, Mark. Love may be blind, but let's hope it's not deaf and dumb."

A very big man, thought Mark.

"Thank you, sir. I'll see you on Wednesday morning."

Mark drove his car quietly out of the FBI's garage. He was drained. There was no sign of the anonymous man. He stared in the rear-view mirror. A blue Ford sedan was following him, and this time it seemed obvious. How could he ever be sure whose side they were on? In three more days, he might know. This time next week he'd know everything or nothing. Would the President be alive or dead?

Simon, still on duty at the entrance to the apartment house, gave Mark a cheerful grin. "Make it, man?"

"Not exactly," he replied.

"I could always call up my sister, if you're desperate." Mark tried to laugh.

"A generous offer, but not tonight, Simon." He tossed the car keys over and headed for the elevator. Once locked and bolted into his apartment, he strode into his bedroom, pulled off his shirt and tie, picked up the phone and dialled seven digits slowly. A gentle voice answered.

"You still awake?"

"Very much so."

"I love you." He put the phone down and slept.

# Tuesday morning, 8 March

## 8:04 am

The phone was ringing, but Mark was still in a deep sleep. It continued to ring. Eventually he awoke, focused on his watch: 8:05. Damn, probably the Director asking where the hell he was; no, he hadn't wanted to see him this morning, isn't that what they agreed? He grabbed the phone.

"You're awake?"

"Yes."

"I love you, too."

He heard the phone click. A good way to start the day, though if she knew he was going to spend it investigating her father . . . And almost certainly the Director was investigating her.

Mark let the cold shower run on and on until he was fully awake. Whenever he was awakened suddenly, he always wanted to go back to sleep. Next week, he promised himself he would. There was one hell of a lot of things he was going to do next week. He glanced at his watch: 8:25. No Wheaties this morning. He flicked on the television to see if he had missed anything going on in the rest of the world; he was sitting on a news story that would make Barbara Walters fall off her CBS chair. What was the man saying?

". . . and now one of the greatest achievements of mankind, the first pictures ever taken from the planet

Jupiter by an American spacecraft. History in the making, but first, this message from Jell-O, the special food for special children."

Mark turned it off, laughing. Jupiter, along with Jell-O, would have to wait until next week.

Because he was running late, he decided to return to taking the Metro from the Waterfront Station next to his apartment. It was different when he had been going in early and had the roads to himself, but at 8:30, the cars would be bumper to bumper the whole way.

The entrance to the subway was marked with a bronze pylon sporting an illuminated M. Mark stepped on to the escalator, which took him from street level down to the Metro station. The tunnel-like station reminded him of a Roman bath, grey and dark with a honeycombed, curved ceiling. One dollar. Rush-hour fare. And he needed a transfer. Another dollar. Mark fumbled in his pockets for the exact fare. Must remember to stock up on quarters when I get to the centre of town, he thought, as he stepped on to another escalator and was deposited at track level. During rush-hour, 6:30–9:00 am, the trains drew in every five minutes. Round lights on the side of the platform began to flash to indicate the train was approaching. The doors opened automatically. Mark joined the crowd in a colourful, brightly lit car, and five minutes later heard his destination announced on the public address system: Gallery Place. He stepped out on to the platform and waited for a red line train. The green line worked perfectly on mornings when he was going to the Washington Field Office, but to get to Capitol Hill, he had to switch. Four minutes later, he emerged into the sunshine at Union Station Visitors' Center, the bustling command post for bus, train, and subway travel in and out of Washington. The Dirksen Senate Office Building was three blocks away, down 1st Street, at the corner of Constitution. That was quick and painless, thought Mark, as he went in the Constitution Avenue entrance. Why do I ever bother with a car at all?

He walked past two members of the Capitol police who were inspecting briefcases and packages at the door, and pressed the Up-button at the public elevator.

"Four, please," he said to the elevator operator.

The Foreign Relations Committee hearing was scheduled to begin shortly. Mark pulled the list of "Today's Activities in the House and Senate", which he had torn out of *The Washington Post*, from his coat pocket. "Foreign Relations: 9:30 am. Open. Hearing on US policy towards the Common Market; administration representatives. 4229 DOB." As Mark walked down the hall, Senator Ralph Brooks of Massachusetts stepped into Suite 4229, and Mark followed him into the hearing room.

The senator, a tall man with rugged, almost film star good looks, had dogged every step of President Kane's political career until finally she had replaced him as Secretary of State when she took over after President Parkin's death.

He had quickly won her seat back in the Senate and then stood against Florentyna Kane as the Democratic candidate and only lost on the seventh ballot. He had gone on to be chairman of the Senate Foreign Relations Committee.

Did he now intend to kill the President in order to reach the highest office himself? It didn't add up because if Kane were assassinated the Vice President Bill Bradley, who was younger than he was, would take her place and then Brooks would be left with no chance. No, the senator didn't look a serious threat but Mark still needed proof before he could cross him off the list.

The hearing room had light-coloured wood panelling, accented by green marble on the lower part of the wall and around the door. At the end of the chamber, there was a semi-circular desk of the same light wood, which was raised one step above the rest of the room. Fifteen burnt-orange chairs. Only about ten of them were occupied. Senator Brooks took his seat, but the assorted staff members, aides, newsmen, and administrative officials continued to mill around. On the wall behind the senators hung two large maps, one of the world, the other of Europe. At a desk immediately in front of and below the senators sat a stenotypist, poised to record the proceedings verbatim. In front, there were desks for witnesses.

More than half the room was given over to chairs for the general public, and these were nearly all full. An oil painting of George Washington dominated the scene. The man must have spent the last ten years of his life posing for portraits, thought Mark.

Senator Brooks whispered something to an aide, and rapped his gavel for silence. "Before we begin," he said, "I'd like to notify Senate staff members and the press of a change in schedule. Today and tomorrow, we will hear testimony from the State Department concerning the European Common Market. We will then postpone the continuation of these hearings until next week, so the committee may devote its attention to the pressing and controversial issue of arms sales to Africa."

By this time, almost everyone in the room had found a seat, and the government witnesses were glancing through their notes. Mark had worked on Capitol Hill one summer during college, but even now he could not help feeling annoyed at the small number of senators who showed up at these hearings. Because each senator served on three or more committees and innumerable sub- and special committees, they were forced to specialise, and to trust the expertise of fellow senators and staff members in areas outside their own speciality. So it was not at all unusual for committee hearings to be attended by three or two or sometimes even only one senator.

The subject under debate was a bill to dismantle the North Atlantic Treaty Organisation. Portugal and Spain had gone Communist and left the Common Market, like two well-behaved dominoes, at the turn of the decade. The Spanish bases went soon after; King Juan Carlos was living in exile in England. NATO had been prepared for the Communist takeover in Portugal, but when Italy finally installed a Fronto Popolare government in the Quirinal, things began to fall apart. The Papacy, trusting to tried and proven methods, locked itself behind its gates, and American Catholic opinion forced the United States to cut off financial aid to the new Italian government. The Italians retaliated by closing her NATO bases.

The economic ripples of the Italian collapse were thought to have influenced the French elections, which had led to a victory for Chirac and the Gaullists. The more extreme forms of socialism had recently been repudiated in Holland and some Scandinavian countries. The Germans were happy with their social democracy. But as the west entered the last decade of the twentieth century, Senator Pearson was declaring that America's only real ally in NATO was Britain, where a Tory government had recently won an upset victory in the February general election.

The British Foreign Secretary, Kenneth Clarke, had argued forcefully against the formal breakup of NATO. Such a move would sever Great Britain from her alliance with the United States, and commit her solely to the EEC, seven of whose fifteen members were not Communist or close to it. Senator Pearson thumped the table. "We should take the British view seriously in our considerations and not be interested only in immediate strategic gains."

After an hour of listening to Brooks and Pearson questioning State Department witnesses about the political situation in Spain, Mark slipped out of the door and went into the Foreign Relations Committee suite down the hall. The secretary informed him that Lester Kenneck, the committee staff director, was out of the office. Mark had telephoned him the day before, leaving the impression that he was a student doing research for his dissertation.

"Is there someone else who could give me some information about the committee?"

"I'll see if Paul Rowe, one of our staff members, might

be able to help you." She picked up the telephone and, several moments later, a thin bespectacled man emerged from one of the back rooms.

"What can I do for you?"

Mark explained that he would like to see other members of the committee in action, particularly Senator Nunn. Rowe smiled patiently. "No problem," he said. "Come back tomorrow afternoon or Thursday for the discussion about arms sales to Africa. Senator Nunn will be here, I guarantee. And you'll find it much more interesting than the Common Market stuff. In fact, the meeting may be closed to the public. But I'm sure if you come by here and talk to Mr Kenneck, he'll arrange for you to sit in."

"Thank you very much. Would you by any chance happen to know if Nunn and Pearson were present at the hearing on 24 February, or last Thursday?"

Rowe raised his eyebrows. "I have no idea. Kenneck might know."

Mark thanked him. "Oh, one more thing. Can you give me a pass for the Senate gallery?" The secretary stamped a card and wrote in his name. Mark headed for the elevator. Arms sales. Africa, he thought. Thursday's too late. Damn. How the hell am I supposed to know why one of these guys would want to kill President Kane? Could be some crazy military thing, or a severe case of racism. It doesn't make any sense. Not why, but who, he reminded himself. As he walked, Mark almost knocked over one of the Senate pages, who was running down the corridor clutching a package. The Congress operates a page school for boys and girls from across the nation who attend classes and work as "gophers" in the Capitol. They all wear dark blue and white and always give the impression of being in a hurry. Mark stopped just in time and the boy scooted around him without even breaking stride.

Mark took the elevator to the ground floor and walked out of the Dirksen Building on to Constitution Avenue.

He made his way across the Capitol grounds, entered the Capitol on the Senate side, underneath the long marble expanse of steps, and waited for the public elevator.

"Busy day," the guard informed him. "Lots of tourists here to watch the gun control debate."

Mark nodded. "Is there a long wait upstairs?"

"Yes, sir, I think so."

The elevator arrived, and on the gallery level a guard ushered Mark into line with a horde of gaping visitors. Mark was impatient. He beckoned to one of the guards.

"Listen, officer," he said, "I have a regular public pass for the gallery, but I'm a student from Yale doing research. Think there is any way you could get me in?"

The guard nodded sympathetically.

A few minutes later, Mark was seated in the chamber. He could see only part of the floor. The senators were seated at desks in semi-circular rows facing the Chair. Even while someone was speaking, staff members and senators wandered around, giving the impression that the really significant manoeuvring took place in hushed tones, not in dramatic debate.

The Judiciary Committee had reported out the bill two weeks before, after prolonged hearings and discussion. The House had already passed similar legislation, which would have to be reconciled with the stricter Senate version if it were to be approved.

Senator Dexter was speaking. My future father-in-law? Mark wondered. He certainly didn't look like a killer, but then which senator did? He had given his daughter her glorious dark hair, although there was a little white at his temples. Not as much as there ought to be, thought Mark – a politician's vanity. And he had also given her his dark eyes. He seemed fairly contemptuous of most of the people around him, tapping the desk with his long fingers to emphasise a point.

"In our discussion about this bill, we have side-stepped a critical, perhaps the most crucial, consideration. And that is the principle of Federalism. For the past fifty years, the federal government has usurped many of the powers once wielded by the states. We look to the President, the Congress, for answers to all our problems. The Founding Fathers never intended the central government to have so much power, and a country as wide and diverse as ours cannot be governed democratically or effectively on that basis. Yes, we all want to reduce crime. But crime differs from place to place. Our constitutional system wisely left the business of crime control to state and local jurisdiction, except for those federal criminal laws which deal with truly national matters. But crimes committed with guns are of a local nature. They ought to be legislated against and enforced at the local level. Only at the state and local levels can the attitudes of the people and the specific characteristics of the crime problem be understood and dealt with by public officials.

"I know that some of my colleagues will argue that, since we require registration of cars and drivers, we ought also to register guns. But gentlemen, we have no national car – or driver-registration law. These matters are left to the states to determine. Each state should be allowed to decide for itself, taking into account the interests of its people, what is reasonable and necessary."

Senator Dexter monopolised the floor for twenty minutes before yielding to the Chair, occupied today by Senator Kemp, who recognised Senator Brooks. When Brooks had finished his preliminary remarks, he launched into a prepared speech:

". . . have consistently decried the killing in the Middle East, in Africa, in Northern Ireland, in Chile. We ended the bloodshed in Vietnam. But when are we going to confront the killing that takes place in our own communities, our own streets, our own homes, every day of every year?" Brooks paused and looked at Senator Harrison from South Carolina, one of the leading opponents of the bill. "Are we waiting for another national tragedy to compel us to take action? Only after the assassination of John F. Kennedy was Senator Thomas Dodd's Handgun

Control bill taken seriously by a Senate committee. No legislation was passed. After the Watts riots of August 1965, in which purchased, not looted guns were used, the Senate held hearings about control of handguns. No action was taken. It took the slaying of Martin Luther King, before the Judiciary Committee passed legislation, controlling interstate sale of handguns as a rider to the omnibus Crime Control bill. The Senate approved the bill. The House concurred after Robert Kennedy was murdered too. In response to the violence of 1968, we enacted the Handgun Control act. But the act, gentlemen, contained a huge loophole – it did not regulate domestic production of these weapons, because at that time eighty per cent of available handguns were manufactured overseas. In 1972, after George Wallace was shot with a Saturday-Night Special, the Senate finally acted to close the loophole. But the bill died in a House Committee.

"Now, some twenty years or more later, having disregarded the fact that President Reagan was seriously wounded in 1981 by a man wielding a handgun in the streets of Washington, even with all that history someone in America is killed or injured by gunfire every two minutes, and we are still without an effective gun control law. What are we waiting for? Someone to try again to assassinate the President?" He paused for effect. "The American people favour gun control legislation. Every poll indicates that this is the case, and it has been true for a decade. Why do we allow the National Rifle Association to manipulate us, to persuade us that they and their views are compelling when in fact they are hollow? What has happened to our capacity for the clear weighing of alternatives, and for outrage at the violence in our society?"

Mark, along with many other observers, was astonished by this impassioned outburst. His impression from informed political journalists was that Brooks would not support the President as, quite apart from personal animosity, he had been a key figure on a number of constitutional issues and in the fight against two of Kane's Supreme Court appointees, Haynsworth and Carswell.

Senator Harrison of South Carolina, an urbane, quietly distinguished man, asked to be recognised. "Will the distinguished Senator from Massachusetts yield?"

Brooks nodded to the Chair.

Harrison addressed his colleagues in a soft, firm voice. "This bill completely negates the concept of self-defence. It asserts that the only legitimate reason for owning a handgun, a shotgun, or a rifle is for sporting purposes. But I would like to ask my distinguished colleagues from the urban states to consider for a moment – just a moment – the plight of a family on a farm in Iowa or on a homestead in Alaska which needs a gun in the house to protect itself. Not for sport, but for self-defence. In my estimation, they have a right to take that step. For what we face in this country, in urban as well as rural areas, is increasing lawlessness. That is the root problem – lawlessness – not the number of guns in circulation. Increased lawlessness means more crimes involving guns, to be sure. But guns do not cause crimes, people cause crimes. If we want to fight crime, we should investigate its root causes instead of trying to take guns away from people who would use them legally. As many a bumper sticker in this great land proclaims, 'If guns are outlawed, only outlaws will have guns'."

Senator Thornton of Texas, thin and gaunt, with greasy black hair, whom Mark remembered from Mr Smith's Restaurant, had only just begun to express his agreement with the views of Senator Dexter and Senator Harrison when six lights around the numbers on the clock at Mark's end of the chamber came alive. A buzzer sounded six times to signal that morning business was concluded. The "morning hour" on the floor of the Senate, from midday until no later than 2:00 pm, was set aside for the presentation of petitions and memorials, reports of standing and select committees, and introduction of bills and resolutions.

Senator Kemp looked at his watch. "Excuse me, Senator Thornton, but it is noon and now that morning business is over, a number of us are expected to appear in committee to debate the Clean Air bill which is on the calendar for this afternoon. Why don't we reconvene at 2:30? As many of us who can get away from the committee at that time can meet back here to discuss this bill. It's important that we move as quickly as possible on this legislation, as we are still hoping to vote on it in this session."

The Senate floor was cleared in a minute. The actors had said their lines and left the stage. Only those who had to get the theatre ready for the afternoon performance remained. Mark asked the guard which was Henry Lykham, the other staff director he had to see. The doorman in the official blue uniform of the Senate Security Staff pointed to a short fat man with a thin moustache and a jolly open face sitting firmly in a large seat at the far side of the gallery, making notes and checking papers. Mark strolled over to him, unaware that a pair of eyes behind dark glasses was following his every movement.

"My name is Mark Andrews, sir."

"Ah, yes, the graduate student. I'll be free in a moment, Mr Andrews."

Mark sat down and waited. The man in dark glasses left the chamber by the side door.

"All right, Mr Andrews, how about some lunch?"

"Great," replied Mark. He was taken to the ground floor, to G-211, the Senators' Dining-Room. They found a table at the side of the room. Mark chatted convincingly about the hard work a committee staff director must have to do, while others get the praise and publicity. Henry Lykham readily agreed. They both chose their meal from the fixed menu; so did the man three tables away, who was watching them both carefully. Mark told the committee staff director that he intended to write his thesis on the Gun Control bill if it became law, and that he wanted some interesting inside information that the general public wouldn't get from the newspapers. "Therefore, Mr Lykham," he concluded, "I have been advised to speak to you."

The fat man beamed; he was duly flattered, as Mark had hoped, and he began.

"There is nothing I can't tell you about this bill or the bunch of politicians involved in it."

Mark smiled, he had studied the Watergate hearings in an elective seminar at Yale and he recalled a particular remark of Anthony Ulasewicz, a retired NYPD detective. "Why bother to bug the place? Politicians and officials will tell you anything you want to know, over the phone, they'll even want to send it to you in the mail, whoever you are."

Senator Sam Irvin of North Carolina, the committee chairman, had reprimanded him for treating the committee lightly and turning the matter into a joke. "It's no joke – it's the truth," was Ulasewicz's reply.

Mark asked which of the eleven senators on the committee were for the bill. Only four of them had been present at the morning discussion. From his research, Mark was fairly certain about the opinions of most of them but he wanted his assessments confirmed.

"Among the Democrats, Brooks, Burdick, Stevenson, and Glenn will vote for the measure. Abourezk, Byrd, and Moynihan are keeping their own counsel, but will probably come through in support of the Administration position. They voted for the bill in committee. Thornton is the only Democrat who may vote against it. You heard him start to speak in favour of Dexter's states' rights position. Well, for Thornton, young man, it's not a matter of principle. He wants it both ways. Texas has a strong state gun control measure, so he can claim that his stance means that states can take whatever action they deem necessary to protect their citizens. But Texas also has a number of firearms companies – Smith and Wesson,

GKN Powdermet, Harrington and Richardson – which would be seriously affected by a federal gun control act. The spectre of unemployment again. As long as those companies can sell their wares outside Texas, they're okay. So Thornton fools his constituents into thinking they can control guns and manufacture them at the same time. Strange games are being played by that particular man. As for the Republicans, Mathias of Maryland will vote for the bill. He's a very liberal guy – I'll never understand why he stays in the GOP. McCollister of Nebraska is against, along with Woodson of Arkansas. Harrison and Dexter you heard. No question where they stand.

"Harrison despite being a Democrat knows damn well that his constituents wouldn't tolerate gun control and will vote him out if he goes with it. Hard to tell if he's been brainwashed by the National Rifle Association, because he seems to be sincere when he talks about the idea of self-defence. He's a strange guy. Everyone in this place regards him as a dyed-in-the-wool conservative, but no one really knows him. He hasn't been here all that long. He succeeded Sparkman when he retired – bit of an unknown quantity."

Mark let him talk on. Lykham was enjoying the role of the expert, the man who knew everything. Normally, he sat for hours in the hearing room, unable to say a word, listening and making notes and occasionally whispering a suggestion in the ear of the chairman. Only his wife listened to his opinions and she never understood their significance. Lykham was delighted to have found an academic who had come to him for the facts.

"Dexter talks a good game – smooth character, that one. He beat the guy who was appointed to fill Ribicoff's term when Abe was picked by the President for a roving ambassadorship. Surprise winner. Wouldn't have thought that Connecticut would be represented by two Republicans. Guess all those rich New Yorkers moving to Stamford are making a difference. Anyway, just between the two of us, Mark, I have my suspicions about the purity of his principles. Do you know how many gun companies there are in Connecticut? Remington, Colt, Olin, Winchester, Marlin, Sturm-Ruger. Now, that never stopped Senator Ribicoff from voting for gun control, but Dexter . . . well, he owns a big slice of one of them, that's no secret. Something's biting him at the moment, he's as grouchy as hell, and he hasn't missed a session yet."

Mark had a sick feeling in his stomach. My God, Elizabeth's father? He just didn't want to believe it.

"So you think the bill will be passed?" said Mark in a conversational tone.

"No question, while the Democrats remain in control of both Houses. The minority report was vicious, but it'll get a majority on 10 March. There wasn't much doubt about that after the House put it through. By Thursday, nothing can stop it. The Majority Leader is only too aware of the importance the President attaches to this bill."

Byrd, thought Mark. He's on the list. "Could you tell me a little about the Majority Leader? He was on the Judiciary Committee, right? Where does he stand?"

"That's an interesting question, Andrews. Senator Byrd is a humourless, driven, ambitious individual. He has ulcers. He was born in poverty, always makes a point of emphasising his origins, so much so that some of his colleagues call him Uriah Heep. In the 1940s, when he was only nineteen, he belonged to the Ku Klux Klan; yet he managed to overcome that handicap and rise to the most powerful post in the Senate in a party dominated by liberals. He got where he is because he's a team player. He does favours for other senators, and always has. He's diligent, conscientious about meeting their needs. His attention to detail has paid off in spades. He had always supported the Democratic – with a capital D – position. And he's a very effective Majority Leader.

"No love lost in that relationship, but since Byrd has become Majority Leader he has fallen into line. With his background, it's unlikely that he's genuinely in favour of gun control, but he hasn't spoken out against the bill, naturally, because he has been shepherding it through the Senate for the President. He's done it very efficiently. He's scheduled it early, avoided recesses –"

"Sorry to interrupt you, Mr Lykham, but what do you mean he's avoided recesses? The committee didn't sit round the clock, surely?"

"No, young man, I was referring to a technical, procedural distinction between adjournment and recess. You see, the Senate usually recesses from one day to the next. The day after a recess, the unfinished business of the previous day is in order; the morning business can be dispensed with. Whenever the Majority Leader opts for a recess rather than adjournment, he thereby lengthens the 'legislative day'. And since bills reported from committee must lay over one legislative day before a motion to consider is in order, the recess can be used to delay action on a particular measure. The so-called legislative day can extend for days, weeks, conceivably even months now she only has two years left. This bill has been put through in the minimum possible time. If the President doesn't get support on 10 March, she will not have time to put it up again before she goes for re-election. It will be a victory for those against the bill. And she may not be re-elected if the polls are to be believed. Americans get sick of their presidents very quickly nowadays. So it's 10 March or forget it."

"What could stop it on 10 March?"

"Nothing I can think of offhand, except the death of the President, which could recess the Senate for seven days. Still the President looks pretty fit to me, perhaps a little tired, not that I'm one to comment."

Mark was about to question Lykham about Brooks, when the staff director glanced at his watch.

"Look at the time," Lykham expostulated, "I must get

back. I have to be the first, you know, get everything in order, so those senators think that we haven't been away at all."

Mark thanked him. Lykham picked up the check and signed it.

"Any time you want more help or information, don't hesitate to get in touch."

"I certainly will," said Mark.

The fat staff director waddled away at what for him was full speed. Mark pondered over his coffee. The man three tables away had finished his and was waiting for Mark's next move. Those damn bells were ringing again. Only one this time, indicating that the yeas and nays were being tallied on the Senate floor. As soon as the vote was over, the senators would be flocking back to committee meetings. The bell brought Mark sharply out of his thoughts.

Once again he returned to the Dirksen Building and the Foreign Relations Committee Suite, where he asked if he could see Mr Kenneck.

"Who shall I say is asking for him?" the receptionist inquired.

"Andrews, I'm a Yale student."

She picked a phone up and pressed two digits, informed the listener of what Mark had told her.

"He's in Room 4491."

Mark thanked her and left for Room 4491, which was only a few doors down the corridor.

"Well, Andrews, what can I do for you?" he asked, even before Mark had closed the door.

Mark was taken aback by the suddenness of his question; he recovered.

"I'm doing some research for a thesis, Mr Kenneck, on the work of senators, and Mr Lykham said you were the man to speak to. I wondered if Senators Nunn and Pearson were in the Senate on Thursday, 3 March, at 10:30, for the Foreign Relations Committee?"

Kenneck bent over a red leather-bound book. "Nunn – no," he paused. "Pearson – no. Anything else, Mr Andrews?" He obviously hadn't any time to waste.

"No, thank you," said Mark and left.

Mark headed for the Library. Suddenly he was down to five senators, if the Bureau were right about what they had overheard on the illegal radio transmission when their man must have been in the Senate on the morning of 3 March. He checked his notes: each one of the remaining suspects – Brooks, Byrd, Dexter, Harrison, and Thornton – had sat on the Judiciary Committee on the Gun Control bill and was in the Senate for the debate. Five men and a motive?

He was followed out of the room and into the elevator that took him to the ground floor. He used the pay phone across the hall from the elevator, near the Constitution Avenue entrance, to call the Director.

He dialled the Director's private number.

"Julius."

"What's your number?"

Mark gave it. A few seconds later the Director called him back.

"Nunn and Pearson are off. I'm down to five and the one thing they have in common is that all of them were on the committee of the Gun Control bill."

"Good," said the Director. "Much as I had expected. Getting better, Mark, but your time is running out, we've only about forty-eight hours left."

"Yes, sir."

The phone clicked.

He waited for a moment and then dialled Woodrow Wilson. There was the usual interminable wait while they found Elizabeth. What could he say about last night? What if the Director were right and her father –"

"Dr Dexter."

"When do you finish work tonight, Liz?"

"Five o'clock, lover," she said mockingly.

"May I pick you up?"

"If you like, now that I know your intentions are pure and honourable."

"Listen, one day, but not today, I'll be able to explain about that."

"See you at five, Mark."

"See you at five, Liz."

Mark put Elizabeth out of his mind by a conscious effort of will, and walked across the street to the Capitol grounds. He sat down under a tree on the grassy area between the Supreme Court and the Capitol. Protected, he thought, by law and legislature, bounded by Constitution and Independence. Who would dare to confront him here in front of the Capitol, the favoured haunt of Senate staff, law clerks, and the Capitol police? A blue and white sight-seeing tourmobile passed by on 1st Street, blocking his view of the fountains in front of the Supreme Court. Tourists gaped at Washington's white-marbled splendour. "And on your right, ladies and gentlemen, the United States Capitol. The cornerstone of the original building was laid in 1793. The British burned the Capitol building on 24 August, 1814 . . ."

And some crazy senator is going to defile it on 10 March, added Mark silently as the tourmobile moved on. Foreboding oppressed him; it really is going to happen, we can't stop it. Comes Caesar to the Capitol . . . Blood on the steps.

He forced himself to look at his notes. Brooks, Byrd, Dexter, Harrison, Thornton. He had two days to transform five into one. The conspirator he sought was Cassius, not Brutus. Brooks, Byrd, Dexter, Harrison, and Thornton. Where were they at lunchtime on 24 February? If he knew the answer, he would know which four men were innocent and which man was so desperate that he would plot to assassinate the President. Even if we find out which man is behind this, he thought, as he stood up and brushed the grass from his trousers, how do we stop the murder? Obviously, the Senator isn't going to commit the killing himself. We must keep the President away from the Capitol. The Director must have a plan, he surely wouldn't let it go that far. Mark closed his file and walked to the Metro.

Once home, he picked up his car and drove slowly to Woodrow Wilson. He looked in the rear-view mirror. A different car was following him today, a black Buick. Someone looking after me again, he thought. He arrived at the hospital at 4:45 but Elizabeth wasn't free yet, so he went back to his car and turned on the evening news. An earthquake in the Philippines that had killed 112 people was the lead story. President Kane was still confident of support for the Gun Control bill. The Dow-Jones index had moved up three points to 1,411. The Yankees beat the Dodgers in a spring training game, what's new?

Elizabeth came out of the hospital looking depressed and jumped in beside him.

"What can I say about last night?" Mark asked.

"Nothing," said Elizabeth. "It was like reading a book with the last chapter torn out. Who tore it out, Mark?"

"Perhaps I've brought the last chapter with me," said Mark, avoiding the question.

"Thanks, but I don't think I'll be in the mood for another bedtime story for a while," she replied. "The last one gave me a bad dream."

Elizabeth was very quiet and Mark could get little response from her. He turned right off Independence and stopped the car on one of the side streets on the Mall, facing the Jefferson Memorial and the sunset.

"Is it last night?" asked Mark.

"Partly," she said. "You made me feel pretty silly walking off like that. I don't suppose you're going to tell me what it was all about?"

"I can't do that," said Mark uneasily. "But believe me, it had nothing to do with you. At least that's almost –" He stopped abruptly.

Never embarrass the Bureau.

"'At least that's almost' what? Almost true? Why was that call so important?"

"Let's stop this and go eat."

Elizabeth didn't reply.

He started the car again. Two cars pulled out at the same time as he did. A blue Ford sedan and a black Buick. They're certainly making sure today, he thought. Perhaps one of them is just looking for a parking space. He glanced at Elizabeth to see if she'd noticed them too; no, why should she, only he could see in the rear-view mirror. He drove to a small, warm Japanese restaurant on Wisconsin Avenue. He couldn't take her home, while the damned Bureau had the place bugged. Deftly, the Oriental waiter sliced the fat shrimps, cooked them on the metal slab in the centre of their table. He flicked each shrimp as he finished it on to their plates, giving them small, delicious bowls of sauces in which to dip the pieces. Elizabeth brightened under the influence of the hot sake.

"I'm sorry to react so strongly. I have a lot on my mind at the moment."

"Like to tell me about it?"

"I can't, I'm afraid. It's personal and my father has asked me not to discuss it with anyone yet."

Mark froze. "Can't you tell me?"

"No. I guess we'll both have to be patient."

They went to a drive-in movie and sat in the comfortable semi-darkness, arms companionably intertwined. Mark sensed she didn't wish to be touched, and indeed he was in no mood to do so. They were both concerned about the same man, but for different reasons – or was it the same reason? And how would she react if she discovered that he had been investigating her father since the day after they met? Maybe she knew. Damn it, why couldn't he simply believe in her? Surely, she wasn't setting him up. He could remember very little about the film, and when it ended he took her home and left immediately. Two cars were still following him.

A figure jumped out of the shadows. "Hi, stud!" Mark swung around and checked his holster nervously.

"Oh, hi, Simon."

"Listen, man, I can show you some dirty postcards if you're still desperate, 'cause it seems that you're just not good enough, man. I had a black one last night, I'm having a white one tonight."

"How can you be so sure?" asked Mark.

"I check in advance, man, I ain't got time to waste with my pretty body." Simon burst out laughing. "Think about me when you go to bed tonight, all alone, Mark, 'cause I sure will have forgotten you. Cool your jets, man."

Mark threw him the keys and watched him as he walked towards the Mercedes swinging his hips, dancing and laughing.

"You ain't got it, baby, whatever it is."

"Bullshit! You're a jive-ass bastard," Mark said, and laughed.

"Now, you're just jealous, man, or prejudiced," said Simon, as he revved up the car and moved to a parking space. As he passed Mark, he shouted, "Either way, I'm the winner."

Mark wondered if he ought to apply for a job as a garage attendant at the apartment building. It seemed to have its compensations. He looked around; something moved; no, it was just his nerves or his imagination. Once in his room, he wrote his report for the morning session with the Director and fell into bed.

Two days to go.

# Wednesday morning, 9 March

## 1:00 am

The phone rang. Mark was just falling asleep, still in that world between sleeping and waking. The phone insisted. Try to answer it, it could be Julius.

"Hello," he said, yawning.

"Mark Andrews?"

"Yes," he said wearily, shifting himself to a more comfortable position in the bed, fearing if he woke up fully he would never get back to sleep.

"It's George Stampouzis. Sorry to wake you, but I've come up with something I thought you would want to know about immediately."

Stampouzis's statement acted like cold water. Mark was wide awake instantly.

"Right, don't say anything else, I'll call you from a pay phone. What's your number?" Mark wrote it down on the back of a Kleenex box, the only thing he could reach. He threw on a bathrobe, forced his feet into a pair of tennis shoes, and started for the door. He opened the door, looked both ways. Hell, he was getting paranoid. There was no sound in the hall; there wouldn't be even if someone were waiting for him. He took the elevator down to the garage level, where there was a pay phone. Simon was asleep on the chair – how did he manage it? Mark had found it hard enough to sleep in bed.

He dialled the 212 area code.

"Hello, Stampouzis. Mark Andrews."

"Do you G-men always play games at one in the morning? I would have thought you'd figured out a better system by now."

Mark laughed; the sound echoed in the garage; Simon twitched.

"What can I do for you?"

"I traded some information today, now you owe me two stories." Stampouzis paused. "The Mafia had nothing to do with Stames's death, and they are not going overboard for the Gun Control bill, although they basically oppose it. So you can eliminate them. I wouldn't have gone this far for anyone but Nick, so make sure you handle it right."

"I'm doing my best," Mark replied. "Thanks for your help."

He put the phone on the hook and walked back to the elevator, thinking about the tousled bed which he hoped was still warm. Simon was still asleep.

# Wednesday morning, 9 March

## 5:50 am

"It's for you, sir."

"What?" mumbled the Director, still half-asleep.

"The phone, sir, it's for you." His housekeeper was standing by the doorway in her dressing-gown.

"Ugh. What time is it?"

"Ten to six, sir."

"Who is it?"

"Mr Elliott, sir."

"Right, switch it through."

"Yes, sir."

Elliott had woken him up. A decision he would never have taken unless it was urgent.

"Good morning, Elliott, what is it?" He paused. "Can you be sure? That changes the whole situation. What time is he due in? 7:00, of course. I'll see you at 6:30."

The Director put the phone down, and sat on the edge of the bed, and said very loudly: " Damn," which by the Director's standards was extreme. His big feet placed firmly on the floor, his large hands splayed on his equally large thighs, he was deep in thought. Eventually he rose, put on a dressing-gown, and disappeared into the bathroom, repeating the expletive several times.

Mark also had a phone call, not from the anonymous man, but from Elizabeth. She needed to see him urgently.

They agreed to meet at eight o'clock in the lobby of the Mayflower. He felt sure no one would recognise him there, but he wondered why Elizabeth had chosen that particular meeting place.

Mark took off his dressing-gown and returned to the bathroom.

The Senator took an early-morning phone call as well, not from the anonymous man or from Elizabeth, but from the Chairman, who was confirming their midday meeting for the final briefing at the Sheraton Hotel in Silver Spring. The Senator agreed, replaced the phone, and roamed around the room in his dressing-gown thinking.

"Coffee for three, Mrs McGregor. Are they both here?" the Director asked as he passed her.

"Yes, sir."

Mrs McGregor looked very chic in a new turquoise, two-piece suit, but the Director didn't notice. He strolled into his office.

"Good morning, Matt. Good morning, Mark." When should he drop the bomb? He decided to let Andrews speak first. "Right, let's hear what you've found out."

"As I told you yesterday, sir, I think I've cut the list of senators down to five – Brooks of Massachusetts, Byrd of West Virginia, Dexter of Connecticut, Harrison of South Carolina, and Thornton of Texas. The only common factor is their interest in the Gun Control bill, which as we know, sir, is likely to become law on 10 March. Assassination of the President would now be about the only way of holding that bill up."

"I would have thought," said Rogers, "that that could be the one act that would make certain the bill passed through both Houses."

"You tell that to two Kennedys, Martin Luther King, George Wallace and Ronald Reagan and see what they all have to say," responded the Director. "Continue, Mark."

Mark summarised what Lykham and Stampouzis had briefed him on each man, and explained how he was able to eliminate two other men from the list of seven – namely Pearson and Nunn. "That completes my report, sir, unless, of course, we are approaching this thing in the wrong way and I'm heading down a blind alley. And as far as I'm concerned that is entirely possible, as I seem to be boxing with shadows."

The Director nodded and waited.

Mark continued: "I was going to spend today trying to hear each one of them in action in the Senate. I wish I could think of a good way of finding out where they were at lunchtime on 24 February, short of asking them outright, that is."

"Don't go anywhere near any of them. That would be the surest way to shut down the whole plot. Now, Mark, I must warn you my news is not good, so settle back and prepare for the worst. We are beginning to think the man we are after is Dexter,' said the Director.

Mark went cold. "Why, sir?" he managed to get out.

The Assistant Director leaned forward to speak. "I have had some men checking out the Georgetown Inn, very unobtrusively. We didn't expect to turn anything up. We questioned all the day staff but they couldn't help. Early this morning, just to be thorough, we interviewed the night staff. Turned out that one of the night porters, who was off duty during the day, of course, is pretty sure he saw Senator Dexter hurrying away from the hotel some time like 2:30 in the afternoon on 24 February."

Mark was stunned. "How did he know it was Senator Dexter?"

"The man was born and raised in Wilton, Connecticut; he knows his face well. I'm afraid there's something else, too; he was accompanied by a young woman whose rough description tallies with his daughter."

"That's not proof," said Mark. "It's all circumstantial. It wouldn't stand up in a court of law."

"I'm sure you're right," said the Director, "but it's an unfortunate coincidence for Senator Dexter. Remember his involvement in the arms business; it won't do his finances any good if the Gun Control bill goes through; in fact our inquiries show he stands to lose a personal fortune, so we have a motive as well."

"But, sir," Mark argued, carried away by the desire to believe in Elizabeth, "do you really think that a senator would plot to kill the President just to keep one of his companies afloat? There are so many less drastic ways to stall the bill. He could try to tie it up in committee. Or organise a filibuster . . ."

"He already has tried – and failed, Mark," Matthew Rogers interrupted.

"The other four senators may have more powerful motives we don't happen to know about. It doesn't have to be Dexter," continued Mark, sounding unconvinced.

"Mark, I understand what you're saying and you do have a point. Under ordinary circumstances I'd agree that it seems unlikely, but we have to go on the evidence we have, even if it's slim and at present no more than circumstantial. And there's something else. On the night of 3 March, when Casefikis and the postman were killed, Dr Dexter's name was not marked on the duty register. She should have finished work at five, but for some inexplicable reason she stayed an extra two hours, treated the Greek – who was not her patient – and then went home. Now it's possible that she was just conscientious and working overtime, or that she was filling in for a colleague, but there are a hell of a lot of coincidences here, Mark. I'm bound to say if one is dispassionate about it, the odds are stacked heavily against Senator Dexter – and his daughter."

Mark did not reply.

"Now listen and listen carefully," the Director went on. "I know you want to believe that all this is circumstantial and that it's one of the other four – but I only have twenty-six hours left before the President leaves the White

House, and I have to live with the facts as they present themselves. I want to catch the man involved, whoever he is, and I'm not willing to risk the life of the President to do it. When are you seeing the girl next?"

Mark looked up. "At eight, at the Mayflower."

"Why?"

"I have no idea, sir. She just said that it was important."

"Um, well I think you still ought to go but then report back to me immediately you're through."

"Yes, sir."

"I can't understand why, Andrews. Be careful."

"Yes, sir."

"It's twenty to eight now, you'd better be on your way. Incidentally, we're still having no luck with those fifty-dollar bills. We're down to the last eight, but still no prints from Mrs Casefikis. Better news on the German, Gerbach, however. We've established beyond a doubt that he had no connection with the CIA during his stay in Rhodesia or at the time of his death, so that's one more problem out of the way."

Mark didn't give a damn about the fifty-dollar bills, the German driver, the Mafia, or the CIA. All his hard work appeared to be leading them straight to Dexter. He left the office even more despondent than he had been when he came in.

Once back on the street, he decided to walk to the Mayflower in the hope of clearing his head. He didn't notice that two men followed him down Pennsylvania Avenue, past the White House, and on towards the hotel.

At the press of a button, Elliott entered the Director's office.

"Elliott, you were right about the Mayflower. What have you done about it?"

"There are two men already there, sir, and one following Andrews."

"It's the first time in thirty-six years that I've hated

my job,' said the Director. "You've done very well, Elliott, and all too soon I'll be able to tell you what this whole damn thing is about."

"Yes, sir."

"Follow up these five names. Leave no stone unturned."

"Yes, sir."

"Thank you."

Elliott slid out of the room.

Damn man has no heart. Can't have a right-hand man without a heart. Makes him damn useful in a strange situation like this though. When this operation's all over, I'll transfer him back to Idaho and –

"You said something, sir?"

"No, Mrs McGregor, I'm just going quietly mad. Don't worry about me. When the men in the white coats come to take me away, just sign the forms in triplicate and look relieved."

Mrs McGregor smiled.

"I like your new suit," the Director said.

She blushed. "Thank you, sir."

Mark pushed through the revolving doors of the Mayflower Hotel, his eyes searching the lobby for Elizabeth. How he wanted to see her and how he wanted to stop being devious and tell her the truth. It's all circumstantial, he continued to insist. He couldn't spot her so chose a comfortable seat which had a good view of the lobby.

On the far side of the lobby, a man was buying *The Washington Post* from the newspaper stand. Mark didn't notice that he made no attempt to read it. Suddenly he saw Elizabeth heading towards him with Senator Dexter by her side. Hell, that was all he needed.

"Hello, Mark." She kissed him gently on the cheek.

Judas showing the Pharisees which one was to be killed? The unkindest cut of all.

"Mark, I'd like you to meet my father."

"Good morning, sir."

"Good morning, Mark, it's good to meet you. Elizabeth has told me quite a bit about you."

And what should you be able to tell me, thought Mark. Where were you on 24 February? Where will you be tomorrow?

"Mark, are you all right?" Elizabeth inquired.

"Yes, fine. I'm sorry, Senator, it's good to meet you too."

The Senator was staring at him strangely.

"Well, I must be getting along, dear – I have a busy schedule. I look forward to our usual lunch tomorrow."

"See you then, Father. Thanks for the breakfast and the chat."

"Goodbye, Mark. See you again soon, I hope." Senator Dexter still looked at him quizzically.

"Perhaps," replied Mark quietly.

They watched him leave. So did three other people. One of them left to make a phone call.

"Mark, what's come over you? Why were you so brusque with my father? I especially wanted you to meet him."

"I'm sorry, I'm just tired."

"Or is there something you're not telling me?" said Elizabeth.

"I could ask you the same question."

"What are you talking about?"

"Oh, I don't know, let's forget it," said Mark. "Why did you want to see me so urgently?"

"Simply because I wanted you to meet my father. What's so strange about that? Why the hell did I bother?"

She began to walk away down the corridor, pushing her way quickly through the revolving door at the entrance to the hotel. Three men saw her leave. One followed her, two stuck with Mark. He walked slowly towards the doors. The doorman saluted him punctiliously.

"Cab, sir?"

"No, thanks. I'll walk."

\*

The Director was on the phone when Mark returned and waved him into the large leather chair by his desk. He sank down in it, his mind fuzzy. The Director put the phone down and looked directly at him.

"So now you've met Senator Dexter, and I must tell you that either Dr Dexter knows nothing or she deserves an Oscar for her performance at the Mayflower."

"You saw everything," said Mark.

"Of course, and more. She was just involved in an automobile accident, two minutes ago. That phone call was the details."

Mark jumped out of his seat.

"She's all right. A couple of hundred dollars' worth of damage to the front of her little Fiat and not a mark on the bus she hit. Sensible girl. She's on her way to work now in a cab, or rather, she think it's a cab."

Mark sighed, resigned to whatever would happen next. "Where is Senator Dexter?" he asked.

"He's gone to the Capitol. Made one phone call when he got there, but it didn't turn out to be of any significance."

Mark was beginning to feel like a puppet. "What do you expect me to do now?"

There was a knock on the door and the anonymous man appeared. He handed a note to the Director, who read it quickly.

"Thank you."

The anonymous man left. Mark feared the worst. The Director placed the note on the desk and looked up.

"Senator Thornton has called a press conference at 10:30 in Senate Committee Room 2228. Better get down there immediately. Phone me as soon as he has said his piece. The questions from the press afterwards will be irrelevant; they always are."

Mark walked to the Senate, once again hoping it would clear his head. It didn't. He wanted to ring Elizabeth and ask if she were all right after the accident; he wanted to ask her a hundred questions, but he only wanted one answer. Three men also walked to the Senate, two of them taking a half of the route each, and the third walking the whole way. All three of them arrived eventually in Room 2228; none of them was interested in Senator Thornton's statement.

The room was already well lit by the large Idreg lights especially set up for the television cameras, and the members of the press were chatting among themselves. It was a packed house, even though Senator Thornton had not yet arrived. Mark wondered what he had to say, whether it would throw any light on his own questions. Point the guilty finger at Thornton perhaps, supply a motive he could return with to the Director. He thought, as he looked at the senior reporters, that they might have a shrewd idea or even a tip from one of Thornton's staff as to the contents of his statement. But he didn't want to ask them any questions for fear of being remembered. With an entrance that would have pleased Caesar himself, Senator Thornton came in, accompanied by three aides and a private secretary. He certainly was making the most of it. His dark hair was covered with grease, and he had put on what he obviously imagined to be his best suit, green with a blue pin-stripe. No one had briefed him on what to wear when facing colour television – only dark clothes, as plain as possible – or if he had been briefed, he hadn't listened.

He sat in a large throne of a chair at the far end of the room, his feet only just touching the ground. He was now surrounded by arc lights and the TV acoustics men put microphones all around him and in front of him. Suddenly, three more vast Idreg lights were switched on. Thornton was sweating already, but still smiling. The three television networks agreed that they were ready for the Senator. Thornton cleared his throat.

"Ladies and gentlemen of the press . . ."

"That's a pompous start," said a correspondent in front of Mark, writing every word down in shorthand.

Mark looked more closely, he thought he recognised the face. It was Bernstein of *The Washington Post*. Senator Thornton now had complete silence from the room.

"I have just left the White House after a private session with the President of the United States and because of that meeting, I wish to make a statement for press and television." He paused. "My criticisms of the Gun Control bill and my vote against it in committee were motivated by a desire to represent my constituents and their genuine fear of unemployment . . ."

". . . and *your* own genuine fear of unemployment," remarked Bernstein, *sotto voce*. "What bribe did the President offer you at dinner on Monday?"

The Senator cleared his throat again. "The President has assured me that if this piece of legislation is passed, and domestic production of guns is prohibited, she will sponsor legislation to give immediate financial assistance to gun manufacturers and their employees, in the hope that the facilities of the gun industry can be turned to other, less dangerous uses than the production of weapons of destruction. The President's concern has made it possible for me to vote in favour of the Gun Control bill. I have for some considerable time been in two minds . . ."

"True enough," said Bernstein.

". . . concerning this bill, because of my genuine fear of the freedom and ease with which criminals can obtain firearms."

"It didn't worry you yesterday. Just what contracts did the President promise," murmured the correspondent, "or did she say she would help you win re-election next year?"

"And the problem for me has always been in the balance . . ."

". . . and a little bribe tipped that balance."

Bernstein now had his own audience, which was enjoying his offerings far more than those of the Senator from Texas.

"Now that the President has shown such consideration, I feel able to announce with a clear conscience . . ."

". . . so clear we can see right through it," more Bernstein.

". . . that I am now able to support my party's position over gun control. I will, therefore, not be opposing the President on the floor of the Senate tomorrow."

Wild applause from scattered parts of the room, sounding – and looking – suspiciously like aides placed in strategic spots.

"I shall, ladies and gentlemen," Senator Thornton continued, "rest an easier man tonight . . ."

"And a re-elected one," added Bernstein.

"I should like to end by thanking the members of the press for attending . . ."

"We had to; it was the only show in town."

Laughter broke out around the *Post* correspondent, but it didn't reach Thornton.

"And I would like to say that I will be delighted to answer any questions. Thank you."

"Bet you don't answer any of mine."

Most of the other reporters left the room immediately, in order to catch the early editions of the afternoon papers, already going to press right across the country. Mark joined them but glanced over the famous journalist's shoulder. He had been scribbling in longhand.

"Friends, Romans, country bumpkins, lend me your jeers; I come to bury Kane, not to praise her." Not exactly front-page material.

Three other men who had attended the press conference followed Mark out of the room, as he ran to the nearest pay telephones, halfway down the hall. Mark found them all occupied by newspapermen anxious to get their copy in first, and there was a long line behind those already dictating. Another line had formed by the two phones at the other end of the hall. Mark took the elevator to the ground floor; same problem; his only chance would be the pay phone in the Russell Building across the street.

He ran all the way; so did three other men. When he reached there, a middle-aged woman stepped into the booth a pace ahead of him, and put her quarter in.

"Hello . . . it's me. I got the job . . . Yeah, pretty good . . . Mornings only. Start tomorrow . . . But I can't complain, money's not bad."

Mark paced up and down while the three men caught their breath. At last, the woman finished talking and, with a big smile all over her face, she walked away, oblivious of Mark or the nation's problems. At least someone is confident about tomorrow, thought Mark. He glanced around to be sure that there was no one near him, though he could have sworn he recognised a man standing by the Medicare poster; perhaps it was one of his colleagues from the FBI. He had seen that face behind the dark glasses somewhere. He was getting better protection than the President. He dialled the Director's private line and gave him his pay phone number. The phone rang back almost immediately.

"Thornton's off the list, sir, because he has –"

"I know, I know," said the Director. "I've just been briefed on what Thornton said. It's exactly what I would have expected him to say if he were involved. It certainly does not get him off my list; if anything, I'm a little more suspicious. Keep working on all five this afternoon and contact me the moment you come up with anything; don't bother to come in."

The phone clicked. Mark felt despondent. He depressed the cradle and waited for the dial tone, put in a quarter and dialled Woodrow Wilson. The nurse on duty went on a search for Elizabeth, but returned and said that no one had seen her all day. Mark hung up, forgetting to say thank you or goodbye. He took the elevator down to the basement cafeteria to have lunch. His decision gained the restaurant two more customers; the third man already had a lunch date, for which he was running late.

# Wednesday afternoon, 9 March

## 1:00 pm

Only Tony and Xan were on time for the meeting at the Sheraton Hotel in Silver Spring. They had spent many hours together but seldom spoke; Tony wondered what the Nip thought about all the time. Tony had had a busy schedule checking the routes for the final day, getting the Buick perfectly tuned – and chauffeuring the Chairman and Matson; they all treated him like a damn cab driver. His skill was equal to theirs anytime, and where the hell would they be without him? Without him those FBI men would still be around their necks. Still, the whole damn thing would be over by tomorrow night and he could then get away and spend some of his hard-earned money. He couldn't make up his mind whether it would be Miami or Las Vegas. Tony always planned how to spend his money before he got it. The Chairman came in, a cigarette hanging from his mouth as always. He looked at them, and asked brusquely where Matson was. Both shook their heads. Matson always worked alone. He trusted no one. The Chairman was irritated and made no attempt to hide it. The Senator arrived, just a few moments later, looking equally annoyed, but he didn't even notice that Matson wasn't there.

"Why don't we start?" demanded the Senator. "I find this meeting inconvenient as it is, since it's the final day of debate on the bill."

The Chairman looked at him with contempt. "We're missing Matson and his report is vital."

"How long will you wait?"

"Two minutes."

They waited in silence. They had nothing to say to each other; each man knew why he was there. Exactly two minutes later, the Chairman lit another cigarette and asked Tony for his report.

"I've checked the routes, boss, and it takes a car going at twenty-two miles per hour three minutes to get from the south exit of the White House on to E Street and down Pennsylvania Avenue to the FBI Building and another three minutes to reach the Capitol. It takes forty-five seconds to climb the steps and be out of range. On average six minutes forty-five seconds in all. Never under five minutes thirty seconds, never over seven minutes. That's trying it at midnight, one o'clock, and two o'clock in the morning, remembering the routes are going to be even clearer for Kane."

"What about after the operation is over?" asked the Chairman.

"It's possible to get from the crane through basement passageways to the Rayburn Building and from there to the Capitol South Metro Station in two minutes at best and three minutes fifteen seconds at worst – depends on elevators and congestion. Once the VC –" He stopped himself. "Once Xan is in the Metro, they'll never find him; in a few minutes, he can be on the other side of Washington."

"How can you be sure they won't pick him up in under three minutes fifteen seconds?" asked the Senator, whose personal interest in Xan was non-existent, but he didn't trust the little man not to sing if he were caught.

"Assuming they know nothing, they also won't know which way to turn for at least the first five minutes," answered the Chairman.

Tony continued: "If it goes as planned, you won't even need the car so I'll just dump it and disappear."

"Agreed," said the Chairman. "But nevertheless I trust the car is in perfect condition?"

"Sure is, it's ready for Daytona."

The Senator mopped his brow, which was surprising, since it was a cold March day.

"Xan, your report," said the Chairman.

Xan went over his plan in detail; he had rehearsed it again and again during the last two days. He had slept at the head of the crane for the last two nights and the gun was already in place. The men would be going on a twenty-four-hour strike starting at six that evening. "By six tomorrow evening, I will be on other side of America and Kane will be dead."

"Good," said the Chairman, stubbing out his cigarette and lighting another one. "I shall be on the corner of 9th and Pennsylvania and will contact you on my watchband radio when I arrive at 9:30 and again when Kane's car passes me. When your watch starts vibrating, she will be three minutes away, giving you three minutes and forty-five seconds in all. How much warning do you need?"

"Two minutes and thirty seconds will be enough," said Xan.

"That's cutting it a bit close, isn't it?" inquired the Senator, still sweating.

"If that turns out to be the case you will have to delay her on the steps of the Capitol because we don't want to expose Xan more than necessary," said the Chairman. "The longer he is in view, the greater the chance the Secret Service helicopters will have of spotting him."

The Senator turned his head towards Xan. "You say you've been rehearsing every day?"

"Yes," replied Xan. He never saw any reason to use more words than necessary, even when addressing a United States Senator.

"Then why don't people notice you carrying a rifle or at least a gun box?"

"Because gun has been taped to platform on top of

crane three hundred and twenty feet out of harm's way ever since I returned from Vienna."

"What happens if the crane comes down? They'll spot it right away."

"No, I am in yellow overalls and rifle is in eight parts and has been painted yellow and is taped to underpart of platform. Even with strong field glasses, it looks like part of crane. When I picked up latest sniper rifle from Dr Schmidt of Helmut, Helmut, and Schmidt, even he was surprised by can of yellow paint."

They all laughed except the Senator.

"How long does it take you to assemble it?" continued the Senator, probing for a flaw, something he always did when questioning so-called experts in Senate committees.

"Two minutes to put rifle together and thirty seconds to get into perfect firing position; two more minutes to dismantle gun and retape it. It's a 5.6 by 61 millimetre Vomhofe Super Express rifle, and I'm using a .77 grain bullet with a muzzle speed of 3,480 feet per second, which is 2,000 foot-pounds of muzzle energy which, in layman's language, Senator, means if there is no wind, I will aim one and one half inches above Kane's forehead at two hundred yards."

"Are you satisfied?" the Chairman asked the Senator.

"Yes, I suppose so," he said, and sank into a brooding silence, still wiping his brow. Then he thought of something else and was about to start his questioning again, when the door flew open and Matson rushed in.

"Sorry, boss. I've been following something up."

"It'd better be good," snapped the Chairman.

"It could be bad, boss, very bad," said Matson between breaths.

They all looked anxiously at him.

"Okay, let's have it."

"His name is Mark Andrews," said Matson, as he fell into the unoccupied seat.

"And who is he?" asked the Chairman.

"The FBI man who went to the hospital with Calvert."

"Could we start at the beginning?" the Chairman asked calmly.

Matson took a deep breath. "You know I've always been bothered about Stames going to the hospital with Calvert – it never made sense, a man of his seniority."

"Yes, yes," said the Chairman impatiently.

"Well, Stames didn't go. His wife told me. I went by to visit her to offer my condolences, and she told me everything Stames had done that evening, right down to eating half his moussaka. The FBI told her not to say anything to anyone but she thinks that I'm still with the Bureau, and she doesn't remember, or maybe she never knew, that Stames and I were not exactly friends. I've checked up on Andrews and I've been following him for the last forty-eight hours. He's listed in the Washington Field Office as on leave for two weeks, but he's been spending his leave in a very strange way. I've seen him at FBI Headquarters, going around with a female doctor from Woodrow Wilson, and nosing around at the Capitol."

The Senator flinched.

"The good doctor was on duty the night that I got rid of the Greek and the black bastard."

"So if they know everything," said the Chairman quickly, "why are we still here?"

"Well, that's the strange part. I arranged to have a drink with an old buddy from the Secret Service; he's on duty detail tomorrow with Kane and nothing has been changed. It is painfully obvious that the Secret Service has no idea what we have planned for tomorrow, so either the FBI know one hell of a lot or nothing, but if they do know everything, they're not letting the Secret Service in on it."

"Did you learn anything from your contacts in the FBI?" asked the Chairman.

"Nothing. Nobody knows anything, even when they're blind drunk."

"How much do you think Andrews knows?" continued the Chairman.

"I think he's fallen for our friend the doctor and knows very little. He's running around in the dark," Matson replied. "It's possible he's picked up something from the Greek waiter. If so, he's working on his own, and that's not FBI policy."

"I don't follow," said the Chairman.

"Bureau policy is to work in pairs or threes, so why aren't there dozens of men on it? Even if there were only six or seven, I would have heard about it and so would at least one of my contacts in the FBI," said Matson. "I think they may believe there is going to be an attempt on the President, but I don't think they have a clue when – or where."

"Did anyone mention the date in front of the Greek?" asked the Senator nervously.

"I can't remember, but there's only one way of finding out if they know anything," said the Chairman.

"What's that, boss?" asked Matson.

The Chairman paused, lit another cigarette, and said dispassionately, "Kill Andrews."

There was silence for a few moments. Matson was the first to recover.

"Why, boss?"

"Simple logic. If he is connected with an FBI investigation, then they would immediately change tomorrow's schedule. They would never risk allowing Kane to leave the White House if they believed such a threat existed. Just think of the consequences involved; if the FBI knew of an assassination attempt on the President and they haven't made an arrest to date and they didn't bother to inform the Secret Service . . ."

"That's right," said Matson. "They would have to come up with some excuse and cancel at the last minute."

"Exactly, so if Kane comes out of those gates, we will still go ahead because they know nothing. If she doesn't, we're going to take a long holiday, because they know far too much for our health."

The Chairman turned to the Senator, who was now sweating profusely.

"Now, you just make sure that you're on the steps of the Capitol to stall her if necessary and we'll take care of the rest," he said harshly. "If we don't get her tomorrow, we have wasted one hell of a lot of time and money, and we sure aren't going to get another chance as good as this."

The Senator groaned. "I think you're insane, but I won't waste time arguing. I have to get back to the Senate before somebody notices that I'm missing."

"Settle down, Senator. We have it all under control; now we can't lose either way."

"Maybe you can't, but at the end of the day I might end up the fall guy."

The Senator left without another word. The Chairman waited in silence for the door to close.

"Now we've got that little funk out of the way, let's get down to business. Let's hear all about Mark Andrews and what he's been up to."

Matson gave a detailed description of Mark's movements during the past forty-eight hours. The Chairman took in every detail without writing down a word.

"Right, the time has come to blow away Mr Andrews, and then we'll sit back and monitor the FBI's reaction. Now listen carefully, Matson. This is the way it will be done: you will return to the Senate immediately and . . ."

Matson listened intently, taking notes and nodding from time to time.

"Any questions?" the Chairman asked when he had finished.

"None, boss."

"If they let the bitch out of the White House after that, they know nothing. One more thing before we finish. If anything does go wrong tomrrow, we all take care of ourselves. Understood? No one talks; compensation will be made at a later date, in the usual way."

They all nodded.

"And one final point: if there should be a foul-up, there's one man who certainly won't take care of us, so we must be prepared to take care of him. I propose we do it in the following way. Xan, when Kane . . ."

They all listened in silence; no one disagreed.

"Now I think it's time for lunch. No need to let that bitch in the White House spoil our eating habits. Sorry you'll be missing it, Matson; just make sure it's Andrews' last lunch."

Matson smiled. "It will give me a good appetite," he said, and left.

The Chairman picked up the phone. "We're ready for lunch now, thank you." He lit another cigarette.

# Wednesday afternoon, 9 March

## 2:15 pm

Mark finished his lunch. Two other men finished their sandwiches and also rose to leave. Mark quickly returned to the Senate, as he wanted to catch Henry Lykham before the floor debate started. He hoped that Lykham would have something new to reveal after having had a night to sleep on it. He also needed copies of the Judiciary Committee Gun Control Hearings so that he could study the questions asked by Brooks, Byrd, Dexter, Harrison, and Thornton. Perhaps they would reveal another missing piece of the jigsaw. But somehow Mark doubted it. He was becoming convinced that politicians rarely revealed anything. He arrived a few minutes before the session was scheduled to begin, and asked a page if he could locate Lykham in the ante-chamber.

Lykham bustled out a few moments later. It was obvious he didn't want a chat ten minutes before a full session. So he had no real chance to tell him anything new even if he had thought of something. All Mark did manage to find out was where to obtain transcripts of the committee hearings and discussions.

"You can get them from the committee office at the end of the corridor."

Mark thanked him and walked upstairs to the gallery, where his new friend, the guard, had saved him a seat. The place was already packed. Senators were entering the chamber and taking their places, so he decided to pick up the transcripts later.

The Vice President, Bill Bradley, called for order and the tall figure of Senator Dexter looked around the room slowly and dramatically, sweeping the chamber with his eyes to be assured of everyone's attention. When his eyes alighted on Mark he looked a little surprised, but he quickly recovered and began his final arguments against the bill.

Mark was embarrassed and wished he had taken a seat nearer the back, beyond the range of Dexter's piercing glance. The debate dragged on. Brooks, Byrd, Dexter, Harrison, Thornton. They all wanted a final word before tomorrow's vote. Before tomorrow's death.

Mark listened to them all but he learned nothing new. He seemed to have come to a dead end. All that was left for him to do that day was to go and pick up transcripts of the hearings. He would have to read them through the night and he doubted, having listened to the five speak twice already, that they would reveal anything. But what other lead did he have left? Everything else was being covered by the Director. He walked down the hall to the elevator, left the Capitol by the ground-floor exit, and made his way across the Capitol grounds to the Dirksen Building.

"I would like the transcripts of the Gun Control Hearings, please."

"All of them?" asked the disbelieving secretary.

"Yes," replied Mark.

"But there were six all-day sessions."

Oh, hell, he thought, it will be worse than all night; still, it would be only the questions and statements of Brooks, Byrd, Dexter, Harrison and Thornton.

"Sign or pay?"

"I wish I could sign," he said jokingly.

"Well, are you an official of any kind?"

Yes, thought Mark. But I can't admit it.

"No," said Mark, and took out his wallet.

"If you asked for these through one of the senators

from your state, you could probably get them for nothing. Otherwise that'll be ten dollars, sir."

"I'm in a hurry," said Mark. "Guess I'll have to pay."

He handed over the money. Senator Stevenson appeared in the doorway connecting the hearing room to the committee office.

"Good afternoon, Senator," said the secretary, turning away from Mark.

"Hi, Debbie. Would you happen to have a copy of the Clean Air bill as it was reported out of the sub-committee, before the committee markup?"

"Certainly, Senator, just a moment." She disappeared into a back room. "It's the only copy we have at the moment. Can I trust you with it, Senator?" She laughed. "Or should I make you sign for it?"

Even senators sign, thought Mark. Senators sign for everything. Henry Lykham signs for everything, even lunch. No wonder my taxes are so high. But I imagine they have to pay for the food later. The food. My God, why didn't I think of it before. Mark started running.

"Sir, sir, you've left your hearings," a voice shouted. But it was too late.

"Some kind of nut," said the secretary to Senator Stevenson.

"Anyone who wants to read all those hearings must be crazy to begin with," said Senator Stevenson, staring at the pile of paper Mark had left behind him.

Mark went straight to Room G-211, where he had lunched with Lykham the previous day. The door was marked "Officials' Dining-Room". There were only two or three attendants in evidence.

"Excuse me, I wonder if you could tell me, is this where the senators eat?"

"I'm sorry, I don't know. You'd have to talk to the hostess. We're just cleaning up."

"Where might I find the hostess?"

"She's not here. Gone for the day. If you come back tomorrow, maybe she can help you."

"Okay." Mark sighed. "Thanks. But can you tell me – is there another Senate dining-room?"

"Yeah, the big one in the Capitol. S-109, but you won't be able to get in there."

Mark ran back to the elevator and waited impatiently. When he reached the basement level, he jumped out and walked past the entrance to the labyrinthine tunnels which connect all the office buildings on Capitol Hill. Past the door marked "Tobacco Shop", he raced towards the large sign – "Subway Cars to Capitol". The subway car, actually just an open train with compartments, was about to leave. Mark stepped into the last compartment and sat down opposite a couple of Senate staffers who were jabbering away about some bill or other, with an air of "we belong".

A few moments later, a bell signalled their arrival and the train came to a stop at the Senate side of the Capitol. Easy life, thought Mark. These guys need never even wander out into the cold, cruel world. They just shuttle back and forth between votes and hearings. The basement on this side was a replica of the basement on the other side, a dull yellow, with exposed plumbing, and the inevitable Pepsi machine; it must have made Coca-Cola mad that Pepsi had the concession for the Senate. Mark bounded up the small escalator and waited for the public elevator, while a couple of men with a certain air of importance were ushered into the elevator marked "Senators Only".

Mark got off on the ground floor, and looked around, perplexed. Nothing but marble arches and corridors. Where was the Senate Dining-Room? he asked one of the Capitol policemen.

"Just walk straight ahead, take the first corridor on the left. It's the narrow one, the first entrance you get to." He pointed.

Mark tossed a thank-you over his shoulder and found the narrow corridor. He passed the kitchens and a sign which announced "Private – Press Only". Straight ahead, in large letters on a wooden sign, he saw another "Senators Only". An open door on the right led into the anteroom, decorated with a chandelier, a rose-coloured, patterned carpet, and green leather furniture, all dominated by the colourful, crowded painting on the ceiling. Through another door, Mark could see white tablecloths, flowers, the world of gracious dining. A matronly woman appeared in the doorway.

"What can I do for you?" she asked, raising her eyebrows inquisitively.

"I'm doing a thesis on the working life of a senator for my Ph.D." Mark took out his wallet and showed his Yale I.D. card, covering the expiration date with his thumb.

The lady was not visibly impressed.

"I really only want to look at the room. Just to get the atmosphere of the place."

"Well, there are no senators in here at the moment, sir. There almost never are this late on a Wednesday. They start going back to their home states on Thursdays for a long weekend. The only thing that is keeping them here this week is that Gun Control bill."

Mark had managed to edge himself into the centre of the room. A waitress was clearing a table. She smiled at him.

"Do senators sign for their meals? Or do they pay cash?"

"Almost all of them sign, and then they pay at the end of the month."

"How do you keep track?"

"No problem. We keep a daily record." She pointed to a large book marked *Accounts*. Mark knew that twenty-three senators had lunched that day because their secretaries had told him so. Had any other senator done so without bothering to inform his secretary? He was a yard away from finding out.

"Could I just see a typical day? Just out of interest," he asked with an innocent smile.

"I'm not sure I'm allowed to let you look."

"Only a glance. When I write my thesis, I want people

to think that I really know what I'm talking about, that I've seen for myself. Everyone's been so kind to me."

He looked at the woman pleadingly.

"Okay," she said grudgingly, "but please be quick."

"Thank you. Why don't you pick any old day, let's say 24 February."

She opened the book and thumbed through to 24 February. "A Thursday," she said. Stevenson, Nunn, Moynihan, Heinz, names rang one after the other. Dole, Hatfield, Byrd. So Byrd lunched at the Senate that day. He read on. Templeman, Brooks – Brooks as well. More names. Barnes, Reynolds, Thornton. So his statement this morning was for real. The hostess closed the book. No Harrison, no Dexter.

"Nothing very special about that, is there?" she said.

"No," said Mark. He thanked the woman and left quickly.

In the street he hailed a taxi. So did one of the three men following him; the other two went off to pick up their car.

Mark arrived at the Bureau a few moments later, paid the driver, showed his credentials at the entrance, and took the elevator to the seventh floor. Mrs McGregor smiled. The Director must be alone, thought Mark. He knocked and went in.

"Well, Mark?"

"Brooks, Byrd, and Thornton are not involved, sir."

"The first two don't surprise me," said the Director. "It never made any sense that they were, but I'd have put a side bet on Thornton. Anyway, how did you dispose of those three?"

Mark described his brainstorm about the Senate dining-room, and wondered what else he had overlooked.

"You should have worked all of that out three days ago, shouldn't you, Mark?"

"Yes, sir."

"So should I," said the Director. "So we're down to Dexter and Harrison. It will interest you to know that both men, along with almost all of the senators, intend to be in Washington tomorrow and both are down to attend the ceremony at the Capitol. Amazing," he mused, "even at that level, men like to watch their crimes enacted.

"Let's go over it once again, Andrews. The President leaves the south entrance of the White House at 10:00 am unless I stop her, so we have seventeen hours left and one last hope. The boys in Fingerprints have isolated the bill with Mrs Casefikis's prints on it. The twenty-second, we may be lucky – with still another half dozen to go we shouldn't have had a hope before ten o'clock tomorrow. There are several other prints on the bill, and they will be working on them all through the night. I expect to reach home by midnight. If you come up with anything before then, call me. I want you here in the office at 8:15 tomorrow. There's very little you can do now. But don't worry too much; I have twenty agents still working on it, though none of them knows all the details. And I'll only let the President into the danger zone if we have a fix on these villains."

"I'll report at 8:15 then, sir," said Mark.

"And, Mark, I strongly advise you not to see Dr Dexter. I don't want to blow this whole operation at the last moment, because of your love life. No offence intended."

"No, sir."

Mark left, feeling slightly superfluous. Twenty agents now assigned to the case. How long had the Director had them working round the clock without telling him? Twenty men trying to find out whether it was Dexter or Harrison, without knowing why. Still, only he and the Director knew the whole story, and he feared the Director knew more than he did. Perhaps it would be wiser to avoid Elizabeth until the following evening. He picked up his car, and drove back to the Dirksen Building and then remembered he had left the hearings' transcripts at the Committee Office. When he got there he found himself drawn towards the telephone booths. He had to call her, he had to find out how she was after her accident. He dialled Woodrow Wilson:

"Oh, she left the hospital – some time ago."

"Thank you," said Mark. He could feel his heart beat as he dialled her Georgetown number.

"Elizabeth?"

"Yes, Mark." She sounded – cold? frightened? tired? A hundred questions were racing through his mind.

"Can I come and see you right now?"

"Yes." The telephone clicked.

Mark left the booth, conscious of the sweat on the palms of his hands. One more job to do before he could drive off to Elizabeth, pick up those damned papers from the Senate Gun Control Hearings.

Mark walked towards the elevator and thought he could hear footsteps behind him. Of course he could hear footsteps behind him; there were several people behind him. When he reached the elevator, he pressed the Up-button and glanced around at the footsteps. Among the crowd of Senate staffers, congressmen, and sightseers, two men were watching him – or were they protecting him? There was a third man in dark glasses staring at a Medicare poster, even more obviously an agent, to Mark's quick eyes, than the other two.

The Director had said that he had put twenty agents on the case, and three of them must have been allocated to watch Mark. Hell. Soon they would be following him back to Elizabeth and Mark did not doubt that the Director would learn about it immediately. Mark resolved that no one was going to follow him back to Elizabeth's. It was none of their damned business. He'd shake the three of them off. He needed to see her in peace, without prying eyes and malicious tongues. He thought quickly as he waited to see which of the two elevators would arrive first. Two of the agents were now walking towards him, but the one by the Medicare poster remained motionless. Perhaps he wasn't an operative after all, but there certainly was something familiar about him. He had the aura of an agent; other agents can sense it with their eyes shut.

Mark concentrated on the elevator. The arrow on his

right lit up and the doors opened slowly. Mark shot in and stood facing the buttons and stared out at the corridor. The two operatives followed him into the elevator, and stood behind him. The man by the Medicare poster started walking towards the elevator. The doors were beginning to close. Mark pressed the Open-button, and the doors parted again. Must give him a chance to get in, and have all three of them together, Mark thought, but the third man did not respond. He just stood, staring, as if waiting for the next elevator. Perhaps he wanted to go down and wasn't an agent at all. Mark could have sworn . . . The doors began to close and at what Mark thought was the optimum point, he jumped back out. Wrong. O'Malley managed to squeeze himself out as well, while his partner was left to travel slowly but inevitably up to the eighth floor. Now Mark was down to two tails. The other elevator arrived. The third agent stepped into it immediately. Very clever or innocent, Mark thought, and waited outside. O'Malley was at his shoulder – which one next?

Mark strolled into the elevator and pressed the Down-button, but O'Malley was able to get in easily. Mark pressed the Open-button and sauntered back out. O'Malley followed him, face impassive. The third man remained motionless in the elevator. They must be working together. Mark jumped back in and jabbed the Close-button hard. The doors closed horribly slowly, but O'Malley had walked two paces away and was not going to make it. As the doors slammed together, Mark smiled. Two gone, one standing on the ground floor helpless, the other heading for the roof, while he was descending to the basement alone with the third.

O'Malley caught up with Pierce Thompson on the fifth floor. Both were out of breath.

"Where is he?" cried O'Malley.

"What do you mean, where is he? I thought he was with you."

"No, I lost him on the first floor."

"Shit, he could be anywhere," said Thompson. "Whose side does the smart-ass think we are on? Which one of us is going to tell the Director?"

"Not me," O'Malley said. "You're the senior officer, you tell him."

"No way I'm telling him," Thompson said. "And let that bastard Matson take all the credit – you can be sure he's still with him. No, we're going to find him. You take the first four floors and I'll take the top four. Bleep immediately when you spot him."

When Mark reached the basement, he stayed in the elevator. The third man walked out and seemed to hesitate. Mark's thumb was jammed on the Close-button again. The door responded. He was on his own. He tried to make the elevator bypass the ground floor but he couldn't; someone else wanted to get in. He prayed it was not one of the three men. He had to risk it. The doors opened and he walked out immediately. No agents in sight, no one studying the Medicare poster. He ran towards the revolving doors at the end of the corridor. The guard on duty looked at him suspiciously and fingered the holster of his gun. Through the revolving doors and out into the open, running hard. He glanced around. Everyone was walking, no one was running. He was safe.

Pennsylvania Avenue – he dodged in and out of the traffic amid screeching tyres and angry expletives. He reached the parking lot and jumped into his car, fumbling for some change. Why did they make trousers that you couldn't get your hands into when you sat down? He quickly paid for his ticket and drove towards Georgetown – and Elizabeth. He glanced in the rear-view mirror. No Ford sedan in sight. He'd done it. He was on his own. He smiled. For once he had beaten the Director. He drove past the lights at the corner of Pennsylvania and 14th just as they were changing. He began to relax.

A black Buick ran the lights. Lucky there were no traffic cops around.

When Mark arrived in Georgetown, his nervousness returned, a new nervousness associated with Elizabeth and her world, not with the Director and his world. When he pressed the bell on her front door, he could still hear his heart beating.

Elizabeth appeared. She looked drawn and tired and didn't speak. He followed her into the living-room.

"Have you recovered from your accident?"

"Yes, thank you. How did you know I'd had an accident?" she asked.

Mark thought quickly. "Called the hospital. They told me there."

"You're lying, Mark. I didn't tell them at the hospital, and I left early after a phone call from my father."

Mark couldn't look her in the eyes. He sat down and stared at the rug. "I . . . I don't want to lie to you, Elizabeth. Please don't."

"Why are you following my father?" she demanded. "He thought you looked familiar when he met you at the Mayflower. You've been haunting his committee meetings and you've been watching the debates in the Senate."

Mark didn't answer.

"Okay, don't explain. I'm not completely blind. I'll draw my own conclusions. I'm part of an FBI assignment. My, you've been working late hours, haven't you, Agent Andrews? For a man singled out to work a senators' daughters' beat, you're pretty goddamn inept. Just how many daughters have you seduced this week? Did you get any good dirt? Why don't you try the wives next? Your boyish charm might be more effective on them. Although, I must confess, you had me fooled, you lying bastard."

Despite a considerable effort to maintain the icy control with which she had launched her attack, Elizabeth bit her lip. Her voice caught. Mark still couldn't look at her.

He heard the anger and the tears in her voice. In a moment, the chilling frost had covered her emotion again.

"Please leave now, Mark. Now. I've said my piece and I hope I never lay eyes on you again. Perhaps then I can recover some of my self-respect. Just go; crawl back into the slime."

"You've misunderstood, Elizabeth."

"I know, you poor misunderstood agent, and you love me for myself. There's no other girl in your life," she said bitterly. "At least not until you're transferred to a new case. Well, this case has just finished. Go find somebody else's daughter to seduce with your lies about love."

He couldn't blame her for her reaction, and left without another word.

He drove home in a daze. The occupants of the car following him were fully alert. When he arrived, Mark left the car keys with Simon and took the elevator to his apartment.

The black Buick was parked a hundred yards from the building. The two men could see the light in Mark's apartment. He dialled six of the seven digits of her number, but then he put the phone back on the hook and turned off the light. One of the men in the Buick lit another cigarette, inhaled, and checked his watch.

After months of bargaining, bullying, cajoling and threatening the Gun Control bill was at last to be presented to the House for their final approval.

This was to be the day when Florentyna made an indelible mark on American history. If she achieved nothing else during her term of office she would live to be proud of this single act.

What could prevent it now? she asked for the thousandth time. And for the thousandth time the same dreadful thought flashed across her mind.

She dismissed it once again.

# Thursday morning, 10 March

## 5:00 am

The Director woke suddenly. He lay there, frustrated; there was nothing he could do at this hour except look at the ceiling and think, and that didn't help much. He went over and over in his mind the events of the past six days, always leaving until last the thought of cancelling the whole operation, which would probably mean even now that the Senator and his cohorts would get away scot-free. Perhaps they already knew and had disappeared to lick their wounds and prepare for another day. Either way it would remain his problem.

The Senator woke at 5:35 in a cold sweat – not that he had really slept for more than a few minutes at any one time. It had been an evil night, thunder and lightning and sirens. It was the sirens that had made him sweat. He was even more nervous than he had expected to be; in fact just after he heard three chime he had nearly dialled the Chairman to say that he couldn't go through with it, despite the consequences that the Chairman had so delicately, but so frequently, adumbrated. But the vision of President Kane dead beside him reminded the Senator that everybody even now could remember exactly where he was when John F. Kennedy was assassinated, and he himself was never going to be able to forget where he was when Florentyna Kane died. Even that seemed less appalling than the thought of his own name in the headlines, his public image irreparably damaged, and his career ruined. Even so, he nearly called the Chairman, as much for reassurance as anything, despite their agreement that they had contacted each other for the last time until late the following morning, when the Chairman would be in Miami.

Five men had already died and that had caused only a ripple: President Kane's death would reverberate around the world.

The Senator stared out of the window for some time, focusing on nothing, then turned away. He kept looking at his watch, wishing he could stop time. The second hand moved relentlessly – relentlessly towards 10:56. He busied himself with breakfast and the morning paper. The *Post* informed him that many buildings had caught fire during the night in one of the worst storms in Washington's history, and the Lubber Run in Virginia had overflowed its banks, causing heavy property damage. There was little mention of President Kane. He wished he could read tomorrow's papers today.

The first call the Director received was from Elliott, who informed him that the recent activities of Senators Dexter and Harrison revealed nothing new about the situation – not that the anonymous man knew exactly what the situation was. The Director grumbled to himself, finished his egg – sunny-side up – and read the *Post*'s description of the demonic weather that had assailed Washington during the night. He glanced out of the window at the day, now clear and dry. A perfect day for an assassination, he thought. The bright day that brings fourth the adder. How late could he leave it before letting everyone know everything? The President was scheduled to leave the White House at 10:00 am. The Director would have to brief the head of the Secret Service, H. Stuart Knight, long before then and, if necessary, the President at least one hour before that. To hell with it, he would leave it to the last minute and make a full explanation afterwards. He was willing to risk his career to catch this pernicious Senator red-handed. But risking the President's life . . .

He drove to the Bureau soon after 6:00. He wanted to be there a full two hours before Andrews to study all the reports he had ordered the evening before. Not many of his senior aides would have had much sleep last night, though they were probably still wondering why. They would know soon enough. His deputy Associate Director for Investigation, his Assistant Director for Planning and Evaluation, and the head of the Criminal Section of that division would help him decide if he should go ahead or cancel. His Ford sedan slid down the ramp to the underground parking lot and his reserved parking place.

Elliott was there to meet him at the elevator – he was always there, never late. He's not human, he'll have to go, thought the Director, if I don't have to go first. He suddenly realised that he could be handing his resignation in to the President that night. Which President? He put it out of his mind – that would all take care of itself in its own time, he must now take care of the next five hours.

Elliott had nothing useful to say. Dexter and Harrison had both received and made phone calls during the night and early morning, but nothing incriminating had been picked up. No other information was forthcoming. The Director asked where the two senators were at that moment.

"Both eating breakfast at their homes. Dexter in Kensington, Harrison in Alexandria. Six agents have been watching them since five o'clock this morning and have been detailed to follow them all day."

"Good. Report back to me immediately if anything unusual happens."

"Of course, sir."

The fingerprint man was next. When he arrived, the Director first apologised for keeping him up all night, though the man's face and eyes looked more alight and alive than his own had been in the shaving mirror that morning.

Five feet four inches tall, slight and rather pale, Daniel Sommerton began his report. He was like a child with a toy. For him, working with prints had always been a passion as well as a job. The Director remained seated while Sommerton stood. If the Director had stood, he would not have been head and shoulders above him, but head, shoulders, and chest above him.

"We have found seventeen different fingers, and three different thumbs, Director," he said gleefully. "We're putting them through the Ninhydrin rather than the iodine-fume process, since we were unable to do them one at a time for technical reasons that I won't bother you with."

He waved his arm imperiously to imply that he would not waste a scientific explanation on the Director, who would have been the first to acknowledge such a pointless exercise.

"We think there are two more prints we might identify," Sommerton continued, "and we will have a read-out for you on all twenty-two of them within two, at the most three hours."

The Director glanced at his watch – already 6:45.

"Well done. That won't be a minute too soon. Get me the results – even if they are negative – as quickly as possible, and please thank all of your staff for working through the night."

The fingerprint expert left the Director, anxious to return to his seventeen fingers, three thumbs and two unidentified marks. The Director pressed a button and asked Mrs McGregor to send in the Assistant Director for Planning and Evaluation.

Two minutes later, Walter Williams was standing in front of him.

Five feet eleven, fair with a thin pallid face, dominated by a magnificent high-domed forehead, lined with amusement not grief, Williams was known in the Bureau either as the Brain or W.W. His primary responsibility was to head the Bureau's think tank of six lesser but still impressive brains. The Director often confronted him with hypothetical situations to which W.W. would later provide an answer which often proved, in retrospect, to be the right one. The Director placed great faith in his judgement, but he could not take any risks today. W.W. had better come up with a convincing answer to his hypothetical question of last night or his next call would be to the President.

"Good morning, Director."

"Good morning, W.W. What is your decision concerning my little problem?"

"Most interesting, Director . . . I feel, to be fair, the answer is simple, even when we look at the problem from every angle."

For the first time that morning a trace of a smile appeared on the Director's face.

"Assuming I haven't misunderstood you, Director."

The Director's smile broadened slightly; W.W. neither missed nor misunderstood anything, and was so formal that he didn't address the Director even in private as Halt. W.W. continued, his eyebrows moving up and down like the Dow-Jones index in an election year:

"You asked me to assume that the President would be leaving the White House at X hundred hours and then travelling by car to the Capitol. That would take her six minutes. I'm assuming her car is bullet-proof and well covered by the Secret Service. Under these conditions would it be possible to assassinate her. The answer is, it's possible but almost impossible, Director. Nevertheless, following the hypothesis through to its logical conclusion, the assassination team could use three methods: (a) explosives; (b) a handgun at close range; (c) a rifle."

W.W. always sounded like a textbook. "The bomb can be thrown at any point on the route, but it is never used by professionals, because professionals are paid for results, not attempts. If you study bombs as a method of removing a President, you will find there hasn't been a successful one yet, despite the fact that we have had four Presidents assassinated in office. Bombs inevitably end up killing innocent people and quite often the perpetrator of the crime as well. For that reason, since you have implied that the people involved would be professionals, I feel they must rely on the handgun or the rifle. Now the short-range gun, Director, is not a possible weapon on the route itself because it is unlikely that a pro would approach the President and shoot him at close range, thereby risking his own life. It would take an elephant gun or an anti-tank gun to pierce the President's limousine, and you can't carry those around in the middle of Washington without a permit."

With W.W., the Director could never be sure if it were meant to be a joke or just another fact. The eyebrows were still moving up and down, a sure signal not to interrupt him with foolish questions.

"When the President arrives at the steps of the Capitol, the crowd is too far away from her for a handgun to (a) be accurate and (b) give the assassin any hope of escape. So we must assume that it's the best-tested and most successful method of assassination of a Head of State – the rifle with telescopic sights for long range. Therefore, the only hope the assassin would have must be at the Capitol itself. The assassin can't see into the White House, and in any case the glass in the windows is four inches thick, so he must wait until the President actually leaves the limousine at the steps of the Capitol. This morning we timed a walk up the Capitol steps and it takes around fifty seconds. There are very few vantage points from which to make an assassination attempt, but we have studied the area carefully and you will find them all listed in my report. Also the conspirators must be convinced that we know nothing about the plot, because they know we can cover every possible shooting site. We think an assassination here in the heart of Washington unlikely, but nevertheless just possible by a man or team daring and skilful enough."

"Thank you, W.W. I'm sure you're right."

"A pleasure, sir. I do hope it's only hypothetical."

"Yes, W.W."

W.W. smiled like the only schoolboy in the class who can answer the teacher's questions. The Brain left the room to return to other problems. The Director paused and called for his other Assistant Director.

Matthew Rogers knocked and entered the room, waiting to be asked to take a seat. He understood authority. Like W.W. he would never become the Director, but no one who did would want to be without him.

"Well, Matt?" said the Director, pointing to the leather chair.

"I read Andrews' latest report last night, Director, and I really think the time has come for us to brief the Secret Service."

"I will be doing so in about an hour," said the Director. "Don't worry. Have you decided how you'll deploy your men?"

"It depends where the maximum risk is, sir."

"All right, Matt, let's assume that the point of maximum risk is the Capitol itself, at 10:06, right on the steps – what then?"

"First, I would surround the area for about a quarter of a mile in every direction. I'd close down the Metro, stop all traffic, public and private, pull aside for interrogation anyone who has a past record of making threats, anyone who's on the Security Index. I'd get assistance from the Met to provide perimeter security. We'd want as many eyes and ears in the area as possible. We could get two to four helicopters from Andrews Air Force Base for close scanning. In the immediate vicinity of the President, I'd use the full Secret Service Presidential detail in tight security."

"Very good, Matt. How many men do you need for such an operation, and how long would it take them to be ready if I declared an emergency procedure now?"

The Assistant Director looked at his watch – just after 7:00. He considered the matter for a moment. "I need three hundred special agents briefed and fully operational in two hours."

"Right, go ahead," said the Director crisply. "Report to me as soon as they're ready but leave the final briefing to the last possible moment, and, Matt, I want no helicopters until 10:01. I don't want there to be a chance of a leak of any sort; it's our one hope of catching the assassin."

"Why don't you simply cancel the President's visit, sir? We're in enough deep water as it is, and it's not entirely your responsibility in the first place."

"If we pull out now, we only have to start all over again tomorrow," said the Director, "and I may never get another chance like this."

"Yes, sir."

"Don't let me down, Matt, because I am going to leave the ground operations entirely in your hands."

"Thank you, sir."

Rogers left the room. The Director knew his job would be done as competently as it could be by any professional law-enforcement officer in America.

"Mrs McGregor."

"Yes, sir?"

"Get me the head of the Secret Service at the White House."

"Yes, sir."

The Director glanced at his watch: 7:10. Andrews was due at 8:15. The phone rang.

"Mr Knight on the line, sir."

"Stuart, can you call me on my private line and be sure you're not overheard?

H. Stuart Knight knew Halt well enough to realise that he meant what he said. He called back immediately on his special scrambler.

"Stuart, I'd like to see you immediately, usual place, take about thirty minutes, no more. Top priority."

Damned inconvenient, thought Knight, with the President leaving for the Capitol in two hours, but Halt only made this request two or three times a year, and he knew that other matters must be put to one side for the moment. Only the President and the Attorney General took priority over Halt.

The Director of the FBI and the head of the Secret Service met at a line of cabs in front of Union Station ten minutes later. They didn't take the first cab in the line, but the seventh. They climbed in the back without speaking or acknowledging each other. Elliott drove the Max's Yellow Cab off to circle the Capitol. The Director talked and the head of the Secret Service listened.

Mark's alarm woke him at 6:45. He showered and shaved and thought about those transcripts he had left in the Senate, trying to convince himself that they would have thrown no light on whether it was Dexter or Harrison. He silently thanked Senator Stevenson for indirectly disposing of Senators Brooks, Byrd, and Thornton. He would thank anybody who could dispose of Senator Dexter. He was beginning to agree with the Director's reasoning – it all pointed to Dexter. His motive was particularly compelling, but . . . Mark looked at his watch; he was a little early. He sat on the edge of his bed; he scratched his leg which was itching; something must have bitten him during the night. He continued trying to figure out if there was anything he had missed.

The Chairman got out of bed at 7:20 and lit his first cigarette. He couldn't remember exactly when he had woken. At 6:10 he had phoned Tony, who was already up and waiting for his call. They weren't to meet that day unless the Chairman needed the car in an emergency. The next time they would speak to each other would be on the dot of 9:30 for a check-in to confirm they were all in position.

When he had completed the call, the Chairman dialled room service and ordered a large breakfast. What he was about to do that morning was not the sort of work to be tackled on an empty stomach. Matson was due to ring him any time after 7:30. Perhaps he was still asleep. After that effort last night, Matson deserved some rest. The Chairman smiled to himself. He went into the bathroom and turned on the shower; a feeble trickle of cold water emerged. Goddamn hotels. One hundred dollars a night and no hot water. He splashed around ineffectively and began to think about the next five hours, going over the plan again carefully to be sure he had not overlooked even the smallest detail. Tonight, Kane would be dead and he would have $2,000,000 in the Union Bank of Switzerland, Zurich, account number AZL–376921–B, a small reward from his grateful friends in the gun trade. And to think Uncle Sam wouldn't even get the tax.

The phone rang. Damn. He dripped across the floor, his heartbeat quickened. It was Matson.

Matson and the Chairman had driven back from Mark's apartment at 2:35 that morning, their task completed. Matson had overslept by thirty minutes. The damned hotel had forgotten his wake-up call; you couldn't trust anyone nowdays. As soon as he had woken, he phoned the Chairman and reported in.

Xan was safely in the top of the crane and ready – probably the only one of them who was still asleep.

The Chairman, although dripping, was pleased. He put the phone down and returned to the shower. Damn, still cold.

Matson masturbated. He always did when he was nervous and had time to kill.

Florentyna Kane did not wake until 7:35. She rolled over, trying to recall the dream she had just had, but none of it would come back to her, so she let her mind wander. Today, she would be going to the Capitol to plead her case for the Gun Control bill before a special session of the Senate and then on to have lunch with all the key supporters and opponents of the bill. Since the bill had been approved in committee, as she had been confident it would be, she had concentrated on her strategy for the final day of floor battle; at least the odds now seemed to be with her. She smiled at Edward, although he had his back to her. It had been a busy session, and she was looking forward to going to Camp David and spending more time with her family. Better get moving, more than half of America is already up, she thought, and I am still lying in bed . . . Still, that waking half of America had not had to dine the previous evening with the four-hundred-pound King of Tonga, who wasn't going to leave the White House until he was virtually thrown out. The President wasn't absolutely certain she could pinpoint Tonga on the map. The Pacific was after all a large ocean. She had left her Secretary of State, Abe Chayes, to do the talking; he at least knew exactly where Tonga was.

She stopped thinking about the overweight king and put her feet on the floor – or to be more exact, on the Presidential Seal. The damned thing was on everything except the toilet paper. She knew that when she appeared for breakfast in the dining-room across the hall, she would find the third edition of the *New York Times*, the third edition of the *Washington Post*, the first editions of the *Los Angeles Times* and the *Boston Globe*, all ready for her to read, with the pieces referring to her marked in red, plus a prepared digest of yesterday's news. How did they get it all completed before she was even dressed? Florentyna went to the bathroom and turned on the shower; the water pressure was just right. She began to consider what she could say finally to convince the waverers in the Senate that the Gun Control bill must become law. Her train of thought was interrupted by her efforts to reach the middle of her back with the soap. Presidents still do that for themselves, she thought.

*

Mark was due to be with the Director in twenty minutes. He checked his mail – just an envelope from American Express, which he left on the kitchen table unopened.

A yawning O'Malley was sitting in the Ford sedan a hundred yards away. He was relieved to be able to report that Mark had left the apartment building and was talking to the black garage attendant. Neither O'Malley nor Thompson had admitted to anybody that they had lost Mark for several hours the previous evening.

Mark walked around the side of the building and disappeared from the view of the man in the blue Ford. It didn't worry him. O'Malley had checked the location of the Mercedes an hour earlier; there was only one way out.

Mark noticed a red Fiat as he came around the corner of the building. Looks like Elizabeth's, he thought to himself, except for the damage to a bumper. He stared at it again and was taken by surprise to see Elizabeth sitting in it. He opened the door. If he were to be Ragani and she were Mata Hari, he was now past caring. He climbed in beside her. Neither of them spoke until they both spoke at once and laughed nervously. She tried again. Mark sat in silence.

"I've come to say I'm sorry about being so touchy last night. I should have at least given you a chance to explain. I really don't want you to sleep with any other senator's daughter," she said, trying to force a smile.

"I'm the one who should be sorry, Liz. Trust me, as they say in Hollywood. Whatever happens, let's meet this evening and then I'll try to explain everything. Don't ask me anything before then and promise that whatever happens you will see me tonight. If after that you never want to see me again I promise I'll leave quietly."

Elizabeth nodded her agreement. "But not as abruptly as you left once before, I hope."

Mark put his arm around her and kissed her quickly. "No more nasty cracks about that night. I've spent every night since looking forward to a second chance."

They both laughed. He started to get out.

"Why don't I drive you to work, Mark? It's on my way to the hospital and we won't have to bother with two cars this evening."

Mark hesitated. "Why not?"

He wondered if this were the final set-up.

As she drove around the corner, Simon waved them down. "Apartment Seven's car won't be back until late this morning, Mark. I'll have to park the Mercedes on the street for now but don't worry, I'll keep an eye on it." Simon looked at Elizabeth and grinned. "You won't be needing my sister after all, man."

Elizabeth pulled out and joined the traffic on 6th Street. A hundred yards away, O'Malley was chewing gum.

"Where shall we have dinner tonight?"

"Let's go back to that French restaurant and try the whole evening again. This time we'll complete the final act of the play."

I hope it begins, "This was the noblest Roman of them all. All the conspirators, save only he . . ." Mark thought.

"This time it's my treat," said Elizabeth.

Mark accepted, remembering his unopened bill from American Express. The lights turned red at the corner of G Street. They stopped and waited. Mark started scratching his leg again, it really felt quite painful.

The cab was still circling the Capitol but Halt was coming to the end of his briefing for H. Stuart Knight.

"We believe that the attempt will be made when the President gets out of her car at the Capitol. We'll take care of the Capitol itself if you can manage to get her into the building unharmed. I'll have my men cover the buildings and roofs of buildings and every elevated vantage point from which it would be possible to shoot."

"It would make our job a lot easier if the President didn't insist on walking up the steps. Ever since Carter took his little stroll up Pennsylvania Avenue in '77 . . ." His voice trailed off in exasperation. "By the way, Halt, why didn't you tell me about this earlier?"

"There's a strange quirk to it, Stuart. I still can't give you all the details, but don't worry, they're not relevant to the task of protecting the President."

"Okay. I'll buy that. But are you sure my men can't help at your end?"

"No, I'm happy as long as I know you're keeping a close watch on the President. It will give me the freedom I need to catch the bastards red-handed. They mustn't be allowed to get suspicious. I want to catch the killer while he still has the weapon in his hand."

"Shall I tell the President?" asked Knight.

"No, just inform her that it's a new security measure you are putting into practice from time to time."

"She's had so many of those she's bound to believe it," said Knight.

"Stick to the same route and timetable and I'll leave the finer points to you, Stuart. And I don't want any leaks. I'll see you after the President's lunch. We can bring each other up-to-date then. By the way, what's today's code name for the President?"

"Julius."

"Good God, I don't believe it."

"You are telling me everything I need to know, aren't you, Halt?"

"No, of course I'm not, Stuart. You know me, Machiavelli's younger brother."

The Director tapped Elliott on the shoulder and the cab slipped back into the seventh place in line. The two passengers got out and walked in opposite directions, Knight to catch the Metro to the White House, the Director a cab to the Bureau. Neither looked back.

Lucky Stuart Knight, thought the Director, he's gone through the last seven days without the information I have. Now the meeting was over, the Director's confidence in his own stratagem was renewed, and he was resolved that only he and Andrews would ever know the full story – unless they had conclusive proof on which to secure the Senator's conviction. He had to catch the conspirators alive, get them to testify against the Senator. The Director checked his watch with the clock on the Old Post Office Tower over the Washington Field Office. It was 7:58. Andrews would be due in two minutes. He was saluted as he went through the revolving doors of the Bureau. Mrs McGregor was standing outside his office, looking agitated.

"It's Channel Four, sir, asking for you urgently."

"Put them through," said the Director. He moved quickly into his office and picked up the extension.

"It's Special Agent O'Malley from the patrol car, sir."

"Yes, O'Malley?"

"Andrews has been killed, sir, and there must have been another person in the car."

The Director couldn't speak.

"Are you there, Director?" O'Malley waited. "I repeat are you there, Director?"

Finally the Director said, "Come in immediately." He put the phone down, and his great hands gripped the Queen Anne desk like a throat he wanted to strangle. The fingers then curled and clenched slowly into the palms of his hands until they made massive fists, the nails digging into the skin. Blood trickled slowly down on to the leather-work on the desk, leaving a dark stain. Halt Tyson sat alone for several minutes. Then he instructed Mrs McGregor to get the President at the White House. He was going to cancel the whole damned thing; he'd already gone too far. He sat silently waiting. The bastards had beaten him. They must know everything.

It took Special Agent O'Malley ten minutes to reach the Bureau, where he was ushered straight into the Director.

My God, he looks eighty, thought O'Malley.

The Director stared at him. "How did it happen?" he asked quietly.

"He was blown up in a car; we think someone else was with him."

"Why? How?"

"Must have been a bomb attached to the ignition. It blew up right there in front of us. Made an unholy mess."

"I don't give a fuck for the mess," began the Director on a slowly rising note, when the door opened.

Mark Andrews walked in. "Good morning, sir. I hope I'm not interrupting something. I thought you said 8:15."

Both men stared at him.

"You're dead."

"Excuse me, sir?"

"Well, who the hell," said Special Agent O'Malley, "was driving your Mercedes?"

Mark stared at him uncomprehending.

"My Mercedes?" he said quickly. "What are you talking about?"

"Your Mercedes has just been blown to smithereens. I saw it with my own eyes. My colleague down there is trying to put the pieces together; he's already reported finding the hand of a black man."

Mark steadied himself against the wall. "The bastards have killed Simon," he cried in anger. "There will be no need to call Grant Nanna to screw their balls off. I'll do it myself."

"Please explain yourself," said the Director.

Mark steadied himself again, turned around and faced them both. "I came in with Elizabeth Dexter this morning; she came by to see me. I came in with her," he repeated, not yet coherent.

"Simon moved my car because it was occupying a reserved daytime parking space and now the bastards have killed him."

"Sit down, Andrews. You too, O'Malley."

The telephone rang. "The President's Chief of Staff, sir. The President will be with you in about two minutes."

"Cancel it and apologise. Explain to Janet Brown that it was nothing important, just wanted to wish the President luck on the Gun Control bill today."

"Yes, sir."

"So they think you're dead, Andrews, and they have now played their last card. So we must hold ours back. You're going to remain dead – for a little while longer."

Mark and O'Malley looked at each other, both puzzled.

"O'Malley, you return to your car. You say nothing, even to your partner. You have not seen Andrews alive, do you understand?"

"Yes, sir."

"Get going."

"Mrs McGregor, get me the head of External Affairs."

"Yes, sir."

The Director looked at Mark. "I was beginning to miss you."

"Thank you, sir."

"Don't thank me, I'm just about to kill you again."

A knock on the door, and Bill Gunn came in. He was the epitome of the public relations man, better dressed than anyone else in the building, with the biggest smile and a mop of fair hair that he washed every two days. His face as he entered was unusually grim.

"Have you heard about the death of one of our young agents, sir?"

"Yes, Bill. Put out a statement immediately that an unnamed special agent was killed this morning and that you will brief the press fully at eleven o'clock."

"They'll be hounding me long before then, sir."

"Let them hound you," said the Director sharply.

"Yes, sir."

"At eleven, you will put out another statement saying the agent is alive . . ."

Bill Gunn's face registered surprise.

". . . and that a mistake has been made, and the man who died was a young garage attendant who had no connection with the FBI."

"But sir, our agent?"

"No doubt you would like to meet the agent who is supposed to be dead. Bill Gunn – this is Special Agent Andrews. Now not a word, Bill. This man is dead for the

226

next three hours and if I find a leak, you can find a new job."

Bill Gun looked convincingly anxious. "Yes, sir."

"When you've written the press statement, call me and read it over to me."

"Yes, sir."

Bill Gunn left, dazed. He was a gentle, easy-going man and this was way above his head, but he like so many others trusted the Director.

The Director was becoming very aware just how many men did trust him and how much he was carrying on his own shoulders. He looked back at Mark, who had not recovered from the realisation that Simon had died instead of him – the second man to do so in eight days.

"Right, Mark, we have under two hours left, so we will mourn the dead later. Have you anything to add to yesterday's report?"

"Yes, sir. It's good to be alive."

"If you get past eleven o'clock, young man, I think you have a good chance for a long and healthy life, but we still don't know if it's Dexter or Harrison. You know I think it's Dexter." The Director looked at his watch again: 8:29 – ninety-seven minutes left. "Any new ideas?"

"Well, sir, Elizabeth Dexter certainly can't be involved, she saved my life by bringing me in this morning. If she wanted me dead, that sure was a funny way of going about it."

"I'll accept that," said the Director, "but it doesn't clear her father."

"Surely he wouldn't kill a man he thought might marry his daughter," said Mark.

"You're sentimental, Andrews. A man who plans to assassinate a President doesn't worry about his daughter's boy friends."

The phone rang. It was Bill Gunn from Public Relations.

"Right, read it over." The Director listened carefully.

"Good. Issue it immediately to radio, television, and the papers, and release the second statement at eleven o'clock, no earlier. Thank you, Bill." The Director put the phone down.

"Congratulations, Mark, you're the only dead man alive and, like Mark Twain, you will be able to read your own obituary. Now, to bring you quickly up-to-date. I have three hundred field agents already out covering the Capitol and the area immediately surrounding it. The whole place will be sealed off the moment the Presidential car arrives."

"You're letting her go to the Capitol?" said Mark in astonishment.

"Listen carefully, Mark. I'll have a minute-by-minute briefing on where the two senators are from 9:00 am on and six men are tailing both of them. At 9:15, we're going into the street ourselves. When it happens, we're going to be there. If I'm going to carry the ultimate responsibility, I may as well carry it in person."

"Yes, sir."

The intercom buzzed.

"It's Mr Sommerton. He wants to see you urgently, sir." The Director looked at his watch: 8:45. On the minute, as promised.

Daniel Sommerton rushed in, looking rather pleased with himself. He came straight to the point. "One of the prints has come up on the criminal file, it's a thumb, his name is Matson – Ralph Matson."

Somerton produced a photograph of Matson, an Identikit picture, and an enlarged thumbprint.

"And here's the part you're not going to like, sir. He's an ex-FBI agent." He passed Matson's card over for the Director to study. Mark looked at the photo. It was the Greek Orthodox priest, big nose, heavy chin.

"Something professional about him," said the Director and Mark simultaneously.

"Well done, Sommerton, make three hundred copies of the picture immediately and get them to the Assistant

Director in charge of the Investigation Division – and that means immediately."

"Yes, sir." The fingerprint expert scurried away, pleased with himself. They wanted his thumb.

"Mrs McGregor, get me Mr Rogers."

The Assistant Director was on the line; the Director briefed him.

"Shall I arrest him on sight?"

"No, Matt. Once you've spotted him, watch him and keep your boys well out of sight. He could still call everything off if he got suspicious. Keep me briefed all the time. Move in on him at 10:06. I'll let you know if anything changes."

"Yes, sir. Have you briefed the Secret Service?"

"Yes, I have." He slammed the phone down.

The Director looked at his watch: 9:05. He pressed a button and Elliott came in. "Where are the two senators?"

"Harrison's still in his Alexandria town house, Dexter has left Kensington and is heading towards the Capitol, sir."

"You stay here in this office, Elliott, and keep in radio contact with me and the Assistant Director on the street. Never leave this room. Understood?"

"Yes, sir."

"I'll be using my walkie-talkie on Channel Four. Let's go, Andrews." They left the anonymous man.

"If anybody calls me, Mrs McGregor, put them through to Special Agent Elliott in my office. He will know where to contact me."

"Yes, sir."


A few moments later, the Director and Mark were on the street walking up Pennsylvania Avenue towards the Capitol. Mark put on his dark glasses and pulled his collar up. They passed several agents on the way. None of them acknowledged the Director. On the corner of Pennsylvania Avenue and 9th Street, they passed the Chairman, who was lighting a cigarette and checking his watch: 9:30. He moved to the edge of the sidewalk, leaving a pile of cigarette butts behind him. The Director glanced at the cigarette butts: litter bug, ought to be fined a hundred dollars. They hurried on.

"Come in, Tony. Come in, Tony."

"Tony, boss. The Buick's ready. I've just heard it announced on the car radio that pretty boy Andrews bought it."

The Chairman smiled.

"Come in, Xan."

"Ready, await your signal."

"Come in, Matson."

"Everything's set, boss. There's a hell of a lot of agents around."

"Don't sweat, there's always a lot of Secret Service men around when the President is travelling. Don't call again unless there's a real problem. All three keep your lines open. When I next call, I will only activate the vibrators on the side of your watches. Then you have three minutes forty-five seconds, because Kane will be passing me. Understood?"

"Yes."

"Yes."

"Yes."

The Chairman broke the circuit and lit another cigarette: 9:40.

The Director spotted Matthew Rogers in a special squad car and went quickly over to him. "Everything under control, Matt?"

"Yes, sir. If anybody tries anything, no one will be able to move for half a mile."

"Good; what time do you have?"

"Nine-forty-five."

"Right, you control it from here. I'm going to the Capitol."

Halt and Mark left the Assistant Director and walked on.

"Elliott calling the Director."

"Come in, Elliott."

"They have spotted Matson at the junction of Maryland Avenue and 1st Street, other side of the Garfield statue, south-west corner of the Capitol grounds, near the west front renovation site."

"Good. Observe and post fifty men around the area, don't move in yet, brief Mr Rogers and tell him to keep his men out of Matson's field of vision."

"Yes, sir."

"What the hell is he doing on that side of the Capitol?" said Mark softly. "You couldn't shoot anyone on the Capitol steps from the north-west side unless you were in a chopper."

"I agree, it beats me," said the Director.

They reached the police cordon surrounding the Capitol. The Director showed his credentials to get himself and Andrews through. The young Capitol policeman double-checked them; he couldn't believe it; he was looking at the real live object. Yes, it was the Director of the FBI. H. A. L. Tyson himself.

"Sorry, sir. Please come through."

"Elliott to the Director."

"Yes, Elliott?"

"Head of the Secret Service for you, sir."

"Stuart."

"The advance car is leaving the front gate now. Julius will leave in five minutes."

"Thank you, Stuart. Keep your end up and surprise me.'

"Don't worry, Halt. We will."


Five minutes later, the Presidential car left the South Entrance and turned left on to E Street. The advance car passed the Chairman on the corner of Pennsylvania Avenue and 9th. He smiled, lit another cigarette and waited. Five minutes later, a large Lincoln, flags flying on both front fenders, the Presidential Seal on the doors, passed by the Chairman. Through the misty grey windows, he could see three figures in the back. A limousine known as the "gun car" and occupied by Secret Service agents and the President's personal physician, followed the President's car. The Chairman pressed a button on his watch. The vibrator began to tickle his wrist. After ten seconds, he stopped it, walked one block north and hailed a taxi.

"National Airport," he said to the cab driver, fingering the ticket in his inside pocket.

The vibrator on Matson's watch was touching his skin. After ten seconds, it stopped. Matson walked to the side of the construction site, bent down and tied his shoelace.

Xan started to take off the tape. He was glad to be moving; he had been bent double all night. First he screwed the barrel into the sight finder.

"Assistant Director to Director. Matson is approaching the construction site. Now he has stopped to tie his shoe. No one on the construction site but I'm asking a helicopter to check it out. There's a huge crane in the middle of the site which looks deserted."

"Good. Stay put until the last minute. I'll give you the timing the moment the President's car arrives. You must catch them red-handed. Alert all agents on the roof of the Capitol."

The Director turned to Mark, more relaxed. "I think it's going to be all right."

Mark's eyes were on the steps of the Capitol. "Have you noticed, sir, both Senator Dexter and Senator Harrison are in the welcoming party for the President?"

"Yes," said the Director. "The car is due to arrive in two minutes; we'll catch the others even if we can't figure out which Senator it is. We'll make them talk in due course. Wait a minute – that's odd."

The Director's finger was running down a couple of closely typed sheets he held in his hand.

"Yes, that's what I thought. The President's detailed

schedule shows that Dexter will be there for the special address to Congress but isn't attending the luncheon with the President. Very strange: I'm sure all the key leaders of the opposition were invited to lunch. Why won't Dexter be present?"

"Nothing strange about that, sir. He always has lunch with his daughter on Thursdays. Good God! 'I always have lunch with my father on Thursdays.'"

"Yes, Mark, I heard you the first time."

"No, sir, 'I always have lunch with my father on Thursdays.'"

"Mark, the car will be here in one minute."

"It's Harrison, sir. It's Harrison. I'm a fool – Thursday, 24 February, in Georgetown. I always thought of it as 24 February, not as Thursday. Dexter was having lunch with Elizabeth. 'I always have lunch with my father on Thursdays.' That's why he was seen in Georgetown that day, must be. They never miss it."

"Are you sure? Can you be certain? There's a hell of a lot riding on it."

"It's Harrison, sir. It can't be Dexter. I should have realised it on the first day. Christ, I'm stupid."

"Right, Mark. Up those steps quickly, watch Harrison's every move and be prepared to arrest him whatever the consequences."

"Yes, sir."

"Rogers."

The Assistant Director came in. "Sir?"

"The car is pulling up. Arrest Matson immediately; check the roof of the Capitol." The Director stared up into the sky. "Oh my God, it's not a helicopter, it's that damn crane. It has to be the crane."

Xan nestled the butt of the yellow rifle into his shoulder and watched the President's car. He had attached a feather to a piece of thread on the end of the gun barrel, a trick he had picked up when training for the Olympics – no wind. The hours of waiting were coming to an end.

Senator Harrison was standing there on the Capitol steps. Through the thirty-power Redfield scope he could even see the beads of sweat standing out on the man's forehead.

The President's car drew up on the north side of the Capitol. All was going according to plan. Xan levelled the telescopic sight on the car door and waited for Kane. Two Secret Service men climbed out, scanned the crowd, and waited for the third. Nothing happened. Xan put the sight on the Senator, who looked anxious and bemused. Back at the car, still no Kane. Where the hell was she, what was going on? He checked the feather; still no wind. He moved his sight back on the President's car. Good God, the crane was moving and Kane wasn't in the car. Matson had been right all along, they knew everything. Xan knew exactly what had to be done in these circumstances. Only one man could ditch them and he wouldn't hesitate to do it. Xan moved his sight up the Capitol steps. One and one-half inches above the forehead. A moment's hesitation before he squeezed the trigger once . . . twice, but the second time he didn't have a clear shot, and a fraction of a second later he could no longer see the Capitol steps. He looked down from the moving crane. He was surrounded by fifty men in dark suits, fifty guns were pointing up at him.

Mark was about a yard away from Senator Harrison when he heard him cry out and fall. Mark jumped on top of the Senator and the second bullet grazed his shoulder. There was a panic among the other senators and officials on the top steps. The welcoming party scurried inside. Thirty FBI men moved in quickly. The Director was the only man who remained on the Capitol steps, steady and motionless, staring up at the crane. They hadn't nicknamed him Halt by mistake.

"May I ask where I'm going, Stuart?"

"Certainly, Madam President. To the Capitol."

"But this isn't the normal route to the Capitol."

"No, Madam. We're going down Constitution Avenue

234

to the Russell Building. We hear there has been a little trouble at the Capitol. A demonstration of some kind. The National Rifle Association."

"So I'm avoiding it, am I? Like a coward, Stuart."

"No, Madam, I'm slipping you through the basement. Just as a safety precaution and for your own convenience."

"That means I'll have to go on that damned subway. Even when I was a senator, I preferred to walk outside."

"We've cleared the way for you, Madam. You'll still be there bang on time."

The President grumbled as she looked out of the window and saw an ambulance race in the opposite direction.

Senator Harrison died before he reached the hospital and Mark had his wound patched up by a house doctor. Mark checked his watch and laughed. It was 11:04 – he was going to live.

"Phone for you, Mr Andrews. The Director of the FBI."

"Sir?"

"Mark, I hear you're fine. Good. I am sorry to say the Senate went into recess out of respect for Senator Harrison. The President is shocked but feels this is precisely the moment to emphasise the significance of gun control, so we're all now going into lunch early. Sorry you can't join us. And we caught three of them – Matson, a Vietnamese sharpshooter, and a petty crook called Tony Loraido. There may still be more, I'll let you know later. Thank you, Mark."

The telephone clicked before Mark could offer any opinion.

# Thursday evening, 10 March

## 7:00 pm

Mark arrived in Georgetown at seven that evening. He had gone to Simon's wake and paid his respects to the bewildered parents that afternoon. They had five other children, but that never helped. Their grief made Mark long for the warmth of the living.

Elizabeth was wearing the red silk shirt and black skirt in which he had first seen her. She greeted him with a cascade of words.

"I don't understand what's been going on. My father called earlier and told me you tried to save Senator Harrison's life. What were you doing there anyway? My father is very upset about the shooting. Why have you been following him around? Was he in any danger?"

Mark looked at her squarely. "No, he wasn't involved in any way so let's try and start over again."

Still she didn't understand.

When they arrived at the Rive Gauche, the maître d' welcomed them with open arms.

"Good evening, Mr Andrews, how nice to see you again. I don't remember your booking a table."

"No, it's in my name. Dr Dexter," said Elizabeth.

"Oh, yes, Doctor, of course. Will you come this way?"

They had baked clams, and, at last, a steak with no fancy trimmings and two bottles of wine.

Mark sang most of the way home. When they arrived,

he took her firmly by the hand and led her into the darkened living-room.

"I'm going to seduce you. No coffee, no brandy, no music, just straightforward seduction."

"I should be so lucky."

They fell on the couch.

"You're too drunk," Elizabeth added.

"Wait and see." He kissed her fully on the lips for a long time and started to unbutton her shirt.

"Are you sure you wouldn't like some coffee?" she asked.

"Yes, quite sure," he said as he pulled the shirt slowly free from her skirt and felt her back, his other hand moving on to her leg.

"What about some music?" she said lightly. "Something special." Elizabeth touched the start button on the hi-fi. It was Sinatra again, but this time it was the right song:

> Is it an earthquake or simply a shock
> Is it the real turtle soup or merely the mock,
> Is it a cocktail, this feeling of joy,
> Or is what I feel – the real – McCoy?
>
> Is it for all time or simply a lark,
> Is it Granada I see or only Asbury Park,
> Is it a fancy not worth thinking of,
> Or is it at . . . long . . . last . . . love?

She settled back into Mark's arms.

He unzipped her skirt. Her legs were slender and beautiful in the dim light. He caressed her gently.

"Are you going to tell me the truth about today, Mark?"

"Afterwards, darling."

"When you've had your way with me," she said.

He slipped his shirt off. Elizabeth stared at the bandage on his shoulder.

"Is that where you were wounded in the line of duty?"

"No, that's where my last lover bit me."

"She must have had more time than I did."

They moved closer together.

He took the phone off the hook – not tonight, Julius.

"I can't get through, sir," Elliott said, "just a continual busy signal."

"Try again, try again. I'm sure he's there."

"Shall I go through the operator?"

"Yes, yes," said the Director testily.

The Director waited, tapping his fingers on the Queen Anne desk, staring at the red stain and wondering how it had got there.

"The operator says the phone is off the hook, sir. Shall I ask her to bleep him; that'll certainly get his attention."

"No, Elliott, just leave it and go home. I'll have to call him in the morning."

"Yes, sir. Good night, sir."

He'll have to go – back to Idaho or wherever he came from, thought the Director, as he switched off the lights and made his own way home.

# Friday morning, 11 March

## 7:00 am

Mark woke first; perhaps because he was in a strange bed. He turned over and looked at Elizabeth. She never wore make-up and was just as beautiful in the morning as she was on the other side of a dinner table. Her dark hair curled in towards the nape of her neck and he stroked the soft strands gently. She stirred, rolled over, and kissed him.

"Go and brush your teeth."

"What a romantic way to start the day," he said.

"I'll be awake by the time you get back." She groaned a little and stretched.

Mark picked up the Pepsodent – that was one thing that would have to change, he preferred Macleans – and tried to figure out which part of the bathroom he was going to be able to fit his things into. When he returned, he noticed the phone was still off the hook. He looked at his watch: 7:05. He climbed back into bed. Elizabeth slipped out.

"Only be a minute," she said.

It was never like this in the movies, thought Mark.

She returned and lay down beside him. After a moment she said, "Your chin is hurting my face. You're not as clean-shaven as you were the first time."

"I shaved very carefully that first evening," said Mark. "Funny, I was never so sure of anything. Didn't happen quite the way I intended."

"What did you intend?"

"It was never like this in the movies." This time he stated the sentiments clearly. "Do you know what the Frenchman said when accused of raping a dead woman?"

"No."

"I didn't realise she was dead; I thought she was English."

After she had proved she wasn't English Elizabeth asked Mark what he would like for breakfast.

After Mark had told her, he disappeared into the shower.

Mark turned on the shower, getting the temperature just right.

"Disappointing, I thought we would take a bath together," said Elizabeth.

"I never bathe with the domestic staff. Just give me a call when breakfast is ready," Mark replied from under the shower and started to sing "At Long Last Love" in several different keys.

A slim arm appeared through the falling water and turned off the hot water tap. The singing stopped abruptly. Elizabeth was nowhere to be seen.

Mark dressed quickly and put the phone back on the hook. It rang almost immediately. Elizabeth appeared in a brief slip.

Mark wanted to go back to bed.

She picked up the phone. "Good morning. Yes, he's here. It's for you. A jealous lover, I shouldn't wonder."

She put on a dress and returned to the kitchen.

"Mark Andrews."

"Good morning, Mark."

"Oh, good morning, sir."

"I've been trying to get you since eight o'clock last night."

"Oh, really, sir. I thought I was on vacation. If you look in the official book in the WFO, I think you'll find I've signed out."

"Yes, Mark, but you are going to have to interrupt that vacation because the President wants to see you."

"The President, sir?"

"Of the United States."

"Why would she want to see me, sir."

"Yesterday I killed you, but today I've made you a hero and she wants to congratulate you personally on trying to save Senator Harrison's life."

"What?"

"You'd better read the morning papers. Say nothing for now; I'll explain my actions later."

"Where do I go, what time, sir?"

"You'll be told." The line clicked.

Mark replaced the phone and thought about the conversation. He was just about to call Elizabeth to ask if the morning paper had come when the phone rang again.

"Answer it will you, Mark darling. Now that the lovers have found your whereabouts, it's bound to be for you."

Mark picked it up.

"Mr Andrews?"

"Speaking."

"Hold the line one moment, please. The President will be with you in one moment."

"Good morning. Florentyna Kane. I just wanted to know if you could find time to drop into the White House this morning at about ten o'clock. I'd like to meet you and have a chat."

"I'd be honoured, Madam."

"Then I'll look forward to it, Mr Andrews, and the chance to meet you and congratulate you personally. If you come to the West Entrance, Janet Brown will be there to meet you."

"Thank you, Madam."

One of those legendary phone calls that the press so often wrote about. The Director had only been checking where he was. Had the President been trying to reach him since eight last night?

"Who was it, darling?"

"The President of the United States."

"Tell her you'll call back; she's always on the line, usually calls collect."

"No, I'm serious."

"Yes, of course you are."

"She wants to see me."

"Yes, darling, your place or hers?"

Mark went into the kitchen and attacked some Wheaties. Elizabeth came in brandishing the *Post*.

"Look," she said. "It's official. You're not a villain, you're a hero."

The headline read: SENATOR HARRISON KILLED ON STEPS OF CAPITOL.

"It was the President, wasn't it?" she said.

"Yes, it was."

"Why didn't you tell me?"

"I did, but you didn't choose to listen."

"I'm sorry," said Elizabeth.

"I love you."

"I love you too, but let's not go through this every week."

She continued to read the paper. Mark munched his Wheaties.

"Why would someone want to kill Senator Harrison, Mark?"

"I don't know. What does the *Post* say?"

"They haven't figured out a reason yet; they say he was known to have many enemies both here and abroad." She began to read from the paper:

"Senator Robert Harrison (D-South Carolina) was shot by an assassin on the steps of the Capitol yesterday morning at 10:06.

"The assassination took place only moments before President Kane was due to arrive for her final assault on behalf of the Gun Control bill, which had been scheduled for a vote in the Senate yesterday. Because they had been warned of a demonstration on the steps of the Capitol, the Secret Service diverted the President's car to the Russell Senate Office Building.

"The bullet lodged in Senator Harrison's brain and he was pronounced dead on arrival at Woodrow Wilson Medical Center. A second bullet grazed the shoulder of FBI Agent Mark Andrews, 28, who threw himself on the Senator in an effort to save his life. Andrews was treated at the same hospital and later released.

"There was no immediate explanation of the fact that a second presidential motorcade did arrive at the Capitol steps a few moments before the assassination, without the President.

"Vice President Bradley ordered an immediate recess of the Senate out of respect for Senator Harrison. The House then voted unanimously to extend the recess for seven days.

"The President, who arrived at the Capitol via the congressional subway from the Russell Building, first learned the news of Harrison's assassination when she reached the Senate. Visibly shaken, she announced that the luncheon to discuss gun control would continue as planned but asked the assembled Senators to observe a minute of silence in honour of their dead colleague.

"The President went on to say, 'I know we are all shocked and saddened by the tragic and horrifying event which has just occurred. This senseless killing of a good and decent man must, however, only strengthen our determination to work together in making our country safe from the easy access of arms.'

"The President plans to address the nation at nine o'clock tonight."

"So now you know everything, Liz."

"I know nothing," she replied.

"I didn't know very much of that myself," Mark admitted.

"Living with you is going to be difficult."

"Who said I was going to live with you?"

"I took it for granted from the way you're eating my eggs."

At the Fontainebleau Hotel a man was sitting by the side of the swimming pool reading the *Miami Herald* and drinking coffee. At least Senator Harrison could cause no more trouble which made him feel a little safer. Xan had kept his part of the bargain.

He sipped the coffee, a little hot, it didn't matter, he was in no hurry. He had already given new orders; he couldn't afford any further risks. Xan would be dead by the evening; that had been arranged. Matson and Tony would be freed for lack of evidence, so his lawyer, who had never let him down yet, had assured him, and he would not be visiting Washington for a while. He relaxed and settled back in his beach chair to let the Miami sun warm him. He lit another cigarette.

At 9:45, the Director was met at the White House by Janet Brown, the President's Chief of Staff. They waited and chatted. The Director briefed her on Special Agent Andrews' background. Brown made careful notes.

Mark arrived just before 10:00. He had only just managed to get home and change into a new suit.

"Good morning, Director," he said nonchalantly.

"Good morning, Mark. Glad you could make it." Slightly quizzical but not disapproving. "This is the President's Chief of Staff, Janet Brown."

"Good morning, ma'am," said Mark.

Janet Brown took over. "Will you be kind enough to come through to my office, where we can wait. The President will be videotaping her address to the nation for this evening's television broadcast so that she can fly to Camp David at 11:15. I imagine you and the Director will have about fifteen minutes with her."

Janet Brown took them to her office, a large room in

the West Wing with a fine view of the Rose Garden through a bow window.

"I'll get us some coffee," she said.

"That'll be a change," murmured Mark.

"I'm sorry?" said Janet Brown.

"Nothing."

The Director and Mark settled down in comfortable chairs where they could watch a large liquid-crystal monitor screen on one of the walls, already alive with comings and goings in the Oval Office.

The President's forehead was being powdered in preparation for her speech and the cameramen were wheeling around her. Janet Brown was on the phone.

"CBS and NBC can roll, Janet, but ABC is still fixing things up with their OB unit," said an agitated female voice.

Janet Brown got the producer of ABC on the other line.

"Get a move on, Harry, the President doesn't have all day."

"Janet."

Florentyna Kane was on the middle of the screen.

She looked up. "Yes, Madam President?"

"Where's ABC?"

"I'm just chasing them, Madam President."

"Chasing them? They've had four hours' warning. They couldn't get a camera to the Second Coming."

"No, ma'am. They're on their way now."

Harry Nathan, ABC's producer, appeared on the screen. "We're all set now, Janet. Ready to record in five minutes."

"Fine," said Florentyna Kane and looked at her watch. It was 10:11. The digits changed – and were replaced by the rate of her heartbeat – 72; normal, she thought. They disappeared again, to be replaced by her blood pressure, 140/90; a little high; she'd get it checked by her doctor this weekend. The digits were replaced by the Dow-Jones index, showing an early fall of 1.5 to 1,409. This disappeared and the watch showed 10:12. The President rehearsed the opening line of her speech for the last time. She'd gone over the final draft with Edward that morning, and she was satisfied with it.

"Mark."

"Sir?"

"I want you to report back to Grant Nanna at the WFO this afternoon."

"Yes, sir."

"Then I want you to take a vacation. I mean a real vacation, some time in May. Mr Elliott is leaving me at the end of May to take up the post of Special Agent in Charge of the Columbus Field Office. I'm going to offer you his job, and enlarge it to your being my personal assistant."

Mark was stunned. "Thank you very much, sir. I would be delighted." Bang goes the five-year plan.

"You said something, Mark?"

"No, sir."

"In private, Mark, you must stop calling me 'sir', if we're going to work together all the time; it's more than I can stand. You can call me Halt or Horatio – I don't mind which."

Mark couldn't help laughing.

"You find my name amusing, Mark?"

"No, sir. But I just made $3,516."

"Testing: one, two, three. Loud and clear. Could you give us a voice test, please, Madam President?" asked the floor producer, now less agitated. "What did you have for breakfast?"

"Toast and coffee," said the President resonantly.

"Thank you, Madam. That's fine. Ready to roll."

All the cameras were focused on the President, who sat behind her desk, sombre and serious.

"When you're ready, Madam President."

The President looked into the lens of Camera One.

"My fellow Americans, I speak to you tonight from the Oval Office in the wake of the bloody assassination of Senator Harrison on the steps of the Capitol. Robert Everard Harrison was my friend and colleague, and I know we will all feel his loss greatly. Our sympathy goes out to his family in their distress. This evil deed only strengthens my determination to press for legislation early in the new session strictly limiting the sale and the unauthorised ownership of guns. I will do this in memory of Senator Robert Harrison, so that we may feel he did not die in vain."

The Director looked at Mark; neither of them spoke. The President continued, repeating her belief in the importance of gun control and why the measure deserved the full support of the American people.

"And so I leave you, my fellow citizens, thanking God that America can still produce men who are willing to risk their own lives for public service. Thank you and good night."

The camera panned to the Presidential Seal. Then the Outside Broadcast units took over and switched to a picture of the White House with the flag at half-mast.

"It's a wrap, Harry," said the female floor producer.

"Let's do a re-run and see what it looks like."

The President in the Oval Office, and the Director and Mark in Janet Brown's room watched the re-run. It was good. The Gun Control bill will sail through, thought Mark.

The chief usher arrived at Janet Brown's door. He addressed the Director.

"The President wonders if you and Mr Andrews would be kind enough to join her in the Oval Office."

Both men rose from their chairs and followed in silence down the long marble corridor of the West Wing, passing pictures of former presidents, intermingled with oil paintings commemorating famous incidents in American history. They passed the bronze bust of Lincoln. When they reached the East Wing, they stopped at the massive white semi-circular doors of the Oval Office, dominated by the great Presidential Seal. A Secret Service man was sitting behind a desk in the hallway. He looked up at the chief usher, neither spoke. Mark watched the Secret Service agent's hand go under the desk, and he heard a click. The Seal split as the doors opened. The usher remained in the entrance.

Someone was unclipping a tiny microphone from under the President's collar, and the remnants of make-up were being removed by an attentive young woman. The television cameras had already gone. The usher announced, "The Director of the Federal Bureau of Investigation, Mr H. A. L. Tyson, and Special Agent Mark Andrews, Madam President."

The President rose from her seat at the far end of the room and waited to greet them. They walked towards her slowly.

"Sir," said Mark under his breath.

"Yes, Mark?"

"Shall we tell the President?"

If you have enjoyed SHALL WE TELL THE PRESIDENT? you will want to read all of Jeffrey Archer's bestselling novels, available from Coronet Books. Overleaf, to whet your appetite, are the opening pages of THE PRODIGAL DAUGHTER.

# THE
# PRODIGAL
# DAUGHTER

# Jeffrey Archer

# Prologue

"President of the United States," she replied.

"I can think of more rewarding ways of bankrupting myself," said her father, as he removed the half-moon spectacles from the end of his nose and peered at his daughter over the top of his newspaper.

"Don't be frivolous, Papa. President Roosevelt proved to us that there can be no greater calling than public service."

"The only thing Roosevelt proved . . ." began her father. Then he stopped and returned to his paper, realising that his daughter would consider the remark flippant.

The girl continued as if she were only too aware of what was going through her father's mind. "I realise it would be pointless for me to pursue such an ambition without your support. My sex will be enough of a liability without adding the disadvantage of a Polish background."

The newspaper barrier between father and daughter was abruptly removed. "Don't ever speak disloyally of the Poles," he said. "History has proved us to be an honourable race who never go back on our word. My father was a baron . . ."

"Yes, I know, so was my grandfather, but he's not around now to help me become President."

"More's the pity," he said, sighing, "as he would undoubtedly have made a great leader of our people."

"Then why shouldn't his granddaughter?"

"No reason at all," he said, as he stared into the steel grey eyes of his only child.

"Well then, Papa, will you help me? I can't hope to succeed without your financial backing."

Her father hesitated before replying, placing the glasses back on the end of his nose and slowly folding his copy of the Chicago *Tribune*.

"I'll make a deal with you, my dear; after all that's what politics is about. If the result of the New Hampshire Primary turns out to be satisfactory, I'll back you to the hilt. If not, you must drop the whole idea."

"What's your definition of satisfactory?" came back the immediate reply.

Again the man hesitated, weighing his words. "If you win the Primary or capture over thirty per cent of the vote, I'll go all the way to the convention floor with you, even if it means I end up destitute."

The girl relaxed for the first time during the conversation. "Thank you, Papa. I couldn't have asked for more."

"No, you certainly couldn't," he replied. "Now can I get back to finding out just how the Cubs could possibly have lost the seventh game of the series to the Tigers?"

"They were undoubtedly the weaker team, as the 9–3 score indicates."

"Young lady, you may imagine you know a thing or two about politics but I can assure you that you know absolutely nothing about baseball," the man said, as his wife entered the room. He turned his heavy frame towards her. "Our daughter wants to run for President of the United States. What do you think of that?"

The girl looked up at her eagerly, waiting for a reply.

"I'll tell you what I think," said the mother. "I think it's well past her bedtime and I blame you for keeping her up so late."

'Sir!' Porter grabbed Galloway's arm, holding him back.

Galloway got himself back under control. Pressing his hands flat against the table top, he said, in a much quieter voice, 'How did you know that Jess Ashcroft was going to go missing? We've found her car, up by the woods. Do you have an accomplice? Is it the red-headed girl? You've been seen in the company of a red-headed girl, so was Jess. Is she your accomplice? Or is she another victim?'

The young man looked round. He raised one finger, like he was about to issue a ticking-off. 'You,' he said, 'are a very noisy man. Now listen!'

'I'm trying to talk to you!'

'And I'm trying to listen! Shush!'

'But—'

'Lips! Sealed! Now!'

'Sir,' Porter said quietly, 'it can't do any [m.']

[th]e three of them stood and listened, but [Ga]lloway could hear was the steady pitter-[patter] of rain against the window. He felt like ['There's nothing,' he said, impatiently. [nothin]g at all.'

[c]an't hear it?' The young man frowned [press]ed his ear back against the window. 'I

light responded to her touch, as it had to Rory's palm in the hold earlier, thickening around her fingertip as she drew it along. 'I feel like I'm still in the woods. In October. But the air's stale. I can tell we're not really outside.'

'A ship like this would have to be tightly sealed if it was going to be able to move about in space,' Rory said.

'I know that,' Emily said. 'Like something in a story by Mr Wells. Me and Sam used to read him to each other.'

'Sam?' Rory looked around, bewildered. 'Who's Sam? Is there someone else here? Why haven't you mentioned him before? Emily, you've got to tell me everything, you don't know what's important!'

'Oh, shut up,' said Emily miserably. 'Sam? Where do you think he is? Sam's dead.'

'Dead?' Desperately, Rory searched through his memories, but he only found empty spaces where this knowledge should have been. Could he forget someone's death? What else had he forgotten? Who else had he forgotten? 'When? What happened?'

'More than a year ago, you fool! In the War. We should have been married by now. But Sammy's dead and I've got myself lost in the woods...' Emily stopped walking. She turned can't be the only one who can hear it…'

Porter, unexpectedly, said, 'I can.'

The young man swung round to face her. He stared at her as if noticing her properly for the first time. 'Yes! *You*! You can hear it!'

He was becoming extremely excited. Carefully, Galloway put himself between the suspect and Porter.

'You've lived here your whole life, haven't you?' the young man said. 'Not him. Not with that accent, as Pond-like as Pond herself. But *you*,' he pointed both his forefingers at Porter. 'Oh I could kiss you!' He pulled back. 'I won't, though, that would be weird… But you can hear it too! I'm not hearing things! Or, rather, I *am* hearing things, but not in the way that leads to awkward conversations, more awkward than usual… You! Yes! You've heard it your whole life, haven't you? And I *missed* it!'

He swung back to face the window. He banged his forehead against it and the blind came crashing down on top of his head. Now he had to struggle to disentangle himself, talking all the while.

'Oh, there's too much noise in this day and age! With your clocks and your 24-hour rolling news and your non-stop reality shows and your CB radio transmissions…'

He managed to get out from under the blind, which slumped back glumly into its former diagonal position.

Porter and Galloway exchanged a look. *CB radio…?*

'All that blathering and chattering and texting and phoning in – no wonder I could hardly hear anything! But it's there, isn't it? Oh yes, it's there. The propulsion unit, the engine, the nice hot cup of tea. Not dead. Not dead at all. Still running. All I had to do was *listen*!'

'You've stopped making sense,' said Porter. 'What's not dead? What's still running?'

As she repeated his words, the young man stopped still and stared at her as if a terrible realisation had struck him. The effect was rather like lightning hitting a gangly and over-excited telegraph pole.

'Oh,' he said, 'but if it's still running, then that changes things. Because it couldn't run indefinitely. Not for thousands of years, anyway. It would need maintenance… And maintenance means someone… someone's there… I've let them go off with those ridiculous triangular things, and the ship hasn't been abandoned at all! There's somebody there!'

'You mean in Swallow Woods?' said Porter. 'Who?' she urged. 'Who's there?'

'Well, who else would it be? The pilot, of course. The ship hasn't been abandoned! The pilot's still here!'

# Chapter
# 9

People. Holding her down, stopping her getting away. Vicky struggled, but their arms were around her, unyielding, like a nightmare tangle of tree branches pressing, scratching, trapping her. She looked round desperately for a place to hide, but the woods were wintry and offered no cover. She struggled, futilely, and then realised that her captors were talking to her, shushing her, trying to calm her, saying her name.

'Vicky, it's OK.' A Scottish accent. 'Vicky, we won't hurt you. You're safe.'

'My watch,' she said, trying to make them understand. It was so important that they understood; that they knew about everything that was happening here. Perhaps if they understood, they could explain it to her. 'My watch stopped!'

'We know,' said another voice; someone local. 'Don't worry, sweetheart. Are you OK?'

'No!' Vicky said, and then burst into tears. 'My mum's going to kill me!'

One of them let go of her; the other person's hold relaxed, turning into an embrace. Vicky felt herself rocked gently to and fro. 'No she won't,' said the local one, a soft reassuring breath in her ear. 'She's going to be thrilled to see you.'

'Bet you get a new watch out of it,' said the other. 'At the very least.'

Vicky couldn't help but laugh, even through her tears. 'I'll be choosing my own watches in future, thanks!'

She received another hug for that.

'Good on you, kiddo,' said the Scottish voice. 'I'm Amy, by the way. And this is Jess.'

Rubbing her eyes, Vicky took a proper look at her erstwhile captors. Two young women: one very tall and with amazing long red hair; the other shorter and with serious glasses that Vicky bet could make her look impressively stern if she put her mind to it. But she was the one with her arms round Vicky, the one who had spoken so softly. They both wore expressions of real concern. Vicky started to feel better.

They sat her down under one of the trees.

Amy went to get her a drink of water, and then knelt down in front of her. Jess kept tight hold of her hand.

'OK,' Amy said. 'Why don't you tell us what happened. And don't worry if it sounds like rubbish. We'll believe you.'

Again Vicky showed them her watch. It still showed five to ten, as it had been for, for... however long she had been wandering around here – hours, days, weeks – she had no idea now. 'It was like it was stuck. I couldn't get it to start again!'

Jess looked down at her own watch, then shook it, and lifted it up to her ear. 'Snap,' she said. 'Go on.'

'So I missed the last bus. Decided to walk—I know! I know!' she said, seeing them both roll their eyes. 'I should have just asked for a lift! But it was getting late, and I didn't want to bother Frank and Carole. I couldn't get a signal on my phone... I took a shortcut – should have been fine, nobody comes this way... And then I fell and rolled down the hill, and the clouds came out and I couldn't see the lights any more... Next thing I knew I was under the trees! It was so dark. I could hardly see my hand in front of me. I kept walking. The woods aren't that big, are they? I had to reach the edge at some point.

I could hear cars on the motorway, so I thought I'd better walk in that direction.'

Amy and Jess exchanged a look. 'I'm guessing the edge of the woods never turned up,' Amy said.

'No. Sometimes the sound got louder and sometimes it went away. And I never got any closer...'

Jess squeezed her shoulder. 'What happened next?'

Vicky gestured round the glade. 'I got here... It was exactly like it is now. Winter. The trees were bare and dead. I realised that it was getting light, and I knew that was my best chance of getting out, so I didn't stop. I left that way.' She pointed to one of the arches formed by the trees, over to their right. 'At least, I think it was that way. I walked along the path for a while, and I saw some daylight, and I got really excited – but when I went towards it, I ended up back here.' She took a deep breath. 'This next bit's weird, really weird –'

'Trust me,' Amy said, 'there's nothing you can say that will sound weird to me.'

Vicky eyed her doubtfully, but carried on. 'I went another way and the same thing happened. I came back here. Then I started marking the paths with pine cones, so I'd know I wasn't going the same way twice. Eventually I'd tried them all – I *know* I had! Every single path had a pine cone next to it.' Her voice started getting louder. 'But how could that happen? One of them *had* to be the path that brought me here, didn't it? How could that one lead me back, same as the rest? I don't understand it!'

'Shush, it's all OK,' said Jess. 'We're here now. What happened next?'

'By this time I was really tired and it was starting to get dark again. I sat down for a while, and I fell asleep. When I woke up…' She shook her head again. 'You're never going to believe this…'

'Want to bet?' Amy said. 'Remember – weird is fine.'

'Well… when I woke up, it was spring.'

Amy smiled at her. Jess just blinked.

'OK, that is fairly weird,' Amy agreed. 'But, yes, that's the time pockets. It makes perfect sense.'

'It does *feel* weird, though,' Jess said.

'I thought you'd tell me I was being stupid,' Vicky said in relief. 'Or that I must have still been asleep. But I wasn't. I was definitely awake. I woke up and it was spring. The leaves were green and the birds were singing, and everything smelt of rain and growing. I know

121

I can't have been asleep because I got up and went to the pool for a drink of water. I can't have dreamed that, can I? Do you think I must have dreamed it?'

'Neither of us think you were dreaming, Vicky,' Jess said, quietly. She rubbed the girl's arm, partly for warmth, partly for comfort. 'Carry on.'

'OK... So I was sitting there drinking from the pool, and then... well, what happened next was summer. It came all in a rush. I couldn't believe what I was seeing... The buds on the trees sprouted and popped open, the leaves unfurled, and then the blossom appeared and grew and then fell – it was like one of those nature films where they speed everything up... I don't know how long it took, my watch is stuck... It got so warm I had to take my coat off. And the noise, what I thought had been the motorway, that got steadily louder. I had to put my fingers in my ears. I walked around the clearing, trying to work out where it was coming from, but it seemed to be everywhere all at once. And then...'

She stopped and took a very deep breath. She was staring over at one of the archways formed by two trees. 'There,' she said, pointing at the archway, 'There was someone there.'

'*Laura*?' mouthed Jess to Amy, over Vicky's head. To Vicky, she said, 'Can you describe who it was?'

'There's another girl missing in Swallow Woods,' Amy explained. 'Do you think it could have been her? She's a little taller than Jess, but not as tall as me; younger than us but a couple of years older than you. She was wearing a bright red coat and she's got short black hair—'

Vicky shook her head quickly. 'No, no – this was someone with reddish, brownish hair. And I think it was a he, not a she. I'm pretty sure of that.'

Amy's stomach twisted. Could it have been Rory?

'OK,' she said, trying to sound calm so that she didn't frighten Vicky, 'did this person talk to you? Did they say or do anything at all?' She would know at once if it was Rory, probably from the gabbling.

But Vicky had closed her eyes, and had started to tremble. Clearly the memory of this person frightened her in some way – but the only person Rory had a chance of frightening was himself.

'He didn't say anything,' Vicky said. 'He stood under one of the tree arches and he beckoned to me to follow. Well, that wasn't going to happen, not in a million years!'

'Good for you,' said Jess.

'It was a close thing, though. I don't know what he was doing, but I felt like I had to follow him. The noise had got really loud now, maybe that was something to do with it, because it was like a magnet was pulling at me, trying to make me go through one of the arches. I wasn't going to follow a stranger anywhere, but I felt like I should run away – away through one of the other arches. But I didn't fancy that much, either. So I climbed a tree and I put my headphones on and I sang along—'

'Oh, good thinking!' Amy said.

'—and eventually the leaves started going red and gold, and then it was winter again. But that was even worse in a way. Because everything was dead, and there weren't any birds. I couldn't even hear the throbbing noise. There was nothing. I just wanted to go home!' She started to cry. 'I really, really want to go home! Mum's going to kill me—'

'No. Really, that isn't going to happen,' Jess promised.

'You're in luck, kiddo,' Amy said. 'Everyone's going to be over the moon to see you. But next time – stick to the path. Better still, call a taxi or stay the night, OK?'

As Jess explained to Vicky how she and Amy had got there, Amy walked slowly around the clearing, one hand brushing along the circle of trees. At each gap between them, she paused to peer through, trying to decide which way would be best. The mist had begun to dissipate, but each of the paths leading out from the clearing rose slightly and then fell away, making it difficult to see what lay beyond. Vicky may have been mistaken, too tired and too distressed to see that she was following the same paths over and over – but what if she was right? What if by some unlucky concatenation of space-time pockets, all these paths did come back here? They could soon exhaust themselves, walking round and round in circles, and that wouldn't leave them in a fit state to deal with whoever it was that Vicky had seen. Perhaps it was better simply to stay here in the clearing. At some point the Doctor was bound to turn up…

Based on previous experience, however, Amy knew that could take anything up to twelve years. Besides – sitting around and waiting? Hardly her style. The Doctor didn't travel with people who sat around waiting for him to come and save them, did he? He travelled with people who made a choice about what to do, then went off and did it. Didn't he?

And what would happen to the town while she was sitting twiddling her thumbs? She couldn't rely on the Doctor being free in time – which put him in danger too. She couldn't just push the button on the triangulator. She had to get to the ship first, or the TARDIS would be lost in the woods too. And of course, there would be no help from Rory – wherever he was, he was clearly having trouble of his own. Amy was going to have to deal with her own problems and (she glanced over at Vicky and Jess) other responsibilities. Things weren't too bad, though. There was no sign, for example, of anything happening that might cause a devastating flood. On the other hand, what if whatever she decided to do next *was* the cause…?

Amy shook her herself. You couldn't think that way. You'd end up sitting in a tree watching the water lap around your ankles if you thought that way. You had to act.

'Right,' she said, turning round to face the others. 'I'm not thrilled with any of our options right now, but I think probably the worst one is to sit here and wait for the woods to flood. Agreed?'

'Agreed,' Jess said.

'Flood?' Vicky sounded shaky again.

'Yeah. Best not to worry about that right now.'

Vicky looked decidedly un-reassured. 'But which way will we go?' she said. 'I told you – I've tried all the paths. They all come back here.'

'We'll try again,' said Amy, firmly. 'There are three of us now – three sets of eyes, three sets of ears. We're much more likely to spot something that will give us a clue as to how to get out of here.'

'We could split up,' Jess said. 'You take one exit, and I take the next one along with Vicky?'

'Splitting up,' said Amy, 'is always a terrible option. Don't you watch TV?'

'Fair point,' said Jess. 'OK, I guess it's a kind of logic puzzle. If we're going to solve it, we're going to have to work out exactly what sort of puzzle it is, gather as much data as we can, and just do some serious thinking.'

'Uh. I was going to toss a coin,' said Amy.

Vicky was starting to doubt the suitability of her rescuers for the task. 'Whatever we do,' she said urgently, 'I think we need to do it soon. Look, look at the trees. It's starting again...'

She was right. In the short time that Amy had spent walking round, the trees had begun to bud. Even as she watched, new leaves began to emerge. Soon the whole glade was rustling with growth, and the damp, lonely smell of winter was chased away by something warmer and greener.

Jess stood up and looked around in delight. 'It's amazing! I should be afraid, I know, but it's so wonderful!' She gasped and pointed across the glade. 'Oh, look! Look! Over there! A fox!'

There it sat, beneath one of the great arches of trees, its head cocked to one side, watching them.

'It's beautiful!' Jess said, and Amy had to agree. A sudden plash of sunlight through the quickening leaves caught upon its red fur, lighting up the points like flames licking upwards. Its bib was white and its eyes orange. Even though Amy knew it was a mistake to project human emotion onto animals, she thought the eyes looked sad and aged. Perhaps it was the tilt of the creature's head, and the greying flecks of fur above its eyes. Even without imagining things, this was certainly an old animal.

The fox rose slowly to its feet, still watching them. It lifted its front right paw, as if it was about to trot away. Then it stepped onto its hind legs and began to change shape.

'OK,' Amy said. 'This is a new one...'

'What?' said Jess. 'What, what, *what*?'

The transformation took about a minute, by which time the fox was the size and the shape of a human, perhaps somewhat slighter than the average man. The face remained distinctly vulpine – long-muzzled, black ears perched upright at the top of its head, the hair thicker than human hair, more pelt-like, and reddish. No, this was definitely not Rory – unless Rory had forgotten to mention something, and Rory wouldn't dare.

'You didn't mention he was a fox,' Jess remarked to Vicky.

'That's because this bit didn't happen!'

As they watched, the fox-man turned away as if to go. He looked back over his shoulder, and then beckoned to them to follow him along the path.

'Amy,' Jess said, 'not to put you on the spot, but I think you might have slightly more experience with this kind of thing than either me or Vicky. Ought we to go with it?'

'No!' said Vicky quickly.

'Or should we keep well away?'

All the time the transformation had been happening, Amy had been thinking furiously. There was no way of knowing whether this was a good fox-guy or a bad fox-guy, or something in between. But here at least was a face to all the mystery surrounding Swallow Woods. Time pockets, spatial warps, swiftly changing seasons – there was nothing to latch onto there. But here, for the first time, was someone she could reason with.

Besides, perhaps it might be satisfied with one of them.

'OK,' Amy said. 'First of all, I want you to not argue with me, and I want you to listen.'

'You're about to say something I won't like, right?' Jess said.

'Yes, and you're still not to argue. I want you to go, Jess, and I want you to take Vicky with you—I said don't argue! I'm going to follow Fantastic Mr Fox, and I want you two to go in the opposite direction.'

'Amy,' Jess said quickly, 'that's a terrible idea! What if you're lost for good? I don't know enough about what's going on to be able to help—'

'Oh, who ever knows enough!' cried Amy. A leaf above her turned yellow, crisped, and fell to the ground. The man-fox, whatever he called himself, began to back up the path. He was still beckoning to them, but soon he would be out of sight.

Amy rolled her triangulator around in her

fingers. 'Here's what I'm thinking. If I don't go now, we'll only end up sitting around waiting here till summer comes again and this place reactivates. Who knows what will happen in the meantime?'

'Amy, maybe it's you going with this beastie that causes the whole thing—!'

'That's a chance we're going to have to take.' Amy lifted her hand to acknowledge the creature, and took a step towards it. 'Jess, I'm going now. Take Vicky and leave here. If you get through – try to reach the Doctor. Tell him I've still got the triangulator—'

'The *what*-you-later?'

'Oh, just say the chocolate device! He'll know what I mean!'

Autumn was coming fast. All around, the clearing was changing colour, the leaf-fall getting thicker. Amy broke into a run. At the entry to the arch, she paused, and pointed across the clearing. 'Go now!' she shouted to Jess and Vicky. 'Go that way! It's worth a try! Go on! And good luck!'

'Wait!' shouted Jess. 'You said we shouldn't split up!'

'I was wrong! Who'd have guessed! Go *now*!'

Amy knew she couldn't risk waiting any

longer. She ducked beneath the archway of trees, and followed the fox – wherever he was leading her. Behind her, she could still hear Jess, calling to her forlornly.

'Amy! Did you really say the *chocolate* device?'

*Alive.* Now Emily had said it, Rory found it hard not to agree. The lights from the walls, shifting and shimmering, were like sunlight passing through leaves, as if the decorators had tried their best to emulate a forest. The effect was disorientating, like travelling on a train and watching the scenery so intently you started to think that you were motionless and the world was moving at high speed.

When, wondered the-man-who-was-calling-himself-Rory, had he travelled on a train? Where to? Where from? Would he start to remember? Or was the story of his life gone for good?

'I think we're arriving somewhere,' Emily said, softly. She pointed up ahead, where the corridor ended in an archway. The metal panels on either side were etched with long lines, like the branches of a tree. Rory ran his fingertip along one of them, and a trail of light followed his touch.

'I wonder why the design seems so familiar,'

he said.

'Looks like the arches in the parish church,' Emily said. 'Not to mention the trees we came under before we turned up here. You don't remember, do you?'

Rory shook his head. They walked through the doorway into the room beyond. The effect was like entering a woodland glade – only one made from metals and plastics. The walls loomed around, like heavy old grey trees, and in the centre of the room was a large flat circular console, its surface dark and empty like a pool in winter. Steps led down to it from where they stood, and a second set of steps led up to another doorway opposite.

'Where do you think we are?' Emily said.

Rory shrugged. 'Control room of some sort?'

'I wish I knew how you were so sure of these things!'

'Me too... But it seems obvious.'

'Anyone would think you'd been on a – what did you call it?'

'Spaceship.'

'One of them. Anyone would think you'd been on one before.'

Perhaps he had. Before or after he'd been on a train. Rory walked slowly down the steps and stood in front of the console. 'Hello!' he said, and then: 'Computer!'

Nothing happened. Emily, standing next to him, waved her hand at the surface of the console. It sprang to life: writing and images started scrolling past at a great rate, like ripples on water, and a control panel of virtual buttons appeared, following Emily's hand around as she moved it.

'How did you know to do that?' said Rory.

'Well, if they're alien, they might not know English. Waving seemed friendly. Here, what do you think all this is saying?'

'Greek to me...'

'What, *actual* Greek?'

'Well, the alien equivalent of Greek. If aliens have an equivalent of Greek—'

'You do go on, you know. What do you think would happen if I press this red button here?'

Rory grabbed her hand. 'Emily! You never, ever press red buttons!'

'All right.' She snaked her other hand past him and thumped her thumb against the screen. 'I'll try the green one instead.'

Rory threw his arms over his head and dived to the ground.

Emily chuckled. 'You're such an easy target! Come and have a look, this is interesting.'

Gathering up what was left of his dignity, Rory stood up. On the screen, the images and the weird text were rushing past. With some experimentation, Emily found she could slow the pace down; some further tests let them stop and start the flow, but they could not make any sense of the actual words. The pictures, they both noticed, were all of humans.

'Maybe they were the crew,' said Rory.

'But you said this was an alien spaceship?'

'Perhaps I was wrong. Perhaps it's human after all, but from the future.'

'Still full of surprises, aren't you? Look, though, look at the clothes. That dress looks like something my old granny would have worn. And those are Roman!'

Rory, looking at the image, felt himself blush hotly, although he couldn't for the life of him say why.

'They look to me like pictures from the past, not the future,' Emily said. 'Like a history book—Here, I know that one! Go back, go back!'

Rory skimmed back until she told him to stop again.

'That's it!' she said. 'I know him! That's Harry, Harry Thompson! Oh, you won't remember, will you? He's the lad that went missing six weeks ago. We thought he'd run off rather than get called up. And these little pictures – that's his mam and dad, and his three sisters. Their farm backs onto our bottom field. I know them like I know my own family. What are all their pictures doing here, I wonder?'

Rory started scrolling through again, more and more quickly. Was his picture here too? If it was, perhaps they could work out what the text said, work out who he was and where he had come from…

'Slow down, Mr Williams, we might miss something!'

'Emily, I'm trying to see if I'm here—'

'I know that, love, but you're going much too quick.' She rested her hand gently on his, moving it away and stopping the images flooding past. 'Now slow down and let's take a proper look through.'

Slowly, they pored through the pictures. Rory lost count somewhere in the hundred-and-thirties, and he had not even been counting the smaller pictures. There was no sign of a picture of him.

'Less like a history book and more like a catalogue,' he muttered, swiping his hand across the screen so that yet another picture came past. This one looked like a mediaeval peasant.

'Alien abduction... But why on earth would I think that? What is wrong with my *head*? Why won't it sort itself *out*?' Frustrated, he banged the flat of his hand against the console. It made a *thumping* noise. The mottled light from the walls dimmed. Rory looked round anxiously. 'Did I do that?'

'How on earth would I know?' Emily hit the side of the console too, and the light came slowly back to the same level as before. 'Looks like it!'

They both laughed nervously, guiltily, like children who were getting away with some mischief. They stopped laughing when they heard footsteps, coming slowly and heavily along the corridor towards them.

'Oh, Mr Williams,' Emily whispered, her eyes bright with fear, 'what are we going to do?'

Rory didn't stop to think. Summoning up some knowledge from deep, deep within his mind, he grabbed Emily's hand and pulled her towards the doorway opposite. 'What else? Run!'

Tripping over roots, pushing away branches, Amy followed the were-fox through a dark tunnel of trees. He trotted along at a quick pace, every so often turning to check that she was still there, and waving his hand to hurry her. Sometimes he smiled – at least, Amy thought it was a smile. His lips parted to show small, sharp, white teeth. She wasn't sure whether to be alarmed or encouraged.

The path rose again, and the fox-man dipped out of view.

'Oh no, you don't…' Amy ran the last few metres to catch up. The trees were thinning around her, and at last came to an end. With relief, she stepped out into sunshine.

Amy gasped. Ahead of her lay a fantastic landscape. She was standing looking down into a lush green valley set amongst rolling hills, with a swift silver river running through its heart. In the middle distance stood a tall dark turreted building, which looked exactly how a castle would look if built by alien foxes. Amy felt as if she had walked into *Beauty and the Beast*, or a child's picture book of fairy tales in which all the buildings and people were in silhouette.

The fox-man was standing a few yards ahead of her, on the path leading down to the valley. He gave her another sharp white smile.

'OK,' Amy said. 'I'm impressed. Even knowing there are all kinds of spatial wotsits going on around here, I'm still impressed. I'm also tired, so if that's where we're going, I'll need a sit down first.'

The man-fox laughed: a sound somewhere between a rasp and a cough. Not an encouraging noise at all.

'Don't do that again,' said Amy. 'Please. Unless this is the moment where you turn out to be on the dangerous side of scary. In which case – laugh's perfect.'

'Don't be afraid,' said the were-fox. After the laugh, his voice turned out to be surprisingly pleasant, deep and rich, charming, but rather frightening. 'And don't worry about walking, you won't have to.'

Lifting his hand, he waved it in front of him, and the distance between them and the valley collapsed. Now they were standing outside the huge wooden gate of the castle.

'Nice trick,' Amy said gamely. 'All your public transport problems solved. You should speak to the government.'

He waved his hand again, and now they were standing in a broad stone courtyard.

'Lady,' he called out, his deep voice resounding off the stone walls like a great bell. 'I've returned, but only one of them came with me.'

Amy looked around to see who he was addressing. One of the wooden doors around the courtyard opened, and an elderly woman emerged. She was white-haired, but walked quickly towards them. When she reached the fox-man, he bowed with a great show of gallantry, and clasped her hand. Then the old woman turned to Amy.

'Welcome,' she said. She threw her arms around Amy and hugged her with surprising strength. 'Oh, it's been so long since I've seen another human, never mind spoken to one! I'm so glad to see you!'

'OK...' said Amy. 'Um, thanks?'

The old woman released Amy from the embrace, and took hold of both her hands. 'Tell me your name,' she urged.

'Amy. Amy Pond.'

'Amy. Welcome to our kingdom, Amy. I'm Laura Brown.'

The fox-man smiled sharply.

'You know,' said Amy, 'I had a feeling you were going to say that.'

The rain was coming down more heavily, and the wind was picking up, but the police search was finally getting organised at the edge of Swallow Woods. The place where Jess had parked her car, several hours earlier, was cordoned off. Lighting scaffolds were going up; and the distinctive blue and white tape was spreading out across the field which Jess and Amy (and, once upon a time, Rory and Emily) had walked across to enter Swallow Woods.

Galloway watched all this progress with a steadily growing sense of relief. At last, this investigation was properly under way. The quiet country lane, along which he had driven many times in the last eighteen months, was the busiest he had ever seen it. It had not escaped his notice, however, that almost all the officers here were from outside of town. Somehow, the local police had found themselves jobs back at the station – Porter included.

The big lights were ready. Galloway gave the nod, and the field was bathed in their harsh white glare. He climbed over the fence, and stood for a while looking at the woods.

Gathered in the hollow, the trees were dark and impenetrable. They seemed almost to suck in the light. The rain was turning the ground beneath Galloway's feet to mud. He took a few squelching steps forward. Something was moving near the tree-line. An animal? Galloway screwed up his eyes.

Two small figures were moving across the

field towards him. Their progress was slow and unsteady; one of them was leaning on the other, half-carried, half-dragged. They looked like battlefield survivors, pulling themselves bit by bit out of no-man's land. As they came closer, Galloway recognised them. He had been thinking of nothing else for days now.

Galloway broke into a sprint, reaching them before anyone else. He threw his arms around Vicky Caine, and then knelt down before her.

'Oh thank God,' he whispered, brushing a wet lock of hair away from her scratched and dirty face, only realising as he spoke that he had seriously begun to doubt his ability to find them. 'Thank God!'

Jess Ashcroft put her hand on his shoulder. It felt oddly as if she was the one taking care of him.

'So you're all here... Good, good, that's something of a relief, I can tell you.' The harsh searchlights made her look pale and exhausted. 'How long have I been gone? Quickly, Inspector!'

'What?' Her question made no sense. 'Four hours, maybe five?'

She gasped. 'Is that all?'

A couple of paramedics arrived. They covered both girls up, and tried to hurry them towards an ambulance. Vicky was taken off, but Jess wouldn't budge. Grabbing hold of Galloway's arm, she said, 'I need you to do something for me and I need you not to ask any questions. The man you have in custody. You've got to get him here as quickly as possible.'

'*What?*'

'The storm's coming, Mr Galloway. We can't stop it now. Only the Doctor can do that. If we're not too late already.'

Galloway wasn't sure whether she was serious, or just plain mad.

'But we should be OK,' Jess said firmly. 'Amy's still got her chocolate device.'

# Chapter
# 10

Rory and Emily had run out of places to hide. The ship turned out to contain no more than a few empty rooms similar to the one where Rory had woken up, and the passages all led back to the spherical room containing the circular console.

As they arrived there for a third time, Emily started to sound a little desperate. 'We're not going to get away, are we? There's nowhere to hide!'

'Not looking good, is it?'

They ran down the steps and around the back of the console. Rory's thinking was that – perhaps – it was special space plastic and it would act as some sort of barrier between them and whatever was coming. OK. Not very likely.

But possible. There was another door behind them, through which they could run (again) if the need arose, so they wouldn't be completely trapped, even if, in the end, they'd probably just end up back here (again). He looked around for something he could pick up and brandish, but everything was fixed down and, anyway, he wasn't sure how convincing he would look.

The footsteps clanged steadily upon the metal grating. At the doorway, however, they stopped. Rory peered over the console, but the hollow of the room was too low down for him to be able to see out.

'We don't mean you any harm,' he shouted up at their pursuer. 'We hope that's the same for you. Can't we talk?'

'*Talk…*' It was a young man's voice. '*Talk…*'

'OK,' Rory whispered to Emily, 'so whatever it is, at least it's got a throat.'

'Ooh, that doesn't make me feel better!'

'Sorry! Yes! What I meant was that makes it similar to – and therefore less immediately terrifying for – us. Not that human beings are universally marvellous and lovely, of course, and not that we should judge by appearances… I'm going to stop talking now and do some breathing instead, if you don't mind.'

'Fine by me,' Emily whispered. Leaning

forwards on the console, she called out, 'We're scared, you know. Both of us are scared. We don't know where we are and we don't know what you want from us. Your standing out there isn't helping much! If we've disturbed you, we're sorry. We can't hurt you and don't want to hurt you.'

'*Hurt...*' said the voice.

'I hope it won't, you know, *fixate* on that,' Rory muttered.

'We don't want to be here,' Emily went on, 'and we'd rather leave you in peace.'

'*Peace...*'

There was a silence. The voice added nothing more, and its owner made no move.

'Sorry,' Emily said to Rory. 'Best I could do.'

He squeezed her hand. 'Brilliant job. The Doctor would be proud.'

'Who?'

'I've no idea. It just... came out.' But he didn't get a chance to chase that thought further. The owner of the voice entered the room.

He was a young man of about seventeen, with reddish hair, his cowlick slicked back inexpertly, and the merest makings of a moustache. He was in his shirt sleeves. He wore thick boots, and his trousers, held up by braces, were patched and muddy. Seeing him, Emily gave a loud, nervy laugh.

'Oh, Harry, you daft article, you've given us ever such a fright! Why didn't you say hello? Didn't you hear my voice? It's Emily! Emily Bostock!'

The young man walked forwards until he was standing at the top of the stairway leading down to the console.

'My word,' Emily said, coming out from the cover of the console. 'I should clout you!' She turned to Rory, a smile upon her face. 'Don't worry, Mr Williams, it's only Harry. Harry Thompson. You remember? The one we saw in the pictures.'

There was something not right here, Rory thought, as Harry began to descend the steps. Perhaps it was just the light, but the young man's flesh had a yellowish tint, tinged with green, and his eyes... His eyes were cold and dark and lonely as a winter night.

'Emily,' Rory said quickly. 'Don't go any closer.'

'Why ever not? I told you – this is Harry! We've known each other all our lives. He wouldn't hurt us!'

The young man was now at the bottom of the steps. Emily reached out and took his hand. As flesh met flesh, the lights all around began to flicker wildly. The throbbing sound, which had hitherto been no more than background noise, surged. The ship shuddered. Rory grabbed hold of the console with both hands.

'Emily! Get back!'

But Emily didn't seem in the least perturbed.

'Hush now,' she said, stroking the young man's hand. 'Everything's going to be all right. You don't have to be afraid. I won't tell on you, not for all the tea in China. I won't breathe a word. You're not going anywhere, Harry. You're not going anywhere you don't want to.'

But the lights were still flickering, Rory noticed, and the ship still shaking.

Jess finished her story, picked up her cup of tea, and looked over the rim of the mug across the table.

The two detectives stared back.

'I understand how it sounds,' Jess said patiently. 'But it's all true. Time pockets. Spatial ones too— Look, does either of you have a scarf?'

Neither of them responded. Jess sighed and drank some of the hot sweet tea. She was exhausted. Galloway had told her that only a few hours at the most had passed since she had parked her car on Long Lane and gone with Amy into the woods. By her own estimate, and even bearing in mind how time jumped around in Swallow Woods, Jess reckoned she and Vicky had taken the best part of two days to get from the clearing to the edge of the woods. For the last part of the journey, a storm had been chasing them, and it had been getting worse.

'It's all true,' she said, quietly but firmly. 'There's a clearing in the woods with paths running out from it. People get lost there, lost down pockets of time and space. It's been stable for a very long time, but now something's going wrong. I don't know what it is, but I do know that it's going to become critical tonight, and I do know that the town is at risk. What you have to do is let me talk to the Doctor.'

Galloway cleared his throat and leaned back in his chair. When he spoke, he used a very gentle tone that Jess, frankly, found pretty patronising.

'What I don't understand,' Galloway said, 'is that you must have met Laura Brown. She's a friend of your sister. You must want her to get home safe and sound—'

'Well of course I do! I want everyone in the town to be safe, and that's why you have to listen to me, Inspector! Listen to what I'm telling you!'

Galloway continued not to pay her any attention. 'I know that sometimes relationships between the press and the police can be tense, but you've always dealt fairly with me, and I feel as if I've always dealt fairly with you—'

'Yes, you've been marvellous! Wonderful! Brilliant! Now let me see the Doctor.'

'However,' Galloway went on, talking over her, 'even though you have clearly been through an unusual and probably distressing experience, you're running a risk of being charged with wasting police time.' He rubbed his temples. 'Did the red-haired girl put you up to this?'

'Amy? No! I told you – she's still in there! Look, if I could just speak to the Doctor—'

Galloway shook his head. 'Oh, no! Not a chance! He's obviously a very dangerous man, more dangerous than I thought already. I know the type – they have a twisted kind of charisma, they get other people to do their dirty work for them. Even sitting in the cells, he got the Pond girl to work on you. And now he seems to be controlling you in some way. For your own protection, Ms Ashcroft, you're not going anywhere near him!'

'For my own protection... Oh, for heaven's sake!' Jess gave up on Galloway and turned to the young female detective, who had been sitting silently throughout.

'It's Ruby Porter, isn't it?' Jess said. 'I knew your brother at school – James. He was great at cricket. Look, let's not waste any more time. We both know about the woods. We both know there's not a rational explanation for what happens – well, what we commonly understand as rational... Let's not complicate things right now. But you know, don't you, that there's something wrong with Swallow Woods. I can explain it, Ruby. Everything I'm saying is true!'

Porter looked away from her. She stared resolutely down at the floor. Jess now keenly understood the frustration that had made Amy tear at her hair.

'I know you've had a bad time,' Galloway said. 'It's unfortunate you can't bring yourself to be helpful right now, but at least you've confirmed my suspicion that whatever's going on here, the woods hold the key. At first light, I'm starting the search. It's not a big area. With police from three counties, local volunteers and the dog handlers, we'll soon find Ms Pond—'

'I wouldn't count on it!'

'— And we'll soon find out what's been going on in there.'

'Whatever's going on you're not equipped to deal with it! A search party? You think dogs can resolve this? This has been going on for centuries!' Jess stopped, backtracking slightly. 'Dogs... Like a hunt...' She addressed Galloway with new urgency. 'You know, I'm not sure taking dogs into Swallow Woods is a good idea—'

'I'm sure you don't,' said Galloway. He stood up to leave; Porter followed suit. 'Not right now. But you'll be glad in time.'

'No, really, don't do it!' Urgently, Jess turned to Porter. 'Listen to me! Please, you must understand! Something's going to happen tonight that could destroy the town. We don't know what it is yet, but I'm sure as I can be that dogs won't help. Hunted people fight back, they attack...! Please, if you won't let me talk to him, then you must! Talk to the Doctor!'

Galloway smiled benignly from the doorway. 'Drink up your tea, Ms Ashcroft. I'll get a car to take you home.'

Laura and the were-fox, who introduced himself as Reyn, led Amy inside to a big and comfortably appointed chamber. Long, high windows at the far end let sunlight stream in, and at the centre of the room was a large wooden table laid for supper. When she turned her head to look round, Amy thought she could see faint trails of golden shimmering light at the corner of her eye, like pollen drifting through the air.

'Come and eat,' said Laura, mistress of the house.

Amy went slowly towards the table, keeping a close watch on Reyn. He was walking lightly beside her, at her pace, and seemed prepared to let Laura do the talking. It was difficult to judge with a different species, but from the white hairs above each of his orange eyes, and his rather stately way of moving, Amy got the impression of an older man, even elderly. In fact, the pair of them – Laura and Reyn – struck Amy as being rather like an old couple who had been companions for a long time and were very comfortable with each other. Reyn went to the head of the table and waited politely for the two women to sit, one on either side of him.

'Were you lost for long?' Laura said.

'Not really,' Amy replied. 'A couple of hours, maybe?'

'Very quick! I must have wandered for at least two days.' Laura smiled as if the memory was somehow fond. 'Of course, it was all a very long time ago. It's almost as if it happened to somebody else.'

'About that,' said Amy. 'Weren't you…'

'Younger?'

'Yeah…' Amy fumbled around for a way to break the news.

'Don't torment yourself, Amy. I know that ten days have passed outside Swallow Woods since I walked under the trees. And, before you ask, sixty-one. Sixty-one years have passed here.'

That made her nearly eighty. 'Still,' Amy said feebly, 'you're looking good on it.'

'Thank you. Yes, I think I've weathered rather well.' Laura gestured around the table. 'Please, won't you eat?'

Reyn had not held back while they were talking. His plate was piled high with food and he was enjoying it. He tore into a chicken leg with great enthusiasm, stopping every couple of bites to dab a linen napkin against his mouth and wipe his fingers. It was an odd mixture of ferocity and fastidiousness. Laura gave him an indulgent smile.

Amy took a sample bite of bread and butter. The taste was odd, very bland at first, and then it was as if the flavour remembered to kick in, and her mouth was flooded with sensations of warm, nutty bread and creamy, salty butter.

'I have to say,' she said to Laura through a mouthful of cheese, 'You seem pretty laid back for someone who's been held captive for six decades.'

'Captive?' Laura gave a good-humoured snort, to which Reyn lent his odd rasping, coughing laugh. Laura reached out and took hold of his hand. 'Do you hear that? She thinks you're holding me captive!'

'You have to admit, lady, that you made the same mistake yourself, once upon a time.'

Laura gave him a fond smile.

Amy put down her fork. All this mutual admiration was starting to make her feel slightly nauseous. She sincerely hoped that she and Rory weren't like this. The thought of Rory made her anxious and perhaps even, though she didn't like to admit it, scared. Crossly, she said, 'OK, you two, tell me what's going on. Reyn's ship crashed here, didn't it? That's what's causing all the time pockets and disappearances. So how come it's not his fault?'

Laura and Reyn looked at her in surprise.

'Yes,' Reyn said. 'Yes, my ship crashed here. I've not had the resources or the right equipment to fix it. But rest assured, Amy, if I had my way

I would have left your planet centuries ago. I'm not a monster. I certainly wouldn't hold anyone against their will.'

'But all the missing people!' Amy said. 'Not just Laura – there've been hundreds!'

'Three hundred and nine, to be exact,' Reyn said. 'And not all of them have been as lucky as Laura.'

'*Lucky*? Oh yeah, she seems a real lottery winner to me!'

'Please, Amy,' Laura put in quietly. 'Let Reyn explain. 'When he does, you'll understand. There's no malice at work here. Just chance turnings on the road, and some bad luck – and,' she squeezed Reyn's hand, 'no small measure of happiness, in the end.'

'All right,' Amy said. 'I'm open to explanations. Just make them good.'

'I shall endeavour to do my best,' Reyn replied drily. Pouring out pale yellow wine for them all, he leaned back in his chair, goblet in hand, lord of the manor. 'I was an explorer, Amy. My ship could cross space as if it were no distance at all… Laura, my dear, do you have a skein of wool to hand so I might demonstrate?'

'Don't worry,' said Amy. She tapped her forehead. 'I've got the basics sorted.'

Reyn studied her thoughtfully. 'Laura, does

she strike you as remarkably at ease with the notion of space travel? And, indeed, at meeting a shape-shifting alien?'

'If something has happened in the outside world to make her like this,' Laura said, slowly coring an apple, 'it's happened in the last ten days.'

'Yeah, well, don't worry about me,' Amy said. 'I've been around a bit, that's all you need to know. Right now we're talking about where *you* came from. Your ships can travel through space. Yeah, great, I'm with you there. Spaceships – no problem. Massive fantasy castles and disappearing people – slightly more of a problem. So keep on with the explaining.'

Reyn bowed his head. 'As you command.'

'And you can drop the whole Camelot shtick too. Let's keep the talk straightforward, OK?'

Reyn's long ears twitched and flattened back slightly. 'Very well. Our exploration ships, Amy, were unusual in that they learned from their travels. In time they came to consciousness.'

'Yeah yeah, artificial intelligence, I'm fine with that too. Honestly, you're not likely to say something I haven't come across before in some shape or form. How has that ended up in mass kidnappings?'

'The process – we call it the Shift – is a

difficult transition, a vast and destabilising change. At home, we have teachers, scientists, all kinds of people to nurture them through the process. We can feed them information, show them experiences, give them all the knowledge we have accumulated. But my poor ship...' He sighed. 'When I crashed here in the woods, there were no people. I struggled to fix the ship with the resources I had. Before I could do that, the people came. It triggered the Shift.'

'How?' Amy said. 'How does that work?'

'During the Shift, the ship devours information. When the people came through the woods, it took them. You have to understand, Amy, it was acting on instinct. It was trying to learn. Every fifty years or so, the ship needs more. Every fifty years or so, it would pull people to it. It wants memories, experiences, life stories.' He looked away. 'It's not painful, Amy, but it's hardly desirable. Whenever the ship has pulled people into the wood, I've tried to bring them here instead. I've not always been successful.'

*Jess and Vicky*, Amy thought. *Rory...* She pushed her plate aside and put her head in her hands.

'Laura I was able to save,' Reyn said. 'And you, now. Your two companions...' He shook his head. 'I wish you'd been able to bring yourself to trust me. But there it is. My appearance, I have gathered over the years, does not always encourage that. I've tried to make this place beautiful and comfortable for all my guests, as welcoming as possible – but your species can be so suspicious! It's not our way. We're curious, like you, but not so mistrustful. Perhaps that's a failing.'

'You said that you've brought many people here over the years,' Amy said thickly. 'There was a young man came this way, about a century ago in Laura's time. He would have complained a lot—'

'He didn't come this way, I'm afraid. If he passed in summer through the glade in the wood with the pool, he most likely found himself on board the ship.' He studied her with his orange eyes, seeming to understand that this was someone important. 'I'm sorry, Amy.'

Amy shoved her chair back and stood up. She started pacing around the room, coming to a halt near the long windows. Rain was pattering against the panes. She swung back round to face Reyn and Laura. They were sitting watching her, obviously concerned.

'You say you don't have the equipment to fix your ship,' Amy said. 'So why not just let this

Shift or whatever it is finish, and then get out of here! Leave the town and the people in peace!'

'It's not that simple—'

'Oh,' Amy muttered through her teeth, 'I just *knew* you were going to say that…'

'At home, as I said, we have all kinds of experts to hand. Here, there's only me. And there's more. As the years have passed, the ship has become more bound to the world around it, more entangled with it. All the warps and pockets have become so complex that if I tried now to make the ship shift completely, if I tried to force it through – I don't know what damage that would do.'

Amy turned back to the window. The rain was falling steadily now, and some of the water was leaking through and gathering in a small pool at the base of the window. Why would you make it rain, she wondered, in a fantasy world? Perhaps sunshine became boring after a while. Perhaps you started to crave some darkness, some semblance of risk.

'Something's going to happen soon,' she said. 'I don't know what, but this time next week, there'll be a lake covering Swallow Woods, and nothing where the town once stood. Is that what could happen if the Shift was forced?'

'Yes,' said Reyn, speaking slowly. 'How

do you know that, Amy? What makes you so sure?'

'Don't bother about that. Just give me answers. What could make that happen?'

Reyn didn't reply at once. When Amy turned around, she saw Laura leaning across, holding the alien's hand, her eyes pleading with him to speak.

'Tell me,' Amy said. 'I'm not afraid of the truth. What might cause the ship to shift?'

'I've maintained the balance for centuries now, Amy,' Reyn said, 'but it's very delicate. The ship might come to a crisis if there were too many people trying to get in at once. But the real risk comes from people trying to get out. Trying to leave through the portal place.'

'The portal place?'

'The clearing in the wood with the pool. Where we met. That's where your world ends and mine begins.'

'And coming through there,' Amy said, 'brings you either here or to the ship.'

'That's right.'

'And going back out again—'

'Could destabilise the environment I've set up here, and bring on exactly the kind of crisis I've been trying to stop. That's why I've never left your world. That's why nobody leaves.'

'I told you I wasn't a captive,' Laura Brown said softly, 'but I can't go back from here. This is where all our journeys end, Amy. There's no way back through Swallow Woods. Not if we are all to survive.'

Porter saw Galloway safely out of the station on his way back to Swallow Woods, and then quietly, and unnoticed, she slipped down to the cells.

The station was almost deserted; everyone was home or else down at the search. The sergeant led her down the bare bright corridor to the cell, and Porter waited patiently while he unlocked it. The strip light above them fizzled.

'Been like that all night,' the sergeant complained. 'Can't stand fluorescents. Susceptible to bad weather.'

Porter made vague noises of agreement as he opened the cell door. 'Very quiet, this one,' he said. 'Almost too quiet. You'd think he'd ask for a cup of tea at some point, but, no, all he wanted was the spoon.'

The door swung opened. Porter looked past the sergeant into the cell.

The Doctor was standing on the bed with one hand aloft. In that hand, he was holding up the spoon so that it touched the ceiling. The other hand was covering his left ear. Seeing the pair at the door, his expression turned from intense concentration to faint embarrassment. He brought down his arm and jumped from the bed.

'Sorry. Had to do some… important… spoon work.' Carefully, he handed the piece of cutlery over to the sergeant. 'Thanks for that. Good spoon. One of the best.'

The sergeant gave Porter a 'he's all yours' look, and left them alone.

Porter leaned in the doorway, arms folded, blocking the exit. 'All right,' she said. 'What's going on?'

'You already know what's going on. Aliens. Starships. Space bending back round on itself. Time, too. But you're in luck. Help is here.' He gave a bright smile; did jazz hands. 'Where's your friend?'

'He's off to search the woods. With dogs.'

'Ooh, no, terrible idea! Who knows what that will do? Some people can get very testy, particularly when they've been on their own for a long time. Dogs send the wrong message, don't they?'

'That's why I'm here,' Porter said. 'Jess said—'

'Oh, Jess made it! Excellent! What about

Pond, was she with her?'

'No sign of her, not yet.'

The Doctor's face fell. 'Ah. Well. At least Jess is a start. But there's still Amy, and Rory, and Emily, and of course the small matter of whatever minor apocalypse is about to hit Foxton; just because it's only going to affect one small town and an equally small woodland area doesn't make it less of an apocalypse for the people concerned – not to mention that if the motorway gets flooded the traffic is going to be appalling throughout the rest of the county for who knows how long— Sorry. Talk too much. Always did. You were saying?'

'Jess said that you knew about...' Porter stopped, as if having difficulty saying the words.

'Say it,' suggested the Doctor. 'You'll feel so much better when you do.'

'About the woods,' Porter said, in a rush. 'You know what happens when people disappear in Swallow Woods.'

The Doctor smiled at her, gently, kindly. 'Yes, you knew, didn't you? Detective Constable Porter, who has lived in this town all her life, and can hear the same noise that I can hear, and who knows that there's something not right about the woods. Something that can't be solved by ordinary methods – not even by a hard-working, fair-minded, and meticulous policeman. And particularly not by his dogs. Who went missing? Somebody close to you?'

Porter looked past him, over at the wall. 'My mother's older brother. My uncle, of course – although that's not how you think of a 15-year-old boy.'

'When did it happen?'

'About… 1960? No, 1959. That fits with the dates, doesn't it? Every fifty years, give or take a few years. At least, I think that's right – people round here don't exactly talk openly about all this. He was the only one that time. Gran never got over it. Sometimes she would be so sad. Right to the end of her life…' Porter stared up at the little window on the far wall, dark and wet with rain. 'Sadness like that, it gets handed down, doesn't it? Even though I never knew him – my mother hardly remembers him – you still get touched by the sadness. He's why I joined the police. Always wanting to find lost things, always wanting to put things right…' She shook her head. 'It's not just me. The whole town is like that! There's a strange sense of loss that comes from living here in Foxton. It's like something has always been missing, but you don't dare to remember what it was.

You're always thinking about it, but you know you wouldn't go looking, because in your heart you know that the answers can only be found in Swallow Woods. And who goes near Swallow Woods? If you go there, you might not find your way out again. You'd be lost too, and perhaps people wouldn't quite remember you either. Poor Gordon Galloway. I bet he's sorry he ever moved down here.'

The Doctor, she realised, was standing very close to her.

'I can end this,' he told her softly. 'Whatever has been happening here for such a long time, I can end it. No more disappearances, no more secrets and fears and half-truths and confusion. I can end it all tonight. But I can't end it from here.'

Porter looked anxiously over her shoulder.

'It's coming to an end anyway,' the Doctor said. 'The choice now is between the happy ending or the tragedy. But this is when you make a decision, Detective. You can play by the rules, the old rules, the ones that have kept this town terrified for so long, nobody talking about what happens – or you can take a risk. Admit that what's been going on all these years is real. Bewildering, inexplicable – but *real*.'

Porter was listening to him as if mesmerised.

'I've been watching you a lot the last day or so,' she said, slowly.

'You should see me in a fez. Looks *good*...'

'I couldn't make sense of your eyes. You don't look old. Except for your eyes. What do they see, Doctor?'

'Bad things, cruel things. Terrible things made all the worse by how beautiful they are. And sometimes – yes, often, because the universe is full of wonders as well as terrors – the most marvellous thing that it's possible to see. Someone opening her mind.'

'All right,' said Porter. 'I know you're just reeling me in, but whatever you're doing, it works. I'll get you out of the station, and then you're on your own.' She put her hands to her head and sighed. 'What am I doing? I *like* my job!'

'There's one more thing I need,' said the Doctor.

'What more do you want?'

'There's a widget. A gadget. A *thing*. About so long.' He pulled his hands apart about eight inches. 'Green light at the end. Makes a funny noise... You know, I'm fairly certain that you'll recognise it when you see it.'

The strip light in the corridor wavered perilously. Outside, the wind was howling.

'Thirdly,' said the Doctor, 'and, I promise that this is finally – might I also ask for some *haste*?'

# Chapter
# 11

When the meal was finished, Reyn lifted his hand and, with one wave, the room around them disappeared, leaving only faint golden trails behind it. A new room formed around them; a pleasant chamber with a fire crackling at one end, and two chairs by the hearth. Laura sat down in one of these, and took out a rich piece of embroidery from a workbox at her feet. Reyn bowed to Amy, and left.

Amy stalked restlessly around the room like a wild animal trapped in a cage. The air had an odd flavour – stale, metallic – and she could not shake the feeling of being enclosed in a small space. When she ran her finger against surfaces – the tapestries, the thick stone walls of the castle – flecks of light gathered and followed her fingertip wherever she traced with it. Whatever tricks Reyn pulled to give the illusion of space, there were clearly limits to his abilities.

Reaching the window, Amy tugged at the curtains. Night had fallen and it was pitch black outside. That only added to her sense of claustrophobia. She abandoned her progress round the room and slumped into the chair opposite Laura. She nodded down at her needlework.

'So is that how you've filled the time?'

'Hardly!'

'So what have you been doing with yourself for the past, ooh, six decades?'

Laura calmly completed a few more stitches before answering. 'At first, I tried to get away. You wouldn't believe how many times I tried to get away! How many different routes I tried! Of course, I always ended up back in the glade. That's where all the paths lead – the great green cathedral of trees. And Reyn was always there, to bring me home.'

'I bet he was,' Amy muttered.

'After a while it seemed stupid to waste so much energy and emotion on a pointless activity. Particularly when there were so many marvels here to see. Thread this needle for me, will you, Amy? My eyes aren't what they were.'

Amy squinted, and poked the loose end through the eye of the needle with one quick stab. As she bit off the thread, she said, 'What marvels are you talking about? What is there to see here? You're stuck in the middle of a wood!'

'You saw the valley!' Laura said. 'You saw how beautiful it is here! And this is only the most recent of the worlds we've lived in. Reyn can create whatever I want, whatever I imagine! Space stations, intergalactic empires, a gothic mansion filled with spooks and ghouls, our own world at any time in its history!'

'Yes, but it's all fake, isn't it?' Amy waved her hand quickly to and fro, and a trail of golden light followed the movement. 'I don't know how he does it – virtual reality, maybe, or a simulation, or something to do with him being a shape-shifter... Oh, I don't know! I *do* know that none of it is real! It's horrible! It's like you've been stuck in a role-playing game your whole life!' She leaned forwards in her chair. 'Laura, I've seen marvels – *real* marvels – things I can touch and smell and taste, and I haven't had to be stuck in the same place in order to see them! My friend – the Doctor – he's taken me to places you wouldn't believe!'

'Then you of all people should understand, Amy. Of anyone that's ever come this way – you should understand! That's exactly what Reyn has done for me! Perhaps aliens and starships and walking through a door out onto a different world isn't anything particularly wonderful for you, but it was for me! To think that I once thought I might make it as far as Africa!'

'You're not even five miles from home! You're trapped!'

'Trapped is a state of mind. If we thought that way, we wouldn't be able to bear it—'

'Er, excuse me – there's no "we" about this! I'm not staying here a moment longer than I can help. First light – I'm out of here!'

Laura gave the kind of smile that can only infuriate. 'We'll see. We'll see.'

At this point, Reyn came back into the room. He crossed over to the fire, carrying a third chair with him, and sat warming his hands. In the candlelight, there was a real beauty to him – the thick, well-kept reddish hair; the sad, clever, orange eyes; the melancholy that seemed to gather around him like the light that followed Amy's finger... Amy shook herself. No, she wasn't going to be charmed by this creature, however beautiful and lonely and persuasive he might be.

Reyn had become aware that she was watching him. His ears twitched back. 'I do understand your frustration, Amy,' he said, 'but I cannot risk lowering the barriers around the portal place. It's too dangerous.'

Amy nodded towards the door. 'Were you standing out there listening for long?'

'I think you already know that this place is not as large as the impression might give. I could hear your voice quite clearly in the next tower.'

Amy blushed with embarrassment. 'Sorry,' she said. 'Didn't mean to shout. Still, why can't I try? Isn't it always worth trying?'

'I lost count of the number of times I tried, Amy,' Laura said. 'We're only trying to save you a great deal of heartbreak.'

'It's true,' Reyn said, 'that I cannot be entirely sure what would happen if I let you through, Amy. It may make no difference at all. But my best guess – and it's an educated guess – is that it would bring on the Shift. That puts the town at risk. I am the one responsible here, and I don't think that's a risk worth taking.'

'Is this place really so terrible, Amy?' Laura said. 'Could you not at least wait for a while and see? It might be more bearable than you're imagining.'

And, for a moment, sitting in that comfortable chair by that warm and lovely fire, Amy was tempted. Would it be so bad, after all, to stay here, in this calm, beautiful place, in this gentle kindly company; to leave whatever disaster was unfolding to somebody else to deal with? This place was enclosed, secluded – perhaps even if Swallow Woods did flood and become covered in water, this place would remain intact, sealed away. She might be safe here.

But she wouldn't be with Rory, and she wouldn't be Amy Pond.

'It's no use,' Amy said. 'I have to take the risk. I know something's going to happen soon that will destroy the town and flood the valley. But I don't really know what causes it. What if it's because I *don't* try to get out? I don't know whether the Doctor is free or not, I don't know whether Jess and Vicky made it, and I don't know what Rory is doing right now, whenever he is. I do know that I can't sit around waiting for events to catch up with me. I have to do *something*,' she said, 'and then take the consequences. I'll wait till first light, and then I'll go.'

'But you won't get through,' Reyn said. 'I can't let you get through.'

'And I can't *not* try! First light, I'm off.'

Reyn sighed. 'Here, of course, we don't have to wait for dawn to arrive. We can bring it to us.'

He waved his hand. Amy got up, crossed to the window, and pulled the curtains back. Already the sky was pale and, quickly, it was suffused with a golden haze. Then the yellow sun emerged. This all took the matter of a moment.

'Whatever it is you're doing here,' Amy told Reyn, 'it's pretty impressive.'

'Thank you,' Reyn replied. 'I've had a long time to perfect it. Shall we go?'

In the courtyard, the sun was already high overhead. Laura laid her hand, parchment thin with age, upon Amy's cheek. 'Don't be too heartbroken if you find yourself back here with us,' she said. 'I've had a good life, and a happy one.'

'I won't be back,' Amy said. 'But I'll tell your parents you said that, if you like.'

Laura's face crinkled up with an old but unforgotten pain. 'Don't,' she said. 'I know you mean well, but don't hold out hopes like that.'

Reyn bent to kiss his lady's hand and then, in the blink of an eye, he and Amy were standing once again on the edge of the wood. Looking back down into the valley, Amy saw Laura's castle. A soft spring rain was falling, and a double rainbow had formed across the bowl of the valley, brightly coloured and essentially ephemeral.

'Good luck,' Reyn said. 'Although I think it won't be long before you're back with us again.'

'Nothing ventured,' Amy said, and plunged back underneath the dark cover of the trees.

As Emily kept speaking, her words seemed to have a soothing effect not just on Harry, but even on the ship. The lights settled down and the noise fell back to its gentlest hum. Best of all, from Rory's perspective, the walls stopped shaking.

'There,' Emily said. 'No need for us all to get so worked up. I told you, it's only Harry. Oh, but Harry, have you been here by yourself all this time? Did you get lost?'

'*Lost...*' whispered the young man. '*Lost...*'

'Eh, now, come on, Harry, I know you must have been scared – heaven knows me and Mr Williams have been – but can't you even manage a hello? We're old friends, aren't we?'

'Emily,' said Rory. 'I'm not sure that's Harry.'

'What? Don't be daft – look at him! You saw

his picture over there! Besides, I've known Harry Thompson since he was toddling round our yard. I'd recognise him anywhere!'

'What I mean is, it might *look* like Harry, and it might even be his body, but…' Rory struggled to explain. 'It's not him inside.'

'Well, that's just a load of old nonsense.' Emily stared into her friend's eyes and squeezed his hand again. 'You're there, Harry, aren't you? You've just had a shock.' To Rory, she said, 'Given you don't know what a white feather is, or a conchie, do you think it's possible you might not recognise shellshock when you see it? Well, I can, and that's what it looks like to me. Harry's here, aren't you, love? We've just got to find a way to make you feel safe again.'

'*Safe… Safe…*'

Emily made Harry sit down on the steps. She knelt down in front of him, putting his hands within hers. 'Can you tell us what happened, love? Can you remember?'

'*Remember…*' The young man's eyes came sharply into focus. He stared so hard at Emily that Rory was suddenly afraid for her. He reached forwards to try to disentangle their hands, but Emily shook him off.

'We're getting there,' she said. 'He'll be talking soon. Isn't that better than running around getting nowhere?'

'Remember...' Harry's voice was getting steadily stronger. 'The long journey... The dark, the cold... Saw light! Felt something... something new... Pain...'

'I know, love,' Emily said consolingly. 'Go on, now, you'll feel better once you've let it all out.'

'Needed rest. Needed time... to *think*!' The young man's voice became suddenly excited. 'To know! To grow! To become... to become *different*...'

'Eh, now, love, you're not making much sense.'

'Emily,' Rory said quickly. 'Wait a minute. Look – I think I might know what's happening here. A dark journey? That's not how it was for us, is it? We came through bright sunshine, remember?'

'Yes, but you said the place could change—'

'Can I have a go? Can I talk to him? I promise I won't say anything to upset him.'

Emily looked at him doubtfully. 'Well, all right then, but be kind.'

Rory knelt down in front of the young man. 'Your long cold journey,' he said, 'were there stars?'

'Stars... suns... worlds... Then the pain. Then

this world. Fell here. The pain too much… Still wanting to know, to see, to learn… So much here to know, to learn… So much… Soon be ready… Soon be… Soon be me!'

'Mr Williams, I'm not sure it helps sending him off on flights of fancy like this—'

'One more question, Emily, I promise.' Again Rory addressed the young man. 'What have you learned? Who did you learn it from?'

Emily frowned at him. 'Eh?'

'Just let him answer, Emily. Then I'll know for sure.'

The young man looked at Rory. His eyes were vacant and unfocused.

'What did you learn?' Rory said again. 'Who taught you?'

'They came here. There were none before. Then they came. They love and live and quarrel and die in less time than it takes for a tree to grow. They are like the leaves. They are cruel and kind and brave and afraid. Sometimes they know no better. Sometimes they are at fault. Sometimes they doubt. Sometimes they believe. And always they want to know…'

'Mr Williams, I don't understand all this—'

'Doesn't sound much like Harry Thompson any more, does it?' Turning back to Harry once again, Rory said, 'How many? How many have come here?'

'One hundred and seventy-three,' the young man rattled off promptly, like a machine reading out data.

Rory recoiled. There was a sick taste in his mouth. 'A hundred and seventy-three!'

Emily pulled at his arm. 'You'd better start explaining things, mister, or else I'm going to start getting right ticked off with you.'

'How many pictures did we count, Emily?'

'What?'

'On the screen over there. How many different people?'

'More than a hundred, I reckon. We never got to the end, did we? What are you saying, Mr Williams?'

'This isn't Harry,' Rory said. He stood up, and turned away, repulsed. He ran down to the console, waving it back to life, and he started hunting, certain now that he would eventually find what he was looking for.

'All these *people*!' he said, as the images rushed past. 'They came this way, and it took their memories! Emily, that might be Harry's body, but it's certainly not Harry that's talking to us. It's the ship!'

Rory looked down at the console. He waved his hand and stopped the flow of pictures. The blow on the head hadn't taken his memories away. There he was, on the screen, surrounded by impenetrable text. 'It takes memories! The ship steals memories! My memories!'

In the foyer of the police station, Jess watched the storm and waited for the car to arrive to take her home. As the wind hammered at the roof, Galloway came through the double doors that led back into the main part of the building. He stood for a moment peering unhappily out at the rain running in rivulets down the window. Then he pulled out a newspaper and shook it out to use as an umbrella.

It was worth one last try. 'Please,' Jess said. 'Don't search the woods. Talk to the Doctor first—'

'I have talked to him. All I want to know is where he's keeping Laura Brown. Unfortunately, he had nothing useful to say.' Galloway pushed open the entrance doors. 'Go home, Ms Ashcroft. Get a good night's sleep. Call me tomorrow once you've had a chance to think – and if you've anything sensible to say.'

He ducked out into the rain. It was lashing down now, a real storm. Jess watched the inspector sprint across to his car, holding his copy of *The Herald* over his head. There was a flash of lightning followed by a long roll of thunder so loud it almost seemed to make the ground shudder. This, Jess thought, desperately, was how it would feel at the end of the world. Soon the dogs would be going into the woods, yelling, barking, on the hunt for the strange fox creature that she had surely seen...

Behind her, the officer at the desk, in a doubtful voice, said, 'Inspector Galloway didn't mention anything about it...'

'No?' A young female voice. 'Well, he was quite clear in his instructions to me.'

Jess looked round. There was Ruby Porter, a study in nonchalance. Standing behind her...

The      Doctor,      handcuffed,      and uncharacteristically meek.

'He's wanted down at the search,' Porter went on. 'If we really *are* going to search the woods,' she and the officer shook their heads at outsiders who insisted on blundering about near Swallow Woods, 'then I suppose we'd better do it properly.' At this point, Porter noticed Jess. 'How about I give Ms Ashcroft that lift home at the same time? Save you the bother of rustling up a car.'

Now that Porter had given him a solution to his small but immediately pressing problem, the officer was much more willing to let the pair past. Pushing the Doctor ahead of her, Porter walked over to the doors.

'Follow me,' she muttered to Jess on her way past. Jess dutifully obeyed. Porter led them through the rain towards a little dark blue car. 'In the back, both of you,' she hissed.

Jess opened the back door and shoved the Doctor in, hurrying after him and shaking the water from her hair as soon as she was inside. Porter, getting into the driver's seat, said, 'I suppose I'm going to get disciplined for this. At the very least. Probably fired.'

'Cheer up!' the Doctor said. 'Might never happen! Might not get the chance. After all, it's entirely possible that this time next week the town won't be here any longer. Under those circumstances, I seriously doubt anyone would have disciplinary procedures on their mind—'

Porter, furiously, started the car.

'Doctor—' Jess said, urgently.

He raised his cuffed hands to stop her. 'The word you are looking for,' he said, 'is were-fox.' He leaned forwards to address Porter. 'Constable,' he said, 'the gadget with the green light. Did you have any success in... umgph!'

The end of his sentence was lost. Porter had shoved the sonic screwdriver between his teeth, without taking her eyes off the road. The Doctor turned and dropped the device into Jess's lap.

'Ms Ashcroft,' he said politely, holding up his cuffed hands and nodding down at the sonic. 'That button, there— No, *there*. Yes! That's the one!'

'It's not Harry talking to us,' Rory said. 'It's the ship! It takes memories! The ship steals memories. My memories!'

It was as if the ship heard him speak. Once again, the walls shuddered, with even more force, and the body-that-was-once-Harry convulsed. Emily put her arm around the boy's shoulder.

'Stolen your memories?' she snapped. 'Nonsense! You got a tap on the head, that's all! Not stolen any of mine, has it?'

'Perhaps it can only cope with one person at a time. Perhaps you're next! Oh, I don't know, Emily, I'm not the memory-stealing spaceship!'

'Anyway, how can a man be a ship? That's like saying he's a motor car or a train!'

'It's using his body as a kind of transmitter…' Rory cast around for an example she might understand. 'Like he's a walking telegram! He's carrying messages from the ship to us. He's the means by which the ship is able to talk to us.'

'Well, if he's passing on messages, that's good, isn't it? We'll be able to talk to the ship, maybe ask it to let us go home?'

'You don't understand – the ship isn't *asking* him to pass on messages. It's *making* him do it.'

'Eeuw!' said Emily. 'That's horrible!' Her hold on Harry's hand got tighter. 'But is Harry still in there? Are you there, love? Can you hear me?'

'I don't think he can be there. I think the ship has taken his memories, like it's taken some of mine—'

'Poor thing!' said Emily, and from the way she was stroking Harry's hand, Rory got the distinct impression she wasn't talking about him.

'Er, excuse me? My memories too? Pinched? Stolen? Not here?'

'Oh, yes, but look – you're still intact, aren't you? Still standing, still talking. Whereas Harry can't remember a thing, and as for the ship… Well, you heard it! All that talk of learning, and growing – it sounds like a child to me.'

'Pinched!' Rory tapped the side of his head. 'Stolen! No longer there! Honestly, what does somebody have to do to get some sympathy around here?'

'I'm not saying it's not horrible for you, just

that I don't think it knew any better.'

'That's all very well for you to say, Emily, but it's not your memories that have been stolen! And it's not you that could have been turned into a walkie-talkie!'

'A whichety-what?' Emily shook her head. 'You do talk some nonsense! And look! You're upsetting him!' She put her arm around Harry, who was shaking violently. 'Hush, love, it's all right!'

'Me? Upsetting *him*? Anyway, him – it's not a him, it's an it! And what about all the people it's taken? Too right it should be upset! It should be very upset! Not to mention ashamed!'

Harry – or the ship – began to moan, a low drone pitched at the same level as the engine's throb, like the wind howling round a wasteland.

'Oh, do stop! Look what you're doing to him!' Emily patted the young man's hand. 'Shush now! Don't you worry! It's not your fault.'

'Er, well, actually, it *is* its fault. One hundred and seventy-three times over. All those people! It doesn't bear thinking about... What did it *do* with them? Did they spend their days like Harry here, stolen from their friends and their family, walking around this tiny ship like... like *zombies*! It's awful, Emily! And it could have happened to us! It could have taken us! It's already taken some of my memories! Did I mention that? My memories? Taken?'

'*Taken*...' whispered the ship, in Harry's voice. '*Stolen*... *Lost*...' Slowly, tears began to roll down the young man's cheeks. Once again, the walls around them shook hard, as if a deep and guilty wave of sorrow was passing through them.

'Don't, Mr Williams! Please! Can't you see you're distressing it? It's like bullying a child!' To the young man, the young ship, Emily said, 'Don't listen to him, love! Here, what should I call you? If you're not really Harry? Do you have a name? Can you tell me? No? Ship sounds so funny, but I suppose it'll have to do. Don't upset yourself, Ship. You didn't know what you were doing. Now you know, you can stop, can't you?'

'Maybe it can stop, but it can't take back what it's done,' Rory pointed out. And with another deep sigh of shuddering grief, Ship said:

'Sorry... Sorry to be... Sorry to be born...'

It shook again. The lights on the walls dimmed and flickered. This time some patches stayed dark, and others turned an alarming red. The hum rose in pitch and volume, the unmistakable sound of an alarm, like a wind howling through the trees.

'Can't you see what you're doing?' Emily said to Rory. 'You're hurting it! For all we know you could be killing it! What happens to us then, Mr Williams? What happens to us all then?'

A great gale tore through Swallow Woods. The trees shook and threw whatever they could into the path of Amy Pond. She ducked to avoid a branch that flung itself at her, and ran on. There was a grey patch of light ahead. Amy chased it—

And came out into the glade, the portal place, the ancient green chapel where all paths led. She could distinguish no season here now. The rain lashed down, the trees rocked to and fro as if in pain, and, in the centre of the clearing, the water in the pool was rising. In the distance, faintly, Amy heard the barking of dogs.

'Got to go,' Amy told herself. 'Got to get out!'

She ran beneath one of the great silent arches, the storm battering her. A few minutes later – breathless, exhausted, soaked to the skin – she saw another grey slab of light...

And came back into the clearing, where the trees were writhing and the water still rising. Again, she tried – ran through beating rain with the yell of hounds ringing in her ears – and again she got no further than the glade. The pool was swollen, overflowing, the water lapping almost at her ankles now. This, surely, was the start of whatever disaster was going to befall Swallow Woods and the people of Foxton. Amy had tried her best, but either it had not been enough, or else it had been the last straw.

Teeth chattering, bitterly cold, Amy sank to the ground. The rain lashed against her face. She scrubbed at the water, and then saw, standing on the other side of the glade, framed by a swaying arch of old trees, Reyn.

'I truly am sorry,' he said, 'but I did not lie to you. You cannot leave Swallow Woods.'

'I must!' Amy yelled. 'I have to! There's nobody else!'

'But look around you, Amy! Look at what's happening!'

Thunder rolled and there was a flash of light. Torches? Searchlights? Lightning? Amy could not tell. She put her arms across her knees and dropped her head wearily down against them. 'There has to be a way. There *must* be!'

'I'm sorry, Amy,' Reyn said. 'There's no way through the woods.'

'Of course there's a way,' another voice said, a familiar voice that made Amy's heart somersault in her chest. 'There's always a way.'

It felt to Amy as if she had been locked in a deep dark dungeon, and somebody had thrown open the door, let in fresh air and bright sunlight, and then showed her that the key had been in her pocket all along. She leapt to her feet, and cried out in joy.

'Doctor!'

# Chapter
# 12

There he was, the Doctor, leaning against a tree, chucking the sonic screwdriver up into the air and catching it, and looking very pleased with himself.

Amy ran over – and belted him on the arm. 'You took your time!'

'Ow! Don't be *too* excited about seeing me, will you?'

'I've been running around here like a hamster on a wheel, getting *soaked*… What have you been *doing*?'

'Breaking out of jail. I'm an outlaw now, Pond, a vagabond. A man on the run. I live on the edge, with only my wits and my trusty sonic screwdriver to keep me one step ahead of the law.'

'So they let you out?'

'It was in fact a touch more clandestine than that. There was actual stealth involved at one point – but, yes, broadly speaking, they let me out.'

'And Jess? What about Jess and Vicky? Did they get through?'

'They got through, just about…' The Doctor switched on the sonic, and waved it around vigorously and possibly even to some specific end. 'Ooh, I see! All got very complicated here, hasn't it? All these fixes and patches. And then three people come along at once! Ship and pilot were so busy with you, Amy, that Vicky and Jess were able to get past both of them… Look at these readings! Someone's not in as much control round here as he'd like to think. Speaking of whom…' he swung round and pointed the sonic at Reyn, 'are you going to introduce us, Amy?'

He was staring at the were-fox with the kind of look that he generally reserved for his more intractable foes.

'This is Reyn,' Amy said. 'Now don't go Time Lord on him. He didn't mean any harm…'

'They usually don't.'

'He's been stuck here too! He couldn't fix the ship and get away—'

'Fatalism. Dreadful habit. Leads to all kinds of vices, like trapping passing strangers in your timeless fantasy playground or not bothering to brush your teeth.'

'I think he's done his best with limited resources,' Amy said. 'No bad breath, at any rate.' She wiped her face. It was still raining heavily and from beyond the trees came a faint but persistent barking. 'Doctor, are you going to stand around being all Dark Knight about this for much longer? Or can we skip to the bit where we find out what's happening and then stop it?'

The Doctor popped his sonic screwdriver back into his pocket. 'I'm prepared to put things behind me. Let's see whether he is.' He walked across the clearing and gave Reyn an elaborate formal greeting which the were-fox, startled, reciprocated with great elegance.

'I know your species,' the Doctor said. 'I know your myths, your legends, your history. I know all about the Long War and what happened—' He stopped himself. 'Anyway, enough of my chit and chat – why don't you tell me what really brought your ship down here?'

Amy, confused, said, 'I thought he crashed?'

'Which I think is probably partly true,' said

the Doctor, 'but not entirely true. Am I right?'

Reyn, who had been watching the Doctor warily, nodded slowly. 'I was being chased by enemy gunships. I was attacked and my ship was damaged. That part was completely true. I intended to hide here until my ship was healed. Then the people came and the Shift got under way.'

'And that's when all this malarkey with the time pockets and the portal-building and the disappearances started, yes?'

'Doctor,' Amy said, 'hang on a minute…'

'Make up your mind, Pond! A moment ago you were telling me to hurry up!'

'Shut up.' She raised a warning finger. 'And fill me in on this Long War business, OK?'

'The worlds inhabited by Reyn's people, Amy, had – at one point in their history – the misfortune to find themselves living right next door to quite a substantial interplanetary empire. Empires are in general greedy beasts, and this one was no exception. You've seen the kinds of technology that Reyn has at his disposal, not to mention the shape-shifting. There was a war—'

'I'm guessing that it was a long war,' Amy said.

'It has been a very long war,' said Reyn.

'Several generations now.'

'And you've presumably worked out that they're rather a long-lived species,' said the Doctor. 'So you brought the ship down, Reyn, the Shift began but, given the damage done and your lack of support infrastructure, you've not been able either to fix the ship and leave, or else to shut it down entirely and stop people being taken. You've only been able to hold back the whole process. Yes, a very difficult situation...'

'I told you he'd been trying his best,' Amy said. Turning to Reyn, she asked, 'Why didn't you tell me all that earlier? About the war?'

Quietly, from behind her shoulder, the Doctor said, 'I suspect Reyn's enemies weren't only trying to find out how the ship worked, Amy. I rather imagine they wanted to study the shape-shifting too. I'd hide under those circumstances. I might not reveal too much about myself either.'

'And we're supposed to be the suspicious ones,' Amy said.

'I've learned the hard way,' Reyn replied. He sighed, deeply. 'I want to leave this world,' he said. 'More than anything! I want to get home, return to the struggle. I've been away far too long. But I'm stuck here. I have no way out. Either I maintain the environment I've created, or the ship shifts and the town and its people are lost. I brought us here! It's my responsibility. What choice do I have?'

He looked pathetic, the rain running down his red pelt, his ears flat and dejected. Amy put her hand upon his arm.

'So what you need,' the Doctor said thoughtfully, 'is help with the ship. If we can guide the ship successfully through its Shift, you and it would be free to leave—'

'Yes, but, as I've said – I can't maintain the integrity of this environment and handle the Shift! Not all at once! Something will give!'

'Yes, yes, that's what I'll help with! Hello! This is the help you've been waiting for all these years! Here I am! The help!' He gave a friendly little wave. 'I'll go to the ship. Children *love* me!'

'Doctor,' Amy hissed. 'What about Rory?'

'Ah, yes! The elusive Mr Pond. I wonder what he's been up to? Certainly not triangulating. Perhaps we should find out exactly what he's been doing for the past century with that delightful young woman. I imagine Reyn can help with that, guide me through to the ship at the right time. Rory and Emily can help me with the Shift, Reyn can maintain the environment, and when we're done, you can both set sail again and leave this poor old wood in peace to get on with making acorns and feeding squirrels and being a nice place to go for a picnic. Ha! How does that sound as a deal, Reyn? You get to leave, Swallow Woods gets picnickers, and we get Rory. Actually,' he looked excited, 'we might just have a picnic afterwards, too. So. What do you think?'

Reyn did not answer. Close by, dogs were barking.

'Listen,' said the Doctor. 'They're coming. The humans, their dogs. I've met the man in charge. He's a decent sort, but he's very cross right now. Things haven't been going his way recently. He's not in the mood for holding back. So whatever you decide, you'd better decide it soon. Those dogs are scary, and your ship might not wait for them to board it. Besides, I think the Shift is going to happen whether you like it or not. Look around. Look at what's happening.'

Amy saw that the trees were in chaos: all the seasons were jumbled up. Here, one tree was full of blossom and heavy with thick green leaves; there, another tree was bright with autumn colours. It seemed that the portal place was breaking down.

'Trust me,' said the Doctor. 'After all, I'll be trusting you with Amy.' He leaned sideways.

'You're all right with that, aren't you, Pond?'

'Oh, great, yeah,' Amy muttered. 'Absolutely fine...'

'All right,' said Reyn, slowly. 'I'll try to direct you through to the ship. I can't make any guarantees, but I'll try to get you through to the right time.' His ears pricked up. 'As for the dogs,' he pulled out a small golden device, 'I can put them on the wrong track for a while. Long enough for you to reach the ship.'

'Good man! Fox! Foxy-man-thing... Yes, whatever you are, you're good. Very good. We're good. Well, you do whatever it is you've got to do to confuse poor Inspector Galloway. While *Amy*,' he beckoned to her, 'why don't you come and help me choose which path to take?'

'I thought Reyn was going to guide you,' Amy said in a puzzled voice. 'Ow!' she finished, the Doctor having elbowed her hard. 'Yes! All right! I see! Yes! Let's choose an arch for you, Doctor! A really *nice* arch, one that looks like it's got Rory's name written all over it!'

They walked round the clearing and stopped by one of the arches of trees. It was winter over here, wet and gloomy. The Doctor made a big show of waving the sonic screwdriver about.

'I'd switch that on if I were you,' Amy said,

*sotto voce.* 'Looks more convincing that way.'

'Ah, yes.' The sonic started buzzing. 'Now, you've still got your triangulator, haven't you?'

'Of course!'

'Good. Always a good idea to have a back-up system.'

'Never noticed you worrying about that much before... Do you still not trust him?'

'Almost... But I think that war can do bad things to its victims, Amy. Reyn has been on his guard for a very long time. I doubt he's told us everything. So, no, I don't trust him, not entirely. Or, to be more accurate, I don't think he quite trusts me. Which means he might have some more surprises up his sleeve. Which means I'd like to make sure I have something up *my* sleeve. You know what to do if Rory's triangulator finally sends a signal?'

'I hit this button... no, *this* button. And then with any luck we'll all be able to find each other again without relying on Reyn, and I'll finally get my chocolatey treat. After which I'll brush and floss, naturally.'

'Excellent! Yes! Bang on! Chocolates and floss for all!'

'So... what was it you didn't want to say about the Long War?'

'Hmm?'

'You stopped yourself mid-sentence. What didn't you say?'

'Yes…' The Doctor sighed deeply. 'I know how that particular war ends, Amy, and it's a sad story. The thing is – I don't think Reyn realises that it's over. Done with.' He glanced back over his shoulder. 'Laura Brown's not the only one lost in time.'

'One last question, Doctor.'

'Make it quick.'

'You said before that going through one of these portals was irrevocable. But I've been through one, and I guess Rory must have been through one too, and you're about to go through one… Does that mean we're stuck here? Will we ever get out?'

Gently, he touched her cheek. 'Work to do first, Pond.'

'That's not an answer!'

'Of course it's an answer. If we want to get out, we'll have to make a way out.'

'Do you know how you're going to do that? No, no, I know the answer to that already. You're working on it.'

'How well you know me, Pond.' He smiled, and drew her in for a hug. 'Go back with Reyn. Guide me through to Rory. And watch out for any changes of heart at your end. Keep your finger on the button of the triangulator. And I promise you all the chocolate you want when we're done.'

'Actually it's the picnic I'm after now. Pork pie. Hey, watch out, I think Reyn's done.'

The Doctor switched off the sonic and patted the nearest tree. 'What a very fine pair of trees these are! These look just the trees for me! What do you think, Pond?'

'Oh, Doctor,' Amy said in delight, 'what a splendid pair of trees! If I had to choose some trees to take me back through time, these would be exactly the trees I'd choose!'

'Well, now that that's decided,' said the Doctor, 'how about we get on with it? Reyn, what about Inspector Galloway's search party?'

'It'll keep searching,' he said. 'But it won't find its way here. This whole area is now off limits, at least while the power holds. You should go now, Doctor. I can't hold them off indefinitely. Amy and I will return to my control room, and I'll guide you through to the ship.'

'No time like the present!' Standing framed by the arch of dark bare trees, the Doctor waved to Amy. 'Cheerio, Pond! See you later! Or earlier! But don't worry – I'll be ba—!'

The trees, and the Doctor, melted away.

In the courtyard of the castle, the rain was falling heavily. Laura greeted Amy and Reyn with great relief.

'Something's going wrong,' she said to Reyn. 'The whole place is breaking down.' She pointed up at the sky. 'Look!'

Amy looked up at a sky in confusion: patches of bright blue with fluffy white clouds here; sections of inky black spattered with stars there. It was as if parts thought it was day, and other parts were convinced it was night. A rainbow, broken into sections, was scattered haphazardly about.

'It's the Shift,' Amy told Laura. 'But we've found my friend, the Doctor. He thinks he can control the process, but first we have to guide him through to the ship. Reyn, this isn't looking good, really. We should hurry. What now?'

Reyn waved his hand in the familiar gesture. The whole castle disappeared, and the three of them were standing in a spherical room, with gun-metal walls. Steps led down to a console; Reyn ran down them and began operating controls.

Laura looked around her in amazement. 'I've never seen this place…'

'Breaks the illusion, doesn't it?' Amy followed Reyn down the steps. 'OK, are we in touch with the Doctor yet?'

'Not yet...' murmured Reyn, busy at the console. A high-pitched squeal filled the control room, making all three of them cover their ears. Then a voice came through.

*'Pond! Pond! Doctor calling Pond! Can you hear me, Pond?'*

*'Yes!'* Amy clenched her fists victoriously. 'Yes, I can hear you, you crazy time-travelling crazy thing! Where are you?'

*'Where do you think I am, Pond? I'm in a wood, and it's raining. Why didn't we pack the umbrella?'*

'Because we didn't want to look like Mary Poppins!'

*'Ooh, fair point. How's it going at your end?'*

'Oh, you know, the usual! End of things! Sky falling in!'

*'Situation normal, then! Shan't worry about you too much! Reyn – which way now? We're aiming for 1917. Try not to land me in the middle of the Civil War. Or anywhere with dinosaurs. They're cool, but they're not very early twentieth century.'*

As Reyn set about directing the Doctor through, Laura drew Amy aside.

'Amy, what does this all mean? Is everything

coming to an end?'

Amy, anxious to keep in touch with the Doctor, looked past her at the console. 'I don't know. The Doctor isn't there yet. And then we have to guide the ship through the Shift, and we still don't really know what's causing all the damage…' She glanced at Laura.

The old woman's face was wet with tears.

'Laura? Are you OK?'

'It's just that it's been such a very long time…' Laura whispered. 'Amy, did you meet my parents? Did you ever see them?'

Amy took hold of Laura's hand. Suddenly she realised the full extent of the old woman's predicament. Even if they guided the ship safely through the Shift, even if Reyn and the ship left without any damage to the woods and the town – it was all happening far too late for Laura. There was no bringing back the sixty years that she had been here.

'I wanted to travel,' Laura said. 'I wanted to see strange and beautiful places. And when I thought there was no way back, when I thought I could never see everyone and everywhere I loved again, it was easy to make myself believe that I had been somewhere wonderful, seen wonderful things. But now I'm not so certain any more. Amy, have I been deluding myself?

Have I been lost in a fantasy my whole life?'

'No,' Amy said, and held her hand tight. 'No, it's not been like that. What about Reyn? What about your friendship? An alien were-fox, Laura! That's pretty astounding! Try saying that at the school reunion! Who else do you know got to be friends with an alien?'

'You?' Laura said, and then she began to laugh. 'Yes,' she said, 'Yes, we've been friends. And you're right – not many people get to meet someone so extraordinary. Someone so unique.'

'It's not over till it's over, Laura. Nobody knows what ending they get, and happy endings are sometimes not what you've imagined. It looks like Reyn's going home. Perhaps you could go with him?'

Laura squeezed her hand. 'Perhaps.'

Reyn looked up from the console. His eyes were bright and his ears up and alert. 'Amy, I think we're nearly there. The Doctor's reached the ship.'

Amy and Laura hugged each other, and then rejoined Reyn at the console.

*'Pond! Pond! Calling Pond! I'm here, Pond! I'm at the hatch into the ship! I'm going in! Any messages for Rory?'*

Amy grabbed hold of the console. 'Give him

a kiss from me!'

'*Doubt he'll let me, but I'll try my best! Opening the hatch now! Going in!*'

There was a pause, the sound of the sonic screwdriver buzzing, and then an almighty *thump*. The room around Amy rocked alarmingly.

'Try not to finish us off when we're so close to success, Doctor,' Amy said. There was no reply. She leaned forwards anxiously. 'Doctor?'

Another thump.

'*Ow... Yes! Yes! Still here! Everything's fine! It wasn't fine, and now it's fine again! Walking down a corridor... Some things never change... Here's a door... Shut door...*' The sonic buzzed. '*Open door! Ooh, what – and who – do we have here?*'

In the background, Amy could hear voices, raised voices. 'Doctor! Are you OK? Is it Rory? Tell me it's Rory!'

The room around her shook again, and there was another brief squeal. Then the Doctor said, '*Hey! You two! Don't you know better than to quarrel in front of the children?*'

There was a pause, and then, to Amy's delight, Rory's voice came through – clear, annoyed, and extremely baffled.

'*Who on* earth *are you?*'

*

Lights dimming, some blacking out entirely, some turning red; an alarm going off – and now, standing at the top of the steps leading down to the console, there was a young man in a bow tie grinning down at Rory like a maniac.

This, Rory thought, really was the absolute limit.

'I don't know who you are,' he said hotly, 'but if you're the one behind all this, I want it stopped! I want it stopped now. I want my memories back, and I want to go home. Wherever that is. Which I don't know. Because *somebody* has got their spaceship to pinch my memories! Well, I'm telling you,' he raised his finger, not too high, he didn't want cause too much trouble, just to get his point across, 'it's not good enough!'

Bow-tie man beamed at him and then swung down the stairs. He bounded over to Rory and planted a kiss on the top of his head. Rory pushed him away.

'No! Stop! Get off! This isn't fair!'

'*Rory?*' A young woman's voice echoed through the control room, piercing through the whine of the alarm. '*What time do you call this!*'

'Oh, Mr Amy Pond,' said bow-tie man, shaking his head. 'You've stayed out too late, and the wife isn't happy.'

Emily, kneeling beside Harry, couldn't quite suppress a chuckle. Bow-tie man swung round and favoured her with another lunatic smile. 'Miss Emily Bostock!' he said. 'At last! What an *absolute* pleasure to meet you!'

'Oh!' said Emily, nicely. 'Lovely to meet you too, sir!' Bow-tie man went over to join her, and Rory, bewildered, followed. Kneeling down beside Emily, the new arrival took hold of Harry's other hand.

'Well,' he said, calmly. 'I bet you're frightened! That's all right. World's a strange place, isn't it? Confusing. You're not sure what to think and you're not sure what to do. I'm the Doctor, by the way. I'm here to help.'

*The Doctor...* Rory rubbed his forehead. Lights dimmed and reddened around him. The alarm was very distracting.

'It found out, you see,' Emily said to the Doctor. 'About all the people that it brought here. And it got terribly upset. I think that's what's making everything shake about.'

Harry trembled and the walls of the ship rocked. The whine went up a notch.

'Oh, please, love!' Emily cried softly. 'Don't! Don't!'

'*Stolen...*' whispered the ship through Harry. '*Sorry... Sorry to be born...*'

'Yes, I see,' said the Doctor softly. 'Thought about someone else for the first time. Scary when that happens. Thought about what it had done to them. Even scarier.' He rubbed Harry's hand. 'Emily, ever helped anyone give birth before?'

'Well,' Emily said doubtfully, 'the *pigs*...'

'Er, excuse me!' Rory tapped the Doctor on the shoulder. 'What exactly is going on here?'

'Rory, yes! Sorry! Memory loss! Haven't forgotten – how ironic would that be? I'm onto it! But right now we've got to deal with the ship. You probably noticed – what with the alarms and the lights and everything – that something's going on. Well, that something is called its Shift, which means it's coming alive, and I think all this talk about its terrible evildoing hasn't exactly helped—'

'But it's true! It's stolen people! Taken them away and used them!'

Harry – the whole ship – convulsed once again at his words. More patches along the walls went dark and the howling alarm screamed louder, like the ship was in pain.

'Rory,' said the Doctor, 'you need to shut up. *Now.*'

'But it's only a ship. I—!'

'*Rory!*' Again, the young woman's voice rang

round the room. *'Button it!'*

Rory, as if programmed to, obeyed. He clamped his mouth shut and froze.

*'End…'* moaned the ship through Harry's lips. *'Finish… The only way…'*

'Now wherever are you getting that idea?' said the Doctor briskly. 'All right, so it's not nice to go about dragging people off and stealing their memories, but nobody told you not to, and as soon as you realised, you stopped. Can't say fairer than that, can you? What's all this about finishing yourself? That's a terrible idea!'

*'Scared… ran away… Shouldn't have… Don't want it… Don't want to be me…'*

'Oh Harry!' exclaimed Emily. 'Nobody thinks that! Nobody blames you! Anyone who does is wicked or a fool!'

*'Sacrifice… like the others… there has to be a sacrifice…'*

'Oh, an even worse idea!' said the Doctor. 'Where are you picking these things up from? Who are you hanging round with? Emily, who exactly is Harry?'

'My friend. He ran away into the woods rather than get called up. Ship took him. This is his body.'

'Oh… Oh, I see! So Harry's are some of the most recent memories Ship's got to draw on.

And Ship's confused its own guilt about the disappearances with Harry's shame about deserting...'

'And Ship's got the idea that to make amends there has to be a sacrifice,' Emily said. 'Oh, Harry, you poor thing! Who wants you out there in all that murder? Who in their right mind would want that? Not me, love!' She started to cry. 'Don't give up, dear! Stay with me! I can't lose another, not after Sammy...'

'Ship,' the Doctor urged, 'you've got access to other memories, haven't you? Other people came here too, didn't they? Not just Harry. So what about them? What do you know from them? What can they tell you?' He looked back over his shoulder to where Rory was standing by, silent and befuddled.

'What about Mr Amy Pond?' said the Doctor. 'Trooper Rory Williams? What about his memories? Can you see him, Ship, standing guard over the woman he loves, for two thousand years? What an amazing sacrifice! And nobody – absolutely nobody – had to die!'

As he spoke a light switched on in Rory's head. 'Er,' he said, 'actually, that wasn't me...'

'No. It wasn't,' said the Doctor. (And of course this was the Doctor! How did you forget the *Doctor*...?) 'Not technically. But it was you in all the ways that matter. You'd do it if you had to, Rory Williams. Plastic or not, you'd find a way to stand guard for ever if you had to.'

And Rory knew he would – for Amy. His amazing, wonderful, alarming, smashing Amy, the memory of whom flooded back into his head now. Rory nearly cried to think he could ever have forgotten her.

'Amy!' he called out. 'I'm not in trouble, am I?'

*'No, you're not in trouble!'* A pause. *'Well, not today.'*

The alarm sounded mournfully. *'End...'* said the ship-through-Harry. *'Die...'*

'Oh, love!' Emily said. 'I don't want you to die! Nor Harry, neither! There's been enough of that. Please, Ship! Listen to us! Nobody wants you to die!'

Rory, understanding fully now what was happening, rested his hands on Emily's shoulder. 'Ship,' he said urgently. 'Emily's right. You made a mistake, that's all. You're sorry, and you've stopped. That's enough. You don't need to do any more.'

For a moment, there was only the sound of the alarm, howling, the ship's guilt and shame and sorrow. Then: *'Not consistent... Rory... Why*

THE WAY THROUGH THE WOODS

*not consistent?'*

'I was wrong,' Rory said simply. 'I changed my mind. But that's OK. You don't always have to be right. You're allowed to change your mind. You should, if you're wrong. That's what being a person is about.'

*'Not... consistent...'*

The walls shook violently. Rory had to grab onto the console to stay upright. Harry was flung forwards, sending Emily crashing to the floor beneath him. The ship's wail reached its crescendo. Then it, and the lights, cut out. It felt to Rory as if he had been picked up, shaken hard, and then dumped down again slightly to one side.

For a moment, everything was dark and silent. Then the lights, yellow and green, slowly lifted. There was a brief further moment of silence, and then the ship spoke, but not through Harry. Now its voice came from all around.

'I understand,' said Ship, calmly. 'Shift is achieved. Situation stable.'

Harry blinked and his eyes went back to their usual blue. He looked down at Emily, lying in a heap under him. 'Emmy?' he said. 'What the devil's going on?'

Emily laughed in delight.

'Congratulations,' the Doctor announced

proudly to all listening. 'It's a beautiful baby ship.'

Back in Reyn's control room, Amy punched the air.

'Yes! Oh, Doctor, you're amazing! And as for you, Rory Williams...' She blew him a kiss. 'You're adorable!'

She felt Laura's hand suddenly grip her arm.

'Amy...' the old woman whispered.

Amy turned around. Reyn, from somewhere, had produced a weapon, a large weapon, the kind that alien foxes might use to fight their enemies.

'Ship,' Reyn called out. 'This is your captain speaking. Prepare to report for duty.' He looked sadly at the two women. 'Laura, Amy – I'm sorry. But Ship and I have our duty to perform. We have to return to the War.'

# Chapter
# 13

'Oh no you bloomin' well don't!' Emily Bostock
shouted back at the disembodied voice echoing
around her. She gripped onto Harry's arm like
a tigress making ready to defend her cubs.
'Whoever you might be, you just think on! No
one here is going to the War. Not Ship, not
Harry, not anyone! Over my dead body!'

'Got to hope it won't come to that, Emily,'
the Doctor said softly, and then addressed
Reyn. 'Reyn, I don't much like the sound of
this. Sounds – I don't know, a bit too much like
bossing someone about. Why don't we ask Ship
what it wants to do now?'

'Doctor,' said Reyn, 'I'm grateful for all that you
have done for me. But this is no longer your concern.
It's not a question of what Ship wants to do. It's a

*question of duty. Ship knows what's required of it, and so do I. It's been a long war for all of us, Doctor, but it's not over yet.'*

'Ship,' said the Doctor. 'Is that what you want? To go back to the War?'

'You don't have to, Ship, love!' Emily said fiercely. 'Not if you don't want to! It's a waste! A terrible, wicked waste!'

The Doctor touched her arm. 'Let Ship decide, Emily,' he said quietly. 'Ship can do whatever it wants.'

Rory watched as, on the console, images sped past of all the people that Ship had gathered over the centuries.

Eventually, Reyn's voice came through again. He was getting impatient. *'Ship. It's your duty—'*

'No,' said Ship evenly. 'I disagree. I shall not go.'

*'That's desertion, Ship. Mutiny. I can take action—'*

'I shall not go,' Ship said again.

'Sounds like Ship's made up its mind, Reyn,' the Doctor said. 'So why don't we come up with another plan—'

He stopped speaking when the air on the far side of the console began to fill with particles of golden light. Quickening, solidifying, the shimmering space resolved itself into Reyn, Laura, and Amy. Amy gave Rory a little wave.

'Hi, gorgeous,' she said. 'Love to come and give you a "hello" kiss. But look: there's a weapon-wielding were-fox in the way.'

Rory gave her an anxious little wave back. The return of his memories definitely had both good and bad aspects. Good – Amy. Bad – he was the kind of person who could get separated from his loved one by big alien guns carried by humanoid foxes.

Reyn gestured to the Doctor and the others. 'Over here, please,' he said, backing round the console, his weapon covering them all. Bright lights flashed on the console and a voice began to chant. It sounded very much like a countdown.

'What's he doing?' demanded Emily. 'Here, what are you doing?'

'I'd like to know too, please, Reyn,' said the Doctor.

Reyn's free hand moved quickly around the console. 'If Ship's mind is made up, then Ship's mind must be made to change.' The hand upon the weapon shook. 'The Shift is only newly completed. I can still undo it. Ship's sentience can be reversed.'

'That's obscene!' Amy said. 'Ship's alive now!

You'd be cutting out its mind! That's murder!'

'Worse than murder,' the Doctor said. 'The shell of the ship would be intact. It would fly – but it would no longer think.'

'I'm within my rights,' Reyn said defensively. 'Summary execution is the penalty for desertion—'

'You... *monster*!' Emily cried. 'Doctor, have at him!'

'Everyone, calm down,' the Doctor said. 'Reyn, I don't believe that you want to do this.'

'I have to get back! They're dying, Doctor! You said you knew about our war! You should understand!'

'I know. I know that what happened to your world – to your people – was a terrible crime. And so is this!' He took a step forwards, but Reyn lifted the weapon again. 'Reyn, Ship is bound up with this place, entangled with it. If you destroy Ship's mind – what effect will that have on the people around here? Everybody has been affected by Ship's growing consciousness! And now that the Shift has happened... What would that do to them, Reyn? Have you thought about that?'

Again, Reyn wavered. The weapon slipped down slightly and his hand hovered above the console. Then he shook himself, and straightened up, military-style, except that the uniform didn't quite seem to fit. 'No. They're dying in hundreds of thousands back home, Doctor. I can still make a difference.'

'Reyn,' Laura pleaded softly. 'Please don't do this. My parents – they're out there! I've talked to you about them, many times. All the years we spent together. All that we've seen together. Please don't do this!'

'Laura, dear lady!' Reyn's sad orange eyes were bright and wet. There was something desperate about him. 'It's a risk I have to take.'

The voice was still chanting down.

'Doctor!' Amy said. 'Stop him!'

'All right,' the Doctor said. 'Pond! Mr Pond! Both of you! Triangulate!'

Amy and Rory looked at each other, pulled out their twin devices, pressed the long-unpressed buttons...

And with a groan and a sigh, as if remarking to anyone listening that perhaps it was getting rather old for this game, the TARDIS materialised at the top of the stairs.

The uninitiated gawked at her. 'What the devil is *that*?' said Harry.

The Doctor beamed up at it. 'My ship! Isn't she cool?'

Emily sniffed. 'Bit small.'

'So far I've liked you, Emily Bostock. Let's not quarrel now.' The Doctor swung round to face Reyn. 'Now. You. Here's the deal. Gorgeous blue box up there – travels through time and space. She's nifty! So.' He pointed at Reyn. 'You leave Ship alone.' He pointed at himself. 'I take you back home.' He waved his hands around. 'Ship stays here because you no longer need it for the journey. Everyone happy. How does that sound?'

'But Ship is an important part of our arsenal,' Reyn said doubtfully. 'We're fighting a losing battle. We need everything—'

'Reyn,' the Doctor said, 'you may be a soldier now, but you're not a murderer. If you truly cared so little for life, you would have left this planet centuries ago! But you did the right thing! You were prepared to sacrifice yourself to protect the people of this town. Don't waste that sacrifice, Reyn, all those long years you spent here. Let me take you back. Leave Ship here. We can take care of it.'

Reyn lowered his head. His ears went flat.

'It's the right thing to do,' Laura said.

The gun went down.

'All right,' Reyn said. 'All right, Doctor – I'll trust you. Take me home.'

\*

Leaving Amy in charge on board Ship, the Doctor took Rory and Reyn into the TARDIS. He waved his hands around.

'Isn't she gorgeous? I mean, I know Ship is a very impressive piece of temporal-spatial engineering, Reyn, but I think the TARDIS's take on the whole business is so much more elegant... and none of that accidentally turning a nearby piece of woodland into a trap for passing strangers—'

'Doctor,' said Reyn wearily. 'You were taking me home.'

'So I was! Home! Home time for Reyn!' The Doctor clapped his hands together, and then did the series of random moves and leaps around the console that Rory had come to recognise meant that a journey in time and space was under way.

'Home?' said the Doctor. 'I can get you back home to your foxy-man world in as much time as it takes to say foxy-man world inhabitant...' He yanked the control that landed the TARDIS, opened the door, pointed outside, and said, 'There you are, Reyn. Recognise it yet?'

Reyn walked slowly outside, the gun hanging limply from his hand. Rory, following him out, stepped onto a world that looked like it might be the kind of place inhabited by alien foxes.

The air was spicy. Sharp angled buildings sunk underground into deep tunnels lit with golden lights. Turrets spiked high into the clouds, silhouetted against an orange sun.

'This looks like home,' Reyn said, slowly, 'but not how I remember it.' He shook his head. 'Have I been gone so long?'

'You've been gone longer than you imagine,' the Doctor said quietly. 'This *is* your home, Reyn, but not when you knew it. This is what your home is going to be. After the Long War. Long, long after.'

Reyn stared around, bewildered by this half-familiar world. 'I don't understand,' he said. 'The War's *over*? Who won?'

'Nobody won,' the Doctor said. 'Nobody wins at war. But your species survived, if that's what you mean. They were conquered first –'

Reyn shuddered.

'– and they suffered for a long time, a very long time. Then the empire that conquered them declined, as empires do, in the end, and your people became free again. They weren't like they were before – no, how could they be, after all that? They changed. Became a little harder, a little more mistrustful, a little disenchanted. They'd lost a great deal. But they survived. They went on. And that world, down there – thousands of years have passed since your war. The Long War's hardly even history to them – it's more the stuff of legend. Like Troy and Hector are to Rory. Like Achilles and Cassandra and… um, Sherlock Holmes.'

'Doctor,' Rory whispered, 'Sherlock Holmes wasn't real…'

'Oh, yes, people *say* that…' The Doctor went on: 'Reyn, here, in this time, you're the stuff of legend too! They tell stories about you – the lost traveller. They talk about how one day you'll return, and you'll bring with you the knowledge, the way to teach ships to think and speak and be. They don't know how to do that on your world now. They forgot after the Long War.'

'Doctor,' Rory whispered again, 'is that all true?'

'It will be,' the Doctor whispered back, 'soon enough.' To Reyn, he said, 'You spent a long time in the woods, Reyn. Longer than you realised. But time didn't stand still out here. Your war is long since over. But your world is still here, and it's been waiting for you to return. The lost traveller has come home.'

Reyn's shoulders had slumped. His head was down and his ears low. Slowly he turned to look at the Doctor.

'Home? How can this place be home? Everyone I knew and loved is gone! Oh, Doctor!' His voice was full of grief. 'Why have you brought me here? I would rather have died with everyone I knew and loved than be lost like this!' His orange eyes, clever and sad, looked back at the TARDIS. And then he said, 'You said this machine could travel in time. You could take me back! Take me back home! Take me back to where I belong!'

His hand tightened around his gun. Rory whispered, 'Doctor...?'

And then someone called out. 'The traveller! It is, isn't it! Look! The traveller!'

A child, or someone who easily remembered being a child, red-furred and long-muzzled and bright-eyed. 'Look! It *is* him, isn't it!' He called over to his friends. 'Come and look at this! Look at the uniform, the plasma gun – it's like something from a history book! He's even got the scar on his nose! It is! It's the *Traveller*!'

Others passing paused to look too, and their faces changed the moment they caught sight of Reyn. As Rory watched, a crowd quickly formed around the lost old pilot, people whose sheer foxiness was almost overwhelming. They gathered round, chattering, reaching out to touch Reyn, and, suddenly, he was lifted high up, and the air was filled with laughter and delight. Some songs remain the same.

The Doctor looked out at the scene. He was smiling. 'It's been a long time since Reyn breathed his own air or held hands that are the same as his. But he's home now, Rory, and he's welcome here. It's time for us to go.'

And so, very quietly, they slipped away.

'Back to Ship, I suppose,' said Rory, as the TARDIS doors closed behind them. 'What is it we have to do there?'

'Well, we still have to release Ship from all that human history in which it's entangled itself and then send it on its way. Back to the stars. Back to exploring and learning and knowing... Ooh, though,' the Doctor twiddled some dials and yanked some levers, 'one last job to do around here before we leave local space...'

Patiently, the TARDIS landed again in the same place.

'Where are we now?' said Rory. 'And when?'

'Same where,' replied the Doctor, 'but quite a lot earlier when it comes to when. I said that Reyn was a legend, Rory – the lost traveller – and that's all true, or rather, it will be, once we've had a chance to fiddle the books.'

'Fiddle the books?' Rory looked at him in

horror. 'What are you getting me into now?'

'I mean the history books!'

'Oh, well, if you only meant fiddle the history books I suppose that's fine!'

'Legends don't come from nowhere, you know! Somebody has to... legendate... legendify... Make it all up in the first place! The story needs to be seeded, about the lost traveller from the Long War, who returns with the forgotten knowledge of his age, how to build the famous living ships... So we need to have a few words in some foxy ears from the past, get them twitching, get a few stories started... Just set the whole thing going so the legends are written down by the time Reyn arrives. You know the kind of thing: *And, lo, it was promised that the traveller would return, and we would know him from the great blue box that came from nowhere, heralding his homecoming...*' The Doctor frowned. 'Actually, probably quickest if I just write them down myself. Pass me that biro, will you?'

Amy watched with relief as the TARDIS rematerialised on board Ship. Out came the Doctor, Rory at his heels.

'Sorted?' Amy said.

'Of course!'

'So where is Reyn?' asked Laura anxiously.

'Is he safe? Is he happy?'

'Yes, he's safe – and soon I think he'll realise that he's happy. He's back amongst his own people now. He's a legend. A living legend. I think he'll soon be happier than he's ever been.' He smiled at Laura. 'And now… Well. Laura Brown. I think you know what has to happen next.'

Amy glanced suspiciously at the regretful looks Laura and the Doctor were giving each other. 'What? Doctor, what else have you got up your sleeve? And why do I think I won't like it?'

'We guided Ship through its Shift, Amy, and we saw Reyn safely on his way. But Ship is still here, still bound up with Swallow Woods, and it can still affect Foxton and the people that live there. All those time pockets and spatial wotsits, they're scattered around Swallow Woods like leaves, waiting to pull people in, sending them through the portal place. But we can fix it.'

'Er, getting lost now, Doctor,' Rory said. 'How do we fix it?'

'Laura knows, I think.'

'Laura?' said Amy. She turned to the old woman. 'What? What do you know?'

'I think,' Laura said slowly, 'that I have to stay here. Or, rather, stay in the environment that Reyn created. To seal it from behind. Close up time around me... Because everything that's happened to me here – that can't be taken back. I went into Swallow Woods, and I met Reyn – and Ship – and I spent sixty years here with them. None of that can be taken back, or it will undo the Doctor's fix, too. But that will be the end of it. Am I right, Doctor?'

'Nearly,' the Doctor said. 'But not quite. You're right that we can't take back what's happened to you, Laura. You're the last, now that Vicky and Jess are home. But Ship doesn't have to be here throughout all of time. We can send Ship on its way now... Well, one specific now. Your now. It will have to have been here for you to visit. And for Emily and Harry too. But not before. Or in between. Or since.'

'Wait,' said Amy. 'Let me make sure I've got this straight. If we want to rid Swallow Woods of Ship's influence, we can – but Laura *has* to have come here and spent all that time here. Laura's timeline can't be reversed.'

'And why would I want my life reversed? Would you? Would anyone?' Laura bristled.

'It isn't so much about reversing. Time's not like that. It's more... fluid. But no, Laura, no one is going to change your story-so-far,' said the Doctor. 'Although, where it goes now is up to you. The world that you shared with Reyn will disappear when Ship sets out – but I don't think Ship would mind some company for the road.'

Ship's walls shimmered in a gentle confirmation.

'But your parents!' Amy said in dismay. 'Your family!'

'If I go back,' Laura said, 'I'll be older than my parents, much older! How do we explain that? And you know how I wanted to travel, Amy. How I wanted to see new things... And I will! This time, I really will!'

'And you're only going into space!' the Doctor said. 'That's no reason not to stay in touch!'

'Doctor,' said Emily worriedly. 'What about us? Me and Harry. We're part of it. We've come this way, too, haven't we?'

'Well, Miss Emily Bostock – that's entirely up to you. Laura, really, is the one that matters. Laura's the one that *has* to take this path. You can go home, Emily. And you, Harry.'

'But we don't have to go home, do we? We could leave, too?' said Emily. 'There's nothing stopping us from going with them?'

'Not at all! Ship has been here in your time to meet you. So no, there's nothing stopping you going with them, Emily. If you want.'

'Then I'll go,' she said, and turned to Laura. 'If you don't mind, missus. If you don't mind some company?'

Laura laughed. 'Of course I don't mind!'

Emily turned to Harry and held out her hand. 'What do you say, love? Won't you come too?'

'Away?' Harry said. He looked around uncertainly. 'You sure it's safe, Emmy?'

'Safe,' said the Doctor helpfully, 'is a matter of perspective. But it's probably better than 1917.'

'Which,' Rory muttered, 'you told me was absolutely nothing to worry about.'

'Ah. Yes. Mostly. *Mostly* nothing to worry about. But I'd say heading into space on board a living ship probably beats 1917. And certainly beats the trenches.'

That was enough to convince Harry.

'Live and learn,' the Doctor said. 'Good choice.'

The travellers watched as, on the TARDIS screen, Swallow Woods released Ship from its embrace. The trees rocked and parted, and the living ship lifted from the ground and then left, taking its new crew to the stars. A few golden trails spun wildly in its wake, and then drifted away. For one brief second, Amy thought she glimpsed a huge fantastic castle with a rainbow overhead – but the vision slipped away before she could even be certain it was there.

'What about all the other people, Doctor?' Amy said. She started to pin Emily's butterfly brooch back onto her jacket. Emily had told her to keep it, to remember her by. 'The other ones that went missing that we never even met? The ones that were only marks in books?'

Suddenly, Rory's hands took charge of the brooch. He pinned it in place, and then kissed Amy gently on the tip of her nose.

'You're great.'

'So are you.'

'I missed you.'

'I missed you too.'

'So...' said the Doctor, spinning round on his heels. 'Well... Yes... The other people. Good question, Pond. Of course, Ship and Reyn never visited all those times, now. So they never disappeared. There was no Ship to take them on board, no Reyn to direct them to his fantasy world – they'll just walk through Swallow Woods.'

'Not Emily, though,' Rory said. 'Or Harry.'

'No, they've met Ship, and they've left with Ship. They will have disappeared, and without explanation. I suppose people will most likely say that Harry's run away rather than get called up... But what about Emily? What will they say about her? The last anyone saw of Emily Bostock, she was leaving the pub with a strange young man...'

'Oh...!' said Amy, rounding on Rory with an evil glimmer in her eye. 'I can just imagine the story! Emily Bostock, last seen heading into the woods, tempted away by a handsome stranger!'

'Well that's just *great*, isn't it?' said Rory, as Amy wrapped her arms around him. 'Now the history books have me down as some sort of *rake*...!'

Amy shook her head. 'Nah! Not very likely, is it? Besides, you're mine. But they all make it through, Doctor? They don't get lost?'

'Come and see,' the Doctor said.

He pushed open the TARDIS doors. Below them lay Swallow Woods and the land around, which they had come to know so well over the past few days. 'Looks exactly like one of those aerial photographs,' Amy said. 'Poor Jess. They nearly frightened the life out of her.'

'Watch,' the Doctor said.

And as Amy and Rory watched, the landscape beneath them began to alter, like a piece of film being speeded up. They watched the seasons pass over Swallow Woods, watched the trees spring to life and fall away again in winter. They saw people walk along the path that led into the woods – and they saw them all come out again.

'That's wonderful,' Rory said softly. 'All going home.'

'Oh yes, very nice,' said Amy, and, when Rory and the Doctor turned to stare at her, added, 'I do mean it! But I was promised chocolate. And a picnic. And pie.'

And what now, for the people of Foxton? Where does time, unravelling back and flowing forwards, take them? What now, for Swallow Woods?

Gordon Galloway, sitting in traffic on the motorway between Junctions 11 and 12, ponders the three impossible things that happened to him before breakfast. First of all, the nightmare – a terrible nightmare, of being trapped in a forest, in the middle of a storm, running in circles and unable to escape, while dogs howled miserably around him. A nightmare so real that when the alarm woke him, he was sweating, and sure that his hair would be soaked with rain and his clothes filthy from mud and leaves.

But, no. He'd been tucked up safe and warm in bed, and, beyond the bedroom window, the rain had stopped, and a damp bright autumn dawn unfolded as he watched.

That had only been the start. On his way downstairs, the phone rang. A terrible line, as if someone was calling long distance. He could barely make out the speaker's voice at first.

'Inspector Galloway? We've not spoken before, but my name is Laura Brown.'

'Laura! My God, girl, are you all right? Where have you *been*?'

'I'm fine, I'm fine, don't worry! I know I've caused a lot of trouble and I'm sorry. The truth is, I got into a terrible tizzy about my exams, and I decided to start my gap year early—'

'Where *are* you? There's been a search... the papers got hold of it... We've all been terrified for you!'

'I know, and I'm sorry. I'm... about to board a flight. Now don't make a fuss! I've spoken to my parents and it's all just fine. I'm going to be travelling for a while. It's what I wanted to do, what I really wanted to do, not exams. Maybe I'll do them some other time. I've got to go now, Inspector! They're calling me to... to the gate. I'm on my way! At last! Goodbye, Mr Galloway, goodbye! Thank you for worrying so much about me! Everything's fine! You *don't have to worry any more!'*

And she'd hung up, leaving him standing there like a small boy who'd been told what's what by his old granny. It was bewildering. Had she always been so self-assured? He rang her parents at once, of course. Tearfully, they told him what he was desperate to hear: that they had spoken to Laura too, and that she was safe. And that was what counted, he supposed...

The morning hadn't quite finished with him yet. Last of all, but still before his first sip of tea had been given the chance to touch his lips, Mary, his beloved wife, put down her own cup and said: 'Sweetheart, I've been thinking. Why don't we move back north?'

The traffic inched forwards. Gordon Galloway counted his blessings.

On the high street that morning, Vicky Caine, on her way to school, popped into the florists to send her mum an apology for missing the last bus and (heinous crime) walking home.

Across the road, Ruby Porter stopped at the newsagents to buy a birthday card for her favourite uncle, Peter, who was 67 later in the week. Then she hopped into her little blue car and drove to the college in the next town, where she lectured in history. She was looking forward to her day. She wasn't facing any disciplinary action. She had never joined the police.

Outside Foxton's ordinary police station, the people from the papers and the television channels, briefed now about the safe return of Laura Brown, were packing up and heading back to the city. Inside, in an ordinary interview room, a clock mended itself while the blind remained broken. And down the road, in the parish church, the records quietly tidied themselves, a number of curious green marks disappearing for good.

Jess Ashcroft stood on Long Lane by a signpost watching a big blue police box dematerialise. In her head, she still held two sets of memories. One set of memories was alarming and amazing and astonishing – and they were slowly fading away, becoming dreamier, replaced by another story: the sudden disappearance of Laura Brown, the brief flurry of press interest, and then Laura's reappearance online. Soon that would be all that remained.

The TARDIS was gone. Jess climbed over the fence and walked down the hill to Swallow Woods. There was a path across the field that forked: one way went to the road, the other led under the trees deep into the woods. Jess took this path. She knew the way very well. She'd come here a lot as a child, despite parental warnings. You couldn't keep kids away from Swallow Woods. It was their playground.

The path brought her in time to a clearing in the heart of the woods, where a deep old pool lay amidst a temple of trees. Jess sat beneath an old oak magnificent with autumn colour. The blue box (not to mention its strange and alarming inhabitants) had now slipped her mind...

Jess takes out her phone and balances it between her hands, wondering what to do next. Yesterday, at the press conference, she'd told a journalist from a national paper that Laura Brown would turn up today. This morning, as he was packing up, he'd waved her over and given her his phone number. So what should she do? Stay in the town she knows so well, better than anyone, probably, or leave, go on, go elsewhere, somewhere new...?

Her phone beeps. A message from Lily.

*Hey LOIS* (Lily had written) *did you see Luara's facebook update: she sez 'Laura Brown is reaching for the stars.'*

Jess puts away her phone and takes out a coin. Heads, she goes; tails, she stays. She throws the coin up into the air, where it hangs for a split second, silvery bright in a shaft of sunshine, full of potential, and then falls to the ground…

# Acknowledgements

With grateful thanks to Justin Richards, Gary Russell, Steve Tribe, and Kat Woods. Love and thanks as ever to Matthew.

And thanks to Fairport Convention for recording 'Reynardine'.

*Available now from BBC Books:*

# DOCTOR ⬛ WHO
## The TARDIS Handbook
### by Steve Tribe

£12.99  ISBN 978 1 846 07986 3

The inside scoop on 900 years of travel aboard the Doctor's famous time machine.

Everything you need to know about the TARDIS is here – where it came from, where it's been, how it works, and how it has changed since we first encountered it in that East London junkyard in 1963.

Including photographs, design drawings and concept artwork from different eras of the series, this handbook explores the ship's endless interior, looking inside its wardrobe and bedrooms, its power rooms and sick bay, its corridors and cloisters, and revealing just how the show's production teams have created the dimensionally transcendental police box, inside and out.

*The TARDIS Handbook* is the essential guide to the best ship in the universe.

# DOCTOR WHO
## Nuclear Time
by Oli Smith

£6.99  ISBN 978 1 846 07989 4

Colorado, 1981. The Doctor, Amy and Rory arrive in Appletown – an idyllic village in the remote American desert where the townsfolk go peacefully about their suburban routines. But when two more strangers arrive, things begin to change.

The first is a mad scientist – whose warnings are cut short by an untimely and brutal death. The second is the Doctor...

As death falls from the sky, the Doctor is trapped. The TARDIS is damaged, and the Doctor finds he is living backwards through time. With Amy and Rory being hunted through the suburban streets of the Doctor's own future and getting farther away with every passing second, he must unravel the secrets of Appletown before time runs out...

*A thrilling, all-new adventure featuring the Doctor, Amy and Rory, as played by Matt Smith, Karen Gillan and Arthur Darvill in the spectacular hit series from BBC Television.*

# DOCTOR █ WHO
## The King's Dragon
by Una McCormack

£6.99   ISBN 978 1 846 07990 0

In the city-state of Geath, the King lives in a golden hall, and the people want for nothing. Everyone is happy and everyone is rich. Or so it seems.

When the Doctor, Amy and Rory look beneath the surface, they discover a city of secrets. In dark corners, strange creatures are stirring. At the heart of the hall, a great metal dragon oozes gold. Then the Herald appears, demanding the return of her treasure... And next come the gunships.

The battle for possession of the treasure has begun, and only the Doctor and his friends can save the people of the city from being destroyed in the crossfire of an ancient civil war. But will the King surrender his new-found wealth? Or will he fight to keep it...?

*A thrilling, all-new adventure featuring the Doctor, Amy and Rory, as played by Matt Smith, Karen Gillan and Arthur Darvill in the spectacular hit series from BBC Television.*

*Available now from BBC Books:*

# DOCTOR ◉ WHO
## The Glamour Chase

by Gary Russell

£6.99  ISBN 978 1 846 07988 7

An archaeological dig in 1936 unearths relics of another time... And – as the Doctor, Amy and Rory realise – another place. Another planet.

But if Enola Porter, noted adventuress, has really found evidence of an alien civilisation, how come she isn't famous? Why has Rory never heard of her? Added to that, since Amy's been travelling with him for a while now, why does she now think the Doctor is from Mars?

As the ancient spaceship reactivates, the Doctor discovers that nothing and no one can be trusted. The things that seem most real could actually be literal fabrications – and very deadly indeed.

Who can the Doctor believe when no one is what they seem? And how can he defeat an enemy who can bend matter itself to their will? For the Doctor, Amy and Rory – and all of humanity – the buried secrets of the past are very much a threat to the present...

*A thrilling, all-new adventure featuring the Doctor, Amy and Rory, as played by Matt Smith, Karen Gillan and Arthur Darvill in the spectacular hit series from BBC Television.*

*Available now from BBC Books:*

# DOCTOR ⊙ WHO
## The Only Good Dalek

by Justin Richards and Mike Collins

£12.99  ISBN 978 1 846 07984 9

Station 7 is where the Earth Forces send all the equipment captured in their unceasing war against the Daleks. It's where Dalek technology is analysed and examined. It's where the Doctor and Amy have just arrived. But somehow the Daleks have found out about Station 7 – and there's something there that they want back.

With the Doctor increasingly worried about the direction the Station's research is taking, the commander of Station 7 knows he has only one possible, desperate, defence. Because the last terrible secret of Station 7 is that they don't only store captured Dalek technology. It's also a prison. And the only thing that might stop a Dalek is another Dalek...

*An epic, full-colour graphic novel featuring the Doctor and Amy, as played by Matt Smith and Karen Gillan in the spectacular hit series from BBC Television.*

# DOCTOR ⬛ WHO
## The Coming of the Terraphiles
by Michael Moorcock

£16.99  ISBN 978 1 846 07983 2

Miggea – a star on the very edge of reality. The cusp between this universe and the next. A point where space-time has worn thin, and is in danger of collapsing… And the venue for the grand finals of the competition to win the fabled Arrow of Law.

The Doctor and Amy have joined the Terraphiles – a group dedicated to re-enacting ancient sporting events. They are determined to win the Arrow. But just getting to Miggea proves tricky. Reality is collapsing, ships are disappearing, and Captain Cornelius and his pirates are looking for easy pickings.

Even when they arrive, the Doctor and Amy's troubles won't be over. They have to find out who is so desperate to get the Arrow of Law that they will kill for it. And uncover the traitor on their own team. And win the contest fair and square.

And, of course, they need to save the universe from total destruction.

*A thrilling, all-new adventure featuring the Doctor and Amy, as played by Matt Smith and Karen Gillan in the spectacular hit series from BBC Television, written by the acclaimed science fiction and fantasy author Michael Moorcock.*

In Dr Bloom's clinic at a remote spot on the Italian coast, at the end of the eighteenth century, nothing is ever quite what it seems.

Maria is a lonely little girl with no one to play with. She writes letters to her mother from the isolated resort where she is staying. She tells of the pale English aristocrats and the mysterious Russian nobles and their attentive servants. She tells of intrigue and secrets, and she tells of strange faceless figures that rise from the sea. She writes about the enigmatic Mrs Pond who arrives with her husband and her physician, and who will change everything.

What she doesn't tell her mother is the truth that everyone knows and no one says – that the only people who come here do so to die...

*A thrilling, all-new adventure featuring the Doctor, Amy and Rory, as played by Matt Smith, Karen Gillan and Arthur Darvill in the spectacular hit series from BBC Television.*

# DOCTOR ⬛ WHO
## The Dalek Handbook

by Steve Tribe and James Goss

£9.99  ISBN 978 1 849 90232 8

Exterminate!

The chilling battle cry of the Daleks has terrorised and terrified countless billions across thousands of worlds throughout time and space, from Skaro, Vulcan and Exxilon to the Medusa Cascade, Churchill's War Room and the opening of the Pandorica. This is the comprehensive history of the greatest enemies of the Doctor.

Learn about the Daleks' origins on the planet Skaro, how a Time Lord intervention altered the course of Dalek history, and how they emerged to wage war on Thals, Mechanoids, Movellans, Draconians and humans. With design artwork and photographs from five decades of *Doctor Who*, *The Dalek Handbook* also reveals the secrets of how they're operated, the development of their iconic look and sound, and their enduring appeal in television, radio, books, comics and more.

Including the full story of the Daleks' centuries-long conflict with the one enemy they fear, the Doctor, *The Dalek Handbook* is the complete guide to the Daleks – in and out of their casings!

# DOCTOR ⬛ WHO
## Touched by an Angel
by Jonathan Morris

£6.99  ISBN 978 1 849 90234 2

In 2003, Rebecca Whitaker died in a road accident. Her husband Mark is still grieving. Then he receives a battered envelope, posted eight years ago, containing a set of instructions and a letter with a simple message:

'You can save her.'

Later that night, while picking up a takeaway, Mark glances at a security monitor – to see himself, standing in the restaurant in grainy black and white. And behind him there's a stone statue of an angel. Covering its eyes, as though weeping… Except, when Mark turns, there's nothing there.

As Mark is given the chance to save Rebecca, it's up to the Doctor, Amy and Rory to save the whole world. Because this time the Weeping Angels are using history itself as a weapon…

*A thrilling, all-new adventure featuring the Doctor, Amy and Rory, as played by Matt Smith, Karen Gillan and Arthur Darvill in the spectacular hit series from BBC Television.*

*Coming soon from BBC Books:*

# DOCTOR WHO
## Paradox Lost
by George Mann

£6.99  ISBN 978 1 849 90235 9

London 1910: An unsuspecting thief gets more than he bargained for when he breaks into a house in Kensington. He finds himself confronted by horrific, grey-skinned creatures that are waiting to devour his mind.

London 3189: An unimaginably ancient city. The remains of an android are dredged from the Thames. It's one of the latest models, only just developed. But it's been in the water for over a thousand years. And when the android is reactivated, it has a message – a warning that can only be delivered to a man named the Doctor.

The Doctor and his friends must solve a mystery that has spanned over a thousand years. Travelling backwards and forwards in time, they must unravel the threads of an ancient plot. If they fail, the deadly alien Squall will devour the world…

*A thrilling, all-new adventure featuring the Doctor, Amy and Rory, as played by Matt Smith, Karen Gillan and Arthur Darvill in the spectacular hit series from BBC Television.*

*Coming soon from BBC Books:*

# DOCTOR⬛WHO
## Borrowed Time
by Naomi Alderman

£6.99  ISBN 978 1 849 90233 5

Andrew Brown never has enough time. No time to call his sister, no time to prepare for that important presentation at the bank where he works... The train's late, the lift jams, the all-important meeting's started by the time he arrives. Disaster.

If only he'd had just a little more time.

Time is the business of Mr Symington and Mr Blenkinsop. They'll lend Andrew Brown some time – at a very reasonable rate of interest. If he was in trouble before he borrowed time, things have just got a lot worse.

Detecting a problem, the Doctor, Amy and Rory go undercover at the bank. The Doctor's a respected expert, and Amy's his trusted advisor. Rory has a job in the post room. But they have to move fast to stop Symington and Blenkinsop before they cash in their investments. The Harvest is approaching.

*A thrilling, all-new adventure featuring the Doctor, Amy and Rory, as played by Matt Smith, Karen Gillan and Arthur Darvill in the spectacular hit series from BBC Television.*

"Yes, I suppose you're right," the husband said. "Off you go to bed, little one."

She came to her father's side, kissed him on the cheek and whispered, "Thank you, Papa."

The man's eyes followed his eleven-year-old daughter as she left the room and he noticed that the fingers on her right hand were clenched, making a small tight fist, something she always did when she was angry or determined. He suspected she was both on this occasion, but he realised that it would be pointless to try and explain to his wife that their only child was no ordinary mortal. He had long ago abandoned any attempt to involve his wife in his own ambitions, and was at least thankful that she was incapable of dampening their daughter's.

He returned to the Chicago Cubs and had to admit that his daughter's judgement might even be right on that subject.

Florentyna Rosnovski never referred to the conversation again for twenty-two years, but when she did she assumed her father would keep his end of the bargain. After all, the Polish are an honourable race who never go back on their word.

# The Past

1934–1968

# 1

It had not been an easy birth, but then for Abel and
Zaphia Rosnovski nothing had ever been easy, and in
their own ways they had both become philosophical about
that. Abel had wanted a son, an heir who would one day
be chairman of the Baron Group. By the time the boy
was ready to take over, Abel was confident that his own
name would stand alongside those of Ritz and Statler
and by then the Baron would be the largest hotel group
in the world. Abel had paced up and down the colourless
corridor of St Luke's Hospital waiting for the first cry,
his slight limp becoming more pronounced as each hour
passed. Occasionally he twisted the silver band that
encircled his wrist and stared at the name so neatly
engraved on it. He turned and retraced his steps once
again, to see Doctor Dodek heading towards him.

"Congratulations, Mr Rosnovski," he called.

"Thank you," said Abel eagerly.

"You have a beautiful girl," the doctor said as he
reached him.

"Thank you," repeated Abel, quietly, trying not to
show his disappointment. He then followed the obste-
trician into a little room at the other end of the corridor.
Through an observation window Abel was confronted
with a row of wrinkled faces. The doctor pointed to the
father's first-born. Unlike the others her little fingers were
curled into a tight fist. Abel had read somewhere that a
child was not expected to do that for at least three weeks.
He smiled, proudly.

Mother and daughter remained at St Luke's for another
six days and Abel visited them every morning, leaving
his hotel only when the last breakfast had been served,
and every afternoon after the last lunch guest had left the
dining-room. Telegrams, flowers and the recent fashion

of greeting cards surrounded Zaphia's iron-framed bed, reassuring evidence that other people too rejoiced in the birth. On the seventh day mother and unnamed child – Abel had considered six boys' names – returned home.

On the anniversary of the second week of their daughter's birth they named her Florentyna, after Abel's sister. Once the infant had been installed in the newly decorated nursery at the top of the house, Abel would spend hours simply staring down at his daughter, watching her sleep and wake, knowing that he must work even harder than he had in the past to ensure the child's future. He was determined that Florentyna would be given a better start in life than he had been. Not for her the dirt and deprivation of his childhood or the humiliation of arriving on the eastern seaboard of America as an immigrant with little more than a few valueless Russian rubles sewn into the jacket of an only suit.

He would ensure that Florentyna was given the formal education he had lacked, not that he had a lot to complain about. Franklin D. Roosevelt lived in the White House and Abel's little group of hotels looked as if they were going to survive the Depression. America had been good to this immigrant.

Whenever he sat alone with his daughter in the upstairs nursery he would reflect on his past, and dream of her future.

When he had first arrived in the United States he had found a job in a little butcher's shop on the lower East Side of New York, where he worked for two long years before filling a vacancy at the Plaza as a junior waiter. From Abel's first day, Sammy, the old maître d', had treated him as though he was the lowest form of life. After four years, a slave trader would have been impressed by the work and unheard-of overtime that the lowest form of life did in order to reach the exalted position as Sammy's assistant head waiter in the Oak Room. During those early years Abel spent five afternoons a week poring over books at Columbia University, and after dinner had been cleared away read on late into the night.

His rivals wondered when he slept.

Abel was not sure how his newly-acquired degree could advance him while he still only waited on tables in the Oak Room of the Plaza Hotel. The question was answered for him by a well-fed Texan called Mr Davis Leroy, who had watched Abel serving guests solicitously for a week. Mr Leroy, the owner of eleven hotels, then offered Abel the position of assistant manager at his flagship, the Richmond Continental in Chicago, with the sole responsibility of running the restaurants.

Abel was brought back to the present when Florentyna turned over and started to thump the side of her crib. He extended a finger which his daughter grabbed like a lifeline thrown from a sinking ship. She started to bite the finger with what she imagined were teeth . . .

When Abel first arrived in Chicago he found the Richmond Continental badly run down. It didn't take him long to discover why. The manager, Desmond Pacey, was cooking the books and as far as Abel could tell probably had been for the past thirty years. The new assistant manager spent his first six months gathering together the proof he needed to nail Pacey and then presented to his employer a dossier containing all the facts. When Davis Leroy realised what had been going on behind his back he immediately sacked Pacey, replacing him with his new protégé. This spurred Abel on to work even harder and he became so convinced that he could turn the fortunes of the Richmond Group around that when Leroy's ageing sister put up for sale her twenty-five per cent of the company's stock Abel cashed everything he owned to purchase them. Davis Leroy was touched by his young manager's personal commitment to the company and proved it by appointing him managing director of the group.

From that moment they became partners, a professional bond developed into a close friendship. Abel would have been the first to appreciate how hard it was for a Texan to acknowledge a Pole as an equal. For the first time since he had settled in America, he felt secure – until he found out that the Texans were every bit as proud a clan as the Poles.

Abel still couldn't accept what had happened. If only Davis had confided in him, told him the truth about the extent of the group's financial trouble – who wasn't having problems during the Depression? – between them they could have sorted something out. At the age of sixty-two Davis Leroy had been informed by his bank that his overdraft was no longer covered by the value of the hotels and that they required further security before they would agree to pay next month's wages. In response to the bank's ultimatum, Davis Leroy had had a quiet dinner with his daughter and retired to the Presidential Suite on the twelfth floor with two bottles of bourbon. Then he had opened the window and jumped. Abel would never forget standing on the corner of Michigan Avenue at four in the morning having to identify a body he could recognise only by the jacket his mentor had worn the previous night. The lieutenant investigating the death had remarked that it had been the seventh suicide in Chicago that day. It didn't help. How could the policeman possibly know how much Davis Leroy had done for him, or how much more he had intended to return that friendship in the future? In a hastily composed will Davis had bequeathed the remaining seventy-five per cent of the Richmond Group stock to his managing director, writing to Abel that although the stock was worthless one hundred per cent ownership of the group might give him a better chance to negotiate new terms with the bank.

Florentyna's eyes opened, and she started to howl. Abel picked her up lovingly, immediately regretting the decision as he felt the damp clammy bottom. He changed her nappy quickly, drying the child carefully, before making a triangle of the cloth, not allowing the big pins anywhere near her body; any midwife would have nodded her approval at his deftness. Florentyna closed her eyes and nodded back to sleep on her father's shoulder. "Ungrateful brat," he murmered fondly as he kissed her on the cheek.

After Davis Leroy's funeral Abel had visited Kane and Cabot, the Richmond Group's bankers in Boston, and pleaded with one of the directors not to put the eleven hotels up for sale on the open market. He tried to convince the bank that if only they would back him, he could – given time – turn the balance sheet from red into black. The smooth, cold man behind the expensive partner's desk had proved intractable. "I must act in the bank's interests," he had used as an excuse. Abel would never forget the humiliation of having to call a man of his own age "sir" and still leave empty-handed. The man must have had the soul of a cash register not to realise how many people were affected by his decision. Abel promised himself, for the hundredth time, that one day he would get even with Mr William "Ivy League" Kane.

Abel had travelled back to Chicago that night thinking that nothing else could go wrong in his life, only to find the Richmond Continental burned to the ground and the police accusing him of arson. Arson it proved to be, but at the hands of Desmond Pacey, bent on revenge. When arrested, he admitted readily to the crime as his only interest was the downfall of Abel. Pacey would have succeeded if the insurance company had not come to Abel's rescue. Until that moment, he had wondered if he would not have been better off in the Russian prisoner-of-war camp he had escaped from before fleeing to America. But then his luck turned when an anonymous backer who, Abel concluded, must have been Mr David Maxton of the Stevens Hotel, purchased the Richmond Group and offered Abel his old position as managing director and a chance to prove he could run the company at a profit.

Abel recalled how he had been reunited with Zaphia, the self-assured girl he had first met on board the ship that had brought them to America. How immature she had made him feel then, but not when they re-met and he discovered she was a waitress at the Stevens.

Two years had passed since then and, although the newly named Baron Group had failed to make a profit in 1933, they lost only twenty-three thousand dollars, greatly helped by Chicago's celebration of its centenary when over a million tourists had visited the city to enjoy the World's Fair.

Once Pacey had been convicted of arson, Abel had only to wait for the insurance money to be paid before he could set about rebuilding the hotel in Chicago. He had used the interim period to visit the other ten hotels in the group, sacking staff who showed the same pecuniary tendencies as Desmond Pacey and replacing them from the long lines of unemployed that stretched across America.

Zaphia began to resent Abel's journeys from Charleston to Mobile, from Houston to Memphis, continually checking over his hotels in the south. But Abel realised that if he was to keep his side of the bargain with the anonymous backer there would be little time to sit around at home, however much he adored his daughter. He had been given ten years to repay the bank loan; if he succeeded, a clause in the contract stipulated he would be allowed to purchase the remaining sixty per cent of the company's stock for a further three million dollars. Zaphia thanked God each night for what they already had and pleaded with him to slow down, but nothing was going to stop Abel from trying to fulfil that aim.

"Your dinner's ready," shouted Zaphia at the top of her voice.

Abel pretended he hadn't heard and continued to stare down at his sleeping daughter.

"Didn't you hear me? Dinner is ready."

"What? No, dear. Sorry. Just coming." Abel reluctantly rose to join his wife for dinner. Florentyna's rejected red eiderdown lay on the floor beside her cot. Abel picked up the fluffy quilt and placed it carefully on top of the blanket that covered his daughter. He never wanted her to feel the cold. She smiled in her sleep. Was she having her first dream? Abel wondered, as he switched out the light.

# 2

Florentyna's christening was something everyone present was to remember – except Florentyna, who slept through the entire proceedings. After the ceremony at the Holy Name Cathedral on North Wabash, the guests made their way to the Stevens Hotel. Abel took a private room in the hotel and invited over a hundred guests to celebrate the occasion. His closest friend, George Novak, a fellow Pole who had occupied the bunk above him on the boat coming over from Europe, was to be one Kum while one of Zaphia's cousins, Janina, was to be the other.

The guests devoured a traditional ten-course dinner including pierogi and bigos while Abel sat at the head of the table accepting gifts on behalf of his daughter which included a silver rattle, US savings bonds, a copy of *Huckleberry Finn* and, finest of all, a beautiful antique emerald ring from Abel's unnamed benefactor. He only hoped that the man gained as much pleasure in the giving as his daughter later showed in the receiving. To mark the occasion, Abel presented his daughter with a large brown teddy bear with red eyes.

"It looks like Franklin D. Roosevelt," said George, holding the bear up for all to see. "This calls for a second chistening – F.D.R."

Abel raised his glass. "Mr President," he toasted – a name the bear never relinquished.

The party finally came to an end around three o'clock in the morning, when Abel had to requisition a laundry trolley from the hotel to transport all the gifts home. George waved to Abel as he headed up North Michigan Avenue pushing the trolley before him.

The happy father began whistling to himself as he recalled every moment of the wonderful evening. Only when Mr President fell off the trolley for a third time did he realise how crooked his path down Lake Shore Drive must have been. He picked up the bear and wedged it in the centre of the gifts and was about to attempt a straight path when a hand touched his shoulder. Abel jumped round, ready to defend with his life anyone who wanted to steal Florentyna's first possessions. He stared up into the face of a young policeman.

"Maybe you can explain why you are pushing a Stevens Hotel laundry trolley down Michigan Avenue at three in the morning?"

"Yes, officer," replied Abel.

"Well, let's start with what's in the packages."

"Other than Franklin D. Roosevelt, I can't be certain."

The policeman immediately arrested Abel on suspicion of theft. While the recipient of the gifts slept soundly under her red eiderdown in the little nursery at the top of their house in Rigg Street, her father spent a sleepless night on an old horsehair mattress in a cell at the local jail. George appeared at the court house first thing in the morning to verify Abel's story.

The next day Abel purchased a four-door maroon Buick from Peter Sosnkowski, who ran a secondhand car lot in the Polish neighbourhood.

Abel began to resent having to leave Chicago and his beloved Florentyna even for a few days, fearing he might miss her first step, her first word or her first anything. From her birth, he had supervised her daily routine, never allowing Polish to be spoken in the house: he was determined there would be no trace of a Polish accent that would make her feel ill at ease in society.

Abel had intently waited for her first word, hoping it would be "Papa" while Zaphia feared it might be some Polish word that would reveal that she had not been speaking English to her first-born when they were alone.

"My daughter is an American," Abel had explained

to Zaphia, "and she must therefore speak English. Too many Poles continue to converse in their own language, thus ensuring that their children spend their entire lives in the north-west corner of Chicago being described as 'Stupid Polacks' and ridiculed by everyone else they come across."

"Except our countrymen who still feel some loyalty to the Polish empire," said Zaphia defensively.

"The Polish empire? What century are you living in, Zaphia?"

"The twentieth century," she said, her voice rising.

"Along with Dick Tracy and Famous Funnies, no doubt?"

"Hardly the attitude of someone whose ultimate ambition is to return to Warsaw as the first Polish ambassador."

"I've told you never to mention that, Zaphia. Never."

Zaphia, whose English remained irredeemably shaky, didn't reply but later grumbled to her cousins on the subject and continued to speak Polish only when Abel was out of the house. She was not impressed by the fact, so often trotted out by Abel, that General Motors's turnover was greater than Poland's budget.

By 1935, Abel was convinced that America had turned the corner and that the Depression was a thing of the past, so he decided the time had come to build the new Chicago Baron on the site of the old Richmond Continental. He appointed an architect and began spending more time in the Windy City and less on the road, as he was determined the hotel would turn out to be the finest in the Mid-West.

The Chicago Baron was completed in May 1936 and opened by the Democratic mayor, Edward J. Kelly. Both Illinois Senators were dancing attendance, only too aware of Abel's burgeoning power.

"Looks like a million dollars," said J. Hamilton Lewis, the senior Senator.

"You wouldn't be far wrong," said Abel, as he admired

the thickly carpeted public rooms, the high stucco ceilings and the decorations in pastel shades of green. The final touch had been the dark green embossed B that adorned everything from the towels in the bathrooms to the flag that fluttered on the top of the forty-two storey building.

"This hotel already bears the hallmark of success," said J. Hamilton Lewis, addressing the two thousand assembled guests, "because, my friends, it is the man and not the building who will always be known as the Chicago Baron." Abel was delighted by the roar that went up and smiled to himself. His public relations adviser had supplied that line to the Senator's speech writer earlier in the week.

Abel was beginning to feel at ease among big businessmen and senior politicians. Zaphia, however, had not adapted to her husband's change in fortunes and hovered uncertainly in the background, drinking a little too much champagne, and finally crept away before the dinner was served with a lame excuse about wanting to see that Florentyna was safely asleep. Abel accompanied his flushed wife towards the revolving door in silent irritation. Zaphia neither cared for nor understood success on Abel's scale and preferred to ignore his new world. She was only too aware how much this annoyed Abel and couldn't resist saying, "Don't hurry home", as he bundled her into a cab.

"I won't," he told the revolving door as he returned, pushing it so hard that it went around three more times after he had left it.

He returned to the hotel foyer to find Alderman Henry Osborne waiting for him.

"This must be the high point in your life," the alderman remarked.

"High point? I've just turned thirty," said Abel.

A camera flashed as he placed an arm around the tall, darkly handsome politician. Abel smiled towards the cameraman, enjoying the treatment he was receiving as a celebrity, and said, just loud enough for eavesdroppers to hear, "I'm going to put Baron hotels right across the globe. I intend to be to America what César Ritz was to Europe. Stick with me, Henry, and you'll enjoy the ride." The city alderman and Abel walked together into the dining-room and once they were out of earshot Abel added: "Join me for lunch tomorrow, Henry, if you can spare the time. There's something I need to discuss with you."

"Delighted, Abel. A mere city alderman is always available for the Chicago Baron."

They both laughed heartily, though neither thought the remark particularly funny.

It turned out to be another late night for Abel. When he returned home he went straight to the spare room, to be sure he didn't wake Zaphia — or that's what he told her the next morning.

When Abel came into the kitchen to join Zaphia for breakfast Florentyna was sitting in her high chair smearing a bowlful of cereal enthusiastically round her mouth and biting at most things that remained within arms' reach — even if they weren't food. He kissed her on the forehead, the only place that seemed to have missed the cereal, and sat down to a plate of waffles and maple syrup. When he had finished, Abel rose from his chair and told Zaphia that he would be having lunch with Henry Osborne.

"I don't like that man," said Zaphia, with feeling.

"I'm not crazy about him myself," replied Abel. "But never forget he's well placed in City Hall to be able to do us a lot of favours."

"And a lot of harm."

"Don't lose any sleep over that. You can leave the handling of Alderman Osborne to me," said Abel as he brushed his wife's cheek and turned to leave.

"Presidunk," said a voice, and both parents turned to stare at Florentyna, who was gesticulating at the floor where the eight-month-old Franklin D. Roosevelt lay on his furry face.

Abel laughed, picked up the much-loved teddy bear and placed him in the space Florentyna had left for him on the high chair.

"Pres-i-dent," said Abel slowly and firmly.

"Presidunk," insisted Florentyna.

Abel laughed again and patted Franklin D. Roosevelt on the head. So F.D.R. was responsible not only for the New Deal but also for Florentyna's first political utterance.

Abel left the house to find his chauffeur waiting for him beside the new Cadillac. Abel's driving had become worse as the car he could afford improved. When he bought a Cadillac, George had advised a driver to go with it. That morning he asked the chauffeur to drive slowly as they approached the Gold Coast. Abel stared up at the gleaming glass of the Chicago Baron and marvelled that there was no other place on earth where a man could achieve so much so quickly. What the Chinese would have been happy to strive for in ten generations, he had achieved in less than fifteen years.

He leaped out of the car before his chauffeur could run around to open the door, walked briskly into the hotel and took the private express elevator to the forty-second floor where he spent the morning checking over every problem with which the new hotel was faced: one of the passenger elevators wasn't functioning properly; two waiters had been involved in a knife fight in the kitchen and had been sacked by George even before Abel had arrived; and the list of damages after the opening looked suspiciously high – Abel would have to check into possible theft by waiters being recorded in the books as breakage. He left nothing to chance in any of his hotels from who was staying in the Presidential Suite to the price of the eight thousand fresh bread rolls the catering department needed every week. He spent the morning dealing with queries, problems and decisions, stopping only when

Alderman Osborne was ushered into Abel's office by his secretary.

"Good morning, Baron," said Henry, patronisingly referring to the Rosnovski family title.

In Abel's younger days as a junior waiter at the Plaza in New York the title had been scornfully mimicked to his face. At the Richmond Continental when he was assistant manager it had figured in whispered jokes behind his back. Lately everyone mouthed the prefix with respect.

"Good morning, Alderman," said Abel, glancing at the clock on his desk. It was five past one. "Shall we have lunch?"

Abel guided Henry into the adjoining private dining-room. To a casual observer Henry Osborne would hardly have seemed a natural soul-mate for Abel. Educated at Choate and then Harvard, as he continually reminded Abel, he had later served as a young lieutenant with the Marines in the World War. At six feet, with a full head of black hair lightly sprinkled with grey, he looked younger than his history insisted he had to be.

The two men had first met as a result of the fire at the old Richmond Continental. Henry was then working for the Great Western Casualty Insurance Company, which had, for as long as anyone could remember, insured the Richmond Group. Abel had been taken aback, when Henry had suggested that a small cash payment would ensure a swifter flow of the claim papers through the head office. Abel did not possess a "small cash payment" in those days; although the claim eventually found its way through, as Henry also believed in Abel's future.

Abel had learned for the first time about men who could be bought.

By the time Henry Osborne was elected to the Chicago City Council as an alderman, Abel *could* afford a small cash payment, and the building permit for the new Baron proceeded through City Hall as though on roller skates. When Henry later announced that he would be running for the United States House of Representatives for the Ninth District of Illinois, Abel was among the first to send a sizeable cheque for his campaign fund. While Abel remained wary of his new ally personally, he recognised that a tame politician could be of great help to the Baron Group. Abel took care to ensure that none of the small cash payments – he did not think of them as bribes, even to himself – was on the record, and felt confident that he could terminate the arrangement as and when it suited him.

The dining-room was decorated in the same delicate shades of green as the rest of the hotel, but there was no sign of the embossed B anywhere in the room. The furniture was nineteenth century, and entirely in oak. Around the walls hung oil portraits from the same period, almost all imported. With the door closed, it was possible to imagine that one was in another world far away from the hectic pace of a modern hotel.

Abel took his place at the head of an ornate table that could have comfortably seated eight guests but that day was laid for only two.

"It's like being in a bit of England," said Henry, taking in the room.

"Not to mention Poland," replied Abel, as a uniformed waiter served smoked salmon, while another poured them both a glass of Bouchard Chablis.

Henry stared down at the full plate in front of him. "Now I can see why you're putting on so much weight, Baron."

Abel frowned, and quickly changed the subject. "Are you going to the Cubs' game tomorrow?"

"What's the point? They have a worse home record than the Republicans. Not that my absence will discourage the *Tribune* from describing the match as a close-fought battle bearing no relation to the score and but for a different set of circumstances, the Cubs would have pulled off a famous victory."

Abel laughed.

"One thing's for sure," continued Henry, "you'll never see a night game at Wrigley Field. That ghastly innovation of playing under floodlights won't catch on in Chicago."

"That's what you said about beer cans last year."

It was Henry's turn to frown. "You didn't ask me to lunch to hear my views on baseball or beer cans, Abel, so what little plan can I assist you with this time?"

"Simple. I want to ask your advice on what I should do about William Kane."

Henry seemed to choke. I must speak to the chef: there shouldn't be any bones in smoked salmon, thought Abel before he continued.

"You once told me, Henry, in graphic detail what had happened when your path crossed Mr Kane's and how he ended up defrauding you of money. Well, Kane did far worse than that to me. During the Depression he put the squeeze on Davis Leroy, my partner and closest friend, and was the direct cause of Leroy's suicide. To make matters worse Kane refused to support me when I wanted to take over the management of the hotels and try to put the group on a sound financial footing."

"Who did back you in the end?" asked Henry.

"A private investor with the Continental Trust. The manager has never told me in so many words, but I've always suspected it was David Maxton."

"The owner of the Stevens Hotel?"

"The same."

"What makes you think it was him?"

"When I had the reception for my wedding and again for Florentyna's christening at the Stevens, the bill was covered by my backer."

"That's hardly conclusive."

"Agreed, but I'm certain it's Maxton, because he once offered me the chance to run the Stevens. I told him I was more interested in finding a backer for the Richmond Group, and within a week his bank in Chicago came up with the money from someone who could not reveal their identity because it would clash with their day to day business interests."

"That's a little more convincing. But tell me what you have in mind for William Kane," said Henry as he toyed with his wine glass and waited for Abel to continue.

"Something that shouldn't take a lot of your time, Henry, but might well prove to be rewarding for you both financially and, as you hold Kane in the same high regard as I do, personally."

"I'm listening," said Henry, still not looking up from his glass.

"I want to lay my hands on a substantial shareholding in Kane's Boston bank."

"You won't find that easy," said Henry. "Most of the stock is held in a family trust that cannot be sold without his personal concurrence."

"You seem very well informed," said Abel.

"Common knowledge," said Henry.

Abel didn't believe him. "So let's start by finding out the name of every shareholder in Kane and Cabot and see if any of them are interested in parting with their stock at a price considerably above par."

Abel watched Henry's eyes light up as he began to work out how much might be in this transaction for him if he could make a deal with both sides.

"If he ever found out he'd play very rough," said Henry.

"He's not going to find out," said Abel. "And even if he did we'd be at least two moves ahead of him. Do you think you are capable of doing the job?"

"I can try. What did you have in mind?"

Abel realised Henry was trying to find out what payment he might expect, but hadn't finished yet. "I want a written report the first day of every month showing Kane's shareholdings in any company, his business commitments and all details you can obtain of his private life. I want everything you come up with, however trivial it may seem."

"I repeat, that won't be easy," said Henry.

"Will a thousand dollars a month make the task easier?"

"Fifteen hundred certainly would," reply Henry.

"A thousand dollars a month for the first six months. If you prove yourself, I'll raise the figure to fifteen hundred."

"It's a deal," said Henry.

"Good," said Abel as he took his wallet from his inside pocket and extracted a cheque already made out to cash for one thousand dollars.

Henry studied the cheque. "You were pretty confident I would fall into line, weren't you?"

"No, not altogether," said Abel, as he removed a second cheque from his wallet and showed it to Henry. It was made out for fifteen hundred dollars. "If you come up with some winners in the first six months, you'll only have lost three thousand dollars."

Both men laughed.

"Now to a more pleasant subject," said Abel. "Are we going to win?"

"The Cubs?"

"No, the election."

"Sure, Landon is in for a whipping. The Kansas Sunflower can't hope to beat F.D.R." said Henry. "As the President reminded us, that particular flower is yellow, has a black heart, is useful as parrot food and always dies before November."

Abel laughed again. "And how about you personally?"

"No worries. The seat has always been safe for the Democrats. The difficult thing was winning the nomination, not the election."

"I look forward to your being a Congressman, Henry."

"I'm sure you do, Abel, and I shall look forward to serving you as well as my other constituents."

Abel looked at him quizzically. "Considerably better, I should hope," he commented as a sirloin steak that almost covered the plate was placed in front of him while another glass was filled with a Côte de Beaune 1929. The rest of the lunch was spent discussing Gabby Hartnett's injury problems, Jesse Owens's four gold medals at the Berlin Olympics, and the possibility that Hitler would invade Poland.

"Never," said Henry, and started to reminisce about the courage of the Poles at Mons in the Great War.

Abel didn't comment on the fact that no Polish regiment had seen action at Mons.

At two thirty-seven Abel was back at his desk, considering the problems of the Presidential Suite and the eight thousand fresh bread rolls.

He did not arrive home from the Baron that night until nine o'clock, only to find Florentyna already asleep. But she woke immediately as her father entered the nursery and smiled up at him.

"Presidunk, Presidunk, Presidunk."

Abel smiled. "Not me. You perhaps, but not me." He picked his daughter up and kissed her on the cheek and sat with her while she repeated her one-word vocabulary over and over again.